One Last Gift

By Emily Stone

One Last Gift
Always, in December

One Last Gift

A Novel

EMILY STONE

Dell Books
New York

A Dell Trade Paperback Original

Copyright © 2022 by Emily Stone
Book Club Guide copyright © 2022 by
Penguin Random House LLC

Published in the United States by Dell, an imprint of Random House, a division of Penguin Random House LLC, New York.

DELL is a registered trademark and the D colophon is a trademark of Penguin Random House LLC.
RANDOM HOUSE BOOK CLUB and colophon are trademarks of Penguin Random House LLC.

Originally published in the United Kingdom by Headline Review, an imprint of Headline Publishing Group. Published by arrangement with Headline Publishing Group Limited.

LIBRARY OF CONGRESS CATALOGING-IN-PUBLICATION DATA
Names: Stone, Emily, author.
Title: One last gift: a novel / Emily Stone.
Description: New York: Dell Books, [2022]
Identifiers: LCCN 2022018481 (print) |
LCCN 2022018482 (ebook) |
ISBN 9780593598344 (trade paperback) |
ISBN 9780593598351 (ebook)
Subjects: LCGFT: Romance fiction. | Novels.
Classification: LCC PR6119.T6743 O54 2022 (print) |
LCC PR6119.T6743 (ebook) | DDC 823/.92—dc23
LC record available at https://lccn.loc.gov/2022018481
LC ebook record available at https://lccn.loc.gov/2022018482

Printed in the United States of America on acid-free paper

randomhousebooks.com
randomhousebookclub.com

9 8 7 6 5 4 3 2 1

Book design by Virginia Norey
Frontis art adapted from: Gunaonedesign/stock.adobe.com
Part title art adapted from: Drekhann/stock.adobe.com

*There is a path from me to you that I am
constantly looking for.*
—RUMI

One Last Gift

Prologue

Cassie woke while it was still dark, her duvet pulled halfway over her head to hide from the cold. For a moment she frowned into the blackness, groggy from sleep, confused as to what had woken her. Then there was a loud snore from the bed next to hers. She gave the sleeping mass that was her brother a sideways look. He was *always* snoring, and it was so annoying; she'd told him to lie on his side about a *million* times, because her best friend's mum was a doctor and she'd once said that helped. Cassie sighed into her pillow. Maybe if he kept up the snoring, she'd get brave enough to sleep on her own at night and he could sleep in his own room, across the corridor, under the glowing stars he'd stuck to the ceiling. But she hadn't yet worked up the courage, not since Mum and Dad died, nearly two years ago.

Tom gave another snore, making Cassie start. It was only then that she realized, and her heart gave a little leap as she threw her duvet off and sat straight up in bed. It was Christmas Day. It was *Christmas*! How had she forgotten, even for a moment?

Ignoring the chilly air, Cassie stepped down from her bed, careful not to wake Tom, and padded to the window. Maybe there would be snow outside, even though Aunty Claire said it never *really* snowed on Christmas Day. She moved the curtains aside and peered down into her aunt's little garden. It was too dark to see anything at all, the world outside still sleeping.

She turned back around, her eyes adjusting to the darkness. There were no stockings at the foot of the bed because Aunty Claire didn't believe in stockings. Tom had found out Santa wasn't real years ago, and so Claire had decided she didn't want to carry on the "charade" (Cassie wasn't entirely sure what a "charade" was, but Tom had told her it meant acting), even though their parents used to do it every year. The excitement of the day dulled a little in Cassie's chest as she thought about her mum and dad, and the fact that they wouldn't be here to open presents with or make marshmallows on toast for breakfast—a Christmas tradition Aunty Claire hadn't let them continue. She thought about waking Tom up. He'd be OK with it, and they could sneak downstairs and find some chocolate together, before Claire got up. She was pretty sure there were chocolate presents somewhere, wrapped in foil. One of their neighbors had dropped them round—Cassie couldn't remember her name, but she was *really* old and smelled a bit like cocoa and lavender mixed together, and she'd said the chocolates had to be hung on the tree. And there *was* a tree—even though Claire almost hadn't gotten one—because Cassie had cried when Claire had said that maybe they shouldn't have one this year and even *Tom* had looked sad and so she'd given in.

But even as the thought of waking Tom and going chocolate-hunting danced around her mind, something even better occurred to her. She held in the squeal bubbling inside of her, grinning to herself as she grabbed her fluffy socks, the ones with rabbit ears, and tied her pink dressing gown around her, the one her mum and dad had bought for her the Christmas before they died. She was getting too big for it now, she knew she was, but she refused to get another one.

Cassie crept downstairs as quietly as she could, keeping her hand on the banister to guide her in the dark. Her heart was beating faster with each bouncing step she took. They might not do stockings or mince pies for Santa like the rest of her class, but there was one thing that made Christmas morning just the *best* morning ever. She padded into the living room, guided by the fairy lights on the tree, yellow and red and green.

Tom had done it every year for her since she could remember. Well, before that, really, because she didn't actually remember the first time, though her mum and dad had said it was all his idea, even when they were only tiny, and Cassie believed them because Tom was very clever.

She found the first clue under the Christmas tree. It hadn't been there last night—she'd checked before she went to bed, so he must have snuck down in the night to put it there. She pressed her hand to her mouth to stop the excited giggle. Wouldn't it be good if she could do it all by herself this year ... follow the clues and find her present at the end of the treasure hunt before Tom even woke up? He'd be so impressed with that; she knew he would.

So, alone in the dark, under the twinkling lights of the tree, she tore open the envelope, and began to read.

Chapter One

Cassie ducked under the low wooden beam of the doorway and into the warmth of the pub, her hands full, clutching a tray of mince pies. In one corner, logs cracked in the fireplace, and the smell of mulled wine, sherry, pine, and cheese all rolled into one. She walked toward the rustic bar, nodding to a few familiar faces as she passed, the chatter of what must be nearly the entire village washing over her. It made her smile—everyone out together on Christmas Eve, coming out to an event that *she'd* helped organize and looking like they were really enjoying it.

She caught sight of Tom, leaning against a stone wall and laughing as he threw his head back, his blond hair, almost exactly the same color as hers, flopping to one side. He hadn't noticed her coming in: he was chatting away to someone who had their back to her, beer in hand. Someone with messy dark brown hair, relaxed posture, a black jacket showing off those impressive shoulders. Her smile got bigger and she tried to ignore the little lurch in her stomach, the way her skin started to buzz.

It's just Sam, she told herself. Sam, whom she'd known since forever. Sam, her brother's best friend. She glanced at him once more—and nearly stumbled straight into the old oak bar, clutching the tray she was holding and throwing it out in front of her to save the mince pies.

"Watch out, Cassie love—we don't want to see all your hard work ending up on the floor!" Linda, landlady of The Red House, appeared on the other side of the bar, having come through the double doors that led to the kitchen. She tucked a red-and-white tea towel through the belt on her jeans and crossed to Cassie, reached out to take the mince pies, then set them down by the coffee machine.

"Sorry, Linda," Cassie said quickly, slipping out of her coat, "I know I'm a bit late, and I—"

Linda waved her apology away, her many rings glinting in the candlelight from the candles Cassie had helped set up earlier. "Don't be silly. You're a doll for making them, and they look so good I might have to sneak one away before the rabble get their hands on them." She did just that, grabbing one and taking a bite, and groaning in what Cassie thought was slightly overdone pleasure. A crumb of the pastry stuck to Linda's red lip gloss, and Cassie wondered if she should tell her. "I can't believe you whipped these up overnight! You're a girl of many hidden talents, I tell you."

Cassie shrugged modestly and decided not to tell Linda about the three batches of pastry that had ended up in the bin, the state of the kitchen earning many a tight-lipped look from her aunt Claire. But really, what was the alternative? Linda had suggested store-bought mince pies from Sainsburys for the pub's annual Christmas Eve event, but Cassie had known that homemade would be better.

The door to the pub opened again, letting in a blast of cool air that managed to reach even the bar. Cassie looked over to see Hazel, her best friend since the beginning of primary school, coming in with her mum. Hazel spotted Cassie and her eyes— green, not hazel—sparked as she closed the distance between them with a few long, elegant strides. Cassie clocked the heels that Hazel was wearing and tried not to wrinkle her nose. They always looked ridiculous together when she did that, because of the difference in their heights—Hazel tall enough to be a professional model, and Cassie, barely making five foot, still short enough to occasionally fit into children's clothing. Honestly, Cassie had told Hazel that they looked like some kind of double act and that they should be trying to *reduce* the difference in their heights rather than accentuate it, but Hazel didn't care. She was confident in her height and was sure it was going to come in useful one day, if only so that she didn't have to get married just to have someone around to reach the top shelf.

"Happy Christmas Eve!" Hazel gave Cassie a hug—bending down to do so—then stepped back and pursed her lips as she studied Cassie, who twirled a strand of her hair back into place behind her ear. Hazel nodded approvingly. "The dress works," she said decisively, and Cassie felt relief wash over her, as she tried very hard not to glance at the head of messy brown hair behind her. Despite repeatedly telling herself that he was *just Sam*, she knew she'd bought the dress—black, tight-fitting, with silver snowflakes on it—especially for tonight. Because, fine, yes, even if he *was* just her brother's best friend, something had changed since he'd gone away for university this year. She'd missed him. More than she'd thought she would. She'd missed Tom too, obviously, even though she still spoke to him all the time on the phone. But she hadn't expected to miss Sam, his teasing, his easy company, quite so much. Hadn't expected her heart to jump at the sight of him when he came back for the Christmas holidays.

Hazel grinned down at Cassie, shaking back her dead-straight black hair—hair that she dyed to make *more* black, even though Cassie honestly couldn't tell the difference. "Come on then, let's go see the boys."

Linda winked at Cassie, who felt herself flush a little. It was like she knew exactly who Cassie had worn the dress for—and the heels, and the brown eyeliner to frame her brown eyes and make them seem warm rather than murky and boring. Not that Cassie had said anything, but Linda had a habit of guessing these things. She might be her boss, but she was more than that too. She was the person Cassie knew she could rely on, no matter what. She'd spent many days growing up hanging out in the pub and sneaking packets of salt-and-vinegar crisps after school with Tom. When Cassie had hit sixteen, Linda had created a job for her, even though Cassie knew she didn't really need the help. And before that, Linda had done the same for Tom.

Hazel marched over to Tom and Sam, leaving Cassie scurrying behind, trying both to look graceful on her heels, and to keep up with Hazel's long stride. Tom pulled Cassie to him and gave her a one-armed hug, leaving his arm around her shoulders. "Here's my girl, and her sidekick." Cassie smiled, while Hazel waved a hand in the air.

"I'm no one's sidekick, Rivers." True, Cassie thought. She often felt like a sidekick to Hazel rather than the other way around. Tom grinned, dropped his arm away from Cassie, and gave Hazel a quick, tight hug. Cassie, meanwhile, tried hard not to look at Sam directly for too long, even though she could feel his gorgeous blue eyes on her, assessing, as he stood there with his thumbs hooked through the belt loops of his jeans, casual as you like. God, since when did she feel so awkward around him?

"How's the land of university treating you then?" Hazel asked.

Tom wrinkled his nose. "Annoyingly hard work this year." Cassie had been treated to many a moan already, Tom lamenting all the work he was having to do in his second year of university, comparatively to being a fresher. "Well," he clarified, "for some of us anyway. Sam here seems immune." Sam shrugged, and Cassie shifted, relieved to have an excuse to look at him. She smiled, and he nodded back.

"Looking good, Cass." Cassie felt her cheeks grow warm, and she did a sort of shrug-nod thing in acceptance of the compliment.

Tom rolled his eyes. "She ought to, the amount of time she spent with that bloody hair rod." Cassie flushed more, and really hoped it wasn't as obvious as it felt. She shot Tom a glare, which he ignored.

Hazel came to Cassie's rescue, giving Tom a friendly punch on the arm. "It's Christmas Eve, you idiot, we are *supposed* to dress up and look pretty."

"Well, you do," Sam said, looking at Cassie. "Look pretty, that is." He glanced at Hazel, almost like an afterthought. "Both of you."

Hazel shot Cassie the briefest of knowing glances that Cassie didn't dare return, even though the back of her neck was sparking with heat. "Well, Rivers," Hazel said, "I think it's about time you bought me a welcome-home drink, isn't it?"

Tom raised his eyebrows. "Surely if it's me who's coming home, *you* need to buy the welcoming drink, Niagara." *Niagara.* Tom and Sam had come up with the nickname, feeling incredibly clever, because of Niagara Falls, and the fact that it was a tall waterfall. Instead of getting wound up by it, Hazel had decided to own the name, and it had sort of stuck.

Hazel puffed. "Details, details." She walked away on those long legs and Tom, with a slightly helpless glance back at Cassie, followed, leaving Cassie alone with Sam. She suddenly wished she'd thought to get a drink when she first came in, because then it would have given her something to do with her hands. As it was, they felt useless and awkward by her sides. *This is Sam,* she told herself again firmly. But her body wouldn't listen. It was like tonight, the warm lighting of the pub, the smell of pine around them, the fire crackling in the corner, was making her more aware of the looks they'd been shooting each other over the last few weeks. Looks that might not mean anything but, well . . .

"So, umm, you're staying with your mum for the holidays, right?" *Stupid question, Cassie.* She *knew* he was staying with his mum. For God's sake, she could do better than that.

Sam, though, didn't seem to be aware of her thoughts and nodded. "She wanted to come tonight, but she had to work."

"Shame. How is she?" She liked Sam's mum—there was something so warm about her.

"She's great," Sam said, and those blue eyes softened, just a little.

"And . . . your dad?" Cassie asked hesitantly.

Sam narrowed his eyes, and the softness was instantly lost. "No idea," he said harshly. "Last I heard he was off in Sri Lanka surfing or something."

Cassie twirled that same lock of hair that kept wanting to escape her carefully styled half-up, half-down look back into place. "You haven't heard from him?"

"No, and I don't want to." He said it in a way that effectively closed the subject and Cassie bit her lip, wishing she hadn't brought it up in the first place. She knew how Sam felt about his dad, but she had wondered, what with it being Christmas and all . . . She glanced at the bar, where Hazel and Tom were still in a queue—too much for Linda to handle solo, as Cassie had predicted. She felt a squirm of guilt—she should have insisted that she work tonight.

"Anyway, how are you doing, Cass?"

Cassie glanced back at him to see that the tension was lost, chased away like it had never been there. "I'm good," she said, trying for an easy tone to match his. "Finished sending off all my university applications last week." She hadn't meant to say it quite so pointedly, but then, what was the harm in reminding him that she wasn't that much younger than him? Tom and Sam may have taken a gap year together—gone off traveling around Asia and seen the world—but she was still eighteen, and he was only twenty-one.

"Oh yeah?"

"Yeah," she agreed. "Business studies." Working with Linda at the pub had made her realize that she'd love to run her own business one day. And helping to organize the Christmas do had gotten her thinking about events—she had a knack for it, Linda said. Though when Cassie had suggested to Linda that she postpone university, and that Linda hire her as the pub's events manager instead, she had flat out refused. Not only did the pub have no need of an events manager, she'd said, but Cassie did not want to be stuck in this town and this pub forever, according to Linda. Cassie disagreed—she liked the security of the pub, of her hometown, though without Tom it held slightly less of the comfort she knew.

"Business, hey? Where are you—" But he broke off as a group of four vacated the sofa table through the archway, then grabbed her hand, linking his fingers through hers, and sped toward it, tugging her along behind. She laughed at the urgency as he pulled her down next to him on the sofa, her hand still in his. She was still smiling as he shook his head. "Can't let a spot like this go to waste, Cass."

It was one of the best tables, she'd give him that. Right by the crackling fire, the Christmas tree that Cassie had decorated tastefully with gold and red in the corner, a lone candle on the low wooden table, surrounded by empty glasses from the group before. There was another group of young people sitting on stools at one of the high tables next to them, and one of the girls was eyeing Cassie and Sam with disgust, clearly having been hoping to bag the table herself. Though her gaze turned a bit more speculative as it lingered on Sam.

Cassie laughed again as she looked back at Sam. He was sitting very close to her, she noticed now, their legs pressed against one another's, hands still linked together. He reached out, tucked that errant strand of hair behind her ear, where it stayed, listening to his touch where it had not listened to hers. Cassie's heart gave an extra-strong beat.

"You really do look beautiful, you know," Sam murmured, his eyes not leaving hers, and Cassie's skin sparked.

"Excellent! You nabbed us a spot."

Cassie jumped at the sound of Tom's voice, and Sam dropped her hand. She let her breath out in a whoosh as Tom and Hazel sat down on the sofa opposite.

Hazel handed Cassie her mulled gin cocktail, a dark red color with a subtle cherry scent, and gave her a little smirk. "So, what were you guys talking about?" she asked, the picture of innocence.

Cassie narrowed her eyes, though the effect might not have been as severe as she'd hoped, given she still felt flushed from the "beautiful" comment. Seriously, she needed to get a bloody grip.

"Cassie was just saying she'd been applying to uni," Sam replied.

Tom made a disgusted noise in the back of his throat. "Yeah. Business." Sam raised his eyebrows at Tom's tone of voice and he shook his head. "Boring."

"Hey!" Cassie exclaimed.

Tom turned to her. "Well, it is. No passion or excitement in studying *business*."

"It's a smart option," Cassie said through gritted teeth. And it was—no matter what she decided to do, surely a degree in business studies gave her a good grounding. Fine, it wasn't the most glamorous or adventurous option—but then, she wasn't exactly the glamorous or adventurous type. And that was the problem, as far as Tom saw it.

She rolled her shoulders to relieve the slight tension, then turned to Sam. "What about you? You really want to tell me you're doing law because it's your true passion?" She couldn't say the same thing to Tom—he really *did* love geology, though he managed to get away with it and not slip into nerd territory because he was also sporty, good-looking, and charming. And, unlike her, he had grand plans to follow in their parents' footsteps—to go into environmental work, make a difference to the world. That was the second problem, Cassie admitted to herself—her brother, like her parents, would do something important and meaningful, while she . . . Well, her plans were less far-reaching than that.

"Nah, but I'm going to be rich, Cass, and then I'll be able to do whatever I like." Sam grinned, first at her, then at Tom, who grinned back in solidarity.

"Money's not all that matters," Cassie said, a little primly, mainly because she thought that was something she *ought* to say.

"No, but it helps," Sam said, and though he was clearly trying for jokey, Cassie heard the subtle edge to his voice. She bit her lip. She knew, didn't she, how hard Sam's mum had to work, how Sam had spent more hours at work than at school during his A-level year—and *still* got the grades to get into Manchester.

She opened her mouth to say something, to take it back, somehow, but caught sight of Linda practically jogging over to their table, tea towel bouncing in time with her bob.

Cassie frowned. "Is everything—?"

"The fairy lights have gone out," Linda said, a little breathlessly. "Outside." Cassie glanced at the window behind her, saw that the lights decorating the windows had indeed stopped shining. "And I know it's not that big a deal, but I—"

Cassie held up her hand as she got to her feet. "I'll sort it." She got it. No matter what Linda said about shop-bought mince pies, this pub was Linda's baby, and the Christmas event was one of the highlights of the year.

"Thanks, Cassie love."

"I'll help," Hazel declared, setting down her drink on the table and coming alongside Cassie as Linda scurried back to the bar.

"So," Hazel said as she linked an arm through Cassie's. "What's going on with Sam, hey?"

"Nothing," Cassie said. "What do you mean?" Her attempt at breezy might have worked better if her voice hadn't sounded *ever* so slightly too high-pitched.

But she was saved from further interrogation by Hazel's mum, Mel, who grabbed Hazel as they were walking past. Mel pouted, in a way that suggested that might be her second glass of red wine in front of her.

"You haven't talked to me properly yet," Mel said to Hazel. "Come on, your dad's gone to the loo. Keep me company for five minutes—it's Christmas!" Hazel rolled her eyes at Cassie, then sighed, as if to say that she might as well get it over with now, and Cassie nodded—she could fix the fairy lights alone. In all honesty, Hazel wouldn't have been much help anyway—Cassie had stayed over at Hazel's once when Hazel hadn't bothered to replace the dead lightbulb in the overhead light *or* the bedside lamp and was using her phone light to get around her room in the dark instead.

"Where's Claire, Cassie?" Mel asked.

Cassie shrugged. "Probably in bed by now. She's not really into Christmas." Not really into socializing in general—Claire tended to stay locked away during any of the village social events if she could help it. Mel gave a disapproving "hmmm" in response.

Cassie left Hazel with her mum, laughing as Hazel grimaced over Mel's shoulder. She couldn't help feeling a little pang as she waved and headed for the exit though. At least Hazel had parents to come here with. Mostly, she thought she had a handle on it—the fact that she was, technically, an orphan—but there were times when the loss of it flared up, and Christmas was one of those.

She watched her breath mist out in front of her as she stepped outside. It was cloudless tonight, the stars out in force. The chatter from inside was muted through the walls and Cassie allowed herself a moment to look up, to breathe in the cold night air. To imagine that her parents were up there, watching. She didn't often give in to that—the idea that they were "out there" somewhere—but tonight, on Christmas Eve, with the stars twinkling above her, felt like a night to allow herself the fantasy of it.

That moment didn't last long, though, because it was bloody freezing. She wrapped her arms around herself as she assessed the fairy lights. It looked like it was only a section of the string of lights that wasn't working—the section that draped over the second window of the pub. So maybe it was just a faulty bulb, then.

The door to the pub opened and Cassie glanced over to see

Sam coming out, clutching her leather jacket. Not the warmest, but "warm" hadn't been the look she was going for. He held it out to her. "Thought you might need this."

"Thanks," she said gratefully, and slipped it on.

"And I saw Hazel get commandeered by her mum, so just wanted to check if you needed a hand, while Tom gets another round in." He stuck his hands into his pockets, rocked back a little on his heels, standing, Cassie thought, a careful distance away from her.

She turned her attention back to the lights and tried to ignore the fact that it was just the two of them out here. "I think it's just a bulb." She walked closer, frowning as she inspected them. "They're old lights," she admitted. "Someone tried to chuck them out and I said we'd use them here."

"Feeling sad for inanimate objects again?"

She glanced over her shoulder to see him grinning at her. "I just don't like to see the waste," she said, a little defensively. And yes, fine, she also didn't like to see old things thrown away or stuffed out of sight, just because they weren't new and shiny anymore. With a bit of work, old things could shine again.

She worked a few of the bulbs, smiling to herself at the fact that Sam was content to let her do it, not step in and insist he'd fix it, as Tom most likely would have. She found the problem—a loose bulb—and pressed it firmly into its socket. The lights lit up, a gorgeous white. *Et voilà!* she exclaimed, clapping her hands as she stepped back—right into Sam. She lost her balance, felt his arms come up to her shoulders to steady her.

She turned, slowly, tilted her chin up to see his face, eyes softly illuminated by the fairy lights and the stars above. His hands stayed where they were and as she hitched in a breath, she felt them tighten their hold, just for a moment, before they dropped to his sides. She made herself take a step away from him, though the smell of his subtle aftershave stayed with her.

She cleared her throat. "Shall we . . . ?" She gestured inside.

He nodded. "Yeah."

She tried to ignore the lurch of disappointment in her gut. What, exactly, had she expected? *No, Cassie, I want to stand outside with you and make out?* She almost snorted to herself as she headed toward the pub entrance.

"But first . . ." She turned back to him to see him flush a little. "I, err, got you a present." He reached into his coat pocket, drew something out. She took a step toward him, staring at the tiny cardboard box in his hand. Plain, not wrapped. No ribbons. Rustic, she decided.

She bit her lip as she took another step. She hadn't gotten him anything. Sometimes they did jokey presents—and the four of them had done Secret Santa for a few years, but they'd said nothing about it this year, and she hadn't thought to get him something. OK, fine, that wasn't entirely true—she *had* thought about getting him something, but she'd worried it would look weird or he'd be awkward or something, and then she hadn't been able to think of what to get him that wouldn't look as though she'd gone overboard but wasn't, like, socks or a pen or something.

He thrust the box into her hands, not quite making eye contact. "Come on," he said, a bit gruffly. "Open it."

"I didn't get you anything," she admitted.

He rolled his eyes in a way that diffused some of the subtle tension between them. "Just open it, Cass."

She lifted the lid from the box. A necklace, she saw, and took it out to examine it, the silver chain cool against her already cold fingers. Her breath caught when she saw the pendant. It was a stone. A stone, from when they'd all gone to the beach together *months* ago, over the summer holidays. She'd found some beautiful ones and it had felt sad that they were there unappreciated; they'd seemed almost lonely out there on the beach, so she'd collected the best ones and given one each to Tom, Sam, and Hazel.

"It's the stone you gave me at—"

"I remember," Cassie murmured, embarrassed to find that there was a lump in her throat. She traced the stone with her fingertips.

"Right." Sam cleared his throat. "I just . . . This is making it beautiful, right? Giving it time to . . . whatever."

She looked up at Sam to see him running a hand across the back of his neck, looking incredibly embarrassed—more than she thought she'd ever seen him before.

"I took it into a shop and they made it into a necklace for me. It's stupid," he continued, words coming quickly, "you don't have to keep it—I just thought . . ."

"I love it," she said, firmly but softly. And then, after a brief moment of hesitation, she reached up on tiptoes and kissed his cheek. It was something she'd never done before, and it felt very grown up, like they were both on the verge of something else, something older, something new. She felt Sam go very still, felt the whisper of his breath on her ear as he exhaled. "Thank you," she murmured.

They stared at one another, and Cassie saw the stars reflected in his eyes. She felt like she couldn't breathe. Like she didn't *dare* breathe, in case it ruined this moment. She should smile or squeal and throw her arms around him. Something she'd done so many times before. But she couldn't bring herself to.

"Cassie," Sam said, his voice husky. He reached out to toy with that lock of hair again, and her neck tingled. "I—"

"*There* you guys are!"

Cassie jolted away from Sam as Tom came outside.

"Come on. Hazel's guarding the table, and Linda will be forcing us all to sing Christmas carols soon—you can't leave us alone for that."

Cassie snorted. "I hear you practicing your singing in the shower often enough—I'm surprised you don't want a solo." Together, Sam and Cassie crossed to where Tom was standing. Cassie didn't dare look at Sam, though she was still clutching the necklace and the cardboard box in her hand.

"Jealous of my incredible singing voice, Chipmunk?"

Cassie wrinkled her nose at the nickname he only pulled out when he was being deliberately annoying—referring to her height and the fact that when she was growing up her front teeth had looked way too big for her. Something which she'd been self-conscious enough about without him reminding her of it—not that he ever seemed to get that.

"Don't worry, I'm sure you'll show us all up with that squeaky little chipmunk voice of yours."

"I do *not* have a squeaky chipmunk—"

"Ah, there it is."

Cassie scowled at Tom, resisting the urge to stick her tongue out at him like a four-year-old. She glanced up at Sam, whose face was carefully neutral—clearly determined not to get in the middle. Something he'd practiced enough, she supposed. He was always on Tom's side really, Cassie knew—he was Tom's friend before he was hers—but she appreciated the effort he made not to make that obvious.

"Ah, come on," Tom said, swinging his arm around Cassie and pulling her back into the warmth of the pub. "You can't be too annoyed with me, or I won't give you your first clue tomorrow."

She wrinkled her nose, then sighed, leaning into him. "It better be rhyming, that's all I can say."

"Of course," Tom said, putting his hand on his heart dramatically. "Do you think I want a repeat of the tantrums of '03?"

She ignored the jibe and just said, "Good. It's not a treasure hunt if it doesn't rhyme."

"So you've told me—multiple times."

Cassie glanced over her shoulder at Sam. He met her gaze, gave her a little smile, then came up on the other side of Tom, clapping him on the back as they reached their table. And as she sat down, Cassie slipped the necklace into the pocket of her leather jacket before she took it off. She didn't want it on display just yet. She'd tell Hazel later, and no doubt Tom would find out, one way or another, but for tonight, on Christmas Eve, she wanted it to be something that was just hers.

Two Years Later

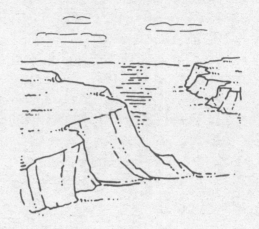

Chapter Two

Up high in the Alps, the snow glittered in the sunlight beneath Cassie, spanning out under a blue sky broken occasionally by wispy clouds. The mountains stretched out around all sides, almost unnerving in their vastness, the white giving way to gray rock in places where snow had melted or not quite settled. The nearest pine trees were topped with white, looking like something right out of a snow globe, and a brisk, biting breeze tried to cut through her hefty ski jacket, which did *not* look quite as effortlessly fashionable as it had on the online model.

Cassie struggled to properly take in any of the beautiful surroundings, however, due to the fact that she and Hazel were climbing slowly up the mountain, suspended in air and hanging off what looked like nothing more than a telephone wire in a moving chair. Her legs felt vulnerable, dangling beneath her, and she kept feeling like her skis would drop off and hit an unsuspecting skier below. She was gripping the bar in front of her tightly, remembering the one and only time Tom had forced her onto a roller coaster when they were growing up, and how much she had hated it—hated the horrible, sickening feeling in her stomach, and the way she'd almost collapsed from the rush of adrenaline after they'd gotten off. And this time it was worse, because when they got off, she'd actually have to ski down the bloody mountain.

"Ready?" Hazel asked brightly. She took hold of the bar, and

Cassie gripped it more tightly, trying to hold it in place. She saw Tom and Sam, two seats in front of them, gliding off the chair lift and onto the snow, both with seemingly effortless grace.

"No," she hissed out through gritted teeth.

"Yes, you are," Hazel said firmly, and she shoved the bar up, forcing Cassie to let go. "You're going to have to get off, otherwise you'll be like Bridget Jones and end up doing a loop and heading back down again, and that will be more scary."

The launch-off place, or whatever you were supposed to call it, was getting closer now. Cassie swallowed, her throat dry.

"Just stand up, OK? It's easy. Easier than it looks, anyway, trust me."

"Right," Cassie muttered. "OK." It wasn't like she had a choice, was it? She'd only done one of those tiny practice slopes before Hazel had declared her ready to go, which she definitely did not feel.

When her skis touched the ground, Cassie stood before she could think too hard about it, and felt the chair lift give the back of her knees a little bump as she did so. Then she was sliding away with Hazel toward where Tom and Sam were waiting. She stumbled but didn't fall. OK, good. Point for her. Because falling on her face in front of Sam as she got off the chair lift would not be in keeping with the poised, confident, sexy vibe she'd planned to portray during this holiday. Because maybe— just maybe—something might actually happen between them this time, now that they had a week together, with the possibility of some time for just the two of them in among the foursome activities. Maybe—just maybe—the last two years of glances and occasional touches that lasted a bit too long to be considered only friendly might finally come to something. Not that she was putting pressure on the holiday or anything.

She had a feeling, however, that even though she'd planned the pale-blue ski outfit, she looked more like a pale-blue marshmallow, or a thirteen-year-old girl, given her height, than sexy skiing chic. She'd like to say that *no one* looked good when skiing, but Hazel was pulling it off in a purple-and-black outfit, her black hair striking against the white of the snow. Then again, Hazel had had several skiing holidays with her family to get it right. Tom and Sam had been a few times together too. Which left Cassie, who had never been skiing before—Claire wasn't exactly the family-holiday type, and skiing was expensive. Plus, in all honesty, the concept of strapping wooden slats onto your feet and going as fast as you could down the side of a mountain had never appealed to her. Tom had been insisting that they went as kids once, before their parents died, but she was too young to remember it, so she didn't think that counted. And how much skiing could she really have done at that age anyway?

Tom moved his sunglasses onto his mop of blond hair and grinned at Cassie as she approached him, reaching out to grab her arm to slow her to a complete stop. She took a deep breath, which made both him and Sam laugh.

"Don't look so pleased to be here, Cass," Sam said, his eyes hidden by dark, expensive-looking sunglasses, "you'll make the rest of us look like we're having a bad time."

She just rolled her eyes. Partly because, now that they were at the top of the slope, with people darting around everywhere, going over what looked like the edges of cliffs, in her opinion, her mouth was feeling dry and she wasn't sure she actually *could* form coherent sentences.

"Come on then," Hazel said, her green eyes glinting. She grinned at Tom and Sam. "Bet you two a pint that I can beat you down the run."

Tom pffed. "Whatever, Niagara. You'll be eating my snow-dust."

Hazel cocked her head. "Is it called snowdust?"

Tom shrugged. "No idea." He looked at Cassie. "Ready?"

"No," Cassie said bluntly. She was fine here, she decided, standing very still.

"You are," Hazel said again, like by saying it she would im-mediately change how Cassie felt just through force of will.

"I'm not. How about I stay up here, and we'll all meet up later?"

Hazel put one hand on her hip, the other clutching her two poles. "And how exactly are you planning on getting down?"

"I'll walk," Cassie shot back. It had to be easier than skiing, anyway.

"You did fine on the baby slope," Hazel insisted. Though calling it a "baby slope" was hardly inspiring confidence. "And this is an easy blue run, you'll be fine." There were three differ-ent ways to go, as far as Cassie could tell, but Hazel gestured toward the slope that they were apparently aiming for. It didn't look easy to Cassie, it looked steep, and there were loads of peo-ple skiing down already—more people to crash into. She could feel all three of them looking at her, though, so opted for silence, trying to balance acting cool and confident with being genuinely terrified.

Hazel moved away gracefully to the start of the slope, glanc-ing back over her shoulder to check that the rest of them were following her.

"You'll be OK, Cassie," Tom said softly, starting to move slowly toward the edge and taking her gloved hand in his to drag her with him. "It'll be fun, trust me—you'll be glad you've done it when you get to the bottom."

"On three," Hazel said firmly. She was giving Cassie that

look you just couldn't say no to, so Cassie nodded. Tom let go of
Cassie's hand, slid his sunglasses onto his face, and gave her an
encouraging smile as he took a pole in each hand. Cassie felt
Sam come up behind them, her body always aware of his position in relation to hers.

"One, two, three."

But she couldn't do it. Sam, Hazel, and Tom all pushed away,
Hazel and Tom heading left, Sam heading right . . . leaving her
behind, where she was rooted to the spot, her legs having forgotten how to obey the instruction from her brain to move.

"Come on, Cassie," she muttered to herself, and with great
effort, managed to push away. She tried to remember what Tom
and Hazel had been trying to teach her earlier. Skis parallel and
weight down on right foot to turn right, right? She tried it, felt
herself speeding up, and her heart lurched. She immediately
pointed the tips of her skis together as Hazel had shown her to
slow down.

"Looking good, Cassie!" She looked up from where she was
staring at the snow to see Hazel give her a thumbs up sign. She
saw Tom, his red ski jacket standing out, gliding into action
from where he'd been standing at the side of the slope, presumably having been waiting to check that she was following. He
raced right by Hazel.

"Hey!" Hazel shouted, and sped up too. "That's not fair!" The
two of them started zigzagging down the slope, gaining speed
until she couldn't see them anymore.

Well, great. Just great. She hissed out a breath as she tentatively moved her skis again. She managed to keep moving for a
good few seconds this time, before she panicked and jerked to a
stop. Behind her, she heard a soft laugh and spun to face the
noise. Sam was there, his dark hair rumpled, his navy-blue ski
suit putting hers to shame.

She narrowed her eyes at the laugh. "How did you end up behind me?" This wasn't what she wanted—for him to see exactly how ungraceful she was.

"I was just taking a minute to admire the view," he said easily. His lips twitched as she turned from him to scowl down at her skis, which made him laugh again. "Come on, Cass, it's not that bad."

"Easy for you to say. You can actually do it."

"You can too," he said easily. "We can go slowly, come on." He pushed away, looking behind him to check she was following. Grimacing a little, she allowed her skis to slide into motion again, trying to follow exactly where he was going.

"Good," he said as she caught up with him. "Now try to get parallel and keep turning to slow yourself down—you'll end up really aching if you snowplow all the way down."

"If I what?"

"Look, watch, shift your weight." Sam went off again, and Cassie followed, trying to copy. They went through two full turns without stopping, and Cassie felt her lips pull into a smile. She was doing it!

She looked up, smiled at where Sam was waiting for her to catch up. He smiled back, eyes still hidden by his sunglasses. And her stomach lurched, the way it always did around him— the way it did around no one else, including the guy she'd dated for three months at university.

"All right," Sam said calmly as he reached her. "We've got some moguls coming up so . . ."

Cassie frowned. "Some what?"

"They're like bumps on the snow." He gestured and Cassie saw—little mounds of snow positioned randomly, taking up the next section of the slope. "So try not to go straight over

them, OK?" Cassie bit her lip—she wasn't sure she'd have much
say in the matter. Sam gave her a reassuring smile. "Just follow
me."

He set off and she did her best to follow. But after a few more
turns, she messed something up. She turned too early, and felt
herself facing straight down the slope, heading directly for one
of those hill things. *Turn,* she tried to tell herself, but her legs
wouldn't cooperate, and the mound was coming too quickly.
She squeezed her eyes shut, felt herself go straight over it. And
she was fine! Her breath whooshed out with relief. She was fine
and it was no big deal and . . . No. It was not fine. She was speeding up. She was definitely speeding up. Before she could do anything about it, she hit another one, sped up even more.

Don't scream. Don't scream, just think. Her heart was pounding, her legs felt weak as she tried to shift her weight. And then
she felt herself fall, felt her shoulder slam, hard, into the snow,
saw the flashes of someone else's skis as they sped past her. She
rolled twice before she came to a stop, breathing hard. She tried
to move into a sitting position, found her hands were shaking,
her breath coming in short gasps that were dangerously close to
sobs.

Someone stopped near her and she looked up, blinking into
the sunlight. Sam, holding one of her skis, looking like a bloody
hero, framed by that backdrop. She hadn't even noticed losing
the damn thing. "Are you OK?" Sam asked.

She just nodded, swallowing. In truth, her eyes were sting-
ing, and she felt that irrational urge to cry, like a child who has
fallen over and scraped their knee. But she took a breath, con-
trolled herself. She wasn't hurt, was she? At least not as far as
she could tell. A bit bruised, maybe, but that was all.

Sam bent down, attached her ski back onto her foot. His

hand rested on her calf for a moment longer than was necessary, the pressure of his fingers registering even beneath her ridiculous skiing trousers. "Come on, we can make it to the pub halfway down, have a pitstop."

She nodded again, and took his gloved hand when he offered it, letting him pull her to her feet. They went very, very slowly down the slope. Cassie felt like a complete idiot, and a far cry from that cool, sexy persona that she'd wanted to portray—unlike Sam, who looked like something out of an advert from bloody *Skiing Weekly*. Not exactly what she'd imagined for their "alone" scenario.

Sam was right—there was a pub, or restaurant or something, halfway down the slope. They took their skis off and stamped onto the outdoor patio in their ski boots. It was impossible to walk in ski boots, Cassie realized, and she was grateful when she saw an empty picnic bench, crossing to it and sinking down. Her feet were already sore. How did people do this all day?

"I'll get us a drink, OK?" Sam said. Cassie looked up at him, but he was already weaving through the people and heading inside.

She slipped her phone out of her zipped pocket, grateful for the case she'd thought to put it in, being as how she'd undoubtedly rolled over it at some point. She had a message. She hoped it was from Hazel, apologizing for not waiting for her, or in full-blown panic about where she was. But it was Linda, checking in to see if she was having a nice time. Cassie smiled as she tapped out a response—even though she wasn't sure that falling on your face and being so bad at skiing that it was beyond embarrassing qualified as "nice." Still, sitting outside now in the pub was nice, Cassie reasoned, the sun warm on her face, the sprinkling of green tinsel outside the wooden building, along with the snow, creating a lovely festive atmosphere.

Linda messaged back.

Send a pic!

Cassie obliged, getting in what she could of the mountains. It really was beautiful, she admitted, against the bright blue sky. **Amazing!** Linda replied.

Wish you could be here xxx

Cassie had invited her, but Linda had protested that she couldn't come away with the "younguns," as she wouldn't be able to keep up. Cassie missed her, though, being away at university. She hadn't seen her properly since the summer. She knew, too, that the real reason Linda wouldn't come was because she was too worried about leaving her "baby," the pub, in the hands of someone else.

Sam reappeared at the table holding two glasses of hot chocolate, with whipped cream and marshmallows on top and everything. He handed her one with a smile. "Christmas hot chocolate, apparently," he said, swinging his leg over the bench to sit next to her.

She cupped the glass with her hands, letting the warmth seep into them, blew on it, then took a sip, tasting real chocolate—better than the instant cocoa you got at home—alongside a hint of cinnamon.

She gave a little contented sigh, and Sam grinned at her. "The best, right?"

Cassie's phone lit up on the table and she picked it up to see a message from Hazel on their skiing WhatsApp group.

Me and Tom going to tackle a black run!! Then we'll go to a pub at the bottom of the mountain—meet you guys there?

Cassie made a face. She'd known this would happen, had told both Tom and Hazel that she'd hold everyone up, that it would be awful. But would they listen? No. They'd both just said that she'd learn, that it would be fun anyway, that no one minded slowing down for her. And now bloody look at them.

She looked up to see Sam scrolling through his phone too, presumably reading the same message, and sighed. "You can go and join them, if you want." She should offer, she knew, even though she didn't want to be left alone, really—and how the hell would she get down the rest of the slope without him?

He shook his head, slipped his phone back into his ski jacket. He'd taken his sunglasses off now, and the deep blue of his eyes was even more obvious than usual up here, surrounded by the blue sky and sparkling snow. "Nah, I'll leave them to it. Fighting it out on a black run doesn't really appeal." She gave him a look, and he grinned. "OK, fine, it does, but sitting here with you also appeals."

She met his gaze, held it, and offered him a little smile. *Cool and confident, Cassie.* But she didn't quite know how to play it. This wasn't like one of the boys she flirted with at university. Sam knew her. Had known her for basically her entire life. There was no pretending to be someone else with him. He was still looking at her, and his grin had been replaced by that same intense look she noticed sometimes when he watched her—usually when he thought she wasn't looking. She tried to think of something to say, but nothing seemed right. They'd been edging their way toward this for a while now, but both of them, it seemed, were being careful—ever so careful—not to step over that friend line. Or, more accurately, that "sister of best friend" line, she supposed.

Another message popped up on the WhatsApp group, saving her.

How are you doing Cassie? From Tom.

Cassie wrinkled her nose as she typed. **If I make it down in one piece, I'll let you know.**

Her phone lit up immediately, but it was a message from Sam, not Tom. **She's doing great.**

Cassie raised her eyebrows at him, and he shrugged. "You are."

She ignored him and typed back on the group. **I fell.**

She got back up.

She gave Sam a scathing look.

"Well, you did," he said firmly. "Shows more courage to get back up and keep going than it does to be brilliant at something right off the bat, doesn't it?"

That's the spirit, Hazel had written back.

"So how's London?" Cassie asked, trying to take the focus off her. "Everything you hoped it'd be?" He'd started a training contract with a solicitor, she knew, at a pretty impressive London law firm. He was living down there with Tom, who was doing a master's in sustainability at UCL, determined to follow in their parents' footsteps—despite the fact that being environmentalists was the reason their parents had died, crashing in their little plane while they were on a research trip. She hadn't pointed that out to Tom, of course—he knew just as well as she did, and she didn't want to ruin something he was so passionate about by voicing her concerns. She did worry, though. Worry that his ambition and passion for his work would take him away from her—and maybe take him into dangerous areas.

Sam nodded. "It's hard work, but good." Then he let out a little laugh. "I love it, to tell you the truth. London is so goddamn glamorous, Cass." He cocked his head. "When are you coming to visit Tom and me?"

"Soon," she said vaguely, ignoring the little jolt that he *wanted* her to visit. But Tom had only just moved there, and she was letting him settle. "I hear your place is all right?"

Sam wrinkled his nose. "All right being the key word there. It's a bit of a dump, but it won't be forever. The first two years at the firm aren't great money, but from there it's onwards and upwards and I'll be able to afford a better place in no time."

Cassie chose not to say anything to that. Sam had always been like this, a little obsessed with money. It was probably the thing she liked least about him—though she got it. She knew that his mum had struggled a bit while he was growing up—presumably his dad, who was hardly ever around, didn't contribute much to the finances. It wasn't that they were on the verge of homelessness or anything, but she always tried to shop at charity shops for her and Sam, was careful about the food they ate, that kind of thing. Sam had been so self-conscious about having a second-hand uniform at the beginning of one school year that Tom had made him switch, and Tom had used the second-hand stuff instead. Claire didn't notice, of course— she wasn't exactly "present" as far as parenting went. Sam got over it after that, but he'd always been aspiring for more. Cassie hoped he'd be happy, once he got there, once he had the money to rent that fancy place in London and buy the type of clothes he wanted.

"What about you?" Sam asked. "How's Leeds? Heard you met a guy . . . ?" His eyebrows shot up in a way that made her lips twitch.

"I'm enjoying it," she said. And it was true, she was enjoying university more than she thought she would, though the first year had been a bit of a whirlwind—she was very glad she'd chosen a campus university, where everything was all in one place.

"And yes, I met someone"—Why, why was she blushing?—"but we broke up a couple of months ago." *Cool and confident, Cassie. Cool and confident.*

"Oh, sorry." He sipped his hot chocolate.

"You don't *look* sorry." And he didn't—he was smiling.

He shrugged. "You're too young to be settling down."

It wasn't the answer she wanted, but she went with it. "Hmmm, advice I hear you're taking yourself, according to Tom."

"A string of girls," Tom had told her once. And she'd tried to control the jealously. Told herself that—maybe—the reason it was a "string" instead of just one was because he, too, couldn't find one to stick. Because maybe, just as she was comparing the guys at university to him, he was comparing other girls to her.

He cocked his head. "Are you disapproving, dear Cass?"

"Not disapproving," she said primly, "though I do feel sorry for the wave of heartbroken girls you're leaving in your wake." Keep it jokey. She could do that—they were on solid ground if she did that.

"Ah, you're giving me too much credit. What if *they're* all breaking *my* heart, hmm?" He reached out, prodded her teasingly in the ribs, and she swatted him away, then prodded him back. He grabbed her hand to keep her at bay, but held on to it. The cool tips of his fingers sent electricity humming over her skin. He rubbed his thumb over the back of her hand.

She cleared her throat and, because she wanted to link her fingers through his, because she wanted to lean in, right in that moment, and press her lips against his, she pulled her hand back from his gently, and tucked her hair behind her ears.

"So," Sam said, finishing his beer and showing no sign that

he'd noticed her reaction. "Another drink, or shall we brave the rest of the slope?"

Cassie sighed. "If I don't go now, I'll probably wimp out for good."

Sam laughed. "Right you are. Come on then, let's brave Everest."

Chapter Three

Sam unlocked the door to the chalet ahead of Cassie, having declared that it was too late to try to conquer another slope, which she was incredibly glad about—even if she suspected that he might just have said that for her benefit. And yes, she knew, logically, that she had to practice if she was going to get any better, but she'd rather do it at her own pace. There was a green slope, apparently—maybe she'd hire an instructor and do that one, and then there would be less pressure. Or maybe she'd admit that skiing, unsurprisingly, was clearly not her thing, and make the most of the chalet and the fireplace and the books she'd brought with her. For a moment, as she stepped in behind Sam and switched the light on, she imagined a scenario where her parents were still alive, and they'd all come on a family holiday together. Would it just be her, the wimp, staying indoors while the others went off up the mountains? Or would it be her and her dad opting for the quiet time? Her mum had been the brave one, she knew. So like Tom, who was utterly fearless.

Sam shut the door behind Cassie while she shrugged off her ski jacket and hung it up, trying not to react to his presence right *there*, so close. The warmth of the chalet cocooned them, Tom having done some fancy setting with the heating so it would be cozy for them when they got back, and Cassie headed for the kitchen, where the underfloor heating made the tiles warm, even on her now-bare feet. The whole place was like something out of a brochure; it reminded her a little of the cottage in *The Holiday*. It was all wood-paneled, and actually *smelled* of that gorgeous musky wood smell. The floor of the living space, right next to the kitchen, was wooden too, with a white, fluffy rug right by an enormous stone fireplace. A giant squidgy sofa with white blankets stood just off the rug, and two smart armchairs faced the centerpiece of the room—a little wooden coffee table, where a candlestick stood. Cassie had wondered more than once how Tom had found a place like this for the money they were paying, which, because of Hazel and her, was definitely not at the luxury end of the scale. He'd refused to tell her how much it cost, just asked for a specific amount, which made her suspect he might be paying slightly more to cover it. That hadn't surprised her, even though she tried to talk him out of that kind of thing all the time.

Sam followed Cassie to the kitchen, and she looked over her shoulder at him. "Shall I make mulled wine?"

"Sure." He frowned. "By 'make' do you mean 'heat up'? Don't you just buy the stuff from the shop? Do we have any?"

Cassie rolled her eyes. "There's a better way to make it. And I've got the ingredients, don't worry." She took down a bottle of red wine, one of brandy, some cinnamon sticks, a bag of oranges, maple syrup and cloves. She'd picked it all up at the supermarket yesterday; they'd gone on a group outing as soon as they'd arrived here—Tom driving, Hazel and her in the back of the tiny rental car.

"All that, for one glass of mulled wine?"

Cassie laughed. "Yes. I might even make enough for two each, if you're lucky."

The chalet felt oddly quiet as she set about adding things to the pan and slicing oranges, and she felt the weight of Sam's gaze on her, even with her back to him. So she was glad when he said, "Shall I put some music on?"

"Sure. Something Christmassy?"

He shrugged his agreement and crossed to the speaker on the table by the Christmas tree. She'd insisted they decorate it when they got here, and though all three of them had claimed she was ridiculous, taking off the decorations that had already been put up just so they could do it again, she thought they'd secretly enjoyed it. She'd even brought them each an ornament—a decoration that had been somehow broken, but which she'd fixed, so that it could keep being used. Although Tom, obviously, had refused to go along with just one color scheme, and now the tree was a bold combination of red, gold, blue, *and* silver. The presents they'd brought each other were already sitting underneath the tree, and Cassie knew her envelope from Tom was there right on top—the clue that would start her treasure hunt. He'd been getting more adventurous with it in recent years—the clues were no longer confined to the house, but took her on a journey around the local surroundings. She wondered what he'd planned this year, given he didn't know the area. She didn't doubt he'd have figured something out though—he was always creative with it.

Cassie heard Mariah Carey start up on the playlist Sam put on and smiled wryly to herself. "All I Want for Christmas Is You." Well, quite.

Sam came back to the kitchen and leaned against the counter as she stirred the mulled wine. She glanced over at him. "It always makes me think of Linda's pub, mulled wine," she said, almost like a confession. It made her miss it, too. She'd loved working there, and she missed the easy banter with the customers—customers she knew, because the village was small enough that you knew *everyone*—missed Linda's fussing, her easy and direct way. She waitressed in Leeds now, to help cover university costs, but it just wasn't the same. It was a chain restaurant and it lacked . . . soul, she supposed.

"You still think you'll open your own place, one day?" Sam asked.

Cassie hesitated, then shrugged. "Yes," she admitted. "One day. I mean, I've got to work my way up first, get some experience, but I want to set up an events venue, I think. Maybe combine it with a B&B. And I could have weddings there, for instance, and then the bride and groom and the close guests could stay over. Or I could host, like, epic thirtieth birthdays. And it would be in the country, so people could feel like they were really getting away, and I'll pick somewhere that's a bit older, and I'll do it up, make it loved again, and make it *mine*, you know, and . . ." She looked at him again, bit her lip. "Sorry, I'm ranting."

He smiled. "I like hearing you rant. Shows you're passionate about it."

She nodded slowly. She supposed she was. And she sometimes felt stupid, that *this* was what she got excited about, although she couldn't help it, could she? But she didn't like the word: "passionate." It always made her think of her parents, about how they died—how, afterward, everyone said that at least they died because they were doing something they loved, something they were *passionate* about.

Cassie finished stirring and ladled the mulled wine into two mugs, handed him one, blew on her own, and took a sip. It was a whole lot better than the shop-bought stuff the rest of them had wanted to get, if she did say so herself.

Sam's phone buzzed and he slipped it out of his pocket. Cassie saw his lips tighten into a hard line. "Everything OK?" she asked automatically.

He flicked her a glance, said nothing. And she remembered that look. "Your dad?" she asked softly.

He hesitated, then nodded. "How'd you know?"

"You get this look . . ." She shook her head. Maybe it sounded like she'd spent too much time observing him. Maybe she *had* spent too much time observing him. "Want to talk about it?"

"Not really." He set his phone down, scowled at it, then sighed. "He was supposed to be coming to see me and Mum after New Year, when we get back from skiing. But obviously, he's canceled. His new girlfriend needs him, apparently," he added.

Cassie heard the edge of bitterness there. She reached out, laid a comforting hand on his arm, and squeezed.

"Anyway, whatever." He looked at her, gave her a half-smile. "Nothing new, right?"

It was like him to try to make light of it, but she remembered when he was a kid, how he'd be excited about his dad taking him away for the weekend, then how his dad would cancel last-minute, nine times out of ten. Sam would shrug it off, pretend it was no big deal, and he and Tom would inevitably spend the weekend on their bikes or playing on the computer or whatever, but Cassie saw, even then, how much it hurt. She could say what she liked about Claire not being the perfect aunt, but at least Claire had never let them down like that—she was reliable, had always been there, never made promises she wouldn't keep. She couldn't fully imagine what it must be like, to have someone let you down so consistently like that.

"It's more my mum I'm worried about," Sam said quietly. Cassie drew her hand back from his arm, and she clocked the way his gaze flicked to the place her fingers had been. "She was really looking forward to it. Not that she still has feelings for him." He frowned, took a sip of mulled wine. "At least, I don't think she does. It's been, what, nearly twenty years? But it meant a lot to her, the idea that we'd all be there together—she's tried so hard to maintain this friendship or whatever with him over the years, even though he doesn't deserve it. And now she'll be upset. She had this whole menu planned and . . ." He broke off, shook his head.

"You'll be there," Cassie said softly. She wasn't sure it helped—it certainly wouldn't take away the feeling of being let down—but it was true, and she knew his mum would be grateful for it. He met her gaze, held it for a beat.

"Yeah." He shrugged. "Well. I guess that's what happens when you make a commitment you can't keep—someone else pays the price." His tone was harsh in a way that made Cassie wince. "I suppose it's what happens when you can't let go of that commitment, either, like my mum," Sam muttered.

Cassie bit her lip. It seemed a rather bleak outlook to her, though she didn't know quite what to say in response—it wasn't like she had a wealth of experience to draw on here. Linda had met the love of her life years ago, apparently, but they'd made a mutual decision to leave each other, because they wanted different things, and she was happy alone, or so she said. Claire didn't exactly seem happy alone, but then she'd never gone on dates either as far as Cassie could remember. Hazel's parents seemed happy, though. And her parents—by all accounts they'd been very much in love, and happy, and committed to one another.

She caught movement to her right and glanced toward the glass sliding doors that led to their little garden. The light from inside was reflected, so that it almost looked like there were two Christmas trees. It wasn't that, though—she'd noticed something outside. A little flurry of white.

"What is it?" Sam asked, following her gaze to the doors.

"I think it's snowing outside." She leaned forward to check, then put her mug down, ran to the doors, and laughed delight-edly. "It is!" She glanced back at him. "Sam, look, it's snowing!"

Sam laughed, and the sound, the fact that the harshness was gone, made her feel even lighter. "You've been out in the snow all day."

"Yes, but this is different, it's actually falling from the sky."

Sam came to join her by the glass doors. "That's what snow tends to do," he said dryly.

She laughed, hit him lightly on the arm. "Shut up." She opened the door, glanced down at her bare feet, then decided she didn't care. The mulled wine, the Christmas songs, it was making her want to be out in it, enjoy the moment.

"You'll get cold," Sam warned. She only waved a hand at him, stepped out, and twirled in a small circle. Yes, her feet were im-mediately freezing, but she didn't care.

"Stick your tongue out," Sam called from the doorway. She stopped, cocked her head at him. "Isn't that what you're sup-posed to do when it snows? Taste the snowflake or whatever?"

She stuck her tongue out, but at him, feeling wonderfully immature. "Are you thinking of Skittles? And taste the rain-bow?"

Sam laughed, then reached out, grabbed her by the hand, and pulled her back toward him, toward the warmth of indoors. "Tom would kill me if I let you catch a cold or something."

"You know, I'm pretty sure it's a myth that you catch a cold from getting cold." It was impressive, really, how level her voice was, given the way her pulse was spiking just at the touch of him.

He nodded slowly. "OK then." And he stepped out too, pull-ing her back into the snow and making her laugh. "You've got snowflakes in your hair," he murmured, reaching out to brush a few aside and sending a tingle down the back of her neck. Then his eyebrows pulled together slightly, and he moved his fingers to trace the silver chain she was wearing around her neck—the one she'd been wearing all day.

"You're wearing it," he said, sounding dumbfounded.

"Of course," she said. "I wear it all the time." It didn't feel wrong to admit it. She didn't wear it every day or anything—she wasn't *that* obsessive—but it had pride of place in her jewelry box and she wore it on special occasions, as well as every Christmas. Every time she put it on, she felt a little glow, like it was connecting her to Sam, to that moment outside the pub when she knew—she just *knew*—that it wasn't just a crush, that her feelings weren't one-sided.

His hand was still there, resting by her neck. His thumb moved, caressing her jaw, and her breath caught, even as her gaze stayed level on his. Her hand was steady as she reached it up to mirror his, placing it against his neck. And why wouldn't it be steady? Because this was right, she knew it was.

Sam shivered slightly and she wasn't sure if it was because of her touch or because her skin was cold. For a moment, both of them stood there, gazes locked, rooted to the spot. She cocked her head, a question.

And in answer, he leaned in and kissed her. Gently, barely a whisper. Like he was giving her the chance to pull away, if she wanted to. But she didn't want to. She wound her hand around his neck, pulling him closer, and felt her entire body hum. She felt his hands run down the sides of her body, fingertips digging lightly into her waist as she kissed him back. Kissed him in a way that let him know that it was OK, that it was right, that she'd known, for years, that this was meant to be.

Chapter Four

When she broke off the kiss, it wasn't because she wanted to. She could have stayed there all night, kissing him in the snow, but her feet were *freezing*, and she was legitimately concerned that if she didn't go inside soon she'd get frostbite, no matter what she'd said to Sam. She was breathing heavily when they broke apart, and was relieved to see that he was too.

"I'm . . ."

One corner of his mouth crooked up. "Cold?"

She nodded, and he raised one eyebrow.

"Told you."

She hit him lightly on the arm in an attempt to be normal, casual. To pretend that it was no big deal, even though it *was*. She let him pull her inside, let out a little hiss as her feet registered the warmth of the chalet and signaled to her just how cold they'd been.

Sam cleared his throat. "I'm, err, going to have a shower."

"Right." Cassie nodded. "Me too." *Keep it easy, keep it casual.* Even if the energy was still surging through her, even if she didn't *want* to be casual about this.

She showered and changed and tried—and definitely failed—to control the nerves jumping in her stomach. He'd kissed her. He'd actually kissed her—so what now? She hadn't heard the others come back, which meant it was still just the two of them. She gave herself a look in the mirror before going downstairs, her cheeks slightly flushed, her hair still damp. She should dry it so it didn't look so straggly. But then, it would be obvious she'd made the effort, and what if the others got back while she was drying it and she lost the chance to . . . What? *No expectations, Cassie.* But telling herself that didn't help, because this was *Sam* they were talking about.

The fire was on when she got back to the living room. Flames were licking away at the wood, hot sparks jumping and crackling. She glanced over to Sam, who was standing in the kitchen. "You got the fire started, then?" A redundant question, she supposed.

He jumped a little, and it made her lips curve, the fact that he was clearly on edge too. "Yep."

"A man of many talents."

He huffed out a laugh. "Clearly." He held up two mugs as she went to stand with her back to the fire—not that she needed the extra heat, but there was something comforting and calming about it. "Another mulled wine? Don't want it to go to waste."

"Sure," she said, trying to match his easy tone.

He filled the mugs then crossed to her. She was aware of his gaze on her the whole time, blue firelight dancing in his eyes. Her heart picked up speed and she felt the nerves thrumming in her fingertips. But he didn't make a move. Actually stepped back a little, after he'd handed her the mug. But then, who said the guy had to make all the moves?

She put her mug on the fireplace mantelpiece, then reached out, took his mug from him, and set it next to hers. She smiled a little, tried to hide the way her nerves were tumbling in her stomach, and linked her fingers through his. He followed the move, staring down at their joined hands. And swallowed. "Cassie, I—"

But she shook her head, not wanting to hear words of apology or whatever he was about to spout. So she reached up and laid her lips on his. Kissed each side of his mouth softly. She felt the way he was holding himself, so stiffly, so tense. As if those impressive muscles might snap at any moment. His lips stayed still, unresponsive, and she had a moment of doubt that maybe she'd misread this somehow.

Then he swore, quietly. And crushed his mouth to hers, arms coming around her, one hand tangling in her hair, the other going to her hip, where it slid inside her top, just barely, resting on her waist, his fingers tracing circles in a way that made her gasp. She pressed herself closer to him, wanting *more*, and he let out a soft groan. And God, *this*, this was how it felt to be properly kissed, this was what it was supposed to be like, where everything felt right, and perfect, and her body felt unbelievably alive, the fire behind her nothing compared to the heat in her core. She ran her hands under his T-shirt, feeling the hard, toned muscle there, wishing she could stay here, with him, forever.

The front door opened with a bang, and Cassie felt Sam spring away from her, felt the immediate absence of his warmth. She took a slow, shuddering breath, pressed a hand to her lips automatically before dropping it when she heard Hazel.

"It is not true!" Hazel's voice had a petulant tone to it. "And besides, you cut me off and—"

"Details, details, you're just a sore loser, Niagara."

Sam took another step away from Cassie, and she straightened her top, feeling like it would somehow betray what had just happened, even if it had, really, just been a kiss, even though they'd gone no further. Would they have? She tried to push aside the thought before it could take hold, and picked up her mug of mulled wine from the mantelpiece so that she had something to do with her hands.

Hazel and Tom came into the room. Cassie felt too hot. Well, yes, of course she felt hot, she was standing next to a damn fire. But she glanced at Hazel. Surely her best friend could tell, could hear her heart beating from there? But Hazel only wrinkled her nose at Tom. "OK, fine." She sighed, looked at Cassie. "So he *did* win, but I'll beat him tomorrow." She stripped her jacket off, dumped it unceremoniously on the back of the sofa. "But, Jesus, Cassie, you should've seen the speed of him!"

Cassie tried to make her voice casual, even though her body was still intently aware of Sam standing a meter away from her, tactfully not looking at her. "No, thanks." She didn't want to be anywhere near the black slopes, didn't even want to watch Tom do it—seeing him do things like that made her worried that something would happen to him, that he'd break a leg or something. "I, err, made mulled wine, if you fancy it."

"Ah, my little sister, ladies and gentlemen, a hero." Tom winked at her and she smiled, though she caught a movement from Sam out of the corner of her eye. Was that a wince?

"Great," Hazel said, and went over to the little bookcase, the opposite side of the glass double doors. She took one of the board games off the shelf. "And we can play Articulate, boys versus girls."

Tom shook his head in mock sadness. "You just love to lose, don't you?"

Hazel rolled her eyes theatrically. "Does this new girl of yours like this ego, then?"

Sam looked from Tom to Hazel. "New girl?"

"You mean Amy?" Cassie piped up, feeling like she should insert herself into the conversation.

Sam frowned. "Thought you'd only been on like two dates with her."

Tom sighed. "Yes, which is what I told these two." He gestured at Cassie and Hazel. "It was two dates—two *coffee* dates, at that, we haven't even progressed to dinner yet." But Hazel and Cassie exchanged a look, and Cassie knew that Hazel had obviously read what she'd read—that Tom, though he was trying to hide it, had a serious thing developing for this publishing intern. "And now, if you could all stop dissecting my love life . . ." He helped himself to mulled wine, looked over at Cassie. "Ready for round two tomorrow?"

Cassie made a face. "I'm not sure skiing's my thing."

"She was not as bad as she'd have you believe," Sam said.

Cassie crossed her arms, raised her eyebrows at him, forcing herself to pretend that what had happened had not just happened. For now, anyway. "Not that bad, hey? You certainly know how to compliment a girl."

"Did I say not that bad? I meant brilliant. Olympic skier next year, for sure."

She nodded. "That's more like it."

He smiled at her, and it looked almost grateful. Grateful that she was being normal, maybe—which meant that her attempt to sound normal must be working.

"Well, I can't wait to see your new skills on the slope tomorrow, Chipmunk," Tom said teasingly, heading for the sofa and flopping down as Hazel set up the Articulate board on the table. "I'm sure you'll put us all to shame."

Cassie huffed—mainly for his benefit—as she went to sit on the rug next to Hazel, who immediately started squabbling with Tom over who got to be the blue team. She swore neither of them actually cared, but the two of them would squabble over anything given half a chance—Hazel didn't have any siblings, and Cassie knew she'd adopted Tom as a sort of surrogate big brother.

Cassie risked a glance over at Sam, who was sitting next to

Tom on the sofa, but he was looking at the Articulate board, not her. She loosened a breath. They'd just have to tell Tom, she decided. It wouldn't work if they were both too scared to even *look* at each other in front of her brother. So they'd come clean, and Hazel would be thrilled and Tom would deal. It would be fine. It would definitely all be fine.

Chapter Five

Cassie stood in front of the mirror in her and Hazel's shared bedroom, carefully fastening Sam's necklace into place: the finishing touch of her outfit, which she'd spent longer than usual picking out and complimenting with makeup. It shouldn't matter. Sam had already kissed her, already proven how he felt. But still, for their Christmas Eve night out, she wanted to look pretty.

She jolted a little at the knock on her door. "Come in!"

It was Sam who opened the door, peered in almost cautiously. They hadn't really seen each other since last night— Tom and Sam heading off to tackle some of the challenging slopes, while she and Hazel had a more leisurely day that consisted mainly of drinking hot chocolate and eating chips.

"Hey," she said, smiling at him a little. How—*how* was it possible that the very air seemed to spike with electricity between them, even though he was across the room from her? It was like the whole room had woken up. Did other people feel this? Was it normal? She'd certainly never felt it before.

He'd still not spoken, was just watching her, those expressive blue eyes stormy with some kind of emotion she couldn't quite place. "What's up?" she asked. "Are we leaving?"

"No, I . . ." He cleared his throat. "I just came to . . ." He trailed off, and she saw him clock that she was wearing the necklace again, the gray stone sitting neatly against her red top. He dropped his gaze to the floor. "I just came to see if we could . . . talk, for a minute."

Talk? What was that supposed to mean? A jolt ran through her, though she squashed it, raised her eyebrows in a casual way instead. "Sure." She gestured for him to continue. Surely it couldn't be anything bad, could it? There was no way he could kiss her like that and not mean it.

"I just . . . I wanted to make sure that we were on the same page."

She made herself cross the distance between them. "The same page?"

"Yeah. You know, what with, the kiss and everything."

Because she was there, she laid both her hands on his chest—and felt his heart thud against her palms. There. Proof. "Two kisses, if I remember rightly," she said, her voice calm.

"Right," he said. "Well, I—"

"I think we should tell the others," she said, not giving him the chance to finish. She knew that he was worried about Tom—was sure that's what this was about. But if they were open about it right from the beginning, then Tom would have to accept it—and it was better than lying to him. And then Sam wouldn't feel awkward, because he wouldn't be going behind his best friend's back.

But Sam frowned. "What?"

"I think we should tell them. Tom and Hazel. They're going to find out sooner or later, so we might as well come clean."

"Cassie," he said, and his voice was slightly pleading. "It was just a kiss."

The words hurt, and she felt her hands jerk on his chest. She watched something flash across his own face—something pained, like he was already regretting the words. As he should.

Because he knew as well as she did that it wasn't "just" anything. So she shook her head. "Two kisses," she said again.

She kept her gaze level on his as she spoke, so there would be no doubt between them. Because she didn't want to keep pretending. She didn't want to go back to dancing around each other. "I want this, Sam." She smiled a little, even though her heart was hammering, almost like it was warning her to be careful, the way she was putting it on the line like this. "You and me. I've wanted . . ." She blew out a breath. She lifted one hand, traced his cheek, his jaw with her thumb, then rested it on his neck. He didn't move. His body was utterly still, like he wasn't even breathing.

"This is right," she whispered. "I know it."

He took her hands in his, squeezed gently. "Cassie, I—"

But whatever he wanted to say, she didn't get to hear it. "Cassie!" Hazel's voice sounded like a bloody foghorn from the living room. "Come on, hurry up, everyone's ready to go!"

Cassie rolled her eyes at Sam, then stood on her tiptoes and pecked him on the lips. "We'll talk later, OK?" She backed away from him, turned to grab her phone off the dressing table, along with her jacket. Looked back at him. "But it'll be OK, Sam," she said firmly. Like by saying it, she could will it into being. "I know you're worried about Tom," she added softly. "But he'll get it. He might be a bit . . . confused . . . to begin with, but I really think he'll get it."

She patted him on the arm as she came past, then opened her bedroom door, cocked her head at him. "Coming?" And when he followed her out, when she linked her arm through his and he didn't move away, she took it as a good sign.

* * *

The music pounded from inside the wooden bar, reaching where Cassie and Hazel stood, clutching their beers, among the hoard of people outside in the snow. You could just make out the shape of the mountains looming above them in the background, and a massive Christmas tree stood to one side, with a star on top that must have taken a giant ladder to reach.

Hazel grinned as she looked around at the people chatting or just starting to dance as the night took hold. "I love it here," she said contentedly, and Cassie laughed. Her body felt tense, though. Tom and Sam had been gone for a good half an hour and she couldn't see them anywhere. She was being ridiculous. They were perfectly entitled to go off if they wanted to—and she knew they wouldn't actually *leave* them here. But still . . . Her earlier conversation with Sam played on her mind. The way he'd looked at her. She'd been so sure that he was just worried about Tom—which she got. The whole must-not-date-sister thing was some sort of bro-code, right? But what if she'd read the entire thing wrong? It made her stomach tighten.

Hazel caught her looking around—again—and gave her a sly look. "Looking for someone in particular?"

Cassie ignored her and sipped her beer. She hadn't told Hazel about the kiss—kisses—yet. Mainly because she wanted to tell Tom first—and she wasn't quite sure that Hazel would be able to keep the truth hidden when they were all in such proximity to one another.

Cassie jumped, swearing softly under her breath as Tom came up behind them and slung an arm over her shoulder. "Isn't this great?" he asked, his head nodding in time to the music. "We should have Christmas here every year."

Cassie snorted. "Like we could afford it."

He jabbed her in the ribs. "Spoilsport."

She jabbed him back. "Fantasist."

"Oooh, burn," Tom said sarcastically, then laughed, squeezing her shoulder. "Christmas Day tomorrow."

Cassie looked up at him, blinking innocently. "Really? I'd forgotten."

"Oi, be nice, otherwise—"

"No treasure hunt for me." She waved a hand. "Yes, yes, heard the threat plenty of times." And she knew he'd never stick to it—he liked seeing her complete it as much as she liked doing it. She wondered if he'd do it outside, too, make her go hunting in the snow—a real White Christmas.

"So, where's Sam?" she asked, trying to sound casual. Tom shrugged, though she saw Hazel's green eyes snap to her, not missing a thing. "He's over there with some girls." He waved a hand to their left, over to where the Christmas tree was, and Cassie's gaze whirled in that direction, her stomach lurching. *With some girls?*

"You didn't want to try your luck then, Rivers?" Hazel said, as Cassie scanned the crowd.

"Ah, you know me, I wait for them to come to me."

"Sureeee," Hazel said, dragging out the "e." "It has nothing to do with a certain Amy, of course."

There. She saw him. That head of messy brown hair, broad shoulders, in that deep-blue ski jacket. Her heart jumped—and then dropped. Because he *was* with a bunch of girls. And he was standing close to a particular girl with shiny chestnut hair. Running a hand down her arm. Stepping in closer to her, bowing his head.

No. She took a breath, tried to stop watching, but her eyes seemed glued in place. No. What was he *doing?* Was he actually going to . . . ? Yes. Oh my God, he was kissing her. He was actually *kissing* this random stranger after he . . .

She felt sick. Physically sick. She backed away . . . felt, rather than saw, Hazel watching her. "Are you . . . ?" But Cassie shook her head, shoved her half-finished beer into Hazel's hand, and turned away. Dimly, she heard Hazel speak behind her, in a firm, cold voice. "I'll be right back, Rivers."

Cassie kept walking, barging her way through the crowd. She wasn't sure where, exactly, she was going, just knew that she couldn't be *here*. Couldn't be near him, couldn't watch as he . . . Oh God. This wasn't happening. How could he *do* this to her? On Christmas Eve? Right in front of her? This was *Sam*, he was her friend, he was her . . . something. And he'd just . . . Tears were burning her eyes and she let out a muffled sob, even as she tried to keep it in, tried to stop her emotions from overflowing.

"Cassie!" She closed her eyes at the sound of his voice, kept on walking. "Cassie, wait!"

But she would *not* wait. Clearly, Hazel had gone to get him, but it had taken Hazel to go up to him to even make him *think* about her.

She felt a hand on her arm, pulling her around before she shrugged it off. And there he was. Sam, staring at her, his face twisted into a grimace. "Cassie, I'm—"

"Don't," she snapped, a sob bursting through her at the same time. "Don't say that you're *sorry*." Her voice was bitter, scathing. Good.

"But I am," he insisted. He pulled both hands through his hair, the way he did when he was stressed. "I didn't mean to—"

"To what? Get with another girl in front of me? After you kissed *me*?" But it wasn't the kiss—or not just the kiss. She'd told him, hadn't she, how much it meant to her? There was no way he could pretend not to know. She'd opened herself up, admitted it, because she'd felt *sure* he felt the same, and now he . . .

She held in the next sob, tried to turn away from him. She

couldn't do this. Couldn't have this conversation with him. "Go away, Sam."

He blocked her, moving so that he was still in her line of vision. "I tried to tell you," he said, his tone pleading. "I tried to tell you that I didn't . . . that I couldn't . . ."

"Couldn't what?" she snapped. "Be with me?"

His wince was enough to tell her. Yes. Yes—that was what he'd come into her room to tell her. It wasn't *Tom* he was unsure about, it was *her.*

She jerked her chin in the air, tried desperately to stop her lips from trembling. "So, what, this was to prove a point, was it?"

He winced again, but didn't deny it. And she felt something inside her break at the realization that *yes*, he'd done this deliberately—to hurt her, to make it clear that there would be nothing between them. Instead of talking to her, instead of manning up and telling her, he'd decided to show her.

She shoved aside the hurt, the pain, the goddamn grief of it, and focused only on the anger as she drew herself up to stare down at him, no matter her height. "Well, she's welcome to you, whoever she is. I'm sure you have a deep, lasting, meaningful connection after all of, oh, five minutes. What's fifteen years' worth of memories in comparison to that?"

With a surge of inspiration, she reached behind her neck, fumbled with the clasp of the necklace, then thrust it at him. "Here," she said. "You can have this. I don't want it anymore." Didn't want the reminder—of him, of that night outside the pub on Christmas Eve, when she'd decided that her feelings were real, that *this* was real.

He backed away from her. "No, I—" But she shoved it into his hands so that he had to either take it or drop it.

"You've made your point very clear, Sam. And I've got it,

OK?" She was speaking loudly, she knew, but she didn't care right then that anyone could hear, that Tom could be watching. But Sam clearly did. He glanced around them to check, and Cassie laughed bitterly, even as her heart felt like it was splintering. "That's all you care about, is it? What Tom might think?" He flinched as he looked back at her and she considered, for a moment. She could tell Tom. She could cry on his shoulder, let him comfort her. She could work him up into a big-brother rage—and she could very possibly do some serious damage there.

She took a breath, let it out slowly. She wouldn't do it. She wouldn't stoop to it. Tom loved Sam, she knew—and she wouldn't take that away from her brother. She could live with them being friends. And that was part of the problem, wasn't it? He was always Tom's friend, not hers. So, she'd let him keep that friendship. But that didn't mean she'd extend it to herself.

"I'll see you tomorrow," Cassie said, drawing up every ounce of self-preservation she had as she spun from him, as she held the tears in, until she was out of sight. She heard Hazel calling for her and knew she'd catch up. Knew that Hazel would come back with her, would let her cry, and wouldn't ask too many questions. As for tomorrow . . . Well. She'd deal with that then.

"Cassie, please, wait, talk to me, I—"

She glared at him over her shoulder. "Don't," she said sharply. "Either you stop following me, or I'll tell Tom everything that happened."

He stared at her, expression twisted into something she'd never seen before. But when she walked away again, when Hazel came alongside her, linked her arm through Cassie's, Sam did not follow.

And Cassie decided, then and there—she was done with Sam Malone. Done with him for good.

Five Years Later

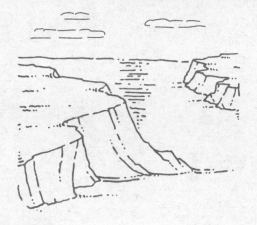

Chapter Six

Cassie almost ran into a bald man in a bright blue suit as she barged through the door into the swanky bar-slash-restaurant in Soho—the type of place she'd never choose to come to if it was down to her, because it all seemed far too expensive to be justifiable. "Sorry!" she squeaked, trying to move her wet umbrella away from where it could do any damage to his designer suit, nearly jabbing him in the ribs in her fluster to get it closed. He gave her a disdainful look before stepping around her to take his coat from the hostess, then headed through the door and out into the cold, a gust of rain swooping in to fill the space he'd left behind.

Cassie felt her cheeks warming as she handed her own coat—damp, despite the umbrella—over to the same woman and self-consciously smoothed down her red top, which she was wearing over a pair of black skinny jeans. She still had her work clothes in her bag and had changed hurriedly in the staff bathroom at the hotel before rushing onto the tube. Now that she was here, surrounded by all these posh business types in among the overly trendy London crowd, she thought that she should have picked a different outfit. But Tom had said it would just be a casual drink.

"I'm meeting my brother here," she said to the hostess, who was wearing big, gold star earrings—a nod, perhaps, to the fact that the two-week Christmas countdown had officially begun.

Or maybe they were just an effort to assert some individuality onto the black-and-white uniform they were all wearing in here. "Tom Rivers?"

The hostess nodded, her earrings glinting in the dim, moody lighting, and gestured for Cassie to follow her without saying a word. Michael Bublé's Christmas album was playing in the background, and Cassie found it a little odd, like the music didn't match up to the classy interior of the place, what with its leather booths, overhead wooden beams, and candles in glass containers around the sides of the room.

Cassie spotted Tom in a corner booth and wrinkled her nose when she saw that, yes, Sam had indeed come along too. She'd been hoping for him to cancel last minute, but the two of them were deep in conversation, leaning toward each other. Sam ran a hand through his dark hair that was so clearly styled to look messy—something he'd taken to doing since he moved to London. Cassie fought to control the scowl that wanted to take up residence on her face.

Tom leaned back and took a sip of his pint of beer, glancing over in time to see Cassie approach. He broke into a smile, his brown eyes, almost exactly like hers, only with lighter tones if you looked closely, crinkling at the corners. She couldn't help smiling back as he grabbed her hand and pulled her into the booth next to him, shifting up so that he was in the middle between her and Sam. "There's my girl! I was getting worried you'd never get here."

"I know, sorry," Cassie said quickly, "I—"

But the waitress with the gold earrings talked over her. "What can I get you to drink?" Cassie noticed that, though she was clearly addressing her, her eyes lingered first on Tom, with his tanned skin—even in winter because of all the traveling he did—and floppy blond hair, then on Sam, his blue shirt unbuttoned at the top, suit jacket shoved on the wooden ledge behind him, far too close to the candle, in Cassie's opinion. He'd probably chosen that shirt deliberately to make his eyes stand out more, she thought scathingly. She couldn't help shifting in her seat a little, though, aware of how scruffy and bedraggled she must look in comparison. Not just her outfit, but the fact that her hair had been attacked by the wind and rain outside—and she was not one of those people who could pull off the beautiful windswept look, her hair just matted and worked itself into wet clumps in bad weather. It was unfair, really, that though she was blond like Tom, *his* hair was soft and amenable, whereas hers was wiry and wild.

"What would you like, Cassie?" Tom prodded.

"Umm," Cassie said as the waitress's eyes moved to her.

"The Malbec's good," Sam said, raising his glass to her in a little salute. In all honesty a glass of red did sound good, and the atmosphere in here certainly lent itself to it, but she didn't want to go with Sam's recommendation.

"I'll have a glass of Sauvignon." The waitress nodded. "Well," she said as the waitress walked away, "this is all a bit posh, isn't it?" She looked over at Sam, raising her eyebrows ever so slightly. "I take it this was your choice?" He was always doing that, trying to pick places that were either expensive and traditional or else trendy, up-and-coming new bars. Trying to prove something, no doubt.

"Yep," Sam said easily, taking a sip of wine. "Allow me to introduce you to some culture, Cass."

"Yes, I *did* hear that 'culture' is all about the table service and posh bars these days and nothing else." She angled herself toward Tom to stop Sam from retorting. "Anyway, sorry I'm late—Robert made me stay on after my shift to sort something out." Sam frowned a little—he clearly had no idea who

Robert was. And why would he? To him, she was very much just an accessory to Tom, a little pet that his best friend wheeled out every now and then. Tom's little sister, nothing more. He'd made that very clear five years ago, and he'd increasingly put distance between them since then—something she didn't have a problem with, given the type of person he'd turned out to be.

Tom, however, wrinkled his nose. "That guy's a dick. I don't know why you're still working for him."

Cassie didn't bother answering. Tom knew full well why she was still working for the hotel—it was good money, and events management jobs were not so easy to come by. It was a step on the ladder, a way to work herself up in the industry. Fine, it wasn't quite the dream she'd been hoping for when she'd come to London, the style of it all a bit cool and clinical rather than warm and personable, but it was a respectable job, she was good at it, and she was grateful for it, Robert be damned.

"You always wanted to do something smaller, didn't you?" Tom prodded. "Set up on your own or whatever?"

Cassie sighed. "It's not quite that easy, Tom." Which he knew—they'd had the discussion often enough. It took a lot of money to fund your own place—as well as the guts to take the risk, when it may very well go wrong, especially in the current climate. "And a lot of people would kill for my job." It was true—something which Robert liked to remind her of at least once a day. Tom said nothing, but he gave her a knowing look.

It was a new waitress who brought over Cassie's glass of wine, the outside of the glass already beaded with condensation. This girl was all smiles and rosy cheeks and she set the glass down on the table with a flourish, her brunette ponytail, tied up with tinsel, swinging with the movement. "There we go! Can I get you anything else?"

Tom shook his head and smiled, and the waitress beamed back, her eyes turning a little soft as she took him in.

"Thanks, gorgeous," Sam said, grinning at her. She glanced at him, then flushed, while Cassie resisted the temptation to roll her eyes.

The waitress walked away, and Cassie saw her glance back over her shoulder, brow slightly furrowed. Cassie imagined she was wondering what she was doing here with two of the objectively most attractive men in the place, when she was plain and still scraggly from the rain.

She noticed that she wasn't the only one watching the waitress walk away, and glared at Sam. "Don't you have a fiancée?" she said sharply. Something which she still struggled to believe. Sam seemed to have made a point of sleeping around throughout the majority of his twenties, and yet he'd met this girl last year, and they were engaged about six months later.

He sipped his red wine. "Doesn't mean you're not allowed to be polite, Cass."

"Oh really?" Cassie asked, raising her eyebrows. "Was that why you started sleeping with the boss's daughter? To be polite? It's super original, I'll give you that." And there was an ugly, scathing part of her that thought that maybe that was the only reason he was marrying her—she didn't doubt that he'd go that far, to move on up in his career. An opinion she was going to have to force aside, given Tom was the best man, and they were having the wedding at the hotel where she worked—Tom had apparently let slip to Sam's fiancée that Cassie was the events manager there, and one thing had led to another and now she was organizing the whole bloody thing, much to her dismay.

"Well, she's marrying me, isn't she? Clearly *she* doesn't mind me being polite to other women. What's got your back up?" He smirked. "Jealous?"

She narrowed her eyes, even as something hot shot to her stomach. She wasn't jealous, not anymore, but it was a low blow. "Sympathetic, I'd say, for any woman brave enough to marry you."

Tom sighed. "Guys, can we not?" He took his arm away from Cassie's shoulder as he picked up his beer. "This is supposed to be a fun evening, the last time we'll see each other before Christmas." He nudged Cassie at that, then flung his arms out overly dramatically, catching each of them around the neck and bringing them into the most awkward group hug in the middle of the booth. "My best friend and my best sister. One big, happy family."

Cassie shoved him away from her, but she couldn't help a little snort of laughter. Tom's expression softened at the sound and Cassie felt her heart give a familiar tug of love. He was used to it by now—playing middleman between Sam and Cassie. Tom might not know *why*, exactly, he had to stop them swiping at each other so much these days—at least, she was pretty sure he didn't know why. He'd asked her about it once—why she and Sam were always at odds—and she'd shrugged, told him that she didn't much like the person he'd grown up to be. Which was true. She'd seen him let Tom down a multitude of times since they'd been in London, prioritizing his posh new friends, worried about how he looked or what money he was earning more than the things that actually mattered. She'd seen him hook up with girl after girl, never bothering to care about their feelings. And bit by bit, she'd watched as he'd changed from the boy she'd once known into someone she didn't like, someone she had no interest in being friends with. So she'd stayed well behind the barrier she'd flung up during that damned skiing holiday, and for whatever reason, Sam had done the same. Tom had told her, in that same conversation, that Sam acted *differently* around her.

She wasn't sure exactly what that meant, and she hadn't asked. It was dangerous, she'd learned, to get too invested in Sam Malone.

She sighed, rested her head on Tom's shoulder. "Maybe I'm just angry because I'm going to miss you," she said. "You'll have to WhatsApp me obsessively with photos."

"If there's signal," Sam piped up. She chose to ignore him.

"It's only ten days," Tom said with a smile. "I've been gone longer before."

"I know." She took a sip of her wine. "So, is Amy coming round for Christmas too? I'm ordering the food tomorrow." They were planning to have Christmas together at Cassie's flat. Hazel was going home to Highclere for Christmas, like she did every year. She'd tried to get Cassie to come home too, but Claire had expressed no interest in spending Christmas with Tom and Cassie since they'd both left for university, and Linda had taken to opening the pub for Christmas Day lunch over the last few years, saying it was a big moneymaker, so she'd be tied up.

To her surprise, Tom looked a little awkward at Cassie's question, not meeting her gaze and looking at his beer instead. She saw Sam shoot him a furtive look, and frowned. Was Tom about to tell her that Sam would be spending Christmas with them too? She'd assumed he'd be spending Christmas with his fiancée, though hadn't wanted to ask, worried that he would take it as an invitation.

"What is it?" she demanded.

Tom cleared his throat and Sam deliberately looked away. "Well, ah," Tom began, "Amy and I . . . We actually broke up."

Her frown deepened. "What? Why?" She couldn't imagine it. Tom and Amy had been together pretty much since he'd moved to London and had seemed solid—they lived on the outskirts, toward Kent, and went on various adventures to-gether while still giving each other the freedom to go off and do things on their own. Cassie liked Amy—she was warm and kind, and always had interesting stories about the books she worked on at her publishing job. Cassie had assumed that Tom would be following in Sam's footsteps soon and getting mar-ried.

"It just didn't work out." But the base of Tom's neck was turning a little red, a sure sign that he wasn't quite telling the truth.

"But what—?"

"Drop it, Cass," Sam said quietly. Her gaze shot to him and she felt her back go up, ready to snap something back at him, but he gave her a very small, subtle shake of the head. She hesi-tated. His tone hadn't been condescending or arrogant, for once, and he was giving her such a sincere look. The kind of look they'd used to exchange, when they'd been able to communicate without speaking, back before everything had changed. So she didn't push, and tried to ignore the little spark of hurt, that Sam knew something about Tom's life that she didn't.

"What about you?" Tom asked in a clear effort to change the subject. "Seeing anyone at the moment?"

She wrinkled her nose. "No."

"Why not?" Tom asked—as if it were that easy, as if she could just pick the right guy from a catalogue or something.

"Because I'm happy being single." It was true—sort of. She and Hazel had both decided they were better off being single than with the wrong guy. And while, OK, she did have mo-ments where she wished she could find someone, she'd never met anyone that made her feel . . . like she was supposed to be with them. And maybe that was stupid, and romantic, and she should just try harder—but she'd seen Tom have it, with Amy.

Or, at least, she thought that's what she'd seen. And her parents—Linda had told her over and over again how much they loved one another. So what if she was holding out for that? At least she tried harder than Hazel—she tried to give guys a chance, whereas Hazel rarely made it past the first date—or half a date, those two times.

Tom sighed overdramatically. "You and Hazel are the worst," he said, like he'd read her mind.

She rolled her eyes, deliberately not looking at Sam, who was staring at his glass of Malbec a little too intently for Cassie to believe he wasn't listening. And that was fine. Let him listen— what was it to her? "What, because you haven't managed to marry us off? Channeling your inner Mrs. Bennet, are you?"

He grinned. "Always."

She was quietly relieved when Sam pulled Tom into a discussion about how epic climbing the Andes in Patagonia was going to be, and after another round Cassie was very ready to call it a night. "I've got to go," she announced, potentially a bit more loudly than was necessary. She stood up for emphasis and tried not to sway on her feet. "I've got work tomorrow and I need sleep if I'm going to deal with Robert for ten hours straight."

"I'll come with you," Tom said, standing with her, and putting a hand on her arm as he helped her out of the booth. Sam was looking down at his phone as Tom and Cassie turned back to him, waiting for him to stand too. He looked up and smiled in that overly cocky way that Cassie hated.

"I'm going to stay out for one more," he said. "Got a few mates who are on their way to meet me." He gestured to his phone and Cassie wondered when, exactly, he'd arranged for said mates to come. Had he been searching for someone more exciting before they'd even announced they were leaving?

"Don't be out too late," Tom said, in a mock warning voice. "We've got an early flight tomorrow."

Sam grinned. "I wouldn't miss it. I've been counting down to this for months now, mate."

Tom reached out and clapped Sam on the back, while Cassie just gave him a nod when he turned his gaze on her. His eyes were bluer, somehow, in the dim, moody lighting of the bar, the candlelight making them shimmer, even though she tried not to notice them.

Cassie walked with Tom to Leicester Square tube station. There were lots of people out, shouting, laughing, or rushing along clutching too many bags, perhaps having been out Christmas shopping for the day. The rain had died down to more of a gentle mist, though the wind was still biting, and Cassie shoved her hands deep into her pockets as she walked, the buzz that had been brought on by several glasses of wine slightly mediated by the outside air.

She glanced up at Tom. "Where are you staying at the moment then?" Presumably not with Amy anymore, if they'd broken up.

"In an Airbnb in north London for a bit. Got a mate up that way." He gave her a smile she knew was meant to be reassuring. "I just need a bit of space. I'll figure it all out when I get back."

They stepped into the tube station, beeping through the ticket barrier together. "Why didn't you tell me, Tom?"

"Because I didn't want you to worry. It's not your job to look after me."

"We look after each other," she said pointedly.

Tom smiled, then sighed. "And you and Amy, you get on. I didn't want to put you in an awkward position."

Cassie shook her head. "You're my brother. That comes first, no matter what." She wanted to ask if he'd cheated on Amy, if that was what he meant by an "awkward position." But then, if he had, she wasn't entirely sure she wanted to know the answer, and she didn't want to push him into telling her if he wasn't ready.

They paused at the bottom of the escalator, each of them about to head onto a different platform—her south, him north. "Well, listen," Cassie said, "have an amazing time in Argentina, but if you ever want to talk about it—or anything—you know I'm here, right?"

"Always." He wrapped his arms around her. "I love you, baby sis."

She hugged him back. "You're just drunk and emotional."

He chuckled. "Maybe a little. But I still love you." He gave her a tight squeeze. "And you love me too," he prompted.

She laughed. "Yes, I love you too."

They pulled away and Tom gave her a little salute in parting. "And hey," he said, as he backed away to head onto his platform, "just you wait until you see the treasure hunt I've got in store for you when I get back. It's an extra special one this year." He gave her an exaggerated wink.

"I can't wait," she said, and meant it. Her train pulled up onto the southbound platform, masking the sound of Tom's final chuckle behind her. Cassie didn't care that some people would think the treasure hunts were silly or childish or whatever. For her, it was the thing that made Christmas special. Besides, it wasn't just for her—she knew that Tom loved putting the treasure hunt together, loved seeing her face when she got to the end. It was something the two of them shared, no matter what, and she couldn't imagine a year without it.

Chapter Seven

"**Is this on straight?**" Hazel looked over her shoulder at Cassie, one hand still on the star that she was placing on top of the Christmas tree.

Cassie laughed. "No. Not even close." The star was sitting crooked to the left, which, to be fair, went with the way the tree tilted to the left too. Hazel frowned, cocking her head. "It needs to move to the right," Cassie prompted. Hazel reached up to move it way too far to the right, then stood back, hands on hips, and nodded in a way that suggested she thought it looked great. Cassie would have loved to put it right herself, but since she couldn't reach even two thirds of the way up the Christmas tree, decided to accept defeat. "Perfect." It went with the slightly mismatched top third of the tree, in any case, where Hazel had had free rein.

They both took a moment to admire their handiwork. The tree was decorated in red and gold, with ornaments they'd bought three years ago, when they'd first moved to London together—Cassie had managed to find ornaments made out of purely recycled materials, loving the chance to give something old time in the limelight. The first year had been an attempt to make their tiny flat look a bit less depressing and distract from the fact that there was no real heating, just electric heaters that they could only afford to plug in for about an hour a day. They'd since moved to a nicer place in Brixton, but it was still tradition to get a tree and make the flat look Christmassy every year, and they always made sure they did it together.

"Right, I say we deserve a mulled wine after that," Hazel said, heading into the open-plan kitchenette just off the living room. She handed Cassie a mug over the counter.

Cassie blew on her mug and took a sip. "So how was your date last night?"

Hazel shrugged. "It was all right, but the guy wouldn't stop talking about his commute, going into detail about the length of time he waited at each tube stop, and then when I politely asked about his job, he took me through a forty-five minute explanation about why working in recruitment was not as easy as people thought it was, and how he had ambitions to win some sort of Recruitment-Consultant-of-the-Year-type award. I mean, I'm not against people having ambition at work or caring about their jobs—but forty-five minutes without interruption, Cassie."

Cassie felt her lips tugging into a smile at Hazel's look of indignation, though she nodded somberly.

"Plus, I have to put up with everyone talking about their boring jobs at work, I don't need it to that degree on dates, too."

Hazel's job was far from boring, in Cassie's opinion—she worked as one of the creatives at an advertising firm, and was constantly coming up with new, inventive ways to grab people's attention—but she understood the sentiment. "So, no second date then?"

"No," Hazel said, padding across the little kitchenette and around to the living side of the room in those ridiculous fluffy socks with a unicorn horn sticking out on top of them. "Somehow I don't think he's The One." Cassie held up her mug and they cheersed to that.

The doorbell rang and Cassie put her mug down. "It'll be Josh," she said.

Since Hazel was slightly closer to the front door on her side of the kitchen counter, she went to buzz him in, and Cassie took the opportunity to grab the game that she'd been up late last night making, while Hazel had been out not meeting the love of her life. It was something she'd made up for a hen party that the hotel had hosted last year. The bride-to-be had asked Cassie to come up with an icebreaker for them all, because a lot of people didn't know each other, and Cassie had gotten quite into it, and had ended up designing a game with different categories, where each person rolled a dice, had to pick a card depending on the number they rolled, and then had a task or a question to answer that was somehow hen-party themed. Only her co-worker Josh had seen what she'd done and had gotten very overexcited and begged her to do one for his mother's "epic" Christmas party. She threw one every year, and last year his sister had organized something special for it, so Josh had been determined to one-up her ever since. Cassie had been invited to said party for the last two years now, but Robert hated giving them both the same days off, because they both worked in the events department, so she hadn't been able to go.

Cassie heard the door open down the corridor of the flat and Hazel say, "Well, well, look what the cat dragged in."

"Hello, light of my life, I was hoping you'd be here."

The two of them were chatting as Hazel brought Josh to the kitchen, his hair looking more ginger in the dull light of the flat than the strawberry blond he claimed it was. He crossed the room to give Cassie a big hug, almost making her topple backward with the force of it. He always gave good hugs, Josh. But right now, her hands were full of carefully organized cards, which she'd used the work computer to print out. "Careful!" She backed away from him, showing him the cards in her hands.

He clapped his hands together. "You did it!"

"No, that's a game she made for me," Hazel piped up from behind him. Cassie only rolled her eyes while Josh made a flapping gesture in her direction. "Mulled wine, Josh?" Hazel asked.

"Go on then." He slipped out of his long black coat and placed it over the back of the sofa. He was wearing tight jeans and an oversized sweater, which seemed to emphasize his skinny frame—one that he often lamented stayed as such, no matter how many hours he put in at the gym.

Cassie laid the cards out on the kitchen counter and started to talk Josh through the rules and the categories. She'd made it Christmas-themed, obviously, and Josh had asked her to arrange it so that each table could have their own pack of cards. There was a general Christmas trivia category, a true-or-false category, a "challenge" card with a Christmassy dare to complete, and a "Have you ever . . . at Christmas?" question.

Josh beamed at Cassie as she finished. "This. Is. Amazing." He hugged her again and she laughed as he lifted her off her feet. "Thank you, thank you, thank you. You are a goddess. A vision of perfection. My everything. The—"

Cassie held up a hand, as Hazel handed Josh a mug. "Yes, I know. I'm brilliant. You can buy me a drink after work sometime to say thanks."

"You'll need to buy her more than a drink," Hazel said, leaning back against the cooker. "She was up until about four A.M. finishing this."

Cassie gave Hazel a look—she didn't really want her boasting about that—but Hazel just shrugged.

"Five drinks," Josh said immediately.

"Ten," Hazel countered.

"The best champagne."

"A magnum of it."

Hazel and Josh grinned at each other as Cassie noticed her

phone light up on the little coffee table in the center of the living room. She crossed to it automatically, leaving Hazel and Josh to chat. It would be Tom, she imagined, sending her another glorious photo of Argentina. Photos that did not include Sam, who had proven himself to be the complete arse Cassie knew him to be by staying out to get so drunk on the night they'd all gone for drinks that he'd overslept and missed the flight. And he hadn't, Tom had told her, been able to get another flight out there in time. Tom had let loose about Sam to her the first night he'd been there alone, which was a sign of just how pissed off he was, because Tom rarely got that annoyed—or at least, he always hid it from Cassie, especially if it was anything to do with Sam.

Still, Tom seemed to be having a lovely time now. He'd met another solo traveler out there called Toby and had been going on all kinds of adventures with him—bonding with a new friend in that instant way that Cassie had never mastered.

It wasn't Tom's number, though, that was flashing on the phone. And it wasn't a message—someone was calling her. A cold caller, maybe? But it was someone calling her on WhatsApp— surely people trying to sell insurance or whatever didn't use WhatsApp? She picked up the phone, hesitating—she hated answering when she didn't know who it was, in case she got caught in some kind of awkward conversation. It was a foreign number, she realized, though she didn't know the different country codes well enough to know where, exactly, it was coming from. As she hovered in indecision, the call stopped.

"You all right, Cassie?" Hazel asked from the other side of the room.

She turned to Hazel, nodding. "Yeah. Someone just—" But the ringing started up again, her phone vibrating in her hand. It must be important, if they were calling again. She turned her back on Hazel and Josh to answer, looking at the Christmas tree instead.

"Hello?"

"Hello?" a man answered. "Am I speaking with Cassie Rivers?" The accent was British, very posh, and it threw her—why was a posh British man calling her from a foreign mobile number?

"I . . . Yes," she said. "This is Cassie. Who are you?" Confusion made her tone a bit blunter than was polite.

"I . . ." There was a hitched breath. "My name's Toby and I—"

"Toby?" Cassie asked. "The Toby that's been hanging out with Tom? What's wrong?" she continued, not giving him a chance to confirm or deny. "Why are you calling? Where's Tom?"

There was a deep breath at the other end of the line, and Cassie found herself gripping her phone more tightly. "Your brother . . . Tom . . ." Her heart pounded at the sound of his name.

"Is he there?" Cassie asked sharply. "Are you with him?"

There was a pause that went on too long and Cassie found herself counting her heartbeats, waiting. "I'm with him, yes," the man said eventually, his words slow, careful. "But he's . . . You're his sister?"

"Yes," Cassie hissed. "What's going on?" The sound of Hazel and Josh laughing washed over her and it sounded wrong, too loud.

"I'm afraid he's . . ." Another deep breath. "He's had an accident."

"An accident?" Cassie asked sharply, as her stomach jolted painfully. Images flashed through her mind: Tom on a stretcher, groaning in pain, in an ambulance being rushed off somewhere. To where? What were the hospitals like in Argentina? God, she didn't even know. "Tom's had an accident?" she repeated. "What kind of accident? Is he OK? Can I speak to him?"

She became aware that the flat had grown quiet, and she turned away from the tree with its sparkling gold baubles to see Hazel stepping toward her, frowning. "Cassie, what—?" But Cassie shook her head frantically, the flat blurring around her. She needed to concentrate, needed to find out what had happened to Tom, needed to focus so she could ask the right things, figure out insurance, call the hospital.

The man—Toby—was speaking again, and the words sounded distant, almost crackling, though the line had been clear a moment ago. Her head thudded and her breathing grew quicker. "I'm so sorry to be the one to tell you this. But he fell and . . ." The man took a breath, but Cassie was unable to. For a moment her heart seemed suspended between beats. On the edge of something, her body waiting to fall.

"By the time we got to him there was nothing we could do. He's . . . He's dead."

Chapter Eight

It was cold inside the church, even in her coat and with Hazel pushed up against one side of her, Linda against the other. But then she felt cold all the time now, so it was hard to tell the difference. The minister's words were washing over her, talking about how they were there today to remember a wonderful man, an adventurous and kind soul, one who would be truly missed. Linda's hand tightened on Cassie's and Cassie heard her muffle a sob. Hazel was crying too, her shoulders shaking, a packet of tissues clutched in her lap.

Cassie's own tears were silent and steady as she stared down at her shoes, unable to look up at the minister, to the coffin that was up there with him at the front of the church. A sleek, wooden coffin, covered in flowers, ones that Cassie had helped choose, mutely nodding as Claire and Linda made suggestions. It was impossible to believe that Tom was inside it, even more so because it was a closed coffin. It could be anyone in there, shut away from the world, ready to be put into the ground. But it wasn't anyone—it was Tom. It was her *brother* in there, the one person she loved more than anyone else, and he was gone.

Cassie took a fragile breath, feeling it quake inside her, and pressed her lips together as the tears came faster. She caught sight of Claire, sitting next to Linda, staring straight ahead, straight-backed, her whole face pinched. It looked grayer and more lined now, the last two weeks taking their toll. Her dyed hair was showing the gray too, patches of white against the bright, fake red, and her brown eyes were blinking furiously. Cassie looked back down at her lap. She couldn't look at Claire or Linda, couldn't take on anyone else's grief today.

She'd been numb since that phone call. The shock had come hard and fast at first, sucking the life from her and leaving her a crumpling, sobbing mess, while Hazel and Josh had tried to figure out what to do with her, tried to get her up, to make her explain, even though she couldn't, because words had been impossible. But after that, she had been overtaken with disbelief. She'd cried, but it had felt like she'd been crying at the *idea* of it. Because the actual fact of it, the true reality that Tom was dead, hadn't hit home until today.

"And now, Tom's sister, Cassie, would like to say a few words."

Cassie jolted at the sound of her name and made herself look up, blink the church into focus. *Would like to.* It was such an odd way of putting it. She didn't *want* to stand up there in front of everyone, didn't want them to witness her grief. She didn't *want* to be here at all. But she was the closest person to Tom, and she needed everyone to see how much he meant. So she got to her feet slowly, extracted her hand from Linda's, and tried to hold her head high as she walked the few meters to the podium.

She'd been to this church only a few times as a child—she had vague memories of carol services and Christingle, which Linda, rather than Claire, had taken her to. It was where her parents were buried, though, as the local church in the village, and so even though Tom hadn't been religious, it felt right that the ceremony should be here, that he should be buried with them. The three of them together in the ground, while she had to keep standing.

She reached the front of the church, took a breath, then turned around to look at the sea of faces, clutching the piece of paper where she'd written down what she wanted to say. She'd tried to sum up, in no more than a few pages, how much her brother had meant to her, tried to come up with something she thought he would have liked, that encapsulated the type of person he was. Now everything she'd written seemed inadequate.

Everyone was looking at her and she blinked a few times, trying to make their faces less blurry. There were still Christmas decorations around the church, she realized, even though Christmas was over: green tinsel along the railings on each side of the podium, fairy lights up above her, dull in the gray lighting. Christmas. It had passed in a grief-stricken blur this year, with her curled up on Linda's sofa and staring into the abyss.

She placed the piece of paper on the stand at the side of her, her fingers shaking too much to hold it steady. "Tom was the most important person in my life," she said, her voice already wavering. "He was the best big brother anyone could hope for. Kind, loving, always looking out for me." She took a slow breath, felt her lips tremble against one another. "He saw the best in me. He saw the best in everyone." She thought of Sam, of how Tom had tried to see the best in him, even when he'd proven, in the end, that he'd never deserved it. Sam was there, she knew. He, his fiancée, and his mum were over on the left-hand side of the church, right near the front. She looked down at her notes to stop her gaze from traveling there, knowing that, if it did, she'd feel a hot ball of anger squeeze her gut.

She went on to tell a story about when they were kids, and how he'd gotten her out of trouble when she'd fallen off her bike, lied to Claire about where they'd been so she didn't get in trouble for riding it without permission, then cleaned her up to hide the evidence. *Tell a story*, Linda had said, when she'd been staring blankly at an empty sheet of paper one evening. So she did, even though it cut her up inside to do so, to remember. To think about the fact that he had always looked out for her and then, in the end, she hadn't been there to do the same for him.

Her hands were shaking as she spoke, for everyone to see. But she didn't care. Why shouldn't she shake? Why shouldn't she crumble?

"Tom was always telling me to be brave," she said, aware that her voice was perhaps too quiet to be heard, but unable to speak up. "To be brave like him, and my mum. He was always trying to push me out of my comfort zone." She squared her shoulders as she looked around the room. "So I'll finish by saying that I think we could all be a bit more like him in that respect." A lump clogged her throat, though she held it back, knowing that she had to keep it together, just a little while longer. "We could all stand to be a bit more brave, to push ourselves, to do exciting things, challenging things. Do things that might be hard, but that will make your life—or someone else's—more enriched because of it." Even if, Cassie thought bitterly, it was that bravery that had killed him.

"For my part, living my life without him will be the bravest thing I'll ever have to do. But it's because of him that I'll be able to do it." Her voice broke on the last word. The tears were coming again now, no stopping them. But she made herself say the final bit. "And for you, every time you do something that, for you, takes courage, think of Tom. Remember him, and celebrate him."

It was such a beautiful speech, Cassie darling." Mel, Hazel's mum, squeezed her shoulder as she approached the bar where Linda, Hazel, and Cassie were all standing. Claire had offered to host the wake at her house, but it turned out that she'd recently decided to move to France, and hadn't gotten around to telling Cassie yet, so the house was half empty, and the rooms that still had furniture were a mess, boxes strewn everywhere. So Linda had said she'd sort it, that they could have it at the pub.

"Thank you," Cassie said automatically. Her voice, her movements, everything seemed to be on autopilot, going through the motions without any real conscious effort on her part.

Mel nodded then, seeming to understand that Cassie couldn't really face much conversation, gave her a small, sad smile, and left, trailing her hand over Hazel's shoulder as she did so. Cassie took a sip of her drink without looking at what it was, tasted something strong and sweet. She wanted to close her eyes, to curl up in a dark room and not leave for weeks on end. In part, the thing that kept her going was the knowledge that, soon, she'd be able to do that and nobody would be able to stop her, not now that the funeral was over.

Linda turned and took a plate from one of her waitresses behind the bar, offering Cassie one of the mini quiches on it. Cassie shook her head. She couldn't face eating, was sure that any food would just get stuck in her throat. Linda put the plate down behind her, looked at Cassie for a moment, and then her face crumpled. She pulled Cassie into a big hug. "Oh, my Cassie. It's not fair, is it?"

"No," Cassie mumbled against Linda's neck. "It's not."

"I know it's not much, but you have me, OK? I'm here for whatever you need." She pulled back, waited for Cassie to nod before she let go of her. Cassie fought the rising heat in her chest. Everyone wanted to touch her today. She knew it was in comfort, but every squeeze, every hug, brought her that little bit closer to the breaking point.

Linda wiped her eyes, her rings flashing in the process, and smoothed down her hair—still the bob Cassie remembered from her teenage years, though with a little more gray threaded through the brunette. Linda's gaze traveled to the walls of the pub, where photos of Tom had been put up all around. Cassie knew it was supposed to be nice, a celebration of him, but she couldn't help feeling torn apart by it each time she saw his smiling face.

Linda chuckled a little, looking at one photo. "That was taken here on his final shift before he and Sam left for Manchester," she said. Cassie saw Hazel turn her head to look. She knew which one Linda meant without looking, though. It had been a lunchtime shift on a Friday, so she hadn't been able to come along, but she'd joined Tom and Sam here at the pub after school, when they were already well and truly on their way to being sloshed. "He tried to get me to open a bottle of my most expensive whisky, just so he could try it."

"And did you?" Hazel asked.

"I most certainly did not," Linda said, smiling again. "He was nineteen and definitely unable to appreciate whisky, and the bottle he was after would've put a severe dent in my profits for the week. But it became a thing—he made a bet with me that if he could convince a customer to buy two glasses of it, we could crack open the bottle. He never managed it, though. Kept trying to turn on the charm, but he never got very far." A little smile was still playing around her lips. "He was a terrible waiter. Kept forgetting to put orders in—that might have had something to do with it."

Cassie frowned and Linda shook her head. "I still loved him." She glanced at the photo again, then turned toward the waitress behind the bar, pointing to something as she spoke. The waitress returned with a bottle, and Linda held it out to Cassie and Hazel. "It's the same brand," she said. "Been on the menu for a good fifteen years—no one ever orders it." She opened it, poured out three measures into glasses that the waitress handed over, and gave one each to Cassie and Hazel. "To Tom," Linda said, and they all took a sip. Cassie immediately started coughing as the harsh liquid slid down her throat and though Hazel managed not to splutter, Cassie saw her eyes water. It nearly made her smile.

"Why whisky?" Cassie asked.

"David—your dad—drank it," Linda said, glancing up again at the photos of Tom on the stone wall behind Cassie's head. "And I made the mistake of telling him that one time." Cassie hadn't known that—about her dad or Tom. And she'd never known that Tom had tried to be like their dad, in this small way. She'd known he'd wanted to follow in their parents' footsteps, of course, but this small, personal need to be connected . . . Well, maybe she hadn't given it enough thought, hadn't tried to talk to Tom about it. Because he'd always been the one looking after *her*, had been almost like a parent, in so many respects. And now it was too late to rectify that, to understand just how losing their parents had affected him, in ways she might never have considered.

"He brought whisky to my birthday party one year. Do you remember, Cassie?" Hazel asked. Cassie nodded, and Hazel started telling Linda the story, but Cassie excused herself under the guise of needing to go to the ladies' room, unable to bear the onslaught of memories. She was fighting a losing battle, though. The whole damn pub was a reminder of him.

A man with a crooked nose, as if it had been broken at some point, and wide upper body intersected her on the way to the loo. "Cassie Rivers?" His accent was very posh, old-school English. She thought she recognized it from somewhere, but no one she knew actually spoke like that. "My name is Toby. Toby Jenkins." He stuck out his hand, like he was introducing himself at a work event, and Cassie took it, a little numbly. His hand dwarfed hers and gripped a bit too tightly. "I . . ." He dropped her hand. "I was the one who called you. I was there, when Tom fell. We'd been spending some time together, both of us on our own, and we went climbing together and I, well . . ."

His eyes, a light gray-green color, focused on her face but Cassie found herself unable to meet his gaze, so she looked down at the floor instead. "Oh." It was all she could think to say. She wanted to flee, to run from this man who had been there, had seen Tom fall, watched him die.

"I'm ever so sorry."

Cassie nodded.

"I saw the funeral announcement and I wanted to . . . well, pay my respects." He put a big hand on her shoulder, rested it there for a moment in comfort. Cassie still couldn't look at him. Where had he been when Tom fell? Had he been close enough to see Tom's face? Had he been close enough to see the moment of impact?

The hand disappeared from her shoulder. Cassie looked up, opened her mouth to speak, to ask one of the questions, to torment herself further with new images of Tom's death. But the man was already walking away, and she didn't have it in her to call him back. Maybe it was better that she didn't ask, didn't know.

She saw Claire at a corner table by the ladies' room, alone, staring into the distance. She hesitated, then crossed to her. "Are you OK?" she murmured. Claire jolted, then ran her hand through her dyed-red hair, nodded.

Claire's gaze traveled away from Cassie's face, toward the photo of Tom on one of the wooden beams above them. "He looked so like your mum," she whispered, her voice hoarse.

Cassie said nothing. She knew that. Her mum—Claire's sister. Maybe it was partly why Claire had found looking after them so difficult—she saw her sister whenever she saw Tom. Maybe it was why she'd never fully been there, in the way a parent should be. She'd taken care of them, yes, but there had never been that emotional connection. And Cassie hadn't minded. She hadn't minded, because she'd had *Tom*, and he was enough. He was the one she'd gone crying to if she fell over, he was the one who had come to comfort her when she'd had a nightmare. And now . . .

"I didn't think I'd have to go through it again," Claire said, her voice breaking. "I didn't think I'd have to lose anyone else before I went myself."

Cassie pressed her lips together and nodded. What else was there to do but nod? They'd never been good at discussing feelings together, and now Cassie didn't know how to bridge that gap, the grief widening the wedge between them rather than bringing them closer.

"So," she said. "Bordeaux?"

"Yes," Claire said with a shaky breath. "I'm sorry I didn't tell you sooner. I was going to tell you and Tom together, once I'd sold the house and everything. I mean, neither of you need me anymore. Or, well . . ." She took a breath. "If you need me now . . ." She brought one hand up to smooth down her hair. "I mean, I could . . . I don't know. I just mean, if you'd rather . . ."

"No," Cassie said quickly. Then she bit her lip, hoping that it didn't sound overly harsh. She appreciated the offer, but Claire was right—it had been a long time since they'd needed each other. "You should go to France," she said.

Claire gave her a brief smile. "You could come and visit."

"Maybe," Cassie hedged.

She left Claire and gave herself a few moments alone in the

bathroom, grateful that no one else was in there. She splashed water over her face, not caring how she looked, just needing to feel the coolness on her skin.

When she came out, Linda and Hazel's parents were still by the bar, so she started toward them. Though she tried not to look for him, she saw Sam out of the corner of her eye, on one of the sofas by the fire, his fiancée next to him. Jessica was her name, Cassie knew, from her correspondence with her about the wedding. Jessica, with glistening auburn hair and high cheekbones.

The man who had spoken to her—Toby Jenkins—was there too, a hand on Sam's shoulder, as it had been with hers. He was saying something and Sam was nodding as he swigged a beer, a few empty bottles already strewn on the table next to him. The thought of him getting drunk at her brother's funeral made her feel slightly sick, and she turned away.

But it was too late—Sam had seen her and had gotten to his feet. He was staggering toward her, leaving his fiancée and Toby on the sofa. Anger whipped through her, hot and hard. She was almost grateful for it, because it took away some of the grief, the numbness. It gave her something to focus on, something to feel that was more bearable.

"Cassie," he started, and she could smell the beer on his breath. He looked awful. His tie was scruffy, hair messed up in a way that suggested he hadn't washed it in days, and there was too-long stubble around his jawline. "Are you OK?"

"No," she said shortly, and then, instead of snapping something she'd regret, something that would make a scene, she turned from him, took a step away. He reached out, grabbed her arm, and she shook it off. He stumbled away from her, unsteady on his feet. "Get off," she said firmly. "I don't want to talk to you."

"I'm—"

"Drunk," Cassie finished his sentence pointedly. "Drunk is what you are." And it became impossible to control, the way *any* emotion had always been impossible to control around him, and she felt the leash on her temper snap. "Are you for real? You're really getting drunk at your best friend's *funeral?* What the hell is wrong with you?" She was breathing too heavily, dangerously close to collapsing into sobs.

His blue eyes narrowed. "No need to get angry," he said, but though he was clearly trying for rational, calm, his words only came out slurred. "I'm just—"

"Well, don't." She crossed her arms protectively over her chest. "Whatever it is, don't. I don't want to hear it."

"What, because you're so perfect?" The people closest to them had gone quiet, Cassie realized, watching and listening even though they were pretending not to. "Because this grief is all yours? Because you're the only one affected?" Cassie felt her stomach tighten, backed away farther. But he wouldn't let her, took a step forward to match. "Look around, Cass, all these people miss him. All of them." His voice broke then, and he hitched in a breath that sounded painful. And she almost caved. She almost let go of the anger that had been on a constant simmer since Tom had died. But then, with his next words, any trickle of sympathy was eclipsed. "Don't be so fucking selfish."

There was a small gasp from somewhere in the room as Cassie and Sam stared at each other. Selfish? *Selfish?* She had lost her *brother,* because he'd fallen, because he'd been *alone* in Argentina with no one to help him, and she was being *selfish?* She dropped her hands to her sides, clenching them into fists. Tears stung her eyes, but she didn't want to cry, not now, not in front of everyone. So, keeping her back as straight as she could, she said nothing at all, and walked away, toward the exit of the pub.

Someone was running after her. She turned, expecting it to be Hazel. But it was Jessica, with the perfect auburn hair and porcelain complexion. "I'm so sorry," she murmured, her voice a soft, Irish lilt. "He's not . . ." She glanced back at Sam, who was heading back to the sofa and picking up his beer again. "He's not doing well."

"No," Cassie managed to get out. "I can see that."

"We're going to leave," Jessica said quickly.

"Good." She closed her eyes. "Sorry." She wasn't sure she really was sorry, though—she didn't want him there. Couldn't bear for him to be anywhere near her, because he was the reason Tom was not here anymore.

"I'm . . . I'm so sorry for your loss, Cassie." *Your loss*. So inadequate, like you'd misplaced someone, rather than having them ripped from you. Cassie watched as Jessica went back to Sam, said a few words, grabbed his arm, and steered him from the pub, him stumbling to keep up with her. Sam's mum was there too, her eyes as blue as his, but her hair lighter, her body and face softer, rounder. Cassie saw her gaze flickering between Sam and Cassie, before she ran after Sam. Of course, Cassie thought. Of course she'd run after her son. He had his mum, his fiancée, to look after him. But the most important person in Cassie's world had been taken.

She gave it a few minutes to be sure they'd gone before heading outside. She needed to breathe, needed to be away from the warmth, the crackling logs, the music. The laughter. Tom was dead, and people were *laughing*. She took a gulp of icy air, headed to one of the outside picnic-style tables, and sat down. She hadn't thought to grab her coat, so she sat hunched in her sweater, arms around herself. She only had a few moments alone before she was joined by someone else. Amy, this time—Tom's girlfriend. Or ex-girlfriend, Cassie supposed. Who, unlike Cassie, had thought to grab a coat before coming outside.

"I saw you come out here," she said as she sat down next to Cassie. "Just thought I'd check if you were OK." Cassie looked at her and Amy sighed, adjusting the black headband she was wearing to keep her curls in place. "Sorry. Silly question." Amy's eyes, usually bright, were red-rimmed and swollen, her hands clasped around a mug of steaming liquid, which smelt of peppermint tea. "I couldn't face drinking," she said, when she saw Cassie looking at it.

They sat in silence for a bit—it was one of the things Cassie had always appreciated about Amy, the fact that she didn't babble for the sake of it, didn't feel the need to fill silences. So it took a few moments for Cassie to realize that Amy wasn't just sitting there in silence. She was *crying* in silence, tears falling off her nose and into her lap, her shoulders shaking with the effort of trying to be quiet.

"Oh, Amy." She moved toward her, put her arm around her—the first person she'd actively tried to comfort since it had happened, rather than the other way around.

Amy tucked one of her brunette curls behind her ear. "Did he . . . ?" But she trailed off, shaking her head.

"What? Did he what?"

"I just wondered if he'd . . . said anything to you, before he left for Argentina? I'm sorry," she continued quickly, "I don't want to make you think about it if you don't want to, it's just, I didn't speak to him for two weeks before he left and I . . ." Amy didn't finish, but Cassie thought she got it. Amy had loved Tom, no matter what happened in the end, and she must have been regretting those weeks of silence, that she didn't get to say the perfect last words. She felt that too. She'd reread the last Whats-App message she'd sent him countless times.

"He just said you'd broken up."

Amy frowned. "Nothing else?"

Cassie hesitated, then shook her head. "I'm sorry." She wished she could say something more profound, tell Amy he'd told her he still loved her, anything to offer comfort. But then again, maybe nothing could. She knew that was the case for her. Her whole world had been shattered, and despite what she'd said at the funeral, in an attempt to do Tom proud, she didn't think she *was* brave enough to get through these next weeks, months, years without him. She'd lost the one person she'd always assumed would be there to lean on, and nothing anyone could say would ever make that better.

Chapter Nine

Cassie curled up on the sofa in Linda's living room, a blanket pulled over her, some kind of daytime show playing on the small television in the corner of the room. Cassie wasn't paying attention to it, though. She was staring into space, her feelings in an "off" setting. There was a mug of cold tea in front of her on the small wooden coffee table, and outside rain battered the window, the storm making the whole room feel gray inside, despite the three vases of flowers positioned around the room, the various paintings on the cream-colored walls.

She'd been staying at Linda's for two weeks now. Hazel had been there off and on too, staying with her parents down the road, and had spent New Year's with them, staying overnight to keep Cassie company. Claire had stayed for a few days too, but she'd gone to France now and Cassie was actually grateful for it—it had been hard to try to keep it together in front of Claire.

Linda padded into the living room in slippers and a fluffy white dressing gown. "I'm just going to have a shower, but can I get you anything, Cassie love?" Her gaze flickered to the cold mug of tea.

"No, thanks." Cassie made herself look at Linda, tried for a weak smile. It made her facial muscles hurt.

"I'll make some nice pasta later, shall I? What do you fancy?"

"Anything's great." Would her voice always sound this dull? she wondered. Had it felt like this, after her parents had died? It was awful that she couldn't quite remember. She knew the general feeling of grief from it, of course, and she still had moments even now when she'd take out old photos of her mum and dad and wish that they were here, that she'd had the chance to really get to know them. But she'd been five when it had happened, and she had no real memory of the immediate aftermath of it, just a sense of blackness around that time. And while growing up without parents left a hole that was a constant ache, this, losing Tom, felt different. More immediate, more acute.

"I've got a great pesto macaroni cheese recipe. Pure comfort food—the only type of cooking I'm good at, as you know."

"Sure. Thanks, Linda." She had to remember that Linda, too, had lost Tom. That she wasn't the only one struggling right now. Just like Sam had told her at the wake, she thought bitterly, though she shoved aside the memory, knowing it would only make her feel worse.

Linda hesitated, then left her alone again. She heard the creak of the stairs as Linda made her way to the bathroom, heard the shower turn on upstairs. Linda would have to go back to work tomorrow, Cassie knew. She'd arranged cover at the pub over the last two weeks, but her stand-in manager was leaving tomorrow, and she'd said she needed to check how everything was doing, after the busy period.

Cassie would have to go back to work soon as well, or risk being fired. Robert had given her a few days' compassionate leave, and she'd combined that with the annual leave she'd already booked off around Christmas—she and Josh took it in turns to work the festive period, and it was her year off. But after that, Robert would expect her back, and he'd have no qualms about "letting her go" if she didn't make it work. Maybe that was for the best, though. Life went on—she still had to earn money, pay rent. She couldn't just stop functioning entirely, much as she wanted to, and work would at least be a distraction.

The doorbell rang. Cassie waited for a moment, but the shower was still on upstairs, so she threw the blanket off and walked to the hallway to open the front door.

Sam. It was Sam, standing there in the rain, barely sheltered by Linda's little porch, his breath misting out in front of him in the cold. Cassie took a step back, pulling her oversized cardigan—one Linda had lent her because she'd packed so haphazardly—around her.

He looked terrible. He was wearing faded jeans and a gray sweater that seemed to hang off his usually toned frame. The stubble had grown even longer since she'd last seen him, into a half-grown beard, and there were dark gray circles under his eyes, which were bloodshot.

"Hazel told me you were staying here," Sam said by way of explanation, his voice a little husky.

Cassie could only stare at him, her palms clammy as they gripped the cardigan. An image of him flashed in her mind, stumbling out of the wake.

Don't be so fucking selfish.

The words cut through her still now, anger and hurt slicing her insides.

"What do you want?" she managed to get out.

He took a breath, his chest rising and falling under his sweater. "I came to apologize. I shouldn't have said that, at the funeral." Cassie felt her back stiffen at the fact he was bringing it up. It was like he knew just where her mind had gone. "I was . . . I was drinking."

"I know," she said shortly, and he winced.

He ran a hand through his wet hair—messy, not deliberately anymore, but from lack of care. "I didn't know how to get through it without . . . Anyway, look, it's no excuse. I didn't mean it, what I said. I wasn't—I'm not, I suppose—coping all that well, but I shouldn't have put that on you." Honesty. She hadn't really expected that from him—he'd never been honest with her before, after all.

Cassie made herself meet his gaze, even though she'd rather have looked anywhere else. She knew she looked just as bad as him—if not worse. Her cheeks were hollowed out, she hadn't washed her hair in days, her complexion was dull, gray. It should have been a comfort, that she wasn't alone in this. That there was someone else grieving the loss of her brother as acutely as her. But she just couldn't get there. She couldn't feel sympathy for him, or invite him to share in her grief, because none of it changed anything. It didn't change the fact that she blamed him.

"You should have been there." It came out as a whisper, and Sam frowned.

"What?"

"In Argentina," Cassie said, her voice a little stronger. "You should have been there, with Tom."

"I know."

"You could have stopped it." Tears were pricking her eyes now, and she didn't bother trying to blink them away. She expected him to tell her that they couldn't know that, that accidents happened, that it wouldn't have made a difference if he was there.

But instead, he nodded. "I know," he said again, his voice hoarse. He pulled a hand through his hair. "Jesus, Cassie, I know, and there won't be a day that goes by when I'm not sorry for it." His eyes were shining like he, too, might break down at any second.

She backed away, shaking her head a little frantically. "I can't do this. I can't deal with you right now."

He took a step toward her, reached out a hand as if to comfort her, but she darted out of reach.

"No!" She was aware her voice sounded high, frantic, but couldn't stop it. "Get out."

"What?"

"Get out! I don't want to see you. I can't *look* at you, do you understand? If you hadn't been so stupid as to get so drunk, so *selfish* . . ." she spat his own word back at him, "then Tom might still be alive. So I want you out. Out of this house and out of my life." She didn't give him the chance to respond. Instead she grabbed the door and slammed it, making him jump out into the cold and rain so as not to get hit. She saw his face just before the door closed, crumpled, mouth twisted. Grieving. But she would not feel for him. He *deserved* to feel that way.

Her shoulders were shaking as she took fast breaths, trying to hold it together. Linda came running down the stairs, a towel wrapped around her, hair dripping wet. "What's going on?" She glanced at the door and then at Cassie. "Are you OK? I heard shouting."

"There was someone at the door. I told them to leave." Linda didn't press, for which Cassie was grateful. She couldn't tell her that it was Sam there, because Linda knew him too—he was another of the teenagers who'd hung around in her pub, another of the sometime-strays.

There were a few letters sitting on the doormat by the front door, and Cassie bent down automatically to pick them up. She frowned as she handed them over to Linda, noticing that there were several from the same bank. One of them had a stamp at the top. *Urgent Correspondence.*

"Is everything OK, Linda?"

Linda took the letters quickly, tapping them on the palm of her hand to even out the stack. "Yes, of course, Cassie love, nothing to worry about."

Linda left to go back upstairs, and Cassie took her place back on the sofa underneath the blanket again. Linda came in after a few minutes, fully dressed, and set a cup of fresh tea down in front of her. Cassie picked it up, grateful for the warmth if nothing else. It was only when she glanced at Linda a second time that she noticed there was something in her hand. An envelope.

Linda rocked back on her heels, a little tentatively it seemed, and Cassie sat up straighter. "I've been starting to sort through Tom's things," she said gently, and Cassie's heart gave a painful tug. It was a job she'd given Linda, unable to face it herself. She knew Linda had gone to clear out the flat he'd been staying in, and had gathered some of his things from Amy's. Everything was in Linda's office at the moment—so few possessions, really, for a whole lifetime.

Linda held out the envelope. "I found this."

Cassie looked at it. It had her name in the middle, and a circled number one in the bottom right-hand corner.

It was her first clue.

She set her tea down and reached out to take the envelope with shaking fingers. Tom had set up the treasure hunt before he'd died.

Of course he would have. He hadn't been due back until Christmas Eve, so he'd have prepared it all beforehand. Did that mean the clues were hidden somewhere, waiting to be found? Waiting for a game that would never happen? She stared at the envelope, at Tom's handwriting. What had he been planning? Something epic, he'd said, the last time she saw him.

There was a hum under her skin. A distant echo of the excitement she'd once felt when she got her first clue on Christmas Day. It wasn't excitement she felt now, but there was something there—a realization that there was something of Tom left behind, that he'd offered her, inadvertently, a way to stay connected with him.

But the hum disappeared as his handwriting blurred behind tears, and she set the envelope down. She couldn't do it. She couldn't bear it: she didn't want to see what he'd written, didn't want to know what the clues led to, because he wasn't here and that was the whole point—he was supposed to be here to do it with her.

She looked up at Linda. "Thanks, I'll open it later."

And when Linda left the living room to start making dinner, Cassie curled into a ball under the blanket, and wept.

Two Months Later

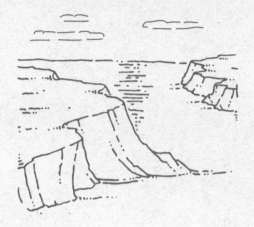

Chapter Ten

"*Shit,*" *Sam swore as* he fumbled to do up his bowtie. He tried to start the knot again, but his hands were shaking enough to make it next to impossible. He blew out a breath, staring at himself in the fancy dressing-table mirror, black tie hanging loosely around the collar of his white shirt, which was tucked smartly into his tailor-fitted black trousers.

What the fuck was he doing? He should be ready to go, maybe outside, smoking cigars with his father-in-law to be. Instead he was here, struggling to finish getting dressed, staring at his pallid reflection.

Jessica had insisted on him having a professional haircut and shave yesterday, but he knew he looked awful. The dark hollows under his eyes were proof that he hadn't been sleeping well for weeks. Months, if he was honest with himself. He could manage no more than four hours at a time, and had gotten used to functioning on that, his brain switching between fog and high anxiety. He was usually good at his job, had worked his way up at a small but well-respected solicitors' firm in London straight out of university, but he hadn't been on good form recently— forgetting things clients had asked him to do, missing emails, getting the times of meetings mixed up. His boss had put it down to being lovesick, suggesting it was all excitement over the big day. Sam was sure he was only willing to go along with that because Sam was marrying his daughter.

There had been no suggestion from anyone at work that it might be something to do with the fact that his best mate had died. The grace period for that kind of bereavement seemed to have ended already—he was supposed to have moved on, put Tom to one side. Jessica had been supportive, yes, but she'd drawn the line at changing the date of the wedding. It was all already organized, she'd said, and they'd lose a chunk of money on the hotel. She'd said it would be good for him, to have something positive to look forward to.

Sam braced his hands on the dressing table—smooth, dark wood to go with the wood-paneled room. He could see why Jessica liked this place—the hotel was indicative of the type of lifestyle he'd always aspired to, that you could only get through money. A far cry from the boy who'd worn second-hand clothes.

He tried to breathe steadily. He felt sick, and knew it wasn't just pre-wedding nerves. He'd drunk too much last night. In his hotel room, alone, ordering up a second bottle of wine through room service. His own private stag party, since he'd canceled the one he'd originally planned. Jessica had tried to convince him to go ahead with it, but it didn't feel right to without Tom, especially as Tom had been organizing the whole thing.

He remembered telling Tom that he was engaged. He and Jessica had gone out with Tom and Amy for drinks at the Ritz. He'd expected Tom to clock something at that, but according to him, Sam and Jessica were *always going somewhere fancy*, so he hadn't thought anything of it. After showing everyone the ring Sam had gotten her—the ring she'd picked out for herself, after looking in four different ring shops—Jessica and Amy had headed off to the bathroom, leaving Sam alone with Tom.

Tom shook his head and clapped him on the back. "Never thought you'd be the one to get married first, mate."

Sam laughed, shaking his head in disbelief as he sipped his champagne. *"Tell me about it."* Especially as Tom had been with Amy for years now, and Sam and Jessica had only been officially dating for six months. But Jessica had been pretty explicit in her hints and he'd known—it was propose, or she'd move on. *"Not making you want to pop the question then?"*

"All in good time, my friend." Tom raised his glass in a toast. *Then his face grew a little more serious, and he glanced behind Sam, toward where the girls had gone. "I like her," Tom said slowly. "Jessica, I mean."*

Sam raised his eyebrows. *"I sense a 'but' in the offing."*

Tom snorted. *"In the offing? You're spending too much time around those lawyer types."*

"You know me," Sam said dryly.

"Yeah. I do." Again, that serious face, the one that Tom wore when he had something to say.

"Out with it. You think it's too quick? You don't think it'll last?"

Tom hesitated, then shook his head. *"It's nothing. Forget about it. If you're happy, I'm happy."* He smiled. *"Your mum is going to lose her shit."*

Sam laughed. *"I know."* She'd be thrilled, Sam knew, that he was "settling down."

A wicked grin spread across Tom's face, making him look younger—more like the teenage Tom Sam knew so well. Sam narrowed his eyes. *"What?"*

Tom chuckled. *"Your stag party is going to be epic."*

Sam rubbed his hands over his face. Tom should be here. He would've been pouring them both a glass of champagne, toasting, making the whole thing feel fun. They'd be laughing and joking, and it wouldn't feel so much like something he had to force his way through. Tom would've listened if Sam said he was having doubts, would've talked him round. He'd known how to have fun, Tom, but he was a solid presence, reliable in the best possible way, and without him, Sam felt like the ground had shifted, like he had nothing to anchor himself to.

And it was his fault. Tom was dead because Sam hadn't been with him, hadn't been there to stop the accident.

There was a knock at the door and he jolted. Had someone come to check up on him? Had Jessica sent up one of her brides-maids to make sure he was on track? He wouldn't have put it past her. He crossed to the door, opened it, and saw his mum on the other side. The knot of tension released a little at the sight of her.

He bent down to give her a kiss. "You look beautiful." And it was true—her hair was done up, curls pinned up against her head, her eyes, so like his, were framed with sparkly eyeshadow, and she was wearing a floaty, flowery dress that suited her round face. It went with the spring wedding theme that Jessica wanted too, although the weather was not cooperating on that front—it was mid-March and still bloody freezing.

His mum patted his hand as she came into the room. "My beautiful boy. Don't you look smart?" She had a bright smile in place, but Sam wondered if it was totally genuine—his mum, he was sure, would be able to see how worn down he was by the last few months. She reached out and smoothed down the arms of his shirt, something she'd done when he was a schoolkid and was trying to reassure him that he looked fine. Then she reached up to where his tie was still hanging around his neck and sig-naled for him to bend down so she could do it up for him.

"There," she said as she stepped back. "You just need your jacket now, then you're all ready." She pulled the jacket off the back of the dressing-table chair, held it out for him to shrug into. Easier to go through the motions when she was making him do it. "I've seen Jessica already. She looks stunning, but that's no surprise, hey?"

No surprise at all, Sam thought. He had no doubt Jessica would look amazing—she always did, no matter what she wore, and she would definitely have gone all out today, after a day in the spa getting ready. She wasn't just film-star gorgeous, though; she was also intelligent and funny. A lawyer herself, too, following in her father's footsteps. It had been risky, sleeping with the boss's daughter—not that he'd given it much thought at the time—but it had turned out well in the end. So why should thinking of Jessica make his stomach squirm, make the nausea swell up in a way that he was pretty sure was not good? Was this normal, ahead of walking down the aisle? Was it just the hangover kicking in?

"Are you all right, my love?"

Sam looked at his mum, nodded, then crossed to the minibar. He'd pretty much emptied the alcohol out of it last night, but he grabbed a sparkling water and took a swig from the bottle.

"Nervous?"

Sam nodded again. Christ, apparently he'd been struck mute now.

His mum perched on the end of the four-poster bed, covers still strewn everywhere from where he'd endured a restless night's sleep. "I remember my wedding day—I was nervous too."

Sam took another sip of water, watching her. This was not something he'd have thought she'd be happy to reminisce about, given the way it turned out, but she was smiling, slightly misty-eyed, as if looking back on a fond memory, rather than thinking about the man who had up and left her twenty-five years ago.

"We got married in Nottingham, where your dad was from, in a lovely little church. I was so nervous, I nearly spilled coffee down my wedding dress—nothing as fancy as Jessica's, but it was still beautiful and the coffee definitely would've ruined it."

She smiled again. "But despite my nerves, it was such a lovely day. One of the best."

Sam flexed his fingers on the glass water bottle. She was sitting there, looking all content, but surely she must regret it, marrying his dad—they were divorced five years later, when Sam was four.

He heard his mum's phone announce a new message—she always had her phone on loud, claiming that it was rude to avoid a message or phone call just because your phone was on silent. She read it, then lifted her gaze to his face. Her expression was carefully neutral. He knew that look—her poker face.

"What is it?" he asked sharply.

She lowered her phone. "It's your dad."

"What about him?"

"He's . . . He's here." Still that damn neutral expression.

"Here?" Sam frowned. "What do you mean, here? He can't be here, Mum. I didn't invite him."

"I . . . I may have told him the wedding was happening, and where."

He stared at her. Surely not. Surely she couldn't have done something so stupid.

"He's your dad, Sam, and he wanted to be here for you."

"Makes a change," he muttered. He started to pace, pulling his hands through his hair. His *dad* was here. Fuck. What was he supposed to do with that? "How could you do this? This is the last thing I need, Mum." He came to a stop in the middle of the hotel room. "Jesus. Why didn't you tell me you'd told him about it?" At least then he could have been prepared, could have messaged his dad explicitly saying he didn't want him there.

His mum bit her lip. "Well, I wasn't sure if he'd—"

"If he'd come," he said bluntly. His mum said nothing, and Sam shook his head. "Exactly." Even his mum, the eternal optimist, had doubted that his dad would show after she asked him to. "That's exactly the fucking point, isn't it?" His mum winced at his language, and Sam muttered "Sorry" automatically.

"I'll go and tell him to leave, if you like," she said. Her voice was calm, but he knew her tones well enough to hear the disappointment there too.

"No, it's fine," he said shortly. "I'll do it." He was already walking to the door, his stride infused with purpose. It felt good, suddenly, to feel that, to have something to do, somewhere to direct his thoughts—something outward to focus on, so he didn't have to look too deeply inward.

"He's on the fifth floor," his mum called behind him.

Of course he was. Of course he'd found a way to put himself in the fucking midst of it, on the floor where the wedding was happening, where guests might see him, where he might see Jessica. Not that he'd recognize her, having never met her.

He got the lift down to the fifth floor, feeling his fingertips pulse as he marched down the corridor. Jesus, what had his dad been thinking? How dare he show up here as if he'd be welcome, as if the last twenty-five years of being let down or showing up drunk could be brushed over? Sam couldn't even remember the last time he'd spoken to him.

He passed the Tapestry Room, which was set up for the ceremony already, and though he tried to rush past it, he still caught a glimpse, and felt himself balk at the sight of all the chairs, underneath that crystal chandelier, facing the front of the walnut-paneled room where he and Jessica would soon be standing, ready to pledge their lives to one another. *Keep walking*, he told himself.

He found his dad out on the terrace. It was long and narrow, all sandstone, with terra-cotta pots spread evenly along the length of it, housing what looked to be mini trees. Standing at one of the tall, round wooden tables, his dad had his back to Sam. He was smoking away, looking out at the view of London's skyline, the top of the Shard and St. Paul's Cathedral forming the centerpieces.

Sam cleared his throat pointedly and his dad spun around.

"Sam!" His dad hurriedly stamped out his cigarette in the plant pot in the middle of the table, then broke into a cough before beaming at him, as if they should be genuinely delighted to see one another. He was wearing a rather shabby gray suit, which clearly didn't fit him well, straining at all the seams. His gray eyes looked tiny, almost sunken in, and the little hair he had left was combed over in a way that was clearly meant to hide his impending baldness. Jesus, what would Jessica think if she saw the kind of man he'd come from?

His dad walked over to him, swinging his arms awkwardly. "It's the big day, then," he said with another cough. "How are you feeling?"

Sam's hands clenched into fists at his sides, and he shoved them into his pockets. Behind his dad, on the table where he'd been standing, stood a half-empty bottle of Becks. So, his dad had already started then.

Sam took a breath, fought for calm. It would do no good to start a shouting match that brought people running outside. "What are you doing here, Dad?"

"I wouldn't miss it!" The fact that he wasn't invited hovered in the air, an unsaid fact.

Sam shook his head. "I don't want you here." To the point was better—quicker and easier.

"But I . . ."

"No, Dad." He felt heat rising in his chest. Right then, he felt the absence of Tom even more acutely. Tom would have known what to say—he'd have gotten rid of his dad and smoothed it all over in a way that didn't create a scene and didn't piss anyone off too much. He would have understood, without Sam having to explain what Sam needed—they'd always been able to do that for one another. Like with Amy—Sam hadn't judged Tom for that, hadn't made him explain. He'd figured Tom had just needed time to process. He'd gotten it, because he got Tom.

"Please," Sam said, biting the word out. "Please leave."

His dad ran a hand over his head. "Well, if that's what you want, of course. But I just thought, you know, maybe we could talk." Sam narrowed his eyes, and his dad carried on hurriedly. "I wanted to check you were doing OK, after, you know . . ."

"What, and you picked my *wedding* day to do that? Because it's the perfect moment to have a heart-to-heart? Because I don't have other fucking things to think about today?" He turned away, chest heaving, and went to stand at the edge of the terrace, placing his hands on the waist-high stone wall at the edge of it.

"Well, it's not like I get many invites, Sam," his dad said defensively.

Sam gave a hollow laugh, still looking out at the skyline of London, the city he'd made his home, through grit and determination. "Of course you're putting this back on me," he said with a sigh. And it was so obvious, so damn predictable, that some of the anger drained from him, giving way to defeat.

"I didn't mean that," his dad said quickly.

"Didn't you? There's always some excuse, isn't there?"

There was a moment of silence, which Sam didn't bother filling.

"I'll go," his dad said.

"Good."

"I'll . . . Right. OK. Well, congratulations and all that."

Sam heard his dad's footsteps, heard the creak of the floor as he stepped through the French doors. It was only then that he turned, watched his dad leave. Bitterness settled at the base of his throat. But what else had he been supposed to do? It wasn't like they were ever going to be able to have some big heart-to-heart, hug it out. Was that what his mum had been thinking? That they'd have a moment, be hanging around together at the wedding, laughing and joking? She didn't get it. There was no point in Sam trying to make up with his dad—he'd just be let down again later down the line.

He scrubbed his hands over his face, then left the terrace—and the lonely beer bottle—behind. He passed the room that he knew was being set up for the immediate aftermath of the ceremony—guests would be ushered here, once he and Jessica had officially tied the knot. This room was white-walled, with black pillars rising up to the domed ceiling. Another chandelier—the hotel did seem fond of them—and flowers *everywhere*. Christ, it must have taken mammoth organization to plan it all out. Not that he would know. He'd mostly stayed out of the wedding prep—he wasn't even sure he could say what the menu was for dinner. Jessica had a whole team of people, though—she hadn't needed his help. A team of people, headed by Cassie. His chest tightened at the thought of her.

He'd been drawn to a stop, staring at the life inside the room, the chaos in there, compared to the quietness of the rest of the floor. There was a cluster of people around one of the tables in the corner, and Sam jolted when he saw Jessica was one of them. She wasn't supposed to be there—she was supposed to be in the spa, surrounded by adoring bridesmaids, putting the finishing touches on her makeup or whatever.

He backed away, but his gaze lingered. She looked stunning, his mum had been right. Her auburn hair was half up, half down, accentuating her high cheekbones, white flowers placed in the curls at the back of her head. Her dress was strapless, corseted at the back, a brilliant combination of sexy and de-mure. She was flushed right now, adding a totally natural rosy-cheeked glow to the heavy makeup she was wearing, and was in full discussion-mode with the member of hotel staff closest to her, gesturing emphatically. His heart started palpitating in a way that made him uncomfortable.

He backed away another step, but too late—Jessica turned, saw him loitering in the doorway. She smiled and raised her eyebrows. He knew what she meant—he wasn't supposed to be there. She mouthed, "Are you OK?"

But Beth, one of her bridesmaids, saw him there too, and came over to usher him away. He took the excuse gladly, be-cause it meant he didn't have to answer Jessica's question.

Satisfied he was leaving, Beth left him to go back to help Jessica with whatever last-minute arrangements she was mak-ing. Sam glanced over his shoulder one last time, and stopped in his tracks. His stomach lurched painfully.

Cassie.

Cassie was there, in that room. She was in the other corner from Jessica, so he hadn't noticed her at first, given the way she blended in with the hotel staff, wearing a black blazer and black trousers, totally unremarkable.

Of course she'd be there. Of course she'd be at the set-up, making it all happen. But there had been a part of him that had expected her to get out of it, the actual day at least, considering what she'd said to him the last time they'd seen one another.

Sam stood rooted to the spot as Jessica crossed the room to talk to Cassie, as she took Cassie's hands in hers. He found him-self watching Cassie, not Jessica. Her blond hair was pulled into a low ponytail, almost scraggy-looking, and her face was a little pale. She wore no makeup—striking in comparison to Jessica's look. She looked . . . fragile, somehow, too thin. And tiny. Why had he never noticed how tiny she was before now? He'd never really thought of her as "short," even though she was, because she always used to sparkle in the room whenever she was there. She lit up, especially around Tom. And, once upon a time, he thought he'd seen her light up around him, too. Before he'd ruined that—and their friendship along with it. But now there was no spark, and a tiny, frail creature had replaced the Cassie he knew. He wished, so much, that he knew what to do to fix it, felt his heart physically ache at the sight of her like this. Wished he could think of something to say, or just go and hug her, tell her that it would be OK, somehow.

But she wouldn't be grateful if he tried, he knew that. There was nothing he could do, and he was too much of a coward to face her again, after last time. So he turned away.

His mum wasn't in his room when he got back. She'd probably decided to give him some space. He crossed to the dressing table and pulled out the chair, intending to collapse there and wait until it was time, but he saw something that made him freeze. A velvet box, the one that held the wedding rings. Placed on the corner of the dressing table. His mum had been looking after them, he remembered. She must have left them here for him. He opened the box and stared at the two gold bands. Tom was supposed to be holding these for him at the ceremony.

He put the box down slowly, leveled a look at himself in the mirror. Thought of Jessica down there, looking beautiful. Thought of her dad, his boss, ready to welcome him as a son-in-law, to prepare him to take over the family firm. Jessica had already talked about how she wanted kids, and no doubt that would follow soon—two children, a well-paid job, a house in London. Then he thought of *his* dad, of the mess that he'd turned out to be. Of his mum, constantly let down by the man she'd chosen to marry.

Of Tom, gone, because of a mistake Sam had made, because he'd been unable to get his shit together. Of Cassie, who had lost her brother because of him.

Jesus, he couldn't breathe. He fumbled to release the bow tie around his neck, found himself gasping. And he knew, in that moment, that he could not do it.

He could not go through with the wedding.

Chapter Eleven

Sam hastily grabbed his things from where they were strewn around the hotel room and shoved them into his brown overnight bag. Thankfully, he didn't have a lot of stuff—the honeymoon was planned for summer, rather than immediately after the wedding. He fumbled to get his bow tie off, felt immediately better when he hid it out of sight at the bottom of his bag. He grabbed his phone off the bedside table last, then hesitated. What was he doing? This was crazy. It would be the end of him and Jessica; there would be no going back after this. And he'd be kissing goodbye to his job; no way would he have a future at the firm after jilting the boss's daughter. He glanced again at the wedding rings on the dressing table, and felt his chest tighten.

No. He couldn't do it. He couldn't walk down the aisle without Tom there to coach him through it. It was an awful, terrible thing to do, to leave her like this. But he was an awful, terrible person, and it was better Jessica knew that now—better to get out of her life while it was still possible, rather than let her down later, like his dad had done to his mum.

So, with slightly trembling fingers from the adrenaline pumping around his body, he unlocked his phone and typed out a text.

I can't do this. I'm so sorry. It's for the best.

He sent it, then practically sprinted from the room, leaving the rings on the dresser. Jessica could sell them, get the money back, pay off the hotel bill. He grimaced. It wouldn't make up for what he was doing. He knew that, but it didn't stop him, didn't make him turn back. He took the stairs all the way down to the ground floor—the lift was too risky.

He hurtled into the hotel lobby, barely thinking, blood pumping in his head, urging him to get out of there. That was his one thought. Get out. He kept his head down, staring at the Art Deco flooring, looking away from the circular red sofa in the middle of the reception area, in case anyone he knew was sitting there. Fuck, he was still wearing his tux. He fumbled in his bag—feeling a rush of guilt as he remembered that Jessica had bought it for him—and got out a jacket to shove over the top, hiding the evidence.

It was halfway across the reception hall, right next to the red sofa, that Sam heard her voice. He was surprised at how instantly he recognized it, how tuned in he was to it. He jerked to a stop. Stayed still, frozen, like somehow just by moving he'd be calling attention to himself.

"Everything is set up and ready," Cassie was saying. "So Josh will be more than capable of handling things from here." He risked a furtive glance around, saw her to his left, on the other side of the sofa, near a gigantic indoor plant. She had her back to him, and was standing with two men—an older man with a receding hairline, and a wiry redheaded man.

"And I'm happy to do it," the redhead said. "Cassie's talked me through the whole thing."

Cassie was bailing, then. Just like him. Though in her case, it was understandable. He carried on moving, slowly now, aware of each step he took. The lobby had been bustling when he and

Jessica had checked in yesterday—where were all the people to hide behind when you needed them?

"Well, I'm not happy for you to leave." Presumably that was the older man, though Sam didn't look over his shoulder to check. "These are *very* important guests—the bride's father owns a London law firm. We can't have anything going wrong here." Sam winced at the reminder of what he was leaving behind, of how he'd managed to completely fuck himself over.

"My aim isn't to let things go wrong, funnily enough." The redhead's voice had turned dry. "And I'm a total hit at weddings, trust me. You can count on me, sir." There was a touch of irony in the "sir."

"You can't leave, Cassie." The voice was final. "You are the events manager, and this is an event. Besides, you were the one who brought these clients in—and that's something that hasn't gone unnoticed up top."

"Fine," Cassie said, her voice weary. Sam wanted to turn, to check her expression. But he didn't give in to the urge. The glass double doors were right there in front of him, and soon he'd be outside, free. "Look, I'll come back in a minute, but I just need to take a beat. Please. It's my brother's . . . It was someone close to my brother, getting married and I . . ."

"Cassie, I've been lenient with you over the last few months, because I know you've had this bereavement, but there comes a time when you have to stop using that as an excuse."

Jesus, the guy was a dick. Sam felt a protective surge toward Cassie, and his stride faltered, half of him wanting to go back and tell this guy that something like this wasn't an *excuse*, that he clearly had no idea what he was talking about, that he should give Cassie a fucking break. There were plenty of times growing up, when Tom hadn't been nearby and someone had been teasing Cassie, when he'd stepped in to do just that.

An elderly couple came in through the glass double doors at that moment, and Sam stepped aside to let them past, unable to get out while they were walking, excruciatingly slowly, into the building. His body twitched. He didn't hear Cassie's response, but presumed she'd made one, because he heard the guy saying, in an annoyingly nasal voice, "Glad that's settled. You can have five minutes, no more."

As the elderly couple let the doors swing shut behind them, Sam risked a glance behind him. Cassie wasn't with the two men anymore, and Sam felt his shoulders relax—she'd gone. But then, "Sam?"

His head whipped around automatically, toward the sound of his name. Somehow, Cassie had gotten behind him, on the other side of where she was supposed to be, and was coming his way. Walking right toward him.

Shit. *Shit!*

But there was no point in pretending he hadn't seen her. "Hey, Cass. How are you? You've, err, done a great job with everything so far." He tried very hard to make his voice casual, like it was no big deal to be caught by her, like he was just stepping out for a sec. Breezy, breezy. But he could hear that it didn't work: the words sounded too strained, and he felt hot under his double jackets as she leveled a look at him. He couldn't help glancing behind him—had Jessica gotten the message yet? Would she come down and look for him? Jesus, he needed to get out of here. What had he been thinking, lingering like that?

"Sam." She said his name pointedly, then frowned. She opened her mouth, clearly trying to think of something to say—this was the first time they'd seen each other in months, after all. Then she closed it, glancing between his face and the bag in his hand. Then toward the exit. She narrowed her eyes, and the brown that was usually so warm turned hard. "What are you doing?"

"I'm . . . Nothing, I'm . . ." But he found himself floundering, unable to think when she was looking at him like that, disapproval and hurt etched across her face. His palms prickled with heat. Fuck, why couldn't he think of an excuse? What was a reason he'd be rushing out of the hotel, bag in hand, still in his tux?

"Are you *leaving?*" Of course she'd immediately think the worst of him, wouldn't she? But then, maybe she was right to do so, because he *was* doing the worst thing, wasn't he? And besides, she'd always seen through him. He'd never been able to bullshit her, the way he could with other people. So it made sense that she'd understand immediately what he was doing, what he was thinking. It didn't stop him from trying to deny it, though.

"No," he said quickly, "I'm just—"

"You are," Cassie said, her tone biting. "You're leaving Jessica. Now? Are you seriously running out on her on the day of your wedding?" Her voice was too loud. Jesus. The dick and the redhead would hear her, would alert the whole bloody hotel if she kept on like this. He acted on instinct and grabbed her by the shoulder, holding firm when she tried to shake him off, and pulled her through the double doors and out onto the pavement.

He ignored her noises of protest, kept a grip on her as he marched away from the white pillars of the hotel building, out of sight and to safety.

"Get off me!" She managed to shake his hand off, her eyes flashing.

He pulled his hand through his hair and found he couldn't even find the energy to lie to her. Everyone would find out soon enough, anyway.

"I can't go through with it," he said flatly.

She stared at him, as if waiting for him to say something more. "Are you serious? You're just going to bail? On your wedding day? What kind of a person does that?"

"I can't do it." His voice had a pleading, panicky edge to it now—he needed her to understand. Even though he knew she wouldn't—of course she wouldn't, how could she? How could anyone? But already the decision felt irreversible, and he knew he couldn't—wouldn't—go back on it.

Her brown eyes were kindling, burning coal at their center. He thought, yet again, of what she'd said to him, the night he went to Linda's. *If you hadn't been so stupid, so selfish, then Tom might still be alive.* And she was right, wasn't she? It was all his fault. He'd partied too hard, lost track of what was important, and let his best mate down. He could've been there to stop the fall, and he hadn't been. So Cassie was right to look at him like that. And when everyone else found out that he'd left Jessica, they'd look at him like that, and they'd be right in their assessment of him too.

She looked for a moment like she might tell him that he *had* to do it, fight with him to make him stay. But then she shook her head, and the fire in her eyes went dull, sparked out. "People always said you were like Tom," she said, her voice low now, barely more than a whisper. "You and him, the brave boys, off doing adventures. The double act."

He remembered it—everyone in their village used to say it, or a version of it, then everyone at secondary school, all their teachers. Linda, his mum, even Claire. At university too, they were the crazy ones, pulling stunts no one else would dream of.

"But they were wrong. You're nothing like Tom. He was brilliant and brave and kind, and *you* . . ." She spat out the last word, her shoulders heaving. "You're a coward and you always have been."

He winced, but didn't contradict her. She was right—he was a coward. He'd been a coward all those years ago, when he'd turned from her, *run* from her, because he didn't like what she was making him feel, didn't want to risk falling for her, didn't want to risk ruining things with Tom, didn't want to risk hurting her if they'd gone any further. He was a coward still, unable to face up to what had happened to Tom, to his part in it. Unable to go through with a wedding he'd agreed to. And he could find nothing, right then, to defend any of it. So all he could do was watch as Cassie turned from him and walked away, just like she had five years ago, her blond hair swishing in the ponytail, her shoulders high. That frailty he'd seen upstairs seemed gone now, chased away by her anger with him.

You're a coward.

Yes, he was. Just like his dad had been. He was nothing, and the best thing he could do right now was to make sure he didn't drag anyone else down with him.

Chapter Twelve

Robert peered down his angular nose at Cassie, to where she was sitting at her desk, flipping through her diary. A paper diary, one that Josh had given her as a Christmas present, because he knew how much she liked having a real one, rather than relying on her computer. A paper diary made with recycled paper, no less, proving how well he knew her.

"I'm just not sure what we can do," Cassie was saying. "We already have the Tapestry Room booked out on that date. The other rooms are too small for this size of event, and we can't—"

"That's not the answer I want to hear, Cassie." Robert's voice was clipped, and he leaned in closer to her. She smelled mint, something that wouldn't usually have been unpleasant, but that felt too sharp when coming off him. Especially when combined with the slightly damp smell he'd brought into work today— understandable, maybe, given the characteristic misty rain of early April, but not exactly nice. His dark eyes watched her from over the top of the computer screen—this close, she could very clearly see the receding hairline that he tried so hard to hide with expensive haircuts and products.

Not the answer I want to hear. Right, so she was just magically supposed to conjure up an extra events room, was she? And anyway, it was *his* fault they were in this mess in the first place— he'd gotten the dates mixed up, told a client that the hotel could definitely host their fiftieth wedding anniversary here, when the events spaces were all booked out. Not that she'd ever say any of that out loud, of course.

Out of the corner of her eye, Cassie saw Josh glance at her from his desk on the other side of the cramped little office, but she didn't dare return the look. Cassie took a breath, trying for calm, even as she felt her stomach curdle with anxiety. She looked through the events list for that date again, but there was no changing what she'd seen the first time—they were fully booked.

"I'm sorry, Robert," she tried again. "We could host them on the eleventh, I think?" She flipped through her diary.

"That's not good enough," he snapped, then turned away to pace the short length of the room. She and Josh were the only two full-time members of the events team, and as such shared a tiny little office, which was surprisingly depressing, given the fact it was housed in a five-star hotel. It had none of the 1920s Art Deco theme of the main hotel, with its plain white walls and beige, slightly frayed carpet, and was on the basement floor, so natural light was limited. In the three years she'd been working here, Cassie had tried to make the office a little nicer, buying a couple of cactus plants, which Josh had named Rosie and Jim, and some paintings for the wall, but she couldn't deny that she much preferred the more active parts of her role, when she was actually at the events, rather than being stuck in here.

"We'll have to move the Spaldings' birthday event," Robert continued.

Cassie frowned. "But the Spaldings have their party here every year."

"Exactly. So they'll be more amenable to moving it."

"But—"

"Enough, Cassie. I've made the decision. We cannot lose this anniversary gig—the client is a property developer in London, and if it goes well it could be very good for us. It's just good business sense." He leveled a look at her, before turning to slide from the room. "Make it happen," he called out behind him, before he let the door shut.

Cassie groaned. "What are we going to do?"

Josh shrugged. "Not much we can do. Don't let it get to you—it's his fuck-up, not yours. See if the Spaldings will move—hopefully they will."

"Easier said than done," Cassie muttered. "It's just not fair on the Spaldings. And they're coming all the way from Scotland."

"Yeah, but, again—not your fault."

"They'll *think* it's my fault, because Robert will leave me to explain, no doubt."

"I'll explain," Josh said easily. Cassie opened her mouth to say something, but the phone started ringing, and Josh answered in his smooth customer voice. The thing was, it was all very well for Josh to say things like that—he was only doing this temporarily, working here in order to be able to afford his part-time master's in graphic design, after which he'd no doubt ditch events and go after his dream job. But for Cassie, this was her career. It *mattered* to her what the guests thought of her and how the events went.

"Cassie?" She glanced over to see Josh gesturing to the phone in his hand. "It's Linda for you."

Cassie frowned. Linda was calling her at work? A knot of anxiety tightened in her gut as she picked up her office phone. "Hey, Linda. Is everything OK?" It was hard to keep the panic out of her voice; she couldn't help but jump to the worst conclusion whenever anyone rang her these days.

"Hello, Cassie love, yes, I'm fine. I'm sorry to worry you. I tried you on your mobile but I couldn't get through."

"Oh, sorry. I have it on silent at work."

"Sensible," Linda conceded. "So, how are you, everything OK your end?" Linda's voice was too bright, and Cassie knew that this question was just filler—Linda wouldn't call her at work without reason.

"What's wrong, Linda?" she asked firmly. "Has something happened?"

"Well, it's just . . ." Linda paused, and Cassie felt her grip tighten on the phone. It couldn't be that terrible, she told herself. Linda didn't sound devastated, just on edge. She tried to breathe, felt Josh glancing at her from his side of the room. Maybe he, too, was remembering the last time she'd gotten a call like this. "It's just, I thought you should know—"

"Thought I should know what?" Cassie didn't mean to snap, but she couldn't help it.

"Yes, sorry. It's the pub."

"The pub? What about the pub?"

"It's . . . I'm going to have to sell it."

"*Sell* it?" Cassie asked incredulously, in a way that made Josh look over at her. She gestured at him to indicate she'd fill him in afterward.

This wasn't what she'd expected. Linda loved that pub. It was her baby. She'd never imagined her selling it—and she hadn't wanted to. That pub, more than Claire's house, held so many memories for her. Memories of her childhood—and of Tom.

"Yes, well, sorry, I'm not explaining this very well." Linda sounded *flustered*, she realized, and Linda never sounded flustered. "We had some broken pipes, and the pub flooded."

"Flooded?" Cassie repeatedly dumbly.

"Yes. Last week. It was all a bit of a nightmare—the ground floor was quite literally underwater, and I had to put my wellies on to wade into the kitchen and make sure all the power was off." Linda laughed, as if trying to make light of it, but Cassie heard the brittleness to it.

"Last week?" Cassie said, realizing she sounded a bit like an echo. "You should've told me! I was off yesterday—I would have come down to help."

"I know you would have, darling," Linda said softly. "But I wanted to get my own thoughts in gear before I burdened you with them."

Sell it, she had said. But . . . "But can't you just . . . fix it? Fix the pipe, sort the flooring? You might have to close for a little bit, but you'll get it back on its feet, I'm sure."

"Well, the thing is," Linda said slowly, "I'm not going to be able to afford to do that." She sighed. "Oh, Cassie love, I just don't have the money. I've been keeping my head above water—just—and I thought we'd turned a corner, thought I'd be able to make it work, but with this . . . It's something I can't come back from. I don't have the money to redo the place, and there's no way I'll be able to borrow any more money. The bank has already been sending me letters, reminding me how much I owe them—as if I didn't already know." The letters she'd seen after Christmas, Cassie remembered. She'd forgotten about them, of course, too torn up by everything else, but she had a flash, then, of the *Urgent* notice. "So I don't really have a choice," Linda finished.

Cassie pressed her free hand to her head, tried to think. "How much money would it cost to fix the damage from the pipe leak?"

Linda hesitated. "About thirty thousand, I think."

"Thirty thousand?" Cassie exclaimed, causing Josh to look at her again. But seriously—what had *happened* with the bloody pipes? "Sorry," she said quickly, aware that she probably wasn't helping. "But, look, that's not completely out of the realms of possibility. Even if you can't get a loan, there must be a way to raise that sort of money. We can think of something. I'll help you."

Linda paused for long enough to let Cassie know that there was something else. "The thing is, there's a developer who's made an offer on the place."

"Already? I thought you said this only happened last week?"

"Yes, but they've been sniffing around for a while now—they must've known I wasn't doing too well, I suppose."

"Well, don't take the offer," Cassie said sharply.

"Cassie love, I'm not in the position to—"

"Please, Linda. Just . . . Wait, OK? At least give me time to . . . think." The office door swung open, and Robert strode in. She jumped. "Sorry, Linda, I've got to go," she said quickly, looking down at the desk as she felt Robert's eyes on her. "But I'll call you back later." She heard Josh calling Robert over, trying to distract him. "I'm going to figure this out, OK?"

"I hope that wasn't a personal call, Cassie," Robert said, the moment she was off the phone. Cassie decided it was safer not to answer that. Robert picked up a pen off Josh's desk and started tapping it against the back of Josh's monitor. Josh watched Robert's hand and the pen with an expression of distaste.

"The Easter egg treasure hunt," Robert demanded. "Where are we with that?"

Cassie shot Josh a panicked look. "I'm doing it," Josh said easily.

Robert paused briefly in his tapping, stared over at Cassie. "But you do it every year." Cassie fought to keep her expression neutral.

"Well," Josh said, "I'm having a go this year. I'm sure it'll be fine."

Robert still looked suspicious, though he resumed his tapping. "Fine isn't really good enough. Cassie is better at this sort of thing than you."

"Consider this me branching out. Growing into my role." Josh's voice was deadpan.

Robert spared him a brief glance, then looked again at Cassie. "You should supervise."

"I will," she said immediately, even though it was a lie. Josh could handle the treasure hunt, she was sure—it was for kids, for God's sake, and he'd watched her do it enough times.

"Fine," Robert said, and left the office, taking Josh's pen with him.

Josh glanced at her. "Are you OK?"

She nodded. It was different, but she couldn't help it—it made her think of Tom, of the treasure hunts he'd done for her, the one he'd set up before he'd died. She still hadn't been able to start it, in the two and a half months since she'd gotten the first clue, even though it had been playing on her mind constantly—wondering what the clues said, what they led to. What he'd been planning for her. Not that she could explain any of this to Robert. He expected her to be running as normal by now, and she was doing her best to convey that.

"I'll take care of it," Josh said soothingly. "Don't worry. Robert can sod off—it's only a stupid treasure hunt." He grimaced. "I didn't mean ..."

"No. I know what you mean. And thanks."

Josh hesitated. "And ... Linda?"

Cassie blew out a breath. "Another story." And she proceeded to fill him in.

* * *

When Cassie got back to her flat that evening, Hazel was making supper, though judging by the steam and the swearing, it was not going well. Cassie walked into the kitchen and peered into the pan to see a congealed mass of rice—Hazel had not gotten any better at cooking since they'd left university. She looked mournfully at Cassie. "I tried."

"And that's what counts."

Hazel held up an open bottle of white wine. "I opened it for the risotto, but since that's not going well it's probably best to drink this, and that way the food might taste better." Hazel poured her a glass, and Cassie took it gratefully.

"So," Hazel said, "how are things going with Robert?"

"OK, I guess," Cassie lied. "He's upset at the moment because I'm not organizing the Easter egg hunt." It wasn't the same, she told herself firmly. It wasn't the same as what Tom used to do, and it was Easter, not Christmas.

Hazel was watching her. A little too carefully, Cassie thought. "Have you . . ." Hazel hesitated, tucking a strand of her ebony hair behind her ear. "Did you ever open that clue from Tom? The one Linda gave you?"

Cassie shook her head, looking at her risotto rather than at Hazel. "I can't bring myself to." A part of her wanted to, though. Wanted to know what he'd written, what he'd been planning. But an equal part of her was terrified at the thought, about the grief spiral that might be waiting for her on the other side.

"Maybe you should," Hazel said softly. "It might help you to—"

"What, move on?" Cassie tried to keep the bitterness from her voice.

"No. Not that. I'm not sure moving on is the right way to put it. Someone like that . . ." Hazel shook her head sadly. "You don't just put them aside and step away from them. But it might help you to process, I guess. Or not." She blew out a breath, picked up her wine. "You don't have to. But if you want to and you want me with you or whatever, then I'm here, OK?"

They ate the rest of the risotto in relative silence, and when they were done, Cassie went to bed early. She didn't go to sleep though. Instead she took out the envelope that she'd been keeping in her bedside drawer, so it was next to her as she slept, always within reach. She traced the edges of it with her fingertips, drinking in the sight of his scrawling handwriting. She'd once accused him of having the ugliest handwriting in the entire world—and he'd managed to take that as a compliment, claiming that if it was going to be ugly, it was best to be *the* ugliest. Like he'd won some sort of competition.

She thought about going to get Hazel. But this first time, seeing what he'd written, it felt like it should be a private moment.

And so, with trembling fingers, she opened the envelope. It wasn't just the clue inside, she saw. There was something else, something more. A little note. Her gaze rushed over the page, too quick to take in the words, frantic in her need to absorb them. She took a breath, forced herself to slow down, and read.

Happy Christmas, Chipmunk! Are you excited? I'm excited. The hunt this year is going to be so much fun. But I feel like I should warn you—so we don't have a repeat of the tantrum of '03 again—that it might be harder this year. You'll get it at the end though. Probably. Hopefully.

Just don't freak out if this takes longer than usual, ok? It's all part of my grand, evil plan.

Underneath that, he'd drawn a little cartoon man with evil eyes, drumming his fingers together, and a little speech bubble with *mwahahahaha* in it. Cassie felt a little snort of laughter build, then bubble over. It was a *terrible* cartoon drawing. But just like his handwriting, she knew Tom would've been proud of it. She could picture him drawing it, writing the note. Could picture his face as she read it. She would've scowled at him, no doubt, demanded to know why, exactly, it would take longer this year—and why he'd felt the need to warn her about it. And he'd shake his head and say something annoying like, "*All in good time, Chipmunk.*" She could actually *hear* him saying it, right now, like he was here with her in the room.

She blew out a breath, put the note aside. Then, heart hammering, she picked up the clue. The first clue that would start the hunt to the very last gift her brother would ever give her.

Chapter Thirteen

"*What do you mean,* you're going to take the offer?"

Cassie jerked forward from where she was sitting on her double bed, her back propped against the pillows. Tom's clue, the one she'd opened last night, fluttered off her lap and onto the duvet next to her, and she snatched it back up. His words had been playing on repeat since she'd read it. *We'll stay close this time but go up high . . .* And he *knew* she didn't like heights—though really, who did? She was pretty sure anyone who said they weren't scared when they were peering down at the ground from high up was lying. Her brain had been whirring, trying to figure out where Tom wanted her to go, and she'd barely been able to sleep because of it. But she was trying to focus, trying to put it aside, because she knew she needed to help Linda.

"Cassie love, I just don't have any options," Linda said with a sigh. Her voice was groggy, not yet fully awake—Cassie had rung her first thing in the morning, and Linda had always been more of a night owl.

"Of *course* you have options. There are *always* options." Cassie took a breath. "Look, Linda, it might not cover it all, but I have my savings, from my parents, and I—"

But the answer was entirely predictable. "Absolutely not, Cassie. That's for your future, not mine."

"But I—"

"No," Linda said. "And that's final."

Cassie wrinkled her nose, but she knew that once Linda decided something, it really *was* final. The thing was, though, when she'd thought about it she'd realized she didn't just have her inheritance now: she had Tom's too, because he'd left it to her in his will. It was less than she would have expected, less than her half—not that she cared about that. She didn't want Tom's money, because it would feel wrong, using it. But she hadn't realized he'd already spent a chunk of his, and she couldn't help wondering what he'd done with it. Wondering why he hadn't told her about it.

"All right," Cassie said. "What about you host some sort of fundraiser in the village?"

"I can't ask the village for money, love," Linda said, and Cassie hated how weary her voice sounded.

"Yes, you can! They'd want to help. We could organize some music, put on some food, ask people for donations and—"

"Where, exactly, can we do this? There's no way I can let anyone near the pub right now—it's a bloody health and safety risk, I tell you, and I swear the mold is already setting in." Linda's voice cracked, just slightly, at the end of her sentence—cracked in a way that might have been easy to hide, if Cassie didn't know her so well. The sound made Cassie's heart break—Linda *loved* that pub. She could only imagine what this was doing to her—seeing it destroyed, feeling like there was nothing she could do. She gripped Tom's clue, the little piece of paper, tighter in her fist, fingernails biting into her palm around it.

"We'll do it at the hall," Cassie said. "I'm sure they'll let us use it for free, if we explain."

Linda huffed out a laugh. "I'm not sure how much money a little village fête will raise us, my love."

"Well, we don't know, do we?" Cassie demanded. "Not until we try."

Linda said nothing, and Cassie read something in the silence. "What?" Still nothing. "Linda, what is it?"

A sigh. "The developers—they've given me two weeks to take the offer, otherwise they're going to withdraw it."

"What? They can't do that! That's like . . . blackmail."

Linda laughed softly. "Indeed. But that's their world for you."

It was wrong, Cassie decided. Wrong that people could manipulate you like that. "You can't let some random people have it," Cassie said, her voice on the edge of a plea. "Who knows what they'd do to it." And she couldn't bear it—the thought that they'd tear it down, build some crap block of new flats or something in its stead. Linda's pub was special *because* it was old. It had history, memories. It needed love, it needed looking after— not tearing down.

"I don't *want* to do this, Cassie—that pub has been my life. But when these things happen, they happen, and you sometimes have to know when to give up the fight. I'm fighting a losing battle anyway—all these chains, and whatnot—village pubs are just not making the money anymore."

Cassie winced. She knew things had changed from when Linda started out, but she didn't like the thought of it. Somewhere deep inside, no matter how she'd tried to push it aside as the impractical dream it was, she still harbored a fantasy of opening her own place in the countryside. She didn't want Linda to give up. It felt like it would prove her dream a façade, once and for all, prove to the sensible part of her brain that she'd be stupid to go down that route.

Linda sighed, and Cassie could imagine the swish of her bob as she shook her head. "I'm getting old, anyway—"

"You're not—"

"And these managers," Linda carried on over Cassie, "they're never any good."

"That's because you don't ever give them a chance." And it was true—Linda didn't trust anyone with her pub longer than a few days.

"What about a crowdfunder?" Cassie asked suddenly.

"A what?"

"A crowdfunder. You know, there are these websites, and you upload details of your project, and then you get people to donate."

"Hmmm, sounds a bit mercenary to me, taking people's money."

"Well, they wouldn't give you the money unless they wanted to—you're not *forcing* anyone to."

"Still, I don't know how I feel about—"

"Or you could give them something in return," Cassie plowed on. "Like a share in the pub or something? I'd do it!" she continued, talking over Linda's automatic protests. "Then if the pub made loads of money, they would too, but more than that, the people donating would feel like they were a part of something, you know?"

"Shares." The way she said it, Cassie could almost see Linda grimacing, the idea of ceding some control there.

"You wouldn't have to let them have any *say* in it—like what you do with it."

"Then what would be the point of being a shareholder?"

Cassie sighed. "Linda, will you just please think about it? If not shares, then we can come up with something else."

"Fine. Fine, yes, I'll think about it. In the meantime though, let's talk about something else, hmm? How are you?"

For now, Cassie thought, she'd let Linda drop the subject—

but she wasn't going to give up on this. "I'm . . . well, I'm OK, I guess." She paused. "I opened Tom's first clue." She looked down at it, sitting in her lap.

"Did you?" Linda's voice changed, became more intent. "What does it say?" Cassie smiled a little at the urgency in her voice. Linda had always loved the treasure hunt. Tom had used her pub more than once, sending Cassie there to a beaming Linda, who would hand over the next clue.

Cassie didn't need to look at the slip of paper—she could recite it from memory.

> "We'll stay close this time, but go up high,
> I talked about taking you, but our plans went awry,
> Now I'm hoping you'll brave it alone,
> Climb to the sky and see the unknown."

Linda laughed delightedly. "I love it! Oh my gosh, the rhyming!"

Cassie smiled again. "He tried to stop doing that one year, and I basically had a fit."

Linda chuckled quietly. "I remember. Do you know, when he was little, he used to ask me for help with the rhymes?"

"Really?"

"Oh yes, he'd sit in the pub after school or when Claire was busy—he'd pick times when you were out of the room or off with Hazel—and we'd go through all the possible rhyming words together." Cassie could imagine it: a young Tom sitting across the other side of the wooden bar during the closed times, before it opened again at 6 P.M., pen poised over paper, frowning in concentration, his floppy blond hair falling into his eyes. The fact that Tom was gone and now soon the pub would be too hung in the air between them.

Cassie cleared her throat. "There's a P.S., too." He did this sometimes, when he thought she might need extra help.

"Oh?"

"*P.S. I've always liked the number thirty-two.*
P.P.S. Once you're there, I hear the afternoon tea is exquisite.
Especially when you order from Rose."

"I can hear Tom's voice when you say that, you know."

The sadness in Linda's voice made Cassie's own throat tighten. "Me too," she whispered, blinking back tears that were always so close to the surface.

Then Linda said, a little incredulously, "He's always liked the number thirty-two?"

Cassie couldn't help laughing. "Apparently so."

"Well," Linda said, in a bolstering tone, "have you figured it out then?"

Cassie hesitated. "I think so." *We'll stay close this time and go up high.* It had clicked in the middle of the night, though she'd then spent the rest of the time she couldn't sleep mulling over whether she'd gotten it right—because the idea of going there and being *wrong* . . . well, she didn't want to put herself through that. And she didn't want to let Tom down like that, either. But she hadn't been able to come up with anything else, and it just felt right. *I talked about taking you* . . . She took a breath. "I think . . . I think it's the Shard."

"The Shard!" Linda exclaimed. "How glamorous."

Exactly the word Cassie had used when she'd come down to London to visit Tom. She'd met Tom at London Bridge, near where he and Sam had been living at the time. She'd been full of nervous anticipation—she and Hazel were planning on moving to London together after university, and she'd wanted to see it, get a feel for it. Tom had met her at the station—and brought along Sam, much to her dismay, given she was still hurting after the skiing incident.

They'd passed the Shard as they walked from the station, and Cassie had stopped, looked up. It seemed to encompass how London in general felt to her—big and imposing and daunting.

"I'll take you up there one day," Tom had said, slinging an arm around her shoulder. She'd smiled at him, just as Sam had come up along Tom's other side.

"Sure you'd be brave enough, Cass? It's pretty high up."

She'd taken the classy route, sticking her chin in the air and not retorting, refusing to engage with him, even though it *did* look pretty high up, and she was kind of glad that Tom didn't suggest they go up right away, because then she'd have to pretend not to be scared in front of Sam. Sam had fallen behind as she and Tom kept walking, catching up with them a few moments later. He'd shrugged when Tom had looked at him. "I was going to see if we could go up now, but you have to have a booking."

"Another time," Tom had said.

Since she'd moved to London, Tom had talked about going there a few times, how cool it would be to go to one of the bars, pretend they were some fancy, rich Londoners and look down on the rest of the city with a cocktail, but it was just one of those things that you talked about and never actually did.

And now, he was sending her up there, and she knew, because of what he'd written in the clue, that *he* knew it would be pushing her out of her comfort zone. He'd have known that she'd have to *brave it*, if she wanted to get the next clue. Which she did. Now that she'd opened it, now that she'd broken that first barrier, something in her had sparked. She *needed* to get it right, needed to find the next one. She wanted to follow the trail, find out what it led to. Even more than that—she knew that it was what Tom would have wanted. He'd gone through all this effort, had laid things out for her, and he'd have wanted her to go through with it, no matter what. So that's what she'd do. She'd go to the Shard, height be damned, and she'd find that next clue.

The spark that had lit up last night intensified, as her mind latched on to the purpose of that. And somewhere inside her, the old echo of childish excitement that these treasure hunts used to bring on flickered.

Chapter Fourteen

Cassie took a breath as she came to a stop outside the pointed glass building. It was so *big*. Why had she never appreciated just how bloody huge it was before now? She felt tiny next to it, dwarfed into insignificance. The Shard stood majestic in front of her, spring sunlight glittering off its glass panes. At the bottom, the glass pyramid gave way to a smaller glass foundation, the edges of the rest of the pyramid propped up by white stone pillars, so that it gave the impression that some of the building was held up on stilts. Cassie eyed the pillars suspiciously—could they really support such a massive glass structure? One that she was about to go up, nonetheless? Her heart jumped nervously at the thought.

She bit her lip as she glanced up to the very top of it, the peak offset against a bright blue sky—a sky that promised more sunny days to come. *I'll take you up there one day.* Tom's voice echoed around her mind. It seemed he was sticking to his word, even now.

With that thought, the determination returned and she squared her shoulders as she marched inside, getting the lift up to the thirty-second floor. The hint had been obvious, once she'd figured it out—there was a restaurant, The Oblix, on the thirty-second floor, and afternoon tea was, according to Google, one of their specialities. She watched the little TV screen at the top of the huge lift count the levels as they shot up—incredibly fast, in Cassie's opinion.

She felt her nerves mount as they hit floor thirty, and slipped her leather jacket off, tucking it under her arm. Smart-casual, the dress code had said when she'd googled the restaurant. So she'd opted for a nice green top over black jeans, hoping that her black pumps would qualify as smart enough.

She smoothed down her hair, which was currently sitting just above her shoulders, as she exited the lift, the only person to do so. Then she came to a halt completely. In the lift, she'd been able to pretend to herself that it was OK, that she wasn't that high up, that she was safe. But now there was no pretending. With glass walls all around her, the fact that she was so much higher up than anything else around her hit her with full force. And oh God, she couldn't look. Actually wanted to squeeze her eyes shut. But refusing to look out of the windows didn't stop her stomach from swooping, her mouth going dry. Why? Why had Tom done this to her? She wanted to turn around, get straight back into the lift, and keep her eyes closed until her feet were safely on the pavement outside—back at ground level.

But she couldn't. She had started this now—and she'd forever regret it if she didn't see it through. So she let out a slow, shaky breath and, keeping her eyes firmly ahead, headed for The Oblix. She stopped at the entrance to the restaurant, glancing around the interior—a classy, semicircular bar with stylish backlighting formed the centerpiece of the room, at which a few people sat on high, white-backed chairs. It was bright inside—*obviously*, Cassie thought scathingly to herself. One entire side of it was glass-paneled, looking out across London. She allowed her eyes a nervous flick. From here she could see the Thames, Tower Bridge bringing the two sides of London together.

It reminded her of the time Tom had tried to make her go on the London Eye. She'd met him and Amy for brunch, and he'd gotten all excited by the idea, given none of them had ever done it before—Londoners who let all the tourist attractions pass them by. She'd adamantly refused. The idea of sitting on what was effectively a giant Ferris wheel and swinging around unstably at the top of it had been too much. She'd ushered Tom and Amy over to it, had told them she had to meet a friend and that it would be a lovely romantic activity for the two of them—not that she had ever felt like a third wheel around them. She'd thought Tom had bought it at the time, but now, looking back, she was increasingly sure he'd seen right through her, as he always did.

A waitress with her hair scraped back into a harsh ponytail, eyes framed by black eyeliner, walked over to her and smiled in a way that indicated she was smiling because she was supposed to, not because she wanted to. Cassie shifted her weight from foot to foot. "I, umm, booked a table. Cassie Rivers." She'd been too nervous to just show up, in case they didn't have room—it was the Shard, after all. Which had turned out to be good foresight on her part—she'd only gotten a table due to a cancellation. It had felt a little like fate, like Tom had somehow, from somewhere, made it so.

The waitress showed her to her table—one right next to the glass window. Or wall? She sat, angling her little brown armchair away from the glass as subtly as she could. Why had they put her right at the edge? Didn't they know that glass could shatter at any moment? She tried to push aside visions of falling—her palms felt clammy enough as it was.

The waitress placed a menu down on the small round wooden table, took away the second place setting in a way that made it very obvious Cassie would be eating alone. "I'll give you a moment to decide what you'd like," she said, sounding bored. Cassie felt self-conscious as the waitress left, unsure of what to do with herself. She should have brought a book or something— no one questioned it when you sat alone reading.

She glanced out through the glass panes. London really did look stunning from up this high, made more so by the bright blue backdrop of the day, the sunlight catching the odd glass window and winking back up at her. Stunning, yes, but was it normal that it still didn't feel like her home, even after more than three years here? She could appreciate the beauty of it, and she loved parts of it, but sitting up here, looking down on the city . . . It made her realize just how exhausting it was, too. In constant movement, everything and everyone. And maybe it was just because *she* was exhausted right now, maybe she was just struggling with everything in Tom's absence, but she felt the weight of it pressing down on her. The need to keep up with London, keep on the treadmill, keep fighting for more money so that she could afford to live here, working her way up the events scene.

The waitress reappeared before Cassie had even picked up the menu. "What can I get you?" She hadn't brought out anything to write with, apparently confident in her ability to memorize Cassie's order.

"Umm . . ." Cassie picked up the menu, then put it back down again. "I'd like the afternoon tea, please." Tom had told her what to order, after all. Though it felt ridiculous, ordering afternoon tea for one—and from the raised eyebrow look she was getting, this woman with her excessive eyeliner was definitely judging her.

"Right. There's quite a few options, though." She indicated the menu, and Cassie frowned down at it. There were far too many options, in her opinion, so that the choice felt constraining rather than liberating. If she ever had her own place, she'd make sure that there were good choices, but not too many. "Do you want me to come back?"

"No," Cassie said, her voice squeaky. "No, it's fine. I'd just like the normal afternoon tea, please, no champagne, and you know, normal tea is great and, umm, do I need to pick the sandwiches and everything?"

"Or you can have a selection?" the waitress asked in that same bored voice.

"A selection," Cassie said firmly. "A selection is great."

The waitress nodded, picked up the menu, and turned.

"And umm," Cassie said quickly, before she could leave, "are you Rose?"

The woman turned and raised her eyebrows again—they were very finely plucked, Cassie noticed. "No."

Right. Helpful. Really bloody helpful. "Do you know someone called Rose?" she asked patiently. "Who works here, I mean."

The woman hesitated before saying, "Yes. Do you know her, then?"

"She, ah, I think she knew my brother. Tom Rivers." Her heart contracted painfully, saying his name, like it always did. "I don't suppose you could . . . ask her?"

The woman gave her a suspicious look, then shrugged. "OK."

The waitress left, leaving Cassie alone once more. She glanced around the room—they'd clearly been going for a contemporary, New York vibe, with the trendy armchairs, dark floor, and low ceilings, and lots of yellow lights and golden details around the room. The buzz of other people's conversations washed over Cassie. In front of her were two women, heads bent toward one another as they talked. The one facing Cassie glanced up, saw Cassie watching. Cassie immediately got out her phone, tried to look busy.

As had become an hourly obsession over the last few days, Cassie checked the progress of her GoFundMe. Eventually, after much wheedling, she'd convinced Linda to go for it—with the compromise that anyone who donated would have a special loyalty card that entitled them to certain perks. Josh and Hazel had been the first to donate. She'd gotten Hazel to tell her mum to spread the word around the village, knowing full well that Linda wouldn't do it herself, and had put it on Facebook. They'd had a few donations already, and Cassie was trying to stay positive, but the odd twenty pounds here and there was not going to cut it, she knew, and the scale of it, combined with the time pressure Linda was facing, was starting to feel overwhelming.

The same waitress with the eyebrows and the eyeliner brought over a pot of tea and a china cup for her, setting both on the table. Cassie bit her lip. Did this mean that Rose wasn't around? Or that she'd refused to come and talk to Cassie?

"She's busy," the waitress said, as if reading Cassie's mind—or her expression. "But she said she'll come over." Cassie felt a wave of relief and nodded in thanks before pouring herself some tea. This was OK, this was good. She was here, and Rose was here—she had to have the next clue, surely.

She lifted her cup of tea, saluting the air. "I'm sorry it's taken me so long," she said quietly, "but I'm here, like you wanted. I wish you were here to see it." She took a sip, used the liquid to swallow away the lump in her throat. She couldn't cry, not in public.

She put the cup down. The china was oddly similar to the china Linda had in her pub to serve coffee after meals—white, with a rim of decorative blue and purple flowers. It made her think of a time when she and Tom were little—she must have been around eight or something. She'd been invited to a friend's birthday party at school—Simone Simmons, who had invited everyone in their class to a birthday tea party. It had sounded so cool and grown up, and Cassie had been so excited, but then she hadn't been able to go, because she'd been ill. Hazel had raved about it at school the Monday after—about how posh it had been, and how there were people actually *serving* them, and there had been so many cakes and sandwiches, and they'd gotten to drink adult tea, and there had been a magician there. Cassie had tried really hard not to cry or be jealous in front of Hazel, but when she got home, she'd locked herself in her room and sobbed into her pillow. It was the type of thing that was ultimately insignificant, but it had felt so important at the time.

Tom knocked on her door. "Cassie, come on, please come out."

"No. Go away."

"Come on."

"No," she said on another sob.

"Please." He used his wheedling voice, then added, "I have something to show you, something that might cheer you up."

The mystery had gotten the better of her then, and she'd opened her door, red-eyed, and followed Tom, past the kitchen, where Claire was cooking. *"Don't be too late," she warned Tom. "School tomorrow." Tom nodded somberly, flashing a grin at Cassie, who didn't understand—be too late where?*

Sam's mum was waiting outside, her blue eyes crinkling when she saw Cassie and Tom. "There you are, my loves. All set?" Tom dragged Cassie to the car that always smelled and sounded a little funny, and bundled her into the backseat ahead of him. Sam was already there, grinning, bouncing in boyish excitement.

"Have you told her then?" Sam asked over Cassie's head, Cassie sandwiched between him and Tom.

"No, it's a secret."

"What is a secret?" Cassie asked, and folded her arms when neither of them would tell her, just grinned in that stupid solidarity

over her head. But she was intrigued, and she didn't feel sad anymore.

Sam's mum had dropped them off at Linda's pub, and Tom had grabbed her hand, dragged her inside. No one else was there—it was only 4 P.M. and the pub wasn't open yet. But there was a table set for three, right by the window. A table with a tray of sandwiches and cake, set with white china.

"See?" Tom said excitedly. "We've brought the afternoon tea to you."

Sam took her hand this time, pulling her to the table, and the three of them sat down.

Linda came out from behind the bar, holding a pot of tea and wearing a silly white apron with red dots that Cassie had never seen her in before. She walked over to the table, and Cassie caught a whiff of that coffee scent that Linda always seemed to smell of.

"Tea, madam?" Linda said in a posh voice. She winked at Cassie, and Cassie giggled.

"Cassie Rivers?" Cassie was jolted out of the memory by a slightly Essex-sounding voice, nearly spilling her tea all down herself. She looked up to see a teenage girl putting a three-tiered stand, filled with sandwiches, cakes, and scones, down on the table.

"Sorry, I . . . Yes." The girl's dark hair was plaited down her back, nearly reaching her waist, and her skin was pale, so pale that Cassie wondered if she ever spent any time outside. It made her dark eyes more pronounced, Cassie thought, and she was looking at Cassie a little suspiciously. She wasn't wearing the same uniform as the rest of the waitresses and Cassie, having worked in hospitality, connected the dots—this girl worked behind the scenes in the kitchen.

Cassie frowned. "Are you Rose?"

The girl nodded, then held out a hand, thrust something

toward Cassie. An envelope, with a number two in the corner. Cassie's heart jumped as she took it. She'd been right. The next clue was here.

"He said to give this to you. Made me memorize your name and everything."

Cassie looked up at the girl. "You knew him?"

"Nah. He paid me to do it. Twenty quid." Rose shifted from foot to foot, awkwardness radiating from her body. "He said you'd be here sooner, though. Around Christmas, he said."

Cassie traced the edges of the envelope with her thumb. "Right. I got delayed." She didn't want to say it out loud. Each time she had to say the words—*He died*—it was like she was reasserting the fact of his absence.

"Well, umm, bye, then."

Rose turned to leave, but Cassie reached out, grabbed her hand. "Thank you," she breathed, feeling tears prick her eyes. She wondered whether to say something more, but she couldn't think of what else that would be. Rose nodded, looking ever so slightly alarmed, and maneuvered out of Cassie's grip, heading back to the kitchen.

Cassie watched her for a moment, before turning her attention to the envelope. Taking slow, measured breaths, she opened it. Both a note and a clue, like last time. Cassie felt her heart spark, the fact that Tom had left her something more to read, something else to connect her with him. The spark warmed her, gave her a sense of lightness—something she'd thought she'd never feel again, after he died.

Ta-da! I give you the Shard! I'm sure you'll tell me all about it, once you finish moaning about me making you do it alone. And you better not have closed your eyes the entire time, ok? More importantly though, the clue! Remember that

time we went to the races with Sam? Well, this is cooler—
and you don't have to dress up. Definitely worth the wait . . .

Cassie smiled as she read the note a second time, allowing herself to savor the sound of Tom's voice in her mind. She stumbled, just a little, over the mention of Sam. She hadn't spoken to him since she'd left him on the pavement outside the hotel. Had no desire to speak with him ever again. And that was perfectly justifiable, she told herself. He'd deserved what she'd spat at him. Deserved to be feeling terrible about it.

She pushed him from her mind as she read the clue itself, welcoming the sense of nervous anticipation that felt so familiar.

One spring day the teams will meet,
But one will go home in defeat,
All of them have brains, it's true,
But this is what it means to be a blue.

P.S. I still can't believe you've never done this—time to fix
that and try something new.
P.P.S. Life is but a dream.

Cassie stared at the little slip of paper as she finished reading. *One spring day . . .* That was now. Spring was *now,* and Tom would have expected her to have months to figure it out, would have enjoyed watching her try, maybe dropping annoying little hints along the way. This was out of character for him—she usually did the treasure hunts in a couple of days, max. *Something epic,* he'd said. Maybe making her wait was a part of that. A part of his *grand plan,* whatever that was.

She read the clue again, feeling her heart pick up speed, her fingertips twitching, unable to keep still. She didn't know. She didn't *know* what he meant, where he wanted her to go.

Life is but a dream. What the hell was *that* supposed to mean?

Her foot started bouncing now, too, the energy rolling through her, the sounds of the restaurant washing over her, distant somehow. But no matter how many times she read it, she couldn't get it.

One spring day . . .

She'd figure it out, she told herself firmly. Soon—before spring was over. She'd figure it out, because she had to. And that sense of determination, of need—it made her feel something she'd not felt since that call in December. It made her feel *hopeful.*

Chapter Fifteen

Sam leaned back on his hands, legs splayed in front of him, sitting on the front of the yacht, the early April wind biting his face, the sea a deep blue. The sun was out, the sky almost cloudless—cold, yes, but bright, a perfect day to be out on the water. He could hear the chatter and laughter behind him, where the rest of their little group were sitting under cover, out of the cold wind, drinking and playing cards. He picked up his beer, took a sip, the bottle icy against his fingers. A shiver ran through him, in a way that made him think he should have packed a better coat. But then, he hadn't really been thinking when he'd stuffed clothes in a bag and bolted for the airport. Hadn't been thinking when he'd opened his wallet, found the card there.

Toby Jenkins's card. Toby Jenkins, who had been in Argentina, as Sam should have been. Had hung out with Tom, while they were both there alone, gone climbing with him. And had seen Tom's fall, had been the one to call, relay the news. Toby, who had come to the funeral, had spoken to Sam. Had made a point of telling him that he was welcome to come and stay with him in New York at any time.

Sam hadn't been sure if Toby had meant it—it was just the sort of thing you said in those situations—but he'd called, from the airport, and Toby had told him to get on a plane, to come.

So here he was, sailing on a fucking yacht in the Hamptons, of all places, because Toby owned a property out here.

He'd been on a yacht a few years ago, when he and Tom had gone on holiday to Croatia. They'd been sitting out in the sun, the sea sparkling blue underneath them. Tom had managed to sweet-talk the owner of the yacht, whom they'd met at a bar the night before, into renting it out to them for a massive discount. Tom was driving the boat, having never done it before but deciding, in that easygoing way of his, that it would all be fine. Sam remembered Tom getting out his phone, smiling at something on the screen.

Sam grinned. "Based on the ridiculous dopey expression on your face, I'm guessing Amy hasn't forgotten all about you yet."

Tom just shot him a raised-eyebrow look.

"What?" Sam said, his voice full of mock innocence. "It's just . . ." He made a point of searching for the right word. "Adorable," he continued, making his voice all pompous, "seeing you loved-up like this."

Tom snorted as he shoved his phone back into his shorts pocket. "You just watch, it'll happen to you one day."

Sam had brushed it off at the time, laughed at the idea of it. He still wasn't sure he believed it, wasn't sure that he'd ever gotten that same ridiculous expression Tom had when he read messages from Jessica. And could he have left Jessica like that, abandoned her on their wedding day, if he'd loved her in that goofy, all-encompassing way that Tom had seemed to love Amy? He didn't think so. He just didn't think he was built that way. He'd never felt so caught up in another person that he couldn't stop thinking about them, that he was terrified he might lose them.

Though if he was totally honest with himself, he'd been on the edge of that, the closest he'd ever come, on that damn skiing holiday. He'd dealt with that the only way he'd known how to, and it had been the right thing, hadn't it? Even if, now, the thought of Cassie sent a fist through his stomach: the idea—no, the *fact*—that he'd lost her, just as completely as he'd lost Tom. Even after what happened between them on that skiing holiday, even after she'd shut him out—shut him out because he'd forced her to—he'd still assumed she'd always be there, a steady presence in his life. And now she and Tom were both gone.

"There you are, Mr. Malone." Toby came around the side of the boat, his voice booming in that way it always did. Sam glanced up as Toby walked over and sat down next to him, knees up, beer propped on one of them, looking out through the metal railings to the ocean in front of them. They were on their way back now, having done a loop, and Sam could see the green of the Hamptons coming up on their left, some of the million-dollar mansions on view from here, dotted among the trees. Quiet this time of year, which is why Toby had arranged the trip, apparently, whisking Sam off practically the moment he'd landed. *No point having the place if we never use it*, he'd said.

"Practicing for your next modeling shoot?" Toby asked, and elaborated when Sam frowned at him. "Sitting out here, staring out at the water, all moody-looking, on a yacht. It's like something out of a music video."

Sam snorted quietly. "A missed career opportunity. And the yacht's not my doing," he said pointedly.

"She's a beaut, isn't she?" Toby patted the boat fondly. He was wearing dark sunglasses, which sat atop his somewhat crooked nose—broken when he fell off a horse at a young age, apparently. Because *of course* Toby was the type to have had horses while growing up. He'd grown up in the countryside somewhere, splitting time between home and boarding school. They'd spent time in New York, too, as a family—just him, no siblings—and Toby had fallen for the place, so he said, and was spending a year out here full time.

"She is," Sam agreed. And Jesus, this life—Toby's life—this was what he'd dreamed of as a kid. Having the money to do what you wanted, jetting off to New York at the drop of a hat, going out sailing on a yacht, just because you could.

"You can take her out, you know, anytime you like. If you fancy having a spin or just getting away from the house or whatever while you're here. Just say the word." Toby clapped him on the back, as if to emphasize the point. He did this a lot, Toby—was always clapping him on the back or shoulder.

"Thanks, Toby."

"Of course, my man."

"No, seriously." Sam took a sip of his beer. "I mean it. Thanks for, you know . . ." He waved a hand to encompass the boat, the surroundings, Toby himself, sitting there in his dark brown Burberry jacket, zipped three quarters of the way up, showing the checked shirt he was wearing underneath. The shirt which, like always, was unbuttoned just one button more than was totally normal, so that you caught sight of his chest hair. Sam had wondered a few times why Toby always wore his shirts like this, but it didn't seem polite to ask. Maybe he just really liked his chest hair or something.

Sam blew out a breath. "Just . . . thanks."

"Of course," Toby said again, in that brilliantly posh voice. "Couldn't leave you stranded at the airport, now, could I?" And he hadn't asked why. Sam had called him—a man who was practically a stranger—and Toby had said yes, no questions asked, come and stay. So Sam hadn't had to explain about Jessica. Toby knew about Tom, of course. They'd spoken about him a couple of times. Toby had only known Tom a few days, but, in that way of his, Tom had managed to form an impression in that short time. And Sam suspected that was part of the reason Toby had been so happy to put him up. Because he felt he owed it to Tom, somehow. And because he felt he needed to make something up, for being the one who'd seen Tom fall. Not that it was in any way Toby's fault.

"So look," Toby said, "I'm heading over to Brooklyn in a few days, wondered if you wanted to tag along? We could head into the city too, take in some of the sights. What do you say?"

Sam hesitated, then shrugged. "Sure." Because why the fuck not? It wasn't like he was doing anything useful, sitting in a mansion all day. "How come you're going?"

"Oh, I'm writing an article on this youth center place for *The New York Times.*"

Sam choked a little on his beer, and Toby thumped him on the back. "What? You're a journalist?" Sam tried to think if Toby had mentioned it before. He didn't think so. But then, he wasn't really sure *what* Toby did, exactly—he mainly seemed to swan around spending lots of money.

"Well, not really, but it's something I've always wanted to have a go at, and my dad's friend practically owns the paper, so he threw the piece my way."

He said it without a trace of irony, without seeming to realize that the world he inhabited was completely alien to the rest of them. And Sam couldn't help laughing. It was a dry chuckle, and it sounded rusty, like his body had forgotten how to laugh. But it was there.

Toby lifted his sunglasses, peered at Sam with those gray eyes. "What?"

Sam laughed a little harder. "Just . . . Your friend's dad owns *The New York Times.*"

Toby frowned. "Well, he doesn't actually *own* it as such, but he . . ." He trailed off. "Ah." He looked at Sam a little sheepishly. "Posh-boy thing?"

Sam grinned. "Posh-boy thing," he agreed.

"My cross to bear, I'm afraid." He slipped his sunglasses back on.

"Can you even write? Like, do you know *how* to write an article?"

Toby wrinkled that crooked nose. "It can't be that difficult, can it?" He clapped Sam on the back again before getting to his feet. "And if it's total shite, I'm sure they won't publish it, and I'll find another calling."

"A calling now, is it?"

"Well, you never know. I've got to be good at *something* other than spending money, buying property, and going traveling."

"And sailing yachts," Sam added. "Don't forget that."

Toby gave a mock headshake. "It's all right for you—you've got a career, skills. Me? All I've got is money and my rugged good looks." He grinned in a way that let Sam know he was joking, but Sam felt his stomach squirm. Because he wasn't sure he still had his career, was he? He'd lost his job, obviously, and Jessica's dad could make it difficult for him to find work as a solicitor. He had savings, though—a lot of savings. Not Toby level of money, but he'd built up a good pot over the last six years, determined not to be caught short, if it ever came to it. No doubt at some point he'd have to sell the flat in London that he and Jessica had bought together—and that would be money too, when it came in. He was trying not to think too far down that line, though—he'd rather save it as a problem for Future Sam.

Besides, he hadn't heard from Jessica. He wasn't surprised— he wouldn't have wanted to be in touch with him either, if he were her. It was easier, really, like that. He could sort of pretend

the whole thing hadn't happened, that he hadn't jilted his fiancée, hadn't been that much of a dick.

Toby started to head to the back of the boat where the others
were, not forcing Sam to come with him, not asking why he was
sitting here alone. He might live in a different world from Sam,
but he was a good guy. He somehow seemed to get it, without
being told. And he was always offering to share everything he
had—the yacht, the house, dinners, drinks. *If it makes people
happy, why not spend it?* he'd told Sam when he'd asked.

"*There* you boys are." Sam glanced over his shoulder to see
Sophia, a dark-haired, curvy girl with golden tan skin and beautiful bedroom eyes coming around the side. She was followed
closely by Zoe—tall, stick-thin, with ash-blond hair—who was
Toby's girlfriend. Sam didn't totally get how they worked as a
couple: Zoe barely said anything and seemed to make it her
mission to be unimpressed by literally everything, which seemed
at odds with Toby's nature, in the short time Sam had known
him. But then, opposites attract and all that.

"We were looking for you," Sophia added unnecessarily, jut-
ting her bottom lip out in a pout. She was wearing a blue dress,
her slim, golden legs on show, and a denim jacket, and definitely
could *not* have been warm enough. Sam supposed that was why
she'd stayed in the undercover bit of the yacht, away from the
wind and sea spray.

Toby went to Zoe and slung an arm around her, while Sophia took another step toward Sam, twirling a lock of hair
around her finger. "Coming, Sam? We're going to have some
champagne, do another loop so we can watch the sunset."

"Are we now?" Toby said.

"Yes." Sophia folded her arms. "We are."

"What if I want to park her up, kick you all off?" Toby said,
his voice teasing.

Sophia huffed out a breath, glancing at Zoe as if to say, *Get your boyfriend under control.* Zoe said nothing, her expression bored. "You're not the only one on the boat, Toby," Sophia said.

Toby laughed, then a grin settled on his face. "We'll just see about that." He grabbed her around the middle, literally lifting her off her feet, making as if to push her over the edge.

She screamed, and Sam was on his feet immediately. He'd stepped toward her, was reaching out as if to grab her, before his brain registered the type of scream. Playful, a bit pissed off. Not scared.

She swatted Toby's hand away. "Not *funny.*"

Toby chortled, put his arm back around Zoe. "Come on. A little funny. Right, S—" He frowned when he looked over at Sam. Sam didn't know what his face must be showing— whether he'd gone pale or looked sick or something, but he tried to smooth out his expression as best he could, his heart still thumping.

Because it was a different scream echoing around Sam's head. One he'd heard countless times in his nightmares. And for a moment, he hadn't been on the yacht. He'd been in the mountains of Patagonia, as he imagined them. He'd been reaching out to grab hold of someone, only to find nothing but air.

Tom's scream, the one that made him wake at night drenched in cold sweat, was still there, vibrating through him. Had he screamed when he fell? He'd never had the guts to ask Toby.

"You all right, Sam?" Toby asked, still frowning at him.

"Yeah." His voice came out a little husky, so he cleared his throat. "Yeah, sorry." He looked at Sophia. "You OK?" Because it would be odd now not to ask, since he'd jumped to his feet to . . . what, save her? Jesus, he needed to get a grip.

"I'm fine," she said, glaring at Toby. But those bedroom eyes turned considering, as she took in Sam. "But maybe I need a bit of help getting back, so that *this one* . . ." she shot Toby another look, "doesn't try anything."

Toby chuckled. "Sure you do."

Sophia didn't give him much of a choice as she came up next to him, linked her arm through his. He caught a whiff of her perfume, a musky scent, undeniably sexy. "Come on, handsome, let's go have some fun."

Toby raised his eyebrows at Sam over Sophia's head so that Sam knew he'd make an excuse for him if he didn't want to come back inside, where music was now blaring, the voices louder as the champagne started to flow. But Sophia's arm was through his, her body pressed next to him. It was easy, so easy, to fall into the pattern. And it would be nice, wouldn't it, to lose himself, just for a bit, to forget how well and truly fucked his life was.

So he gave Toby a little shrug and allowed Sophia to pull him along. Took a glass of champagne when it was handed to him. Allowed the music, the sound of laughter, to wash over him. And when Sophia smiled that sultry smile at him over the rim of her glass, he smiled back.

Chapter Sixteen

"*Here you go.*" *Ted,* one of the longest-standing barmen at Cassie's hotel, smiled as he set down two frothy cappuccinos in front of Cassie and Amy. "Get you anything else?"

"No, that's great, Ted, thanks," Cassie said, pulling the coffees toward her. "You've put it on my tab, yeah?" Ridiculous, really, that they weren't even allowed *coffees* for free here.

"That I have, and I even snuck you a chocolate mint each," he said with a wink, gesturing at the little gold-wrapped chocolates on the side of the saucers.

"It's definitely decaf, right?" Amy said, her eyes flitting between the two coffees, like she'd be able to tell which was which just by looking. Cassie hadn't realized Amy was so worried about caffeine. Maybe it was a recent thing. From the looks of her, she hadn't been sleeping well—there were purple shadows under her eyes, and her face was pale, even though her cheeks were a little flushed now that she was inside the hotel rather than outside in the cold April rain.

Spring. It was definitely spring now, and ten days since Cassie had read Tom's clue: *One spring day the teams will meet . . .*

She tried to ignore the squirm of anxiety that she still hadn't figured it out as Ted smiled at Amy, pushing the nearest coffee over to her. "This one is, hon." With a quick smile for Cassie, he left them where they were, perched on high red stools at the end of the chic wooden bar, and went off to see to another customer.

Amy picked up her stirrer—which also doubled as a chocolate stick—and absentmindedly swirled the froth. She looked like a shadow of the person Cassie had once known—hunched in on herself, wearing a sweater that looked like it might have once been Tom's over leggings. Her curls looked less springy than usual, hanging around her heart-shaped face, a yellow headband atop them being the only nod to the old Amy—the vibrant girl Cassie used to know.

She recognized the way Amy looked, the cloud she carried with her. Not too long ago, that was her. And in some ways, she still felt it—but trying to work out the clues, even if she was terrified she wouldn't figure this one out in time—it was giving her a focus, a distraction. A reason to keep going.

"So how are you, Amy?" Cassie asked, when it was clear Amy wasn't going to start the conversation.

"I'm . . ." Amy put her drink down. "God. I don't know. A mess?" She laughed scathingly, while Cassie grimaced sympathetically. She should have contacted her before now, Cassie thought. Should have tried harder to stay in touch, to realize that Amy might have wanted—needed—to talk to someone who knew Tom, someone else who was grieving. Cassie had Hazel and Linda, but Amy had no one, really. No one who knew Tom in the same way. It had taken Amy contacting her for Cassie to remember that. It was unforgivably selfish of her, she thought now.

"And you?" Amy said, cupping her hands around the coffee, as if she was desperately trying to take some of the warmth from it.

Cassie picked up her own cup and glanced along the length of the bar. No sign of Robert. "I don't know either," she said. "I'm coping, I guess." And, for the first time since Tom's death, it didn't feel like a lie.

"How's work?" Cassie asked. Pointless small talk, she knew, but she thought they both needed it.

"Yeah, it's OK. I've been promoted to commissioning editor."

"Really?" Cassie had no idea what that meant, but it sounded good. "That's great."

"Yeah." She sounded more tired than thrilled about it.

"Does it mean you get to go to more fancy launch parties?"

Amy laughed, and an echo of her lightness came back to her face. "Not quite. And the launch parties aren't fancy, you know— mostly just warm white wine in bookshops, nothing like what you do." The smile faded slowly. She'd met Tom at a launch party, Cassie remembered. One of Tom's friends was celebrating a book release and Tom had gone along to the launch. He'd always seemed to have an endless stream of successful friends, and Cassie often wondered where he picked them up, but then, Tom had been the type of person who could be chatting to someone in the pub one moment and be invited to a party the next. He drew people to him, to that energy and warmth.

"So, Amy," Cassie began, trying to think of a polite way to phrase it, "did you, umm, want to meet me for something specific?" She cringed a little at the overly formal tone of her voice. But she wanted to know. The only thing that drew them together was Tom, and she couldn't help think that the reason Amy had wanted to meet had something to do with him.

"Well, actually . . ."

"Cassie?"

Cassie grimaced, though she quickly smoothed out her expression before twisting around on the stool to see Robert coming over to them, running a hand across his receding hairline. "What are you doing? I thought you were . . ." Robert trailed off,

giving Amy an assessing look, and Cassie just knew he was trying to work out if she was a potential client, if he should switch
on the charm. For a second, Cassie debated lying about it—
claiming that Amy was some important guest who was thinking about hosting one of those not-so-fancy launch parties here
or something. Amy would probably go along with it. But then,
the follow-up questions from Robert wouldn't be worth it—
and she doubted she'd be able to keep up the lie without getting
caught.

"This is Amy," she said. "A friend of mine." Amy nodded politely, and Robert's expression turned sour. He opened his
mouth to press on, no doubt to tell her that she wasn't *allowed*
friends at the bar—which was ridiculous, because there was no
policy against it—but Cassie talked over him before he could
speak. "I'm taking the time out of my lunch break," she said
pointedly. He frowned at her. She never usually spoke so firmly,
never usually showed any sign of a backbone. Maybe it was just
that she didn't want to look weak and pathetic in front of Amy.
Maybe it was that he'd been getting to her more and more recently. Or maybe it was the fact that she'd been feeling stretched.
Not only was half her mind constantly preoccupied with Tom's
clue, but she was still worried about the fate of Linda's pub,
along with trying to keep Robert happy.

And Robert hadn't *cared* when she'd tried to explain about
the pub. He'd refused to let her take a couple of days' holiday at
short notice, so she hadn't been able to go and be with Linda in
person, and he'd shut her down when she'd tried to talk to him.
*It's just a pub, Cassie. There are worse things in the world to get
upset about.* And yes, fine, maybe that was true, but it still meant
something to her.

"I'll catch you at lunchtime, then," he said eventually, and

Cassie heard the unspoken promise—that he'd check up on her, and make sure she was working her lunch break to make up for it.

She wrinkled her nose as Robert walked away. "Sorry about that," she said with a sigh.

"Don't be silly." Amy hesitated. "I guess I don't need to ask you how work's going then . . . ?"

"Oh, it's fine," she said, attempting to brighten her tone a bit for Amy's sake. "Robert might be a dick, but I still love what I do." It was true, she thought firmly. Even if the hotel was feeling a little claustrophobic at the moment, she *did* love the events, the organization of it, the buzz she got when it all came together. She loved the expression on people's faces when the event was just as they'd imagined—or better—and knowing that she'd played a part, no matter how small, in their happiness for that one day. It would feel silly to admit any of that out loud, she knew—she'd never even told Tom, not in so many words. And now she never would.

She noticed Amy watching her, her eyes too understanding, as if she knew exactly where Cassie's thoughts had gone. So she straightened her back. "Sorry, you were saying, before we were so rudely interrupted?"

"Oh." Amy looked down at her coffee, then back at Cassie. "It was nothing really. I just . . . I wanted to see you, I suppose." She offered her a weak smile, so unlike the wicked grin that Cassie remembered from the very first time Tom had introduced them to one another.

They'd been meeting at Gordon's Wine Bar, near the Embankment, and Amy had arrived late, coming up to the outdoor table where Cassie and Tom stood chatting, and apologizing profusely before clasping Cassie's hands and telling her how wonderful it was to meet her. "I've heard all about you, of course. Come on, let's get wine. Do you like wine? If you don't, it's OK, we can still be friends, but I'm getting wine."

"Amy," Tom had said, a touch warningly, to which Amy had given him an eyeroll.

"Relax, I'll be careful with her." She and Tom had exchanged a look, and Cassie had seen how Tom's expression softened, his eyes just on Amy, like they were totally alone in the alleyway. And she'd thought, then, that this was it for Tom. Though it seemed she'd been proven wrong in the end about that, just as she'd been proven wrong about her own "it" moment, all those years ago.

"I'm sorry." Cassie reached out, took Amy's hand in hers across the table. "I should've called."

"No," Amy said firmly. "This is not on you. I . . ." But she shook her head, making her curls bounce, and pressed trembling lips together. "Sorry," she whispered.

"Don't be." Cassie squeezed Amy's hand.

For a moment, neither of them said anything, Amy's eyes firmly on her cappuccino as she clearly fought for some control.

"I started Tom's treasure hunt, you know," Cassie found herself saying, wanting to find something to distract Amy. Amy knew about the annual tradition of the treasure hunt already— it had come up when the three of them had been hanging out at Tom's flat once, and Amy had loved the whole thing. Cassie had recited some of Tom's childhood rhymes, making Amy laugh. "I'm in love with a poet!" she'd declared.

It was the first time Cassie heard either of them say "love" like that and it had made her jolt, but Tom just grinned, then threw a cushion at Amy's head. "You wait, I'll be writing you love sonnets soon."

"Oh, please do, I can give you editorial notes on how to improve."

"Really?" Amy said now. "I'd forgotten about that. But he was working on it, I think, before we . . ." She shook her head. "How's it going?"

"I've only done one clue so far," Cassie admitted. "I'm kind of stuck on the next one."

"What is it?"

Cassie had taken a photo of the clue, and though she didn't need to, could recite it from memory, she got out her phone, read it out.

"One spring day the teams will meet,
But one will go home in defeat,
All of them have brains, it's true,
But this is what it means to be a blue.

P.S. I still can't believe you've never done this—time to fix
that and try something new.
P.P.S. Life is but a dream."

Amy frowned contemplatively. "So it's some kind of sport?"

"I think so," Cassie said slowly. The word "defeat" had initially made her think of boxing, but somehow she couldn't equate boxing with her brother—it just wasn't his sort of thing. Besides, it was a team event, unless there was something she was missing. The only thing she could be certain of was that it was referring to something that happened in spring, and that there were teams—which could be sport, as Amy said. She'd googled soccer because it seemed the most obvious—Tom and Sam had played soccer at school, and going to a soccer match was something she'd never done before, but there were *loads* of matches on in spring and she had no idea how she was supposed to know which one it would be. She'd tried them all after that—rugby, hockey, cricket. But nothing had jumped out at her as some big event—an event that Tom must have assumed she'd know about.

"Blue," Amy said, tapping her fingernails against her mug. "Like second place? Isn't it red for first, blue for second?"

Cassie frowned—she hadn't thought of it that way. Was she supposed to be looking for a team that always came second or something? Worth a try, for sure—as long as she wasn't too late. The sense of time passing—of *spring* passing—pressed down on her, though she tried to hide it from Amy.

"I reckon you'll get it," Amy said confidently. "You haven't ever not finished one before, right?"

"No, but I always had Tom there to help me in person if I got stuck." Both of them went quiet at that. What would he be doing now, if he was here? Would he still be speaking to Amy? Be back together with her? Or would they still be broken up? Would he have helped Cassie with this clue, or given her annoyingly superior hints, making her work for it?

It wasn't fair. It wasn't fair that she'd never know the answer to these questions, that her brother's future had been snatched away, just like that.

She closed her eyes against the threat of burning tears, just as her phone buzzed on the table. She slid it toward herself automatically, saw that it was a GoFundMe alert. The reminder of it, of the fact that she'd not managed to save the pub, made her feel heavy. Linda had been right. It wasn't that easy, getting your hands on that kind of money. Not that Linda had made her feel bad about it.

You tried, she'd said when they'd last spoken. Tried, Cassie thought—and failed.

"It's this thing," she explained to Amy as she unlocked her phone. "Linda, our family friend, is about to lose her pub, and I'm trying to raise money so she can . . ." But she went silent, the words sticking in her throat. Because this was not just another small donation from a friend or family member, doing their best to help out.

Someone had just donated ten thousand pounds.

"Oh my God!" Cassie squealed and jumped to her feet, then sat back down again immediately, her whole body twitching, unable to keep still.

"What?" Amy asked sharply. "What is it?"

"Someone has just . . ." She shook her head, unable to articulate it, and turned her phone toward Amy so she could see for herself.

Amy gave a low whistle. "That's megabucks."

"I know." Sudden adrenaline was pumping around her body, making it impossible to think straight. "Oh my God, Amy, I know, and I think it's enough. All together, I think this is enough." She sprang to her feet again. "Amy, it's enough to save the pub!"

To her credit, Amy jumped on board immediately. "Amazing! This is the pub by your old house, right?"

"Right," Cassie agreed, nodding reverently. "Exactly."

"Who did it? Who donated all the money?"

Cassie frowned, looked down at her phone at the donation. But there was no name, no message. She looked back at Amy blankly. "I have absolutely no idea."

Chapter Seventeen

Sam woke while it was still dark, took a moment to remember where he was, the room in Toby's house still unfamiliar. It was silent around him—noticeable because he'd fallen asleep to the sound of music blaring in the living room, Toby having invited everyone to his place after the yacht. His head was pounding. He figured that was what had woken him. Jesus, he'd drunk too much last night. It had been easy, in the end, to slip into it, to let the party carry him away.

Next to him on the double bed, Sophia stirred, the sheet pulled up around her waist, leaving the rest of her sexy, curvy body on show. It had been so easy to go there with her, too. To flirt back, to kiss her, to let her take him by the hand, lead him to his room. Easy to fall back into old habits, to remember the dance he'd known so well, before Jessica.

Feeling oddly claustrophobic next to her on the bed, he threw the covers off, dressed as quietly as he could in his discarded clothes from the night before and padded from the room, slipping his phone off the bedside table as he did so. He headed for the kitchen, then out the double sliding doors.

It was cold. Really bloody cold outside at night, especially without a coat. He sucked in a breath, walked down over the perfectly mown lawn (by whom, Sam wasn't sure—he'd never seen Toby do it), and headed to the fuck-off massive pool at the end of the garden. He sat on the nearest deck chair, staring at the water. There was just a sliver of a crescent moon tonight, half hidden by cloud, but wisps of moonlight still bounced off the water, in a way that was oddly soothing to watch.

He glanced at the time on his phone, did a quick calculation of the time difference. It would be morning now in the UK; his mum would be up and about, probably having a cup of tea. He called her and she answered immediately.

"Sam?"

"Hey, Mum. Sorry I missed your call yesterday." He hadn't noticed it, his phone on silent, sitting away from him.

"That's OK. How are you, love?"

"I'm OK. I'm still in the Hamptons. It's nice," he added for her benefit. "I'm sitting by the pool right now."

"Oooh, very fancy." She was trying hard to keep her voice light, he could tell. "And are you doing . . . OK? I've been worried about you, out there all alone."

"I'm not alone," he said reassuringly. "I'm staying with friends." He'd slightly amended the truth when he'd told her who he was staying with, had said Toby was a friend from university, rather than a random guy he'd met at Tom's funeral, because he knew the latter would only make her worry.

"Right, I know. But, well. You know what I mean."

"Yeah," he said, because it was easier than arguing. He ran a hand over his head, the pounding still there.

"And have you spoken to . . . anyone . . . back home?" She meant Jessica, but she didn't want to ask directly, he knew, didn't want to upset him by saying it out loud.

"Not yet. I just need some space, to figure stuff out." A feeble excuse, but there it was. He thought back to the last message exchange with Jessica. He'd gotten the message from her on the way to the airport, after haphazardly grabbing some things from their flat. Just one word. *Why?*

He'd not known what to say other than *I'm sorry*, the reasons *why* feeling too big, too messy, to write over text. She hadn't said anything more. He'd imagined her raging, crying, and knew there was nothing he could say to make any of it better.

His mum hesitated for a beat, and Sam could dimly hear the noise of the TV in the background. "Your dad's been trying to get hold of you, you know."

Sam felt his spine stiffen but forced his voice to remain calm. "I do know." He had the missed calls to show for it, didn't he? And now, apparently, his dad was going to his mum, roping her in. "I don't want to talk to him." It felt unnecessary to say it out loud, really.

His mum sighed. "Holding on to this resentment isn't good for you, Sam. It will only eat you up, make you bitter." He said nothing. But in his mind, the alternative wasn't much better. Because the alternative was to let it all go, like her, and open himself up to constant let-down. He didn't know how she did it, how she maintained the positivity she carried around like a light. He realized, though, that he was grateful for it—she *was* always positive, had managed to be so his entire life, and in that moment he felt overwhelmed by the thought of it. Because look what she'd gotten for it. A husband who'd abandoned her, and a son who was turning out to be just as much of a fuck-up. She deserved better than the two of them. And it was turning into a self-fulfilling prophecy, wasn't it? By not wanting to be like his dad, to let people down in that way, he was becoming *exactly* like him—always underpromising, making sure people knew they couldn't depend on him, then letting them down in the end anyway. Like Jessica. And like Cassie.

"You should try not to be too hard on him," his mum continued softly. "He's not a bad person, he's just made some bad choices that led him to where he is now. But he loves you."

"Yeah, well, he has a funny way of showing it," Sam muttered.

"I think your dad—he never really found the right path in life, or, I should say, he never really found *his* path, and so he kept messing up a little, going off the beaten track." Sam frowned, trying to follow the analogy. "I wasn't for him," she continued. "I wasn't where he was supposed to be." And so, Sam thought, by virtue of that, he wasn't either. "I've come to accept that. But your dad, he's been searching ever since for something to hold on to, and I don't think he's ever found it."

"Maybe he hasn't been trying hard enough." Sam tried—and failed—to keep the bite out of his voice.

"Yes, well, maybe."

"And maybe," Sam said, through slightly gritted teeth, "he should've figured out that he didn't want a family *before* he got married, had a kid."

"Maybe," his mum agreed on a sigh. "But life's full of maybes, and if you focus too much on those then you forget to just be. And really, love, you've seen what happens if you force yourself down one path, when your heart is taking you somewhere else." Sam felt an uncomfortable lurch in his stomach. It was the closest she'd come to pointing out that what he'd done to Jessica was not so different from what his dad did to her. He hated that. But she wasn't judging him for it—and that infuriating refusal to judge or condemn his dad was perhaps the same quality of hers that made it easy to talk to her, that meant he hadn't felt the need to cut her out of his life like he'd done with other people, because he knew that she could understand, or at least accept, less than ideal choices.

"I'm sorry, Mum," he said, his throat tight. "With Dad . . . I just can't go there. And I'm sorry for everything else too."

"You don't need to apologize to me, love."

He'd do something for her, he decided. Send her to a spa or something, let her know how much he appreciated her, even if he was a rotten son. For now though, he let it move along. "How are things with you?" he asked.

"Oh, much the same, you know. Did you hear about Linda's pub?"

"No, what about it?"

"She's having to sell it. There was some flooding and she can't afford to keep it." She sighed. "The village just won't be the same without it. It's all very sad, really."

"That's . . ." Sam ran a hand across the back of his neck. "Yeah. Yeah, that is sad." He thought of how much he and Tom used to hang out there, as kids, doing homework or mucking around, then as teenagers, when Sam would wait for Tom to finish his shift. Linda had been like a mum to Tom and Cassie, Sam knew, what with Claire being so absent, and they'd adopted the pub as a second home. He had a distinct memory of sitting there, playing cards with Tom when they were bored and it was raining. Cassie had been working—she'd have been, what, sixteen? She'd only just started there, and it had been impossible not to notice how proud she was of it. Tom had just beaten him at *another* round of trumps, and was teasing him about his terrible card skills, when Cassie had come out of the lunchtime shift. She'd come over, face flushed, hair in a bun on the top of her head, wearing the all-black outfit that the waitresses wore. She'd been pulsing with energy. Sam knew Cassie thought that *Tom* was the one with all that energy, that life—but she was wrong. She had it too, just about different things.

"What are you two doing?"

Tom rolled his eyes. "What does it look like, Chipmunk?"

"Can I play?"

Tom hesitated, looking at Sam questioningly, though Sam knew he was only doing it to wind her up.

"Hmmm, don't know about that," Sam said, "trumps is more of a two-person game, don't you think?" He directed the question at Tom, who nodded seriously.

"Yeah, I reckon so."

"Fine," Cassie said. "Be like that." And she spun away.

Tom grinned at Sam, and even though he knew Tom would call her back, it was still Sam who caved first. She'd barely taken a step when he said, "Ah, come on, Cass, you know we're only joking. Pull out a pew." He pulled the chair away from the table and Cassie eyed it suspiciously, clearly deciding whether or not she was willing to take the teasing. "Come on," he continued. "I'll even let you win the first round."

Tom snorted. "You won't be letting her, mate, she'll wipe the floor with you." And Tom—as usual—had been right.

Sam's head pounded again. "I've got to go, Mum, sorry—it's still night here."

"All right, love. Speak to you soon—please check in, won't you? I love you."

"You too."

He hung up, and then just sat there, staring at the wispy moonlight. Cassie's face swirled around his mind, the face he'd never quite been able to shake, even though he'd always told himself she was off limits. Even though he'd tried to stay behind the wall she'd slammed up, tried to tell himself that it was better that way. Tried to deny how much he missed her—missed their easy conversation, the friendship, the fact that he didn't have to explain anything to her, because she always just got it.

He opened up her Facebook page, unable to help himself.

He wanted to see some evidence that she was doing OK. The first thing he saw up there was a GoFundMe. *Save our local pub!* His heart jolted. Linda's pub. He clicked through. Thirty grand they needed to raise—and they were on just under twenty, with a couple of days to go. Pretty good going, he thought. Though not enough, obviously. He stared at it, the photo of the pub Cassie had put on the page. He wondered who would buy it from Linda. Developers, probably. It'd be destroyed in that case, turned into a soulless block of flats or something. He knew the type, had worked with them. And Cassie . . . Her face flashed in his mind again, bright brown eyes, golden hair. She'd hate this. *Hate* it.

A spark flared inside him—an idea. Cassie had been the most important thing in Tom's life. Nothing he'd ever do would make up for the fact that he hadn't been in Argentina when he should have been, but surely the only way of even *starting* to make it up would be by helping Cassie, Tom's little sister. And here was the opportunity to do that, right in front of him. He had the power, right now, to help Cassie save something she loved.

It was an impulse decision to donate: to take a huge chunk out of his savings and give the rest of the money that Cassie needed. Who cared about savings, anyway? This was something that would make a difference to Cassie, would help her be happy in the face of an awful tragedy. He'd get more money. It had turned out not to matter anyway, hadn't it? He'd spent years and years building it up, determined to always make *more*, to get to some unknown goal. But now, he'd give it all up in an instant if it meant getting Tom back.

So yes, he'd donate this to Cassie, to the pub. But when the page asked for his name, he hesitated. There was a chance Cassie wouldn't take it, knowing it was from him. And maybe he didn't want her to know anyway, not after what she'd said to him the last time they'd seen each other. He didn't want her thinking he had some ulterior motive, didn't want to have to answer questions about *why*. So instead, he ticked the box that said anonymous.

Chapter Eighteen

When Sam woke for the second time, he saw Sophia smiling at him from her pillow, sunlight filtering over her face through the gap in the curtains. She looked alarmingly fresh-faced, eyes bright, lips all glossy. "Hey, handsome," she said.

"Hey, yourself." Unlike hers, his voice was husky from sleep.

"Last night was fun." She reached out, tiptoed her fingers down his bare arm.

"Yeah." And there had been moments of fun, for sure, though he wasn't totally sure it had been a good idea.

He sat up. "Sorry. Got to have a shower." He kissed her on the head before heading into the en-suite bathroom, knowing that sort of thing was expected. He grimaced as he braced his hands against the sink, staring at himself in the mirror. Would she want something from him now? But he hadn't promised anything, had he? And it had been her who had made the move, even if he'd been all too willing to go along with it. Tom used to tease him about that. And he had a flash then of Tom sitting on his single bed, in the tiny room of their first-year university halls, shaking his head, his blond hair flopping with the movement.

"*Girls literally throw themselves at your feet, don't they, Malone?*"

"Ah, come on now, don't get all jealous, green's a bad color on you."

Not that Tom had ever had any trouble on the girl front—he had a line of them waiting, but he'd only had one girlfriend at university, and then he'd met Amy, and that was it.

"Pff, whatever, nothing worth keeping hold of ever came easy," Tom replied.

"Taking a philosophy course on the side that I don't know about?"

Tom answered that by throwing a pen at Sam, which hit him on the arm.

He smiled, just a little, at the memory.

In the shower, turning the temperature right up so that pin-pricks of heat seared his skin, the full scope of last night hit him. Cassie. The pub. His savings.

Shit.

It had been a whim, something he hadn't really thought through, carried away by the need to do something for Tom.

But would he take it back now, if he could, in the cold hard light of day? No, he decided. No, he was glad he'd done it—if it meant Cassie keeping hold of something she loved. If it meant honoring Tom in even a small way, then he'd made the right decision. But it did mean he had to figure out what the hell to do next. He still had a bit of money, but it wasn't going to last indefinitely.

Sophia was gone when he came back out and everyone was already in the kitchen when he got there, coffee and eggs on the breakfast bar. Toby's work, probably. Considering he'd probably had a cook or whatever growing up, the guy was surprisingly good in the kitchen.

Toby caught his eye as Sam pulled up a seat at the granite breakfast bar, and held out an empty mug in question from where he was standing by the wooden cabinets. Sam nodded, and Toby filled the mug with freshly brewed coffee, handing it to Sam.

"Good night?" Toby asked, raising his eyebrows and smirking just a little.

Sam just rolled his eyes and sipped the coffee—black, slightly bitter—and thankfully, Toby said nothing else about it. He clocked Sophia at the end of the breakfast bar, leaning against it rather than sitting, in some sort of intense conversation with Zoe—Sophia doing most of the talking. Both of them were wearing matching black silk dressing gowns, like they'd coordinated or something. The other people from last night—Sam couldn't remember most of their names—seemed to have disappeared, though the house was big enough for triple that number. It had eight bedrooms, a gigantic sitting room, a separate "movie room" with a screen so big it could definitely pass for a private cinema, and two hot tubs, not to mention the pool. The kitchen was actually the least impressive room in the house. Stylish, modern, and bright, yes, but relatively small, with none of the grandeur of the rest of the place. Maybe you weren't supposed to spend much time there. Maybe *other* people were supposed to cook.

Sam tapped his fingers against his mug. "So, Toby, would you happen to know anything about getting a job out here?"

Toby came to lean against the other side of the breakfast bar, opening his mouth to speak, but it was Zoe, down the end of the breakfast bar, who piped up, apparently tuned in to the conversations around her, even if she didn't usually contribute. "What do you need a job for?" she asked with a frown, as if the *idea* of someone getting a job was scandalous.

"Yeah, aren't you just here on holiday?" Sophia added, flicking her dark hair over her shoulder.

"I . . ." Was he? He supposed so, because he couldn't move out here permanently, could he? But he hadn't yet given much thought as to what happened next. He was just trying to get by, day by day, week by week.

"Leave the guy alone, will you?" Toby said with a jokey head-shake at the girls. He turned back to Sam. "Not really sure of the logistics, my man, but I could speak to a few people, put out a few feelers, if you like? Don't sweat the money too much, though, if that's your worry? You know I'm happy for you to crash with me."

"Thanks, mate, but I just want to . . . you know, pull my weight."

"Sure, sure," Toby said easily. "I get that." He grinned—such an easy, instant grin. "You don't fancy journalism, do you?"

Sam laughed a little. "I'll leave that to you, I think."

"Didn't your friend die in a climbing accident?" Zoe asked. Sam winced at the casual way it was tossed out there, at the same time as Toby said "Zoe," in a warning tone.

Zoe swished her hair back. "I thought he could do a first-person piece for one of the papers, that's all. I'm trying to be *helpful*." She looked at Toby accusingly. "It was you who mentioned journalism."

"Sorry," Toby said soothingly. "I know you are." When Zoe and Sophia went back to their own private conversation, Toby mouthed "Sorry" at Sam, who tried to shrug it off, though his shoulders felt brittle.

In the pocket of his jeans—he was the only one dressed, he noticed belatedly—Sam's phone buzzed, and he slipped it out. It was a GoFundMe alert. Cassie Rivers had sent him a message.

His heart jumped. He had done it anonymously, hadn't he? He was sure he had.

**Whoever you are, thank you. This is so incredibly gener-
ous and there are no words to say what this means to me
and Linda. Your donation has made all the difference and
got us over the line.**

There. It had made all the difference. He'd done something
positive, for Tom, for Cassie.

He typed back. **You're welcome.**

He got a reply immediately. **If you don't mind me asking, why
did you decide to donate?**

It was carefully phrased—she clearly wanted to ask who the
hell he was but was too polite to be as blunt as that. Why did he
decide to donate . . . ? How to respond to that? **I'm a friend of
Tom's,** he wrote, then deleted it. It might be too obvious and,
besides, it would lead to a conversation about Tom, and he
wasn't ready for that.

**I'm just someone who appreciates the value of local busi-
nesses. I've worked in law, helping the other side too
much. I decided it was time to give something back.**

It was true, sort of—through working in corporate law he
had often ended up helping the people with the most money
and had been part of the legal team to kill a small business at
least twice. It was a bit of a gray area for him, and not something
he'd loved, but he'd managed to put it aside—people could only
come to them if they had a legal case, after all, so then it was just
about doing his job. This was a different thing—Linda was selling because her business was failing, presumably, not because
she was being sued, but still, here was a chance to help something, rather than tear it down. So if he twisted things a little, it
wasn't a complete lie to Cassie.

"You all right, Sam?" Toby was watching him, like he'd been speaking to him, was expecting some sort of response.

"Yeah. Sorry, yeah."

"I was just saying, maybe you could . . ."

But he couldn't concentrate on what Toby was saying, thinking instead of Cassie. Maybe she'd be smiling now, some of that brilliant light in her eyes as she realized that she'd done it. He missed seeing it, that light. Not just since Tom died, but before that. Once, he'd been a part of it—he'd been a *cause* of it. He used to be able to make her laugh, and he'd caught her looking at him in that warm way of hers when she did so. That quiet, steady way that had such *certainty* that he'd been almost unable to bear it. It had felt like the only option was to destroy it, so that he couldn't make things worse—because if he'd given in, if he'd gone down that line with Cassie, he'd just known he'd fuck it up, sooner or later—and that would have been so much worse for both of them. He'd known that he'd lose her in the end, if they went there.

But he'd lost her anyway, hadn't he? Lost her by betraying her trust back then, and lost her by betraying Tom now. And there was a tiny, selfish part of him that knew—the way his heart had jumped when he'd seen her name wasn't all about his fear of her finding out it was him, or even the thought of Tom. It was the fact that by doing this, by helping her to save the pub, he was keeping her in his life in some small way—even if she could never know about it.

Chapter Nineteen

Cassie tapped her fingertips next to her keyboard as she scrolled through the list Google had brought up. Each tap felt like the ticking of a clock. Counting down until the end of spring—counting down the seconds she still hadn't figured out Tom's clue.

No. *Stop it,* she told herself. Panic was helping no one. She had to focus, think about it. But right now, she also needed to work. So she switched tabs in Google, away from the list of "spring events" and to a list of foods instead.

"What do you think of passion fruit?"

"Huh?" Josh glanced up from his desk, where he was sketching something on a pad, computer screen black from lack of use. "I don't know. Not sure I have strong feelings about passion fruit either way."

"As a cake flavor," she explained. "It's for that eightieth birthday celebration," Cassie went on.

"Right." Josh went back to whatever he was sketching. Cassie couldn't work out what it was from here, though she was ninety percent sure it wasn't work related. Coursework for his master's, maybe. "The Ps."

"Yep." Cassie scrolled through the other possible "P" flavors, and decided passion fruit was still top of her list. The birthday was for a woman name Pauline, and her daughter, who booked the event, wanted everything to be "P" related. Literally every-thing. So it meant the food, drinks, cake, decorations, song choices, all somehow had to begin with a "P." Cassie had man-aged to get around this with the food by pairing things up and making sure the "P" was at the beginning. Pecan and goat's cheese salad. Parsnip and apple soup. Paprika-spiced roasted cauliflower.

"Tea?" Josh asked, pushing his sketch aside and getting to his feet. He did this when he was bored—got up about every ten minutes to get tea, and then every thirty to go to the loo.

Cassie nodded absentmindedly. "Sure."

While Josh was out of the room, she checked her phone, saw a message from Linda.

Meeting with the solicitors scheduled for Monday x

Cassie felt a tiny squirm of nerves. Things had already started moving with the sale of the pub before that final donation had come in, and so Linda was having to meet with the solicitors who'd been handling it before she could back out. She supposed they'd find out on Monday whether they'd been too late. She was trying to be optimistic about it. It would be fine. The meet-ing would go well. They couldn't *make* Linda go through with the final stages of selling it, though admittedly Cassie didn't know much about the legal side of things.

Linda had been dumbstruck when Cassie told her the news over the phone a couple of days ago. She'd asked Cassie to re-peat it, several times. They'd cried on the phone together, and Linda had listed all the ways she was going to make this work, bolstered by the fact that she had another few years in her of running the pub yet, that her baby wasn't being taken away—she was going to make plans, she said, to keep it going even after she passed it on to someone else, because it had made her realize how awful it would have been to have had things ripped away without a choice in what happened to it.

Then they'd both speculated over who the anonymous donation was from.

After sending an email suggesting passion-fruit cake to Pauline's daughter, Cassie opened up the GoFundMe account, reread the message.

> **I'm just someone who appreciates the value of local businesses. I've worked in law, helping the other side too much. I decided it was time to give something back.**

The door to the office opened, letting in the artificial light of the basement corridor, where the two of them were hidden away, and Josh stepped inside. He came over, set her tea down in front of her, and peered over her shoulder at the computer monitor. "Hmmm, no further on figuring out who it is, then?"

Cassie shook her head.

"Maybe it's Jeff Bezos," Josh suggested, heading back to his own desk.

Cassie snorted. "What, because he's such a philanthropist? And so interested in saving a pub he's never been to, has never heard of, and means nothing to him?"

"You never know."

"Shall I ring him and ask?"

Josh grinned. "Yes. Please do that."

"It shouldn't matter," she said, more to herself than Josh. "Why can't I just accept it's a nice thing? It shouldn't matter who it is."

"We're like that though, aren't we, us humans?"

"I just want to know who I'm thanking." It was more than that, though. She didn't quite trust it, the fact that someone anonymous had given them such a big chunk of money. What if it was someone who wanted something in return, later down the line? And so what, she tried to tell herself—she hadn't promised anything. There was no contract, it was a charity donation. But that didn't mean she was giving up quite yet.

She tapped out a reply to the message. **I'd love to keep you updated on the progress. Maybe give you some discount codes, once things are up and running again?** Linda would agree, she was sure. Linda wanted to know who it was as much as she did. **Do you have an email or something I can contact you on?** She drummed her fingers while she waited for a response.

I'd love to see how things are going. Will you post updates on this page?

Cassie wrinkled her nose. She supposed she would do: for everyone, not just the mystery donor, to see—all the people who had given something, big or small, who had tried to help, made it known that they cared. So, he'd neatly sidestepped her hidden demand for a name, then. **I will. Linda will too. Do you know Linda?**

The reply took longer to come this time around. **No. But I have some experience with pubs as businesses, and, like I said, I like the local element.**

Well, that was no help at all, was it? Maybe he really *was* just someone who had happened upon the page randomly and decided to be charitable. She stared at it for a few more seconds but couldn't think of what else to say just now. So instead, she went back to looking at the second clue from Tom—for some reason thinking that if she *looked* at the words rather than just recited them in her head, she'd have a better chance of figuring it out. Her stomach squirmed. What would she do if she didn't figure it out in time? If she missed the spring day he had in mind and the clue passed her by, lost forever? She wouldn't get to the gift, but more importantly, she wouldn't finish the trail that her brother had so clearly wanted her to. And she needed to. She needed to keep going, needed the messages from Tom. It made her feel like he wasn't really lost to her.

"What's wrong now?" Josh asked, paying far too much attention to what she was doing—another thing he did when bored.

"It's my next clue. From Tom." She shook her head a little frantically. "I can't do it, Josh. I can't figure it out."

"OK. It's OK." He came back over to her desk, leaned down so he could read the clue on her phone over her shoulder. "Well, being a 'blue' is an Oxbridge thing, isn't it? Like, their sporting teams?"

Cassie stared up at him. "It is?"

"Pretty sure, yeah. My sister is a Cambridge girl," he added with a shrug.

Cassie looked down, read it again.

One spring day the teams will meet,
But one will go home in defeat,
All of them have brains, it's true,
But this is what it means to be a blue.

Her heart did a little leap as the tips of her fingers tingled with excitement. "So, wait, Josh, that could be it! It's Oxford versus Cambridge, it's . . ." She trailed off, staring at the last "P.S." of the clue. *Life is but a dream.*

A memory, one she didn't realize she still had, came to her, a little hazy. The sound of her mum, singing. Humming the tune as she stroked Cassie's hair, while Cassie drifted toward sleep. *Row, row, row your boat . . .*

She blinked, the memory fading. "Josh."

"Cassie."

"It's the Boat Race." Her face split into a grin and she punched the air. "It's the Oxford-Cambridge Boat Race, Josh, that's where he wants me to go! And it fits, because I've never been before, and he wanted me to try something new!"

"Really, you've never been before? I have—it's great fun, my sister dragged me along three years ago—"

"Not the point, Josh!"

"Right, sorry. But this is great! High five, you did it!" He held his hand out and she hit it, grinning. She'd done it! But then the panic set in again.

"Wait, but when is it, Josh? When is it happening?" Oh God, what if it had already taken place? With frantic fingers, she googled it, letting out a sigh when she saw the date for this year.

"Well," Josh said with a smile, "it looks like we know what we're doing next weekend."

Next weekend. Literally just in time. Then she frowned. "Wait—we?"

"Yes. I'm not letting you have all the fun without me. I want to see how this plays out firsthand—and I'm definitely coming along to your first Boat Race experience."

Cassie shook her head. "There's no way Robert will let us both have the day off."

"Don't worry, darling Cassie," Josh said with a knowing smile. "I have a plan."

Chapter Twenty

Cassie stood with Hazel outside the Pimm's tent in Furnivall Gardens, Hammersmith. Hazel had insisted they watch the Boat Race from here, and when Cassie had asked why, she'd simply said that she'd googled it and it was one of the best places to watch it. She'd even rearranged something to be here, muttering to herself that she couldn't believe she'd forgotten, though Cassie had never realized she'd cared so much about the Boat Race. They were on the green, people everywhere, the pubs nearby completely packed, the whole place buzzing with excitement. The day was perfect—bright blue sky with picturesque wispy clouds, the sun shining down in full force like it, too, was watching with bated breath. It wasn't quite warm enough for the shorts and T-shirts some people were sporting, in Cassie's opinion, but she understood the sentiment.

"Where is he?" Cassie asked, bouncing on her feet outside the red-and-white tent. "We're going to miss it!"

"I'm sure he'll be here any minute," Hazel said soothingly. "But look!" She pointed to the closest screen, which was ready to show the race for those who couldn't get near to the Thames, and which was now showing the two long yellow boats, each holding eight rowers, one team dressed in dark blue, the other in duck-egg blue.

Josh came out of the tent, clutching three cups of Pimm's.

"Sorry," he said, handing out the drinks, "there was a queue. Anyway, come on, let's get a photo!" He got out his phone, maneuvered the three of them so they had their backs to the Thames—which was mainly hidden by the crowd—and snapped.

"You're not going to post that on Instagram, are you?" Cassie asked—Josh was big into Instagram. "Robert will see."

Josh patted Cassie's hand. "You're acting like I'm a beginner at this."

His "plan" to make sure they both got the day off had turned out to be to cajole Robert into giving Cassie the weekend off, citing the quiet events diary and claiming that it was a shame she wouldn't be there all the following week, if she had Monday and Tuesday off instead, to deal with Pauline's daughter's no doubt increasing enquiries as the P party loomed closer. Once that was agreed, he'd made a show of going out to get the greasiest takeaway he could find yesterday, eating it in front of Robert, and then complaining of a funny stomach at the end of the day—so, he had food poisoning today, as it turned out. He had no qualms about doing it, apparently, because it meant Robert would have to do the legwork for once, and the diary really *was* quiet.

"Come on then," Hazel said. "Weren't you worried about us missing it? We're going to have to fight our way through that lot if we want to see it live." She gestured toward the crowd pressed up against the stone wall, looking down on the Thames. Cassie nodded, her heart doing a nervous tumble. She had no clue what she was looking for. There had been no extra hint, no name of the person she was supposed to find. What, was she supposed to look down the entire length of the Thames hoping to find something? Tom would have known she'd be feeling like this. But he'd also planned on being here, hadn't he, according to his last letter? A fist tightened briefly around her heart at the fact that he wasn't here when he should be.

"And they're off!" the tannoy announced, and Cassie yelped, nearly dropping her Pimm's.

"Come on!" Hazel said. The three of them linked hands— Hazel at the front because her height gave her the advantage when weaving through crowds. After much elbow-jabbing, "sorry"s, and "excuse me"s, the three of them managed to make it to the front, right by the little stone wall, Hammersmith Bridge on their left. Below them, the Thames spanned out, water lapping gently at its edges, glistening in the sun, hiding the murky darkness underneath.

"I can't see them!" Cassie's voice was a little too high-pitched.

Hazel crouched down, presumably so she didn't block the view of people behind her. "I don't think we're supposed to see them yet."

Then they came into view, two long yellow rowing boats, oars moving in synchrony. One boat was just pulling ahead of the other, and Cassie found herself holding her breath.

She had a memory, then, of another time she'd watched the Boat Race, the one and only time, as far as she could remember, and even then, she'd almost forgotten it had happened. She'd been sitting on the floor in Claire's little living room behind Hazel, both of them on cushions. Tom and Sam were sitting on cushions next to them, all four of them facing the TV, where the Boat Race was being shown live, pretending to be in boats of their own.

Tom had gotten out the oars that Claire kept in the spare room, up high. He'd had to stand on a chair to get them and he and Sam had made it a mission, Sam standing guard to make sure Claire didn't notice what they were doing. So now each team—she and Hazel versus Tom and Sam—had one oar each.

"We're winning!" Tom was shouting.

"You're not!" Hazel protested. "We can't even tell who's winning, we're not moving!"

"We're rowing faster, though," Tom said with a grin.

Cassie frowned, still moving her arms to row with Hazel. "I didn't know it was a race."

"It's always a race," Sam told her.

"Cassie, concentrate!" Hazel snapped. "We need to win." None of them were paying attention to the real-life Boat Race now.

"Nevarrrrr!" Tom declared. "We are the champions—the finish line is just there!"

The living-room door swung open, and all four of them stopped rowing as Claire came in. Her face went slightly pale, so that her dyed-red hair looked too bright against her skin. "What are you doing?" she asked, her voice a little hoarse. She brought her hand to her throat, staring at the oars in their hands, then at the TV. Cassie felt herself shrink—she wasn't totally sure why, but Claire was not happy about this.

Claire reached down, snatching the oars off them. "These are not toys," she snapped. "Do you hear? You're not to play with them again." All of them just looked at her. She grabbed the remote, switched the TV off. "It's a nice day—go and play outside." She took the remote control with her, so they couldn't switch the TV back on, and shut the door behind her.

The four of them stared at each other. Claire never exactly got their games, but this seemed a bit extreme, even for her. Then Tom got to his feet. "Come on then. We can play outside."

"Play what?" Hazel asked suspiciously.

"This! We can use something else as oars."

"You'll just cheat again."

"It's not cheating, Hazel."

Hazel folded her arms.

"Fine, well, you can be on my team then—that way I can't be cheating."

That seemed to placate Hazel, but Cassie frowned as she followed them out. She didn't want to be the moody one, but Hazel was supposed to want to play with her, not Tom. It wasn't fair that she'd been so easily ditched by her best friend, and maybe then she didn't want to play at all—the three of them could play, and she'd just watch.

Sam was hanging back for her when she reached the back door. "It's OK, Cass, you can be on my team." He held out a hand and, relenting, she took it, and let him drag her out to the garden.

"Who is that in front?" an adult Hazel was saying in the present. Cassie jolted. What was she doing, reminiscing? She was supposed to be focusing!

"The light blue one," Josh said.

"Yes, I know that, thanks—which team is light blue?"

"Cambridge, I think."

"You think? Didn't your sister go to Cambridge?"

"Yes, but that doesn't mean I know the bloody rowing colors, does it?"

Cassie watched both the boats, feeling her heart pounding. She leaned forward, placed her hands on the stone wall, trying to get a better look. The light-blue one was definitely winning. But that didn't help her, did it? She didn't *care* who won, she just wanted to find the next clue and nothing here was proving to be useful at all. Behind her, someone jostled, trying to get a better view, and she was pressed farther into the wall.

"Umm, Cassie?" Josh's voice was a little tentative.

Cassie glanced over at him. "What?"

"Have you seen . . . ?" Wordlessly, he positioned her so she was facing Hammersmith Bridge. There was a line of adverts there, presumably put up for today.

"What?" She frowned, staring at an advert for Nike trainers. "What am I looking at?"

"I see it!" Hazel squealed, clapping her hands and standing up to her full height, earning dark mutters from the people around them. "Right on the left, Cassie."

Cassie whipped her head to the left, eyes frantically searching for whatever had gotten the two of them so excited. And then she saw it. A banner, small in comparison to the rest of them, in bold blue. It was her name. *Cassie Rivers.* Right at the top of the banner.

Her heart spasmed, and she sucked in her breath. It was Tom. It was like Tom was right there, shouting her name, trying to get her attention. And underneath her name, there it was.

It can be cold and wet, it's true,
And also full of sheep, who knew?
It's just across the border you'll find
The little inn I have in mind.

"Oh my God," she whispered. "Oh my God! Guys, what am I supposed to . . ." She grabbed her phone, took a photo of it. Then took several more, just to be safe. Her face felt hot, and she had the urge to cry and laugh at the same time. Around her, everyone was screaming as the boats passed right under her, the heat of many bodies pressing in around her. But she didn't look at the boats. She stared at the sign with her name on. The sign Tom had put up, just for her.

This was insane. *Tom* was insane. How on earth could he have been sure she'd see this?

He'd planned on being here, she remembered again. So she supposed he would have made sure to position her just right. But if it hadn't been for Hazel, insisting they watch it from here . . .

She read the clue again and her stomach turned. It wasn't enough. It wasn't enough to go on. He must have planned on giving her the rest in person, and now . . . She spun to look at Hazel and Josh. "I don't—"

Hazel reached out, grabbed Cassie's hand. Ignored the "Can you bend down, love?" from behind them. "Relax. Take a breath." She slipped something out of her jacket pocket. An envelope.

"You have it?" Cassie breathed. "How?"

Hazel smiled a little. "He asked me for help with the advertising." She paused. "I didn't know if you'd go through with it, and I didn't want to make you if you didn't want to, but . . . Well, he said that in return for helping, I could be a part of it." That smile again, tinged with sadness. "I was teasing him about using my help and getting nothing back, so he told me I could be involved." Cassie could imagine it; it was the type of relationship they'd always had, that teasing, competitive one—almost a more argumentative sibling relationship than Cassie and Tom had had.

"You've had it all this time?"

"He made me promise not to give it to you until you found the clue yourself," Hazel said softly, in a way that made Cassie's eyes sting. She reached out, took the envelope from Hazel. And actually, she was glad Hazel had held on to it, had only given it to her now. She would have felt like she had failed Tom, somehow, if she hadn't followed the treasure hunt as he'd planned.

"If you're not going to watch, do you mind moving along?" a man with slightly graying hair asked from their left. It was a clear attempt to be polite, though he was wearing a scowl as he spoke.

Cassie blew out a breath. "Yeah, maybe we should . . ." The three of them fought their way out of the crowd, back toward the main park.

"I still can't believe you were in on it," Cassie said when they reached the grass area, trading the real view of the Thames for the screens. Josh shifted a little uncomfortably—perhaps feeling like this was a moment between them he shouldn't intrude on.

Hazel shook her head, black hair swinging. "I can't believe I almost let you miss this. Bloody Boat Race, I should have remembered when it was."

Cassie looked down at the envelope in her hands, saw Hazel and Josh exchange a look. "Time for another Pimm's, you reckon?" Josh asked.

"Yes, I think so. Cassie, do you want to wait here and we'll come back?"

She nodded. They were giving her the time, she knew, to read the letter in private. And so, when they walked away, she opened it.

See! Trying new things is not that bad, is it, Chipmunk? And I reckon most of this Oxbridge lot only tried rowing for the first time at university . . .

Speaking of Oxbridge . . . I've never told you this, but I applied to Oxford. And I got in. I can literally hear you right now, screaming at me for not telling you. At least this way, you can get in a huff about it alone first, and then you'll be calmer by the time you see me. But the point is—I didn't go because I was scared to, Cassie. It felt too posh and out there and I didn't want to go without Sam. I don't regret it or anything—honestly, I don't, I had the best time at Manchester and I'd still choose to go there if I could go back.

But I'm imparting wisdom here—I don't want you to be the
same, to be afraid to do something new or different . . .

Cassie frowned. He'd gotten into Oxford? How—how had
he kept that from her all this time? She'd thought they'd told
each other everything. *She* would have told *him*. He knew everything about her life. OK, everything except, maybe, how she'd
once felt about Sam. But that was different. She bit her lip, figured she'd have to digest the information later, and kept reading.

On a different note, did you know that Mum used to row??
I didn't. I only found out recently, because I was trying to
come up with the right clue (it's great, don't you think?), and
remembered the oars at Claire's, so I asked her about it—
apparently Mum was on the team. Shame neither of us got
the gene, hey? I would've looked great in all the rowing lycra.

Cassie paused again, thinking of Claire snatching the oars
away from them. Cassie's mum's oars, maybe? Or even if not, a
reminder of her mum, of a hobby she'd once had. Maybe that's
why she had snapped that day, rather than because of anything
they were doing, specifically. It was easy to forget, sometimes,
that Claire had lost her sister when they lost their parents.

Anyway, in case you need extra help on the clue, because
I know I went a bit wild, here are your P.S.s:
    I'd head westward if I were you.
    I always thought Of Pubs and Men was a good name
for a B&B, don't you agree?
    Also, might be nice for Linda to tag along?

Chapter Twenty-One

Sam couldn't believe how cold New York stayed all through April. He sat hunched on a bench, a gray sky threatening rain overhead, staring at his phone as he waited for Toby, who was meeting him at the youth center, before they went off to explore the wonders of Brooklyn. Toby had an apartment this way as well—rented, not owned, but still—so the plan was to stay for a few days. Toby had been staying with a friend on Long Island last night, so Sam had made his own way here and now he was early, having overestimated the time it would take from the Hamptons house.

He reread the message from Cassie as he waited—yet again. He'd sent her a message last night, unnerved by the lack of updates—what if there were some problems at that end?

We're waiting on a solicitors' meeting on Monday. I'll let you know how it goes though!

He should tell her it was him. He was still feeling guilty about explicitly lying about the fact that he knew Linda, but he'd panicked and hadn't known what to say—because if he'd said "yes," things would have gotten trickier, wouldn't they?

He was going to do it. Going to tell her it was him, so he could stop feeling like he was deceiving her. He actually brought up her number, dialed.

"Hello?" Her voice was a little cold, distant. Of course it

would be. She would have seen his name flash up on the screen, and she'd made it perfectly clear how she felt about him. He felt his throat close. He couldn't do it.

He hung up instead, feeling like a total coward. But he couldn't just turn around and explain. It would sound too weird, and she'd want to know why he hadn't told her in the first place. Besides, he wanted to keep the door open, to be able to help her with the pub again if need be. And OK, he was unlikely to be able to help on the financial front again, but he didn't want her to throw it back in his face, if she found out the money was his. He didn't think she'd actually do that—she wasn't that petty— but best not to risk it.

His phone flashed with an incoming message and he jolted. But it wasn't Cassie.

Can we talk?

Jessica. Shit. Heat trickled down the back of his neck, despite the cool day.

"All right, Mr. Malone?" A hand clapped his back and Sam nearly dropped his phone. He looked up to see Toby standing there in his Burberry coat. "Sorry to keep you waiting, been here long?"

"Nah, it's all right," Sam said, as a way of non-answer. He got to his feet, followed Toby to a slightly run-down-looking building—red-bricked and almost prisonesque in feel, with the smell of weed lingering in the air. "You sure they won't mind me coming in? I can just wait out here."

"Don't be ridiculous, it's freezing. It'll just be a quick sweep of the place—I'll only ask a few questions. The editor basically told me what to write already, piece of cake."

"Right." Sam followed Toby inside and looked around what he assumed was some kind of reception, given the desk at the front. It looked a little like a doctor's waiting room, minus the chairs, though there were posters all along the white walls, clearly in an attempt to brighten up the place.

"Hello, hello." A woman came rushing into the room from a door to the right, smiling at them both politely. "I'm Sheila." Her accent was pure New York, her face open and friendly, dark, wiry hair pulled back in a no-nonsense bun. Despite the smile, there was something shrewd about her dark brown eyes. At a guess, Sam would put her in her late forties. "You the reporters then?"

"That would be me," Toby said, all charm, stepping in and taking her hand in a firm handshake.

"Oh yes, hello." Sheila shook Toby's hand and gave Sam a semi-suspicious look out of the corner of her eye, as if wondering what he was doing here. But after she'd assessed him for a moment, Sam seemed to pass some sort of test and the woman smiled again. "Come on then, I'll show you around." She started talking as she walked them to the door she'd just come from, her words tumbling into one another in a way that was both slightly difficult to understand and oddly soothing. "We get a mix of kids in here," she was saying. "Homeless teenagers, runaways. Some come along because they don't know where else to go, I guess. We don't tend to ask their stories, unless they want to talk about them. It's open all week—we don't have beds or places to sleep, but it's somewhere for the daytime, and somewhere that's always open, always friendly, never demanding or questioning."

She led them into another room, this one brighter, the walls painted pastel green. It looked open and friendly—sofas in one corner around a TV, a pool table taking center stage, alongside table tennis. There was a bookshelf in one corner, full of books and board games that looked a little underused. Sam felt several pairs of teenage eyes on him as they moved in farther—why were teenagers always more judgmental than adults? Was it, like, a hormonal thing?

"We had a big fundraiser a few months ago, managed to do a bit of a remod. The idea was to make it somewhere people actually wanted to come and hang out." She gave them both a smile, as Toby nodded along, saying, "Excellent, yes," and making other noises of amazement and agreement. Sheila raised her eyebrows subtly at him, and Sam wondered if she somehow knew that he wasn't a real reporter.

"So this is what we call the 'chilling room,'" she said, the air quotes obvious in her tone, "but this next room is what a lot of them come for, I think—we've certainly seen a rise in the number of visitors since we did this up."

Sheila took them through a second door and held her arms out to encompass the room. Sam had to admit, it was pretty impressive for a youth center. It looked like some kind of indoor sporting center, though obviously on a mini scale. There was a big indoor basketball hoop; a kid was there, already shooting hoops. A trampoline in the corner, with some kind of hanging contraption that presumably meant you could do flips or whatever; those gym ropes you get that are way harder than they look. And a bouldering wall.

An image of Tom, falling off rocks much bigger than the brightly colored fake ones, slammed into Sam's mind. He took a breath, forced it back. Sheila and Toby were walking away now, Sheila still explaining how it all worked here, and Sam rocked back on his heels, scanning the room. There was a kid climbing the bouldering wall; he stopped about halfway up, face pale, arms shaking a little. A skinny boy, midteens maybe, with slightly greasy black hair. Sam hesitated, then crossed to him.

"You need to use your legs a bit more," he said. "They're stronger than your arms."

He had a flash, then, of Tom saying almost exactly the same thing when Sam had first gone bouldering with him, Claire driving them to the center and waiting around for them to finish. Tom had been a few times already and loved it, but Sam had been nervous, he remembered. They must have been about eleven, something like that, and Sam remembered the feel of his arms shaking at the top of the wall. He'd glanced down, and the ground had seemed a lot farther away than he'd expected.

Tom was next to him, hair flopping into his eyes as he grinned. "Fun, right?" No hint of fear there, as he hung off the wall.

"Yeah." Sam thought he'd done a good job at keeping the shake out of his voice, but Tom cocked his head, noticing something. Sam glanced down again and swallowed.

"Noooo," Tom said, his voice still playful. "Don't look down." He paused, considering. "Though it doesn't matter anyway. They have mats and the ground isn't that far. Look." And with that, he literally launched himself backward off the wall, landing on the thick blue mat with a thump, laughing.

Sam let out a bark of laughter too, hesitated, then, heart thumping, copied Tom. He landed right next to him and Tom whooped, and then they were both laughing in that way you did when you were kids and couldn't stop. By the end of the session, Sam had forgotten about being scared, had gone home to his mum and declared he was going to do climbing for a living, to which she'd made supportive noises as she'd made fish fingers and chips.

Back in the present, the boy on the wall was glaring down at him, saying nothing. He could read it, though, the tension in his body. Could remember, dimly, the feeling of those nerves.

Sam shrugged, kept his voice easy, casual. No big deal. "I'd relax your grip a little. If it's only your fingertips keeping you on, then you're in trouble." It was something both he and Tom had been told once, on a week-long climbing holiday that his mum had saved up for for ages. He got a scowl at his suggestion, but the boy kept climbing, and did seem to be taking Sam's comments on board as he reached the top of the wall. Then, without saying anything or showing any sign of being pleased that he'd made it to the top, the boy started his descent, slow, careful. Coming down wasn't always easier than going up, Sam knew. Around halfway down, the kid looked down at the floor, and frowned. "Hey," Sam said, pushing off the wall he was leaning against. "It's OK, just keep going."

The kid shot Sam a suspicious look, but did keep going, right down to the bottom. "Nice work."

The kid gave him another suspicious look, but this time, it looked like he was trying not to break out into a smile. "It's the first time I've made it all the way up and down again," he said, his voice softer than Sam had imagined it would be.

Sam slipped his hands into the pockets of his jeans. "Yeah?"

The boy nodded. "Yeah."

Toby came up behind him, clapped him on shoulder. "You ready?"

Sam saw the boy slink off at the same time as Sheila came up to join them. "That's Liam," she said, watching the boy leave. "He doesn't talk to many people." She gave Sam a questioning look, and he shrugged.

When they got to the reception area, Sheila slipped a leaflet off the desk and handed it to Toby. "I don't know if you'll be able to get it into the article, but we're hiring at the moment."

"Oh, absolutely," Toby said, with the confidence of someone who has no idea what they're talking about.

"You're hiring?" Sam asked.

Sheila gave him a measured look. "Yes." She handed a second leaflet to him, and he took it automatically. What must it be like, working somewhere like this? "It pays a pittance, obviously, and it's part time, but, well, if you know anyone, tell them to give us a shout."

Both Toby and Sam assured her they would, and Sheila showed them out, Toby making a big deal of thanking her profusely. Sam found himself looking at the leaflet again as they walked away from the youth center and toward some sort of bar that Toby wanted to try out. It was insane. Totally ridiculous to consider it. But there was a small part of him that felt almost hopeful at the idea of it. At the idea of trying something just a little bit different. And that hope made him think that maybe—just maybe—there might be a way out of this hole for him.

Chapter Twenty-Two

Cassie stepped into Linda's pub, feeling that familiar tug of nostalgic love as she took in the wooden bar, the beams, the fireplace, now cold in the corner. She tried not to think about the last time she was here, nearly four months ago. The memory of Tom's funeral resurfaced despite herself, and she took a breath, allowing the grief to wash through her.

This time, though, she wasn't here to mourn him—she was here so that she could collect Linda, as he'd wanted her to, and so that they could find the next clue. Wales. Across the border, to the west. She'd figured it out—Tom was sending her to Wales.

Linda came running out of the door to the kitchen, red-and-white tea towel tucked into the top of her jeans. "Oh, Cassie love!" She rushed toward her, enveloping her in a big hug, and Cassie breathed in that familiar smell of coffee. "It's been too long." She stepped back, holding Cassie at arm's length and giving her a shrewd look up and down. "You look thin. Are you eating properly?"

Cassie gave Linda's arm a squeeze. "I'm fine," she said. "How is everything here, then?"

"Oh, it's good, it's good—and it's because of you that I'm still here, still able to do this." She brought Cassie into another hug, and while Cassie hugged her back, she couldn't help thinking that it wasn't really because of *her* that the pub was still here, but rather because of their mystery donor.

A woman with brown hair streaked with blond highlights stepped out of the kitchen at that moment, wearing smart black trousers and a checked blue-and-black shirt. "Linda, we've still got some of those chocolate mousse pots left, so is it all right if I put them on as a special at dinner?"

Linda flapped a hand. "Fine, fine. Now, come and meet Cassie." Cassie smiled at the woman, who held out her hand as she approached.

"I'm Katie."

"She's my new manager," Linda said, and Cassie couldn't help her eyebrows shooting up in surprise, though she tried to cover it with another smile.

"Lovely to meet you, Katie," Cassie said politely.

Katie beamed—she had the kind of face you immediately warmed to, and Cassie could already imagine her being a big hit with the local customers. "Likewise. I've heard so much about you."

"Now, Katie, have you double-checked the bookings for this evening?"

Katie gave a quick, birdlike nod. "I have."

"And have you—"

"Linda," Cassie said, a little pleadingly. She got it—really—but she was also impatient to get going, to find the clue.

Linda glanced at Cassie. "All right, all right," she said briskly. "We're off, OK, Katie? Please call me if you have any problems."

"I will. But I promise there won't be!" Katie said cheerfully.

Because Linda was opening her mouth to say something more, Cassie linked an elbow through hers and tugged her firmly toward the front door. She gave Linda a sly look as they headed toward the car that she'd rented for this trip. "A new manager, hey?"

Linda wrinkled her nose. "Yes, well, we'll see how she does tonight and tomorrow, and then I'll make a call."

"Does this mean there's no more drama with the solicitors, then?" Cassie asked as she slid into the driver's seat of the little red Kia.

"Well . . ." Cassie gave Linda a look and Linda sighed. "It's just that apparently there was already a deposit put down, so I don't know where we stand, legally speaking."

"What?" Cassie said sharply. "That's . . ." But she trailed off. She had an idea. "What if I knew someone?" she asked slowly. "Someone who might be able to help?"

"Who? Sam?"

"No, not Sam." She was doing her best *not* to think about Sam, especially as she was just starting to feel better, and thinking about him did not help with that. Though he'd called her the other day—called her and hung up without saying anything. She hadn't called him back, but she couldn't help wondering what it had been about. "It's our mystery donor."

"Well, I suppose if you—" Linda slapped a palm to her forehead. "Hang on, I've forgotten my purse. I'll be back in a moment, OK?" And she jumped out of the car, running back across the gravel parking lot to the pub.

Cassie used the opportunity to open up the GoFundMe page and write a message.

> **So we're having some problems with the lawyers—and I know you said you used to be in law? Do you have any experience with property law? If so, I wonder if I could ask you a few questions?**
>
> **Sure, ok.**

She hesitated, but then decided to go for it. **An email would be great, if you don't mind?** She couldn't keep using the page, could she?

Ok. You can get me on sminnnewyork@hotmail.com.

Cassie frowned, surprised that he'd given up his email so easily now, when he hadn't before. She felt a spark of triumph, which was immediately squashed when she reread the email address—no name there.

Still, it was better than nothing and she sent a list of the initial questions that came to mind, getting a response back almost immediately.

Just some quick, easy questions for me to look over, then?

Sorry!! No pressure, of course.

It's no problem—I'll take a look and get back to you later today.

Thanks so much. And because this stranger was being kind, she felt the need to justify. **It's just, thanks to you we've got the money and I don't want everything to be ruined all because of some stupid legal stuff.**

I've always thought legal stuff was quite stupid myself.

Cassie felt her lips twitch. **Not all legal stuff. I suppose some laws are there for a reason.**

Like the law against murdering people, do you mean? That kind of thing?

Cassie felt her lips pulling into a smile. **Yes, that's the kind of legal stuff that probably *isn't* stupid, I'll admit.**

Or, for instance, the law against eating mince pies on Christmas Day.

Cassie snorted out loud. **That's not a law.**

It was in 1644.

You're having me on.

I'm not—Christmas Day fell on a legally mandated fasting day that year.

That's the kind of thing they teach you in law school, is it?

Sure—we have to learn every single law that ever was by heart.

You googled it, didn't you?

Guilty as charged.

Cassie laughed as Linda got back into the car.

Linda frowned. "What?"

"Nothing," Cassie said, a little quickly. "Right—next stop Wales?"

Linda settled her purse on her lap. "Indeed. Wales, here we come."

"*This must* be it," Cassie said, as she followed the GPS and turned right up a winding tarmac drive. A sign that read OF PUBS AND MEN was barely visible by the side, the black lettering on the wooden sign fading, the "Pub" half rubbed away. It wasn't really a pub, either, from what Cassie had gleaned on the internet. It was more of a B&B, but apparently there had *used* to be a pub here, and they hadn't bothered changing the name.

The driveway gave way to an epic house—the photos on the website really didn't do it justice. It was Victorian in style and brilliantly bright green, a beautiful veranda on one side of it and an old oak tree on the other. There was only one other car—an old, slightly rusty-looking Fiat, parked outside. Like the car, the house had a slightly run-down look to it, but in a way that suited it. Cassie couldn't help wondering what it must have been like, back in the day, to live somewhere like this. There were cottages down the driveway to the right, presumably for the workers who had once lived here, and Cassie assumed the drive also led to a separate servants' entrance around the back of the house.

She and Linda got out of the car, and Cassie took a deep breath of the fresh, clean air. The day was glorious—bright blue sky spanning out across the fields—far from the cold and wet picture Tom had painted. There were sheep, though—Cassie could see them in the fields below, with little lambs skipping around after their mothers. It made her smile, and she surprised herself by how instantly she felt content here, out in the rural countryside.

Linda smiled over at Cassie. "You look a picture with that backdrop." She indicated the rolling hills.

Cassie grinned. "I have to say, I kind of love it here." She felt she could breathe, somehow, now that she was out of London, away from the hectic nature of it, away from Robert watching her every move at the hotel.

"You've been to Wales before, haven't you? I remember Claire taking you when you were little."

Cassie nodded absentmindedly. It had been the summer holidays, and Claire had booked a week in Snowdonia. Cassie had been excited about going on holiday for the first time in ages—and about spending time with Tom, just the two of them. At the last minute, though, Sam had ended up coming too. He was supposed to be going on holiday to Greece or somewhere, but his dad had canceled with no notice and his mum had been all panicked, so Claire had invited him along with them.

Cassie grabbed her small rucksack from the trunk of the car. "Hey, Linda. Did you know Tom got into Oxford?"

If Linda was surprised by the abrupt change of subject, she didn't show it. "I didn't," she said, and her voice was a little careful. "You mean, to university there?"

Cassie only nodded. It had been playing on her mind since she'd gotten the last clue, the fact that Tom could have kept something like that from her. It made it better, maybe, that she wasn't the only one who had been in the dark. Had Sam known? she wondered. Would she ever be in the same room with him again, to ask him? They'd only ever been brought together because of Tom, really, and she couldn't imagine just bumping into him, given she'd decided to try to cut him from her life. For the first time, though, she felt a pang of sadness at that. Not for Sam, but for the memories he held of Tom, the bits of her brother he carried with him.

She and Linda walked to the front door. There was no doorbell, so Cassie banged the big brass knocker.

"It's open!" came a voice from inside. Cassie looked over at Linda, who shrugged, then twisted the doorknob. They stepped inside a little porch area, a line of coats hanging to the right and at least four umbrellas leaning against the wall to the left. Tentatively, Cassie stepped through the porch, pushed open another door, and saw a grand entrance hall, red-carpeted steps opening up to a majestic fireplace, a candle chandelier hanging in the middle of the room.

"Welcome, welcome!" An old woman, white-gray hair set in curls atop her head, rushed into the room, beaming at them both. She wore a dress of velvet blue and bright red lipstick, more appropriate for a cocktail party than hosting a B&B, Cassie thought. "Come in, come in, come in." She gestured all the way inside. "You're Cassie Rivers and Linda Hill, is that right?" She had a soft, lilting Welsh accent. "Wonderful. We've got the best rooms in the house set up for you. Though, as you're the only two guests here today, you'd expect that, wouldn't you?" She gave a tinkling laugh.

"Now," she said, taking both Linda's and Cassie's bags with surprisingly toned arms, "I've put a brochure on the things to do in the local area in your rooms—though come to think of it, you're only staying one night, is that right?"

"Yes, sadly," Cassie said. She'd only been able to get the one night away from London because of work. She hadn't wanted to piss Robert off by asking for an extra day off, but on top of that, there was an events exchange weekend coming up in a few months, and she really wanted Robert to send her. It was something some of the hotels did, if they were in the program together, and it meant you could go and manage an event at a different hotel, try to see what they were doing differently that you could take back to your own company, and what you could improve from your own experience. She'd never done it before, and this year it was at this gorgeous manor house in Sussex, and she was hoping that Robert would let her do it.

"It's a shame, it's a shame. But here, I'll show you round. Oh, and I'm Tiff, by the way, but you probably know that." Tiff gave no mention of Tom visiting as she started the tour of the house, but then, Cassie had a feeling she already knew who the next clue was coming from.

"This is amazing," Cassie told Tiff honestly as she finished the tour. There were eleven bedrooms, she'd learned; a billiard room upstairs that was "out of action" at the moment due to a leak in the en-suite toilet but which would be brilliant when up and running; a grand dining room, a living room where you could curl up next to the fire, with the old Victorian kitchen still intact at the back of the house, next to a separate, more demure-looking staircase compared to the one at the front of the house, which presumably the servants would have used. The rundown feel of the house was impossible to ignore, with paint flicking off the walls in places, and cobwebs hanging high in corners in some of the rooms, along with carpets that were tearing off the floor at the back of the house. But despite all that, Cassie loved it. Other than the fact that it was majestic, the house seemed to have a story to tell—she felt it almost waiting expectantly for them as they opened each door, and she couldn't help but feel a tiny bit sad for the old rooms that had been neglected, their doors shut off from the rest of the house, like they were just waiting to shine again.

"Do you do any events here?" Cassie asked, as Tiff led them back into the entrance hall, where two armchairs sat by the window around a coffee table in the corner. Because events would be amazing here, Cassie couldn't help thinking. A majestic Victorian house in the countryside, not too remote but rural enough that you'd have the feeling that you could escape from reality. It would be great for intimate weddings, birthdays, but also longer things too—retreats would be brilliant here, and there was plenty of space to write or do yoga, or whatever your thing was.

"Oh no, I don't have the energy for that anymore," Tiff said. "I'm actually trying to sell the place at the moment."

"Sell it?" Cassie asked.

"Yes. It's lovely, but too much for me now—and I've met someone in Portugal, so I'm going to go and live there, as soon as I'm shot of this place." She gave Cassie a look that she couldn't quite interpret. "Anyway. You both sit down—can I get you a little welcome tipple?"

"That would be lovely," Linda said, sitting herself down on the red armchair and leaving the green for Cassie. "I run a pub, and I'm hardly ever the one being waited on. How about a glass of red wine?"

Tiff pursed her bright red lips. "I don't have any red in at the moment, I'm afraid—I'm running stocks down while I wait to sell up. How about a glass of port? Or sherry?"

"Have you had much interest in the house?" Cassie couldn't help asking.

"Not yet," Tiff said breezily. "It's a big project to take on, I suppose. There was one fellow who was interested a while back, but he said he was waiting for something, so we'll see." It *was* a big project, Cassie thought, but what a place. "I'll get you both a sherry, shall I?" And leaving them with no choice, Tiff disappeared.

Cassie and Linda grinned at each other as they watched her go. "Well," Linda said. "She's certainly . . . something."

"I like her," Cassie said decisively. She was sure Tom would have liked her too, and she wondered if he had ever met her—if that's why he'd decided to send her here.

"Now that we're here," Linda said, "I think it's OK to give you this." She slid an envelope out of her purse. "I know you've been wondering about it," she added softly.

Cassie felt that shock, the way she always did with the enve-lopes, at the sight of Tom's handwriting. Number Four. One more to go after this, if Tom was following the same pattern as previous years—which meant she was over halfway through. What would she find when she got to the end?

"Your parents used to come on holiday to Wales, you know," Linda said.

Cassie looked up at her. "Really?"

Linda nodded. "They took you and Tom one year. I think you might have been too little to remember, but your mum told me all about it when they got back. They attempted to climb Snowdon—your mum's idea, but it was a disaster with you and Tom, apparently."

Cassie smiled. Of course her mum would have tried to climb a mountain with two toddlers. Always searching for the next adventure, like Tom.

"She loved it here, though, your mum. Was always talking about how she and your dad would move to Wales one day. That was the plan, anyway, but they needed to be somewhere on the commuter belt for a bit longer, and Wales was just that bit far out." And they never got the chance, Cassie thought sadly. Just like Tom, now, would never get the chance to do all the things he'd planned to do.

Tiff came back into the room carrying two sherries in mismatched glasses. She popped them down on the coffee table between them. "Now, I think I've got a bit of shortcake to go with that somewhere, bear with."

As she disappeared for the second time, Cassie opened the envelope.

All I can think of when I think of Wales, Chipmunk, is that holiday we went on, and you stamping your little foot and refusing to come in out of the rain, because I'd annoyed you about something, and Sam had to go out and coax you back inside. Do you remember?

She did remember, now that he'd mentioned it. It was on that same holiday she'd been thinking about earlier. Claire had rented a tiny holiday cottage, and Tom and Sam ended up sharing a room, alternating who slept on the floor, because it had only been booked for the three of them. Cassie had been upset, because it was the first time she hadn't been sharing a room with Tom on holiday. She'd stormed out of the house—it had felt like a big deal to her and it should have been *obvious* why she was upset, but clearly she'd not articulated it very well, because Tom didn't get it and thought she was being silly. They'd had a rare sibling fight, ending with him telling her, "*Go away, Cassie, you're so annoying.*"

"*Fine, I will,*" *she said dramatically, intending to go far and leave them all worrying about her—that would teach her stupid brother.* So she had gone away, but she hadn't been brave enough to go farther than the garden, because she didn't want to get lost. So she'd stood out there, folding her arms, refusing to get in out of the rain until Tom apologized.

Claire had called from the house. "*Cassie! Don't be silly, you'll get cold. Come inside now, hmm?*"

"*No.*"

"*Fine. You stay there then.*" *Claire knew, perhaps, that she only had a few more minutes' determination left in her.*

Sam had come out, then. She'd actually forgotten that. "*Come on, Cass. Tom didn't mean it.*"

"*He did. He did mean it. He wants me to go away so it can be just the two of you.*" *And she was jealous, and that was the worst part—she didn't want to share her brother on holiday. It was fine when they were playing at home with Hazel and Sam or whatever, but this was supposed to be her time with him.*

"*He wouldn't actually want that, though.*" *Sam stood, shoulders hunched against the rain, and scuffed his toe on the ground. "I'm sorry for crashing your holiday.*"

And then she felt guilty, because it wasn't Sam's fault. "I'm sorry your dad is rubbish." *Sam had said that word about his dad, so it felt right.*

He laughed. "Come on. We can all sleep in the room together—sleepover style?"

She hesitated—Tom might not want that.

"Or I'll just stay out in the rain with you, until you decide to come in." He rubbed his shoulders dramatically. "It's pretty cold, though. I might get ill."

Cassie laughed, and relented, heading back to the house with him. Tom was hovering in the doorway, looking moody.

"I didn't mean it," he grumbled. "You don't have to be so dramatic."

Claire's voice sounded out from the kitchen. "Now that Cassie's back in, you can all watch something on the TV while I cook dinner."

Tom looked at Cassie. "Coming?"

Cassie nodded.

"You better get changed first, though. You're soaking."

Cassie made a face. "Then you'll pick something I don't like."

Tom rolled his eyes. "We were going to let you pick."

She narrowed her eyes suspiciously. "Even if I say Spirit?"

Tom sighed. "Even then." And so, grinning, Cassie went in to change.

She smiled a little at the memory, though, as always with memories of Tom, her heart tugged in a way that felt painful. She couldn't help thinking of Sam, too. Of the little boy, let down by his dad, who had come to stand with her in the rain. Mostly, she tried to dismiss childhood memories of him, figuring they didn't negate the fact that he'd grown up to be a dick, but she couldn't help wondering if there was still a part of that boy left inside him, somewhere. If he'd still come out into the rain to comfort her.

She went back to the letter, while Linda took a sip of sherry and murmured appreciatively.

Anyway, I just wanted you to see this place—don't you think
it's cool? And I know you're always saying you wouldn't be
able to set up your own thing, like you used to want to,
but look, here is somewhere that's been in business
doing just that.

Tiff *wasn't* making it work though, was she? But there was a
voice in the back of her mind, telling her that maybe *she* could
make it work. Which, she was sure, was exactly what Tom had
wanted. And look at Linda's place—they'd saved it, hadn't they?
Which had felt a little like fate—or even Tom—was proving a
point. Proving that the impossible could happen.

And now, for the clue . . .
 A place far away from the hustle and bustle,
 The waves lap your feet with barely a rustle,
 I won't make you surf now so don't you despair,
 But go and light up a torch for the boats if you dare.

P.S. My friend's name is Greg.

Cassie frowned as she read it again, then glanced up at Linda,
who was trying to read it upside down. She handed the clue to
her, and Linda read with pursed lips.

"Do you know what it means?"

Cassie made a face, shook her head. Surfing—a beach
maybe? Not that that narrowed it down, considering the number of beaches in the UK. She bit her lip. "Do *you* know? Do
you know what he's leading me to, what's at the other end?

Linda paused, then nodded. "Do you want me to tell you?"
she asked quietly. She would. If it helped her to know, to process, then she knew Linda would. For a moment, Cassie consid-

ered it. But just for a moment. Because just as Hazel and Linda
had known that she needed to figure out the clues herself, before they gave her the next one, she knew that she'd never feel
right if she cheated this final time.

"No," she said emphatically. "I think I want to let him show
me instead."

Two Months Later

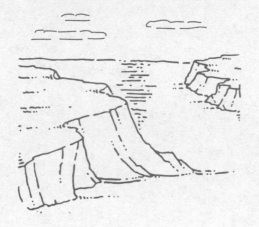

Chapter Twenty-Three

The sound of Sam's phone, which he'd taken to setting to loud after his mum had panicked when he hadn't called her back recently, pulled him out of a deep sleep and he groaned, fumbling around for it. Sheila, from the youth center. What the hell was she doing calling him at this hour? He checked the time before he answered. Five A.M. He wasn't supposed to be up for another hour, and even *that* was early.

"Hello?" His voice was still husky from sleep, and the sound of the AC whirring away—a necessity during a New York summer, he now knew—almost drowned it out.

"Sorry for calling so early," Sheila said. She had her brisk "work voice" on, one that she reserved for journalists, parents, or possible investors, he'd learned, in the two months he'd been working for her. "But I got some bad news last night. Some of our funding's being pulled."

Sam flipped his bedside light on—some fancy designer one. He'd been staying at Toby's apartment in Brooklyn since April, though he was insisting, much to Toby's chagrin, that he at least pay rent. "That's . . . That's not good." It was too early to come up with anything more articulate. "I'm so sorry, Sheila." He wasn't sure why she'd decided to wake him to tell him this, rather than filling him in later, but he genuinely meant it.

"Yes, well, the thing is . . ." She blew out a breath. "The thing is, Sam, it means I can't afford to pay you anymore."

"Oh." So, she was firing him over the phone? Despite the fact he'd not been there long, despite the fact he'd always known it could never last because of the visa situation, he couldn't help but be a little hurt by that.

"I don't want to let you go. Truly. But—"

"It's OK. I get it. Do you still want me to come along today?"

There was a pause that went on too long. "Well, that was why I was calling . . ."

He didn't need her to spell it out. "You can't cancel the trip!" he exclaimed. "The kids have been looking forward to it for ages." And he'd spent ages setting it up, not that that was the point. More of the kids had gotten into bouldering since he'd been there, and so he'd asked if he could organize a climbing trip to the Gunks—the Shawangunk Mountains just outside New York. He'd heard the kids talking about it for weeks now.

"I just don't know how we can afford it," she said with a sigh. "I'm sorry. I really wish—"

"You don't have to pay me," Sam said quickly.

"That's not—"

"And you can use what you haven't paid me from May to put toward it."

Another long pause. "Are you sure, honey?"

Sam smiled as he settled down against his pillows. The "honey" was a sure sign he'd gotten through to her. "Definitely."

"Well, all right then." That was the good thing about Sheila— she never said no to charity. He supposed she'd have to be like that, given her job. "I'll see you in a couple of hours, then."

That's right, Liam," Sam said calmly, watching his skinny frame as he rappelled down the cliff. "You're almost back now." Sam saw Liam glance behind him, checking how close the ground was, saw his legs tremble, just a bit. Despite the bravado that Liam liked to put on, the refusal to ask for help or advice, Sam knew the kid was nervous, running on adrenaline from having completed his first proper outside climb. He coached him all the way to the bottom, knowing that sometimes people were tempted to come down too fast when nice and slow was better and safer. The other seven kids they'd brought were behind him, watching.

Liam's grin when he hit the ground was priceless, and Sam felt his own grin match it. Liam looked up the sheer rock drop he'd just gotten up and down, hard gray stone towering up, with green leafy trees hanging over it. Even though it was a beginner climb, it was still a beauty. Liam turned to Sam, unclipping his rope as Sam had taught him and slipping off his helmet, revealing hair slick with sweat. No wonder—the heat was immense, and Sam was sweating even just belaying. Sam held his hand up for a high five and Liam didn't even roll his eyes as he returned it.

"Good job, mate." Liam laughed as he rejoined the group, everyone getting to their feet to head back to the parking area for lunch.

Sheila handed out packed lunches when they got back to the minibus and they spread out on some picnic benches, glugging water gratefully. The kids headed off in the other direction from where he and Sheila were making camp, and Sam heard Sheila tell them all, "Thirty minutes, you hear me?"

Even here, in the parking lot picnic area, it was beautiful: tall, leafy trees that provided much-needed shade from the beating summer sun merging into a forest that looked like something out of a movie set. And even though he couldn't see the mountains, it was like he could sense them, their presence too big to ignore. Three hours outside New York, and it felt like a different world. If someone had told him three months ago that he'd be teaching a bunch of teenagers he barely knew how to climb at the Gunks, he would've told them to piss off. Not least, he knew, because of the reminder of Tom. Yet here he was.

Sheila groaned as she fell onto the bench next to him, and Sam tossed her a bottle of water. "You're a legend, Sheila."

Sheila's smile was one of the most genuine he'd ever seen—and like her laugh, it was infectious. "This was all you, honey," she said in that brilliant New York accent. "And look," she continued, gesturing to where the kids were now laughing and eating, their expressions maybe not the easy, carefree ones that some people their own age wore, but at least, Sam liked to think, slightly lighter than usual. "It's been a success, right? Been good for them. Good for you too, I'd say." She gave him a look before she bit into her sandwich. "It's taken away a few of those demons, I can see it."

Sam fought the urge to grimace. He supposed she was right. Focusing on other people had helped him to climb out of that dark hole. But still, it made his stomach feel a little tight. Had he done this for the kids? Or to prove something to himself?

Sheila gave him another look—she was good with her looks, was Sheila. Her dark eyes were wide and expressive, and her eyebrows had degrees of up and down that he'd never seen before. "It doesn't mean it's not a good thing to do, even if it was for you too," she said evenly. "Things don't need to be completely selfless to still be doing something good for someone else." Not just observant, Sam thought, a bloody mind reader. It was kind of eerie sometimes.

She glanced over at the kids. "Liam, do *not* throw that there." She got to her feet, walked a few meters toward them.

Sam took a sip of water, looking out across the scenery. Then he raised his water to the sky in a toast. "I wish you were here, mate."

"I just don't know why they don't—" Sheila frowned at him. "Are you OK?"

He cleared his throat, took another sip of water. "Yeah." He wasn't, quite, but the fact that he could be somewhere like this, think of Tom, and not fall apart was, he thought, an improvement. And Tom would have loved it. He would've been out here too, getting involved, making all the kids laugh. Sam could just picture it.

Sheila was still looking at him in that mind-reader way of hers, so Sam picked up his phone as a distraction. There was an email from Cassie, which had come into the fake email he'd set up a couple of months ago. He still felt a bit guilty about that, setting up a separate email account just to message her and hiding who he was—but the alternative had been to refuse to help her, and he hadn't been able to do that, either.

It's official! The pub is ours to keep. Or Linda's, I suppose. But anyway, just thought you'd like to know.

He smiled as he wrote back. **That's amazing!** He sent a line of champagne bottles. A part of him tugged. He kind of wished he was there to celebrate with her, to raise a glass with her and Linda and toast the pub where they'd all grown up. To see the light in Cassie's warm brown eyes, at the fact that she'd done it. And though it was done now, his part in it over, he couldn't help asking a question in the desire to keep the conversation going, keep the connection with her alive.

Are you doing anything to celebrate?

Sort of. I'm heading off to an events exchange thing this weekend.

An events exchange? Sounds ominous . . .

It's this thing where they let me manage an event at a different venue. This gorgeous manor house in Sussex—it's called Gravetye. Anyway, it may be work, but it's been something I've wanted to do for ages, so it's kind of like celebrating!!

Sam snorted quietly to himself, earning a curious look from Sheila. She was *working* to celebrate? Didn't sound like much fun to him. But then, Cassie had always been so sure, when it came to doing what she loved. He envied her that. He didn't think she loved her current job—and he knew Tom had thought that too—but she'd never had any doubt on the type of career she wanted. So, if she wanted this "events exchange," as ludicrous as it sounded to him, then he could imagine it *would* be a kind of celebration. Though he definitely couldn't imagine ever working for fun.

It took a moment to realize that was exactly what he was doing here.

"So, honey," Sheila said. "Now that you're out of a job, what are you gonna do?"

Sam put his phone down, shook his head. "Shit." He winced. "Sorry," he said quickly, but Sheila only snorted quietly.

"Honey, you don't work with teenagers like I do and not get used to a bit of swearing."

"Right." He didn't know what it was about Sheila—she was far from old enough to be his mum, but he still had that kind of protective feeling toward her. "Well, ah . . ." He pulled his hands through his hair, gave her a blank look. "I have no idea." And it was true. The youth center job had kept him going for the last eight weeks, given him some semblance of purpose and helped to pull him out of the hole. And now that it was gone, he had absolutely no fucking clue what he was going to do next.

Chapter Twenty-Four

Cassie stood outside the block of flats staring at number 4a, working up the courage to knock. Amy was waiting for her inside—she'd asked Cassie to come round today. But Cassie needed a moment before the inevitable onslaught of memories, the grief that would punch through her, being in Tom's old flat for the first time since he died.

When she lifted her hand to the wooden door, it felt heavy. "It's open!" Amy called, and Cassie turned the door handle, stepped inside. "I'm in the kitchen!"

Cassie followed the sound of Amy's voice and headed through the living room to the little kitchen. She couldn't help looking around, trying to assess what had changed since Tom had lived here. So much of it was the same—same TV, same coffee table in the living room, same blue sofa. But there were differences, and the lack of Tom's things was a punch to the gut. The bookshelf was less than half full, and some of the kitchen appliances had been put away. A few paintings had been taken down off the walls. The photos of Tom and Amy were still up, though. How Amy could face that every day was beyond Cassie.

There was a part of her, though, that was looking at more than just the memories. She was looking for clues.

Light a torch for the boats if you dare . . .

She hadn't figured it out yet. But Tom was sending her to a beach for the next clue, she was sure of it. And unlike the previous one, there had been no suggestion of a deadline, so she didn't have the anxiety hanging over her that she might miss a specific date. But she hadn't got much further than that. She'd looked at a map of the UK, trying to see if any of the beaches held a particular connection to Tom. They'd been to loads of them together. Cornwall. Bournemouth. Brighton. A beach in Wales. So how was she supposed to know which one?

There was nothing on Amy's bookshelf to help her. No photo of them all at a specific beach, for instance. She'd look later, she reasoned. Maybe see if Amy had any ideas.

Amy had her back to Cassie and was rummaging around in one of the top cupboards when Cassie found her in the kitchen. "What can I get you?" she asked, still not turning to face her. "I'm out of regular tea," she continued, and Cassie thought her voice was a little high. "I've got herbal, though. Mint? Lemon and ginger?"

"Sure," Cassie said. "Anything's fine." Amy took down a box of something from the cupboard, but didn't turn around right away. "Amy? Is everything . . . ?" But she trailed off. Because Amy finally turned around. And despite the fact that she was wearing a loose top, there was no hiding it. No hiding the bump.

Cassie stared at Amy's stomach, before snapping her gaze to her face. "You're pregnant," she breathed. Amy winced, just a little, then nodded. She crossed the kitchen to flick the kettle switch on, and her hands came to rest on her belly, perhaps slightly protectively.

Cassie shook her head, a dull ache starting up there. "What . . . ?" She wet her lips, tried again. "When . . . ?"

The kettle boiled, clicked off, and neither of them did anything about it.

"I'm sorry I didn't tell you. I didn't know how to."

"Is it . . . ?"

"Yes. Tom's the father." She took a breath, her shoulders heaving with the effort. "I'm sorry. I found out a few weeks before Tom died, and then I just didn't . . . I didn't know what to do, whether I wanted to . . ."

"Keep it?" Cassie finished, but her tone was nonjudgmental. She shook her head, not to condemn Amy, just trying to get her head around it. Of course Amy wouldn't have known if she'd wanted the baby. She couldn't imagine having to contemplate it—giving birth when the father was already dead. Cassie took a slow, painful breath. "I think we ought to sit down," she told Amy, who nodded, eyes wide, almost fearful-looking. Like she was worried about what Cassie would think. Cassie tried to smile reassuringly. "I'll finish this," she said, gesturing at the kettle.

She made two peppermint teas while Amy sat down in the living room on the blue sofa, and the mundane action calmed her a little. She brought the mugs through, set one down next to Amy, then sat in the armchair opposite. "So," she said. "Umm . . . wow."

Amy gave a short, breathless laugh. "Yeah. Wow is right."

"How are you feeling?"

Amy shook her head, her curls, kept in place by a blue headband today, bouncing. "I'll be honest. I've been a bit of an emotional mess." She picked up her tea and cupped it in her hands.

"Yeah. I can imagine." Cassie paused. She had absolutely no idea what to say. She should've noticed. She should have *noticed* before now that something was up, should have paid more attention to Amy when they met at the hotel a few months ago. How had Amy managed to hide it? Cassie tried to think back to their meeting. The signs were there. The loose clothing, the decaf coffee. But clearly, she'd been too wrapped up in her own life that she hadn't been looking hard enough at what was in front of her. "Amy, I'm so sorry that I—"

Amy held up a hand to stop her. "Don't. If anyone should be apologizing, it's me. I just . . ."

"I know," Cassie whispered. Because she got it. She really did think she got it. She flicked her gaze around the living room—around *Tom's* living room—again, and Amy followed the movement.

"Linda helped to pack up the flat," Amy said quietly, "but I still find the occasional thing of his, you know? I wanted to move, but at the same time I couldn't bear to part with the place that has all the memories of him, so I've just been . . . in limbo, I suppose." Cassie nodded. She thought she understood what Amy meant—that's how she felt herself. Less so since she'd started the treasure hunt, but it still flared up, now and then. Like she was trying to escape the memories, the pain, and yet trying to hold on to everything at the same time.

Cassie hesitated. But she had to ask, had to know. "Did Tom know?" she asked quietly.

Amy met her gaze, held it. "Yes."

"But he said . . . He said you guys had broken up."

Tears sprang into Amy's eyes. "Yes. I told him and he . . ." She heaved in a breath, apparently unable to finish the sentence. Cassie couldn't speak right away, either. She stared at Amy, not understanding. Or not *wanting* to understand, trying to finish the sentence in different ways in her mind. Amy stemmed a sob. "He said he couldn't handle it, said he needed some time away from it. And I got mad—this was happening to both of us, you know? It wasn't only him who had to deal with it—and I wanted him to commit to it, to me, to say we'd raise the baby together, because I wanted it." Her words were coming more quickly, blurring into one mass. "It was an accident, but I wanted it—and I wanted it with him. I wanted us to be a family. But he just left." She was crying now, her shoulders heaving with the sobs, and Cassie, trying to stem her own tears, stood up and went to sit next to Amy on the sofa, putting an arm around her.

"I . . ." Cassie swallowed. "I'm not sure what to say." It didn't make sense to her. Tom had ditched Amy as soon as he found out she was pregnant? Surely not. That wasn't like him.

She'd been so scathing about Sam leaving Jessica on their wedding day. Was this any better, leaving your long-term girl-friend when she got pregnant? No, Cassie thought firmly. What Sam had done was worse—the wedding had been planned, and there had been plenty of opportunities to get out of it. This would have sent Tom reeling, and it would've been a surprise. She knew, in a distant corner of her mind, that she was trying to make excuses for him. She wanted him to have a clean record, needed to be able to think of him as the perfect big brother.

"Are you going to keep it?" she asked quietly. Surely, with the timeline, Amy had decided to go through with the pregnancy, but there was still a chance she was considering giving the baby up for adoption.

"Yes." Her voice was a little stronger. "Yes, I'm keeping it. And I'm sorry, I wanted to be sure of that before I told you, because I didn't want to make you sad about it—and then I felt like I'd left it too long and I was trying to figure out how to tell you. I wrote a message so many times, but nothing sounded quite right."

"Let's just make a deal that neither of us apologizes, OK?" Amy pressed her lips together, but nodded. "Besides, I'm glad I know now, and that's the most important thing." She reached out, took Amy's hand in hers. "And if you need help, Amy, with anything—I'm here, OK? I'll be around more, I promise, and

I'm totally up for babysitting when the time comes." She glanced at Amy's stomach again. It was Tom's baby in there. She couldn't work out exactly how she felt about that. Tom's baby—a part of him. But something he'd never get to see for himself. Something he'd chosen, apparently, to run from.

Amy smiled, though it was a little watery. "You're going to be an aunt."

"Yeah. I suppose I am." And then the two of them were crying, but the hot, salty tears that traced their way down Cassie's face felt cathartic, so that when she sobbed herself to a stop, something in her had settled a little.

"So," Amy said, wiping her own tears away and brushing a stray curl aside, "how's work?"

It felt so ridiculous, given the enormity of Amy's news, to be talking about work, that Cassie laughed. "It's fine, I guess." She went on to tell Amy about the events exchange weekend that was coming up—about the fact that Robert was actually letting her go to it. In truth though, for the past two months something else had been playing on her mind, too. She couldn't quite shake the image of the house in Wales, the fact that it was for sale, the potential she'd seen there. The idea of taking something a bit run-down and giving it love, making it shine again.

When Amy went to get them another mug of tea—needing, Cassie sensed, a moment alone—Cassie brought out her phone, opened up her email, and stared at it.

It wasn't committing to anything, was it, if she just asked a question? Tom would tell her to, she knew, if he was here. There was no harm in asking someone who knew the industry— someone who had donated to keep a local pub going, who had said they had some experience there. Who would know, perhaps, the types of business that succeeded and failed?

Hi. So I know you said you had some experience with local pubs as businesses, and I wondered if you'd mind talking something through with me?

She took a deep breath and sent it. All she wanted, really, was to talk it through with someone who didn't have any emotional connection—Linda, Hazel, or Josh wouldn't think in that critical way she thought she needed. So she could ask the question, discuss it, realize how ridiculous the whole idea was, and then put it aside.

It must have been the reason Tom had sent her to that house in the first place—he'd have wanted to plant the idea in her mind.

But then again, maybe she didn't know him as well as she'd thought. After all, he'd clearly run from Amy, from the baby, because he was scared of committing, scared of that responsibility. So maybe her fearless older brother hadn't been completely fearless after all.

And if she didn't know him as well as she'd thought she did, if she wasn't able to tap into what he'd been thinking, then how the hell was she supposed to figure out the next clue?

Chapter Twenty-Five

"*So what are you* going to do now?" Sophia asked Sam, looking at him over the rim of her wineglass. He was sitting in a bar in Brooklyn—a trendy, newly opened one—with her, Toby, and Zoe, and had filled them in on the fact that he no longer had the job with the youth center.

"No idea," Sam said truthfully. He shrugged, like it was no big deal, not letting on how much losing the youth center job was making him feel . . . adrift, again.

"We're going back to the Hamptons in a couple of weeks," Toby said. "You should come." Sophia nodded vigorously, dark hair shining in the low lighting. "We'll take the yacht out for another spin—it's unbelievable in the summer. We'll figure something out, don't worry."

"Yeah, maybe." The problem was, though, that his time in the United States was fast running out—he'd gotten an ESTA in order to get in, which was quicker and easier than a visa, but meant that he was only on a ninety-day stay, and those ninety days were approaching an end. So now he had to figure out what next—home, or somewhere else? He'd been looking into some other destinations, unable to deny the allure of traveling somewhere else, of ignoring the problems he'd left back home and putting off figuring out what to do about it all. He had no job, no flat back in London. He had no idea what to do career-wise either, wasn't sure if being a solicitor was still on the table, if his reputation would now be ruined.

He brought up the message Jessica had sent him earlier that day. **Saw your photos of the climbing today on Instagram. I'm proud of you. Tom would be proud too. Let's talk in person, when you're back.**

They'd spoken on the phone, briefly, a couple of months ago, and it had been awkward and painful, and she'd hung up before they'd really said anything. So the message today had come slightly out of the blue. And the tone of it . . . Well, he wasn't quite sure how to read into it.

"Another round?" Toby asked. Nods all around, and Toby slid to his feet. "Mind giving me a hand, Zo?" Zoe sighed a little, her face unimpressed as usual, but got up and followed Toby to the bar.

"Just a sparkling water for me, thanks," Sam said absentmindedly. It wasn't that he'd stopped drinking completely, but he was trying to cut back, rather than relying on it as a crutch as he'd done after Tom had died. He opened up his emails, saw one from Cassie. His heart thumped a little in anticipation, the way it always did with messages from her.

Hi. So I know you said you had some experience with local pubs as businesses, and I wondered if you'd mind talking something through with me?

He stared at the message, felt his heart speed up. He didn't know what she wanted to talk about—she'd kept it vague, perhaps deliberately. It could be something to do with Linda's pub, or something to do with her job, maybe. But whatever it was, she was presuming he had a level of knowledge he didn't. He didn't have the first clue about running anything in the hospitality industry. He shouldn't have said that.

He felt Sophia shift next to him, angle her chair so she was closer. Felt her leg press against his, the smell of her musky perfume wash over him. They hadn't slept with each other since that one time in the Hamptons, but she was making her intentions very clear now. And maybe it would be easy, to go there again, to distract himself from the fact that he was, once again, purposeless.

"So, you still staying with Toby?"

Sam cleared his throat. "Yeah. He's been great, letting me crash with him." And he had—been great. Sam didn't know what he'd have done if he hadn't been offered that lifeline.

"It's not far from here, is it?" She reached out, trailed a hand down his arm, bright red nails scraping lightly against his skin.

So easy, maybe, but not what he needed. He knew, deep down, that it wouldn't make him feel better, not in the long run. So it wasn't fair—to her, or to himself.

He pulled back. "I'm sorry, Sophia, I can't do this."

She stuck out her bottom lip in a pout, but Sam was saved from having to elaborate by Toby and Zoe returning with the drinks.

Sam looked down at his phone, at the email again. He couldn't keep doing this. Couldn't keep lying to her anymore. He took a steadying breath.

How about I talk it through with you in person?

He felt something settle as he pressed *send*.

It was time, it seemed, to go back to London. Time to see Cassie, to tell her the truth, and hope that she didn't slam the door in his face this time.

* * *

Sam looked out the window at the approaching manor house, listening to the crunch of the taxi tires on gravel. It was a stunning building; he could appreciate that. Elizabethan in style, it was gray brick with a hint of peach in places, tall and slightly imposing, with chimneys that looked a little like turrets. The mullioned windows almost seemed to be watching him approach, he thought, like they were the house's eyes, assessing the newest arrival. Assessing him, and his intentions. Whatever the hell they were.

"Here we are then," said the taxi driver. He stopped the engine, coming around to open Sam's door. "Nice place, this, isn't it?" he said conversationally, hooking slightly puffy fingers into his belt loop and turning a circle to take in the whole house.

Sam grunted his assent as he got out of the car. It was warm—not as hot as New York, but sunny and bright, English summer at its best. There was bright green foliage running alongside each side of the stone steps that went up to the entrance of the manor, bushes and trees running out farther to the right, so that they were well and truly surrounded by countryside. Sam was a little surprised that he'd gotten a booking so last-minute, especially given the fact that Cassie's event—an engagement brunch, apparently—was running tomorrow morning.

Was it stalkerish that he knew that, had followed her here? He reckoned it was probably safer not to answer that question.

He'd come straight from the airport—it had taken about an hour and a half from Heathrow. It was weird—he hadn't actually been into London, just skirted around the edges on the M25, but he'd felt the presence of the city, looming and almost suffocating, like it was reminding him of what he'd left behind, reminding him that it was still ready to claim him. He ran a hand through his hair, then took the suitcase the driver offered.

"You have a nice stay then," the driver said, hitching up his trousers before he got back into the car and drove away. Sam raised his hand in thanks, then started up the steps. No point questioning the decision—it was made now.

He'd only taken two steps up, struggling slightly with the heavy suitcase, when a woman with short hair and broad shoulders, wearing a navy-blue blazer over a matching blue dress, came out of the entrance at the top of the stairs. "You leave that there!" she demanded, and Sam jolted enough that he let go of the suitcase. She ran down the steps on tiny little heels, moving with a grace that surprised Sam. Up close, he could see that she was wearing a pearl necklace. "I'll get that—our guests don't carry luggage."

"Oh no," Sam said hurriedly, alarmed at the prospect of this woman hurting her back trying to lift his brick of a case. "It's really heavy, I'm very happy to—" But she'd already nudged him aside and picked it up, lifting it with apparent ease. She marched up the steps in front of him and Sam stared after her, feeling ever so slightly emasculated. Then he jerked into action and quickly followed her into the reception area.

She put the case down, then boomed, "Brian!" Sam saw a thin man with a slightly balding head, wearing a white shirt with a purple tie, scurrying over. "Will you take this to Mr. Malone's room, please?" Sam had no idea how she'd known it was him, or how Brian knew which room he was in, but Brian nodded and smiled in a way that made Sam immediately like him, and wheeled Sam's suitcase away.

"I'm Emma," the woman said, moving through the reception to behind a smart wooden desk. "I'm the front-of-house manager, and you can always just grab me if you have a problem, OK?" Sam nodded. She produced a key, then led him out of the reception area and through the manor.

"Here," Emma said, after they'd climbed two sets of stairs. "This is you." She opened the door and let him step inside in front of her. The room was bright and open: cream wallpaper with green trees on it and a comfortable-looking bed with a gray headboard. It was massive—much bigger than a usual hotel room—with its own sofa, as well as a wooden table and two chairs.

Emma indicated a few features of the room, then gestured to the windows. "You have a view of our gardens, which are set over thirty-five acres." *Thirty-five?!* Sam thought to himself. Jesus. "They were designed by the visionary gardener William Robinson in 1885, and our head gardener carefully maintains them today—if you see him out and about with his collie dog, do feel free to ask him any questions about the grounds." Visionary, Sam thought, smiling a little. It was a good word. "Do you have any questions at all?" Emma pulled her blazer around her with both hands.

Sam noticed his suitcase was already there, at the foot of the bed, and wished he could sink down next to it. "If I want food . . . ?" He was hungry, the type of hunger that was part tiredness, and he hadn't eaten anything on the plane.

"We've reserved a spot for you in our Michelin-starred restaurant downstairs, should you wish, but there's also the option of room service, which is twenty-four hours."

Sam nodded his thanks, thinking he was going to have to be careful about how much he spent this weekend—the two-night stay alone was enough to make him wince, and whereas in previous months he would have happily ordered whatever bottle of wine at a fancy restaurant along with the most expensive main course, he was hardly in a position to do that now.

Emma smiled at him, reiterating that he should shout if he needed anything, then left him alone. Sam glanced around the room, still a little dumbfounded at the fact that he was actually here, doing this. The bed, with its many pillows and soft-looking duvet, was calling to him, inviting him to flop down there fully clothed and not move, but he made himself turn and leave the room. He'd hunt for food first, get that out of the way quickly, then he could crash and think about how the hell he was going to explain everything to Cassie tomorrow.

He headed for the dining room, pausing at the entrance as he waited for someone to come and seat him. Like his room, this was bright and airy—there were glass walls all around it, offering a view of the gardens, and there was a light with several lamp heads hanging from the middle of the ceiling, which looked a bit like a fancy spider.

It took only seconds for someone to come over, holding a menu, and Sam was nodding in assent when asked if he'd like to eat, when he heard a laugh. His heart lurched. He recognized that laugh.

His gaze followed the direction of the sound and he saw her. Cassie. Sitting there, across the other side of the room, Hazel opposite her. It was dusk now, and the evening glow caught Cassie's blond hair, making it sparkle. She was genuinely *smiling*, in a way that she never smiled at him—not anymore.

She was still a little thin, he thought, her cheeks slightly hollow. But she looked better. Healthier. Happier. He couldn't look away. He wanted to watch her, drink in the sight of her. He felt his palms go clammy, his pulse start up at the base of his neck. What was that about?

"Sir?" the waiter prodded, looking over his shoulder to where Sam was still standing. He couldn't do it, he realized. He couldn't go over there, couldn't muster up a cocky grin, couldn't think of what the hell to say to her. So, feeling like a total prick, he cleared his throat. "I'll, err, just get room service."

With that he bolted, leaving the waiter looking slightly be-mused, and fled for the safety of his room.

He let out a slow breath as he closed the door behind him. *Get a fucking grip, Sam.*

He was being ridiculous, overreacting. It must be the shock of seeing her. He told his heart to calm down, actually slammed a fist there to emphasize the point. It was just *Cassie*, for Christ's sake.

Beautiful, strong, smart Cassie.

No, stop that. It was only seeing her for the first time, know-ing that he'd been talking to her. He'd always thought she was hot, so it shouldn't come as a surprise that he'd had a physical reaction to the sight of her. He was just jet-lagged and confused. He'd be over it tomorrow.

God, tomorrow. He thought again of her expression, twisted in hatred the last time they'd seen each other. He wasn't sure he could bear it if he got that reaction again.

Shake it off, he told himself, and he gave his shoulders a literal shake as he crossed to the bed, sank down on it. It was just as soft and inviting as he'd thought, the mattress folding around him. He'd come this far; he had to go through with it now.

So he got out his phone, checked the fake email account.

That would be great! she'd replied, to his suggestion that they meet. **I definitely owe you a drink. Are you based in London?**

He hadn't responded yet. Had wanted to get here first, prove to himself he was actually going to go through with it—that he wasn't the coward she'd once accused him of being.

As chance would have it, I'm around Gravetye tomorrow. I know you have your event in the morning, but would it be ok if I pop by afterward? We could grab a drink at the hotel.

He waited for a response, fingertips tapping his phone, heart beating too fast. He felt a bit like a teenage girl, sitting by a phone, waiting for that call. He got up, looked at the room-service menu, found himself unable to concentrate on it, and sat back down again. After what seemed like an age, the phone lit up in response.

You'll be here tomorrow?

He hesitated, fingers poised. He nearly told her then and there. It would be quicker, more painless if she took it the wrong way, to do it over email.

But no, he needed to do it in person, and let the chips fall where they may. So he settled with **Yeah. I'll see you then.**

How will I know where to meet you?

I'll find you.

I'll find you. The words echoed around his head, like they meant something more. Like maybe he was always supposed to find her.

Chapter Twenty-Six

Cassie paced around the bedroom on the phone, rolling her eyes at Hazel, who was perched on one of the single twin beds, as she filled Robert in on how the brunch event had gone. The cream carpet was soft underfoot—the kind of carpet you *wanted* to walk around barefoot on, just to feel it.

"They seemed really happy," she finished. She would have liked to do something more exciting than a brunch, but it had turned out to be so fun—the couple celebrating their engagement were in their sixties and had wanted something to bring together friends and family, but not a fancy evening event. It had been classy, with plenty to think about in terms of the set-up of the room, and the couple had been effusive in praise. Plus, it meant she had the rest of the day to enjoy the manor house—she had a second night's stay on the house. She'd been allowed to bring someone along for the weekend, if they shared her room, and Hazel had obviously jumped at the chance.

"All right. Well, I'll talk to the manager there later today," Robert said, a little gruffly. She knew that he was regretting not coming himself. It almost sounded like he *wanted* to find some problem here, something that made it seem like she couldn't do it on her own.

"OK," she said. "I'll see you on Tuesday. Thanks so much again for the opportunity, it's been great."

She threw her phone down on the bed next to Hazel, who

grinned at her, raised her arms. "You're free! Now we've just got time to kill until your mystery man *finds you*." Hazel wiggled her eyebrows in a way that made Cassie laugh.

"We don't know if he's a man."

"He writes like a man," Hazel said, which made Cassie snort. Honestly, the whole thing was ridiculous. She didn't have the first clue who she was looking for—and what, she was supposed to wait around to be approached so she could . . . what? Thank him? Ask him whether it was ridiculous, from a financial point of view, to think about starting a business in the current climate?

She stopped in between the twin beds, her gaze lingering on a picture hanging above the headboard. It was a landscape painting of the sea, the waves looking a little stormy, the rocky coastline just visible at the bottom of the painting, a lighthouse stood seemingly on its own in the center of the page, a little lonely-looking. There was something so escapist, so soothing, about the sea, Cassie thought, even photos of it. But right now, something not so soothing was stirring in the back of her mind: a recognition of sorts, her mind trying to tell her something.

She stared at the white speck in the middle of the ocean. The lighthouse. Tom's clue. How could she not have seen it before!

Light a torch for the boats if you dare. That had *got* to be a lighthouse—how thick could she have been not to figure that out beforehand?

"Hazel!" Her voice was loud enough to startle Hazel into sitting bolt upright. "A lighthouse!"

"What?" She stared at Cassie with slightly wide eyes, as if she thought she might have gone a little mad. Cassie gestured toward the painting and Hazel twisted to look at it, then turned back to look at Cassie. "Yes . . ." she said slowly, "I see it."

"Tom's clue!" Cassie's voice was high-pitched, unable to contain her excitement. She stepped toward the foot of Hazel's bed, getting a closer view of the painting. She hadn't even noticed the lighthouse last night, too caught up in the beauty of the rest of the hotel. "The torch for the boats," she explained. "It's a lighthouse." She pushed her hair impatiently out of her face.

Slowly, Hazel's face spread into a grin. "Yes!" She jumped to her feet, came around to stand next to Cassie. She put her hands on her hips as she studied the painting. "You're so right, it's got to be. God, I feel like a total idiot now."

"Me too."

"So, which one?"

"Huh?"

"Which lighthouse?"

Cassie felt the lurch of excitement sink into something else in her stomach. "I have absolutely no idea." And there must be hundreds of lighthouses around the UK, right? How could Tom have expected her to know which one? And why the hell was he sending her to a bloody lighthouse in the first place?

"Well, you're still one step closer, right?" Hazel said, clearly trying to make her tone bolstering. "Stay positive." She gave Cassie's arm a squeeze and Cassie nodded, glancing at the lighthouse one more time before she headed to the bathroom to change for her mystery meet.

Cassie followed Hazel through the small, wood-paneled reception area, taking a moment to admire the little details. Twin lamps hung on the wall across from where they walked, and there were leather notebooks on the reception desk. An ornate-looking chair sat next to what looked like an old wooden writing desk, a bunch of yellow flowers sitting on top of it. It wasn't "old fashioned," not really, but you could still feel the history of the place, like they'd kept the essence of what had made the manor beautiful in the first place and gone with it. It was the type of thing she'd love to do, to take somewhere with history and bring it to life again.

Despite her appreciation for the surroundings, Cassie couldn't help but feel totally ridiculous and overdressed as they stepped into the gardens at the back of the manor. Hazel had insisted she wear makeup, but the brown eyeliner and peach lipstick felt like too much, like she was trying too hard, as did the curls Hazel had insisted on putting in her hair. She was in a floaty dress, and she was sincerely regretting that it was mainly white, though the blue and purple flowers helped to offset it.

"Stop fidgeting," Hazel hissed.

Cassie resisted the urge to scowl up at Hazel, who was wearing a green playsuit that matched her eyes and looked stunning in a casual way. They were walking along a little paved concert path through one section of the gardens, where pink roses poked their heads above the green on both sides and little blue flowers buzzed with the sound of bees. The sun was warm on Cassie's bare shoulders, which were still pale because of all the time she'd spent inside, at the reception desk. She let out a slow breath, allowing herself a moment to take in the ivy creeping up the stone walls of the hotel, the sight of woods up ahead.

She glanced up at the sky—blue with those little wispy clouds. Stupid, really, to look up. Tom wasn't in the sky. She was starting to pull herself together, she thought, to adjust to life without him and find a way to carry on, day by day. But the sense of loss was still there. It still felt like a vital part of her was missing, carved out. Then there were moments, tiny moments like just now, when she felt happy or content, when she laughed, or smiled. And once those moments had passed, she always felt guilty—because how could she feel like that? How could she forget, even for a fraction of a second?

They walked on, taking a few turns until the stone path turned to gravel, and the colors of the flowers changed slightly, more purple and deep green. There were other people in the hotel, of course, but in this part of the gardens it was quiet enough that they felt like they had the place to themselves.

It was because of that that Cassie heard the footsteps behind them, softly crunching on gravel. She and Hazel turned at almost exactly the same time, and Cassie's body jerked back, as if hitting a wall.

Sam.

It was *Sam* walking toward her. Not in his usual lawyer suit, but wearing a dark blue shirt, rolled up at the sleeves to show tanned forearms, and black jeans. He must be hot, was her first, bizarre thought, the only thought that made it through the buzzing in her mind as she tried to process what the hell he was doing here. He didn't *look* hot though—he looked cool, calm, in control, those blue eyes measured as he walked purposefully toward her, completely unsurprised to see her here.

She and Hazel exchanged a glance, and Cassie saw that Hazel had no idea what to make of this either. The last Cassie had heard, Sam had been in New York. He'd been safely across the Atlantic—she wasn't supposed to just bump into him like this. Her heart started beating faster, words sticking in her mind as she tried to think of something to say.

"Hi, Cassie," Sam said, a crooked smile forming on his lips. He nodded at Hazel. "Hey, Hazel." He stopped about a meter away from them, focusing his attention solely on Cassie.

"Sam." Cassie's voice was calm, but his name felt odd, alien, said out loud. All she could think of was the last time she'd seen him, when she'd shouted at him after he'd run out on Jessica, outside her hotel. "What are you doing here?" He couldn't know the couple from brunch, could he? She would have seen him there earlier today.

His gaze stayed level on hers, and she found she couldn't look away—there was something there, an intensity she hadn't seen from him in a while, holding her to the spot. "I said I'd find you."

"You said you'd . . ." But the cogs were turning, the truth rising up to meet her in a wave. Something in her gut wrenched and she stumbled back a step. He said nothing, waiting for her, his gaze careful on her face. "It was you," she whispered, shaking her head as if that would make it less true.

"What are you talking about? What was him?" Hazel frowned, looking between the two of them. "Wait, do you mean . . . ?" She raised her eyebrows at Sam. "It was *you?* You're Mystery Man?" Hazel turned to stare at Cassie, clearly looking for some kind of explanation. But Cassie didn't have one. Her mind wouldn't process this—it couldn't have been Sam, talking to her all this time, it didn't make sense. It couldn't have been Sam, to give that much money, without telling Linda it was him, without taking the credit. But here he was, standing there, looking cool as anything. Something hot was rising in her throat. How could he stand there looking like that, when he'd been lying to her all this time?

Hazel cleared her throat. "Umm . . . I think I'm just going to do a lap of the grounds, take in some air . . ." She glanced at Cassie, then smiled faintly at Sam. "Nice to see you, Malone."

He nodded. "You too, Niagara." *Niagara.* Tom and Sam's nickname for Hazel. For some reason, that jolted Cassie into reality. She reached out, tried to grab Hazel's hand, only for Hazel to neatly dodge her.

"What are you doing?" Cassie hissed, not particularly caring that Sam could probably hear.

"You need to talk to him," she hissed back. She took a step away.

"Hazel," Cassie said warningly, "come back here. Hazel, do not leave me, do you hear me, I'm—" But she was already striding away, covering a lot of ground on those bloody long legs.

Unable to avoid it, Cassie looked back at Sam. He slipped his hands into his pockets, glanced at Hazel's back for a second, then focused on Cassie. Cassie felt her neck grow hot. Why wasn't he speaking?

"It was you, on the GoFundMe?" she asked eventually. It was a redundant question, but she needed to say something.

He nodded. "Yeah."

She backed away, wrapped her arms around herself. She felt exposed, somehow, like she'd been caught in a trick and was now being made a spectacle of. Her chest was tight and she felt, inexplicably, like she might cry. *Sam.* The man she'd spent so long holding on to hatred for, the man she'd blamed for Tom's death . . . This was the man who'd been helping her.

"You lied to me?"

His expression twisted into something she wasn't used to seeing. "No, Cassie, I just . . . I wanted to help you, and I knew you wouldn't take it from me, so I . . ."

"You still lied," she said flatly. "And we were talking, all this time, and you emailed and you . . ." She hitched in a breath. It wasn't fair. It wasn't *fair* that the person who'd saved the pub that meant so much to her, who'd given them a donation that made it feel like *fate*, who'd convinced her that maybe there was hope for her own business idea, was Sam.

He stepped toward her and she backed away, shaking her head. "I can't deal with this right now. I can't deal with *you*. I . . ." She pulled both hands through her hair. "I'm going to get a drink." And with that, she spun away from him, heading back to the manor and leaving him standing there, alone.

Chapter Twenty-Seven

He didn't follow her. She refused to glance back to check, but she didn't hear him behind her, and when she finally looked over her shoulder as she got to the bar, he was nowhere to be seen. She let out a long, slow breath. No sign of Hazel either, who should *not* have left her like that. She realized she was scowling as the man behind the wooden bar, smartly dressed in a suit, smiled over to her, and she tried to smooth out her expression. "A gin and tonic, please," she said. She figured she deserved it.

She propped herself up on one of the cream-backed bar stools as she waited, glancing at the paintings that hung in the white space on the walls above the wood panels of the rest of the room. She didn't really see them, though, found herself thinking of the painting in her room, the lighthouse, the clue. Tom. Tom's best friend, here now. Tom's best friend, helping save the pub they'd both loved.

She heard footsteps and glanced toward the doorway of the room. It was someone Cassie vaguely recognized from the brunch this morning, not Sam. The fact that he hadn't followed her, hadn't tried to stop her, was worsening that pit in her stomach rather than calming it.

The bartender handed her a gin and tonic—fancy, with flowers in it—and she took a big gulp. God, his face, just before she'd left, that twisted expression. It hadn't been put on; it had been hurt. He'd tried to hide it, sure, but she'd seen it in the tight lips, the flash in those eyes. He'd been expecting that reaction from her, hadn't he? That was probably why he hadn't tried to stop her. He'd been trying to help her, all this time, and she'd just laid into him. Yes, she felt confused and uncomfortable and maybe a bit freaked out by it, but . . . She'd been mean, and she shouldn't have been.

A coward. She remembered biting the word at him, back in March. But now who was the coward? She was running, rather than facing up to him, just like she'd accused him of doing. So she took a breath, ordered another gin and tonic, then walked back out into the gardens.

He was still standing where she'd left him, looking out to the wild forest beyond the gardens. He noticed her approaching and turned to face her. For a moment she hesitated, stumbling to a stop. What had he been planning on doing? she wondered. Why hadn't he followed her, grabbed her hand, spun her around? That's what she would've expected him to do—follow her, a little taunting, a little cocky. *"Oh, come on, Cass, surely you must've known it was me, no one else could be that charming."* Or something to that effect. But he was doing none of that. He was just watching her, a little warily.

He took a step toward her, and this time she made herself hold her ground. "Cassie, look, I'm sorry, I—"

"No." She shook her head. "I'm sorry." She held out the second gin, forced it into his hand. That small, crooked smile appeared as he took it, the one that reminded her so much of him as a teenager. One that was pure comradeship. "Look, I shouldn't have reacted like that, I was just . . ."

"Surprised?"

She let out a short laugh. "Yeah. Surprised about covers it, I guess."

Without really thinking about it, they started walking, passing what looked like a little shed in among a wild, overgrown garden and crunching their way on the gravel path toward the lake. An actual lake on the grounds.

Cassie couldn't relax. Her shoulders were too rigid, fingers gripping her glass too tightly.

"So," Sam said, "how was the brunch?" It gave her a jolt, to realize he knew already, that she'd told him, thinking she was telling someone else, over email.

"It went well, I think."

"Do you have to do anything else today, or are you free?"

She checked her watch. "I have to chat to the manager before they go, at four P.M."

"Will you come sit with me until then?" She hesitated, and knew that he clocked it from the way he watched her. But he didn't push, didn't ask again. Maybe that was partly why she nodded, followed him to a wooden bench that looked out across the lake, evergreen trees surrounding it.

She glanced at him when they sat down, a healthy distance between them. "Why?" she asked, a little more bluntly than she'd intended. He looked at her questioningly. "Why did you donate all that money?"

He grimaced—it was clear he'd been hoping that the why of it all would come up a bit later. "Are you angry?"

It wasn't an answer, and her automatic response was to snap back with a yes, to prod at him some way with words. She realized she didn't really know how to talk to him without sniping—it had been so long since she'd tried to. "I'm not *angry*," she said eventually. It was hard to put into words exactly how she did feel. She sat up a bit straighter, looked out at the water, pockets of it sparkling with sunlight while other, darker parts rested in the shadows. "I just . . . I'd hung on to the fact that it was a stranger, I suppose."

His expression twisted again, his face trying and failing to hide the emotion, and she continued, a little hurriedly.

"It's not that it's you, specifically, that's the problem," or at least, she thought to herself, not *just* that, "but the fact that it's someone that I know . . . I don't know." She couldn't really explain it, the way it had made her think maybe she'd be able to set something up herself, because there were people out there who still wanted the small, the independent. It had felt like *fate,* and now, knowing it was Sam all along, it took away from that. She didn't say any of that out loud, though. She didn't want to see him look at her incredulously or scoff at her.

"I did it because I thought it was what Tom would've wanted," Sam said quietly. "I was trying to find a way to . . . I don't know . . . Honor him."

She nodded. That, at least, made sense. Because whatever she thought of Sam, she knew he'd loved her brother.

"I wanted to do it for you, too," he added softly. "Because I knew how much that place meant to you."

She glanced at him, and he met her gaze. She held it for a second, felt her pulse thrum against her wrist. Then she looked down. "I wish Tom was here now." It was easiest, somehow, to admit it to him. Maybe it was because she knew that, of anyone, he might come closest to feeling the same.

Sam smiled, and it was tinged with sadness. "He would've loved it. He would've had all of us out here, exploring the gardens, getting you to pose for photos everywhere so you could remember the day."

Cassie laughed softly. "And he would've forced group shots of the three of us, even if we were arguing."

"And he'd be getting all excited about the little things, making sure that we really made the most of, like, the complimentary shampoo or something."

"And we'd have champagne in hand."

"Oh, definitely."

Cassie was smiling, and she could picture it, him here with them right now. Would Sam still have been here, then? She found that she doubted it. Tom would've come, would've wanted to support her, and would have been set on her having the best day ever. But there would've been no reason for Sam to come.

She thought then of Amy, too. Would she have come with Tom? She was several months pregnant, with Tom's child. Would he really have let her raise the baby alone? Or would he have come to his senses eventually? She wanted, so badly, to bet on the latter, to think he would've gotten up the courage to do what was right. But how could she be sure? She glanced at Sam. She could ask him. He was the only person who might be able to explain some of Tom's state of mind around Amy and the pregnancy. Tom might have talked to him about it, where he didn't talk to her—as much as she hated to admit it. But she couldn't bring herself to. She didn't want the confirmation, if it wasn't the answer she was hoping for.

"I miss him too, you know," Sam whispered, looking out at the lake.

Cassie nodded, a lump in her throat. "I know." Because if nothing else, that much, at least, she knew to be true.

"There were times—still are times—when just the effort of breathing is difficult, painful." She nodded again, felt tears burn the back of her eyes. But despite that, there was something weirdly comforting in it, in knowing that she wasn't alone in her grief. Sam's expression turned anguished. "Cassie, I need to apologize. I never meant—"

And she knew what he was going to say, and found that she didn't want to hear it. Not anymore. So she shook her head. "It wasn't your fault." She'd been coming to accept that for some time now, even if she hadn't been able to at first. She'd needed someone to blame for it, someone to hate, somewhere to direct all her rage so that her emotions didn't turn inward and ruin her. But she'd started to let that go, bit by bit, over the last few months, while she'd been following Tom's clues.

"I should've been there," Sam muttered. "If I'd been there, I could've stopped it."

Cassie felt a fist tighten painfully around her heart. It was what she'd believed, wholeheartedly, and the reminder of it, the *what if*, was still something she found herself grappling with at times. But that didn't make it *Sam's* fault, and she knew that, deep down.

She blew out a slow breath. "Look, I don't know as much about it as you, but from what I *do* know, I've figured some things out. You would've been too far away to reach him, if you'd been there, right?" He frowned, and Cassie made herself say it—it was something she needed to admit out loud, to finally let go of, as much as she knew he needed to hear it. "The equipment failed. It was an accident, Sam," she said softly. And because he looked so anguished, because he didn't seem able to look at her, she reached out, placed her hand over his. Odd, that comforting someone else should make her feel comforted.

"But maybe," Sam whispered, "if I'd been there, it would've played out differently. Maybe we wouldn't have gone to that mountain, or we'd have gone on a different day, so that the ropes weren't dodgy."

"Yeah, maybe." And the "maybe" was something they were both going to have to learn to live with. "Or maybe not." She shook her head. "That doesn't make it your fault, though."

He flipped his hand over, linked his fingers with hers. Then he looked at her, gave her a half-smile that was so painfully familiar, and she felt her heart jump a little, in a way that made her think that, even now, she would have to be a little careful around Sam Malone, in order to keep her heart safe.

Chapter Twenty-Eight

Cassie slumped back into the squishy red-and-white armchair, nursing the rest of her gin and tonic. Well, not so much a "chair" as a sixteenth-century oak throne. She'd just said goodbye to Hazel, who had needed to get back for work, but Sam, it seemed, had his own room at the hotel and now it was just the two of them, sitting in one of the living rooms around a wooden coffee table, next to a huge old fireplace engraved with Tudor flowers and a coat of arms. Neither of them was speaking. With Hazel there, the quiet had felt peaceful, lulling her toward sleep almost, but now the silence felt weighted and she found herself wishing Hazel would turn around and change her mind, come back, be a buffer between her and Sam.

"So," Sam said. He was leaning back against his chair, still looking casual as ever, blue shirt unbuttoned slightly, dark hair scruffy, less perfectly styled than he used to wear it. She liked it better that way, she decided. "Do you fancy one more drink?"

Cassie hesitated—would he take it personally if she refused? She felt on uneven footing, not sure how to behave around this Sam, the less cocky version than the one she'd gotten used to. But she thought she might *really* fall asleep in this chair if she had one more drink. "No, better not. I think . . . If it's OK, I think I'm going to go to bed, actually. I'm knackered." She expected him to protest, to tell her she was boring, to say one more wouldn't hurt—the type of thing he used to do. But he got to his feet.

"I'll walk you to your room." She frowned to herself as she followed him out of the sitting room. He kept doing the opposite of what she was expecting, and it was confusing. She wondered if he'd changed since Tom's death—if it had changed him—or if this side of him had always been there, buried somewhere, and she hadn't seen it. Hadn't looked for it. Or if, maybe, this was a front, some weird game he was playing. She didn't think so, but then, she was sensible enough to at least consider it.

Cassie glanced up at him as they started up the stairs and he noticed, smiled at her. She felt herself flush, and looked down at the wooden steps, carpeted down the middle. "So I've been wondering," she said, directing her voice at the floor.

"Wondering in general or about something specific?" She gave him a light punch on the arm as his lips twitched.

"You don't *really* know anything about the hospitality industry, do you?"

He winced a little as he shook his head.

"And you don't really have an interest in local pubs in general?"

"Ah, no." Even though she'd known that, it still felt a little like something was hitting her in the gut, like the tiny kernel of hope she'd felt when she'd seen that house in Wales was being guttered out. It was stupid. It shouldn't make a difference. But there it was. He glanced at her. "I just . . . I didn't think I could tell you right away, because I was worried you wouldn't take the money."

"I would've taken the money," she said firmly. And it was true. Wasn't it? Would she really have been so petty as to throw the offer back in his face, if she'd known it was him? She doubted it. Not when the stakes had been so high. But the fact that she was asking herself the question at all helped her to see why he'd decided to keep his identity a secret.

They reached her room and Cassie stopped, jerking her head to indicate this was her. They faced each other, her with her back to the door. She couldn't help noticing how close they were to one another. It would be so easy to reach out, run a hand through his hair. Silly thought. It must be all the gin.

Sam slipped his hands into his pockets. "So, what are you doing tomorrow?" The question made her jolt a little. Why did he want to know? Was he going to ask her to spend the day with him? Her stomach did a sort of uncomfortable twist and she crossed her arms to try to hide it. It was normal, if he was going to ask her—they'd known each other practically their whole lives after all and they were . . . friends? It had been a long while since she'd described him as such, but was that where this was going?

"Not sure," she said in the end. "Breakfast here and then home, I guess." It was a true enough answer—tomorrow was Monday and she had work on Tuesday so should really be getting herself home and getting sorted tomorrow.

He nodded, looked away from her, down the corridor. His eyes seemed a little glazed and she could tell that he wasn't really taking in their surroundings. "Tom and I were supposed to go away this week," he said quietly. "Thursday and Friday. We booked this festival ages ago."

"Oh," Cassie said, unsure how to respond, even as it pulled at her, the reminder that Tom would have no more festivals.

"Yeah. I'd actually completely forgotten until today, but I got a reminder email about it. I've still got the tickets." He smiled sadly.

"Do you still want to go?"

He shook his head. "It would feel wrong, without him. Maybe in the future, but . . . not yet."

Cassie nodded. She got it. There were still things she couldn't do—things she thought she'd never be able to—without her brother. And maybe because he'd offered up this nugget to her, she felt she could confess something too. "I've been doing the treasure hunt," she said. "The one he did for me before he died. You know, to find my Christmas present."

Sam stared at her and she felt her face warm at the intensity of his gaze. "You've got the clues?"

"Yeah. Linda found the first one, gave it to me." She didn't tell him *when* she'd gotten the first clue—right after she'd slammed the door in his face.

Sam pulled a hand through his hair, dropped it to his side. "I can't believe I didn't think of that. I guess I just thought . . ." But he didn't finish the sentence. She knew what he'd been thinking, though—he'd thought the clues would be lost, like Tom was.

"I've done the first few already. It's weird, they're bigger than usual, almost . . . almost like he knew that it would be the last time." It was impossible, of course, because his death had been an accident. She knew it must just be her brain, molding things that way, but still.

He smiled. "I remember him talking about it. He wanted this year to be bigger and better." She nearly asked him if he knew what the gift was at the end, but changed her mind immediately. Her reasoning still stood: Tom wanted her to figure out the clues, so that's what she'd do. Help, though: she didn't think that was cheating, not when Tom would have given her hints if he'd been here—and not when she'd figured out *most* of it by herself.

"I can't work out this most recent one, though, so I'm stuck."

"What's the clue?" She told him and he frowned. "I feel like that's somehow familiar."

"I know that it's about a beach and a lighthouse, but that's as far as I've gotten." She chose not to tell him that she'd only figured out the lighthouse part this morning.

He nodded slowly. "If I think of anything, I'll let you know." He looked at her for a moment, then ran one hand across the back of his neck. "See you at breakfast?"

"Yeah, sure," she said, working up a smile. It shouldn't feel difficult to do that. She shouldn't be feeling disappointed that he didn't suggest something else to do tomorrow. This was *Sam*—she shouldn't want to spend time with him. But it was a new him, and it seemed to change the rules of play, neither of them sniping, both of them treading carefully around each other. He was still looking at her, and she cleared her throat, gestured to her door behind her. "Well, I'll get to bed then."

He hesitated, then leaned in, pressed his lips softly against her cheek. The tingle ran from there all the way to the back of her neck, where it stayed. She heard herself suck in a soft breath, unable to stop it.

"Night, Cass," he whispered, his breath softly caressing her ear, in a way that lingered after he had walked away down the corridor.

She woke to the sound of banging and went from groggy to alert in a matter of moments. Why was someone trying to hammer down her door? She jolted upright in bed, switched on her lamp, and stared at the door, heart beating extra fast. A murderer, trying to break in? She scrambled out of bed at that thought, glanced frantically around the room. But no, a murderer was unlikely to knock, bad tactic. A fire maybe? But surely they had alarms for that?

The banging stopped and she waited, hovering by her bed. When it started up again, she crossed the room tentatively. "Hello?" she called out, still with the door safely shut.

"Cassie?" His voice was a little muffled. "It's me."

She let out a whooshing breath and opened the door. "Sam! What the hell's going on?" She pushed her hair out of her face. "What time is it?" Had she overslept and missed breakfast or something? The curtains in the room were too good—they effectively blocked out all morning light.

"Six A.M.," he answered impatiently, as if that were completely irrelevant.

She stared at him incredulously. "Six A.M.?! But . . . it's my day off." OK, so maybe she was still a bit groggy from sleep, if that was the best she could come up with. Slowly, she became aware that she was standing in front of him in her old pajama top, no makeup on, her hair surely a complete mess. She crossed her arms over her chest.

Sam, on the other hand, was bright-eyed and looked like he was fizzing with energy, just about bouncing on the spot. He had his jeans and shirt on again, but it was buttoned up wrongly, like he'd thrown clothes on impatiently at the last minute. "I figured it out!"

"What?"

"I figured it out," he repeated. "The clue!" He looked so young then, face all alight, and so damn cute. No, she corrected herself immediately. Not cute. Annoying. It was *annoying* to be woken at six A.M.; there was nothing cute about it.

She shook her head, trying to keep up with him. Then it dawned on her and she dropped her arms, momentarily forgetting to be embarrassed about what she looked like. "You know where it is."

"You do too," he said, smiling. "Surfing. He won't make you surf this time. Do you remember?"

Cassie only frowned at him.

"We went on holiday," Sam continued. "You, me, Tom, Claire, Mum."

And she remembered then—they'd gone to Cornwall, all together. They'd gone, and Tom and Sam had gone surfing and forced her to come too and she'd hated it, coughed up water and gotten hit over the head with her surfboard.

"Cornwall," she breathed and he nodded, actually *did* bounce this time. But Cassie shook her head, pulled a hand through her hair. She was right—it was matted at the back. "He wants me to go to a bloody lighthouse in Cornwall?" There was a pit in her stomach at the thought of it—Cornwall was *miles* away—but Sam was looking positively delighted.

"Yes! And I looked it up, and I think it must be Pendeen lighthouse, because we were in Penzance and that's the closest one there. And I've been on trainline and there's a train in an hour." He clapped his hands in front of him.

Cassie took a step back, feeling like she wanted to back away completely, at speed. "Wait, hang on, you want us to go today? Now?"

"Yeah, why not? You've been trying to work it out for ages, right? So why not now?"

"Because . . ." Because it was last-minute and spontaneous and so many things could go wrong, and she hadn't packed for Cornwall. Because Cornwall was bloody miles away and would surely take hours to get to. But Sam was smiling at her, so excited, and something tugged at her heart, looking at him like that. She thought of Tom, and how he'd be grinning at her right now, trying to get her to just do it. Stop overthinking and just roll with it. She took a slow breath, let it out, and tried to quiet the gnawing in her stomach. "OK. I'll go today." She'd look up the return journey on the way—surely she'd be able to figure something out, get back in time for work tomorrow. As long as she found the clue quickly, that was. She hesitated. "Does this mean you're coming with me?"

"Sure, if you want me to." His voice was casual—almost, Cassie thought, a little careful. Putting the ball firmly in her court.

This time, she did not hesitate, but squared her shoulders. If she was doing this, then she might as well go all the way. "Yes. I want you to come." She tried, very hard, to match his easy, casual tone. It was natural, wasn't it, that she'd want company? "Give me twenty minutes to pack and I'll meet you downstairs."

Chapter Twenty-Nine

The taxi pulled up outside the lighthouse, the midafternoon sun shining down on it, and Cassie stared, unable to believe that they were really here. It was a tall white building, contained within a little wall, with a couple of smaller buildings next to it, also white, all with a turquoise stripe running around the bottom. Cassie noticed that Sam had already gotten out of the car and was paying the taxi driver and she made herself open the door and get out too. She turned away from the lighthouse to the sea and felt her heart stutter.

It was stunningly beautiful, the type of place that was impossible ever to capture on camera. Green grass gave way to epic cliffs, where waves crashed underneath, foaming white hands clawing at the rock. Beyond it was wide, vast ocean, all the way out to the horizon. A white boat bobbed in the distance, but apart from that there was nothing but blue. She took a breath, enjoying the feel of being outside after so long on a train. The air was warm, though there was a hint of humidity, like a storm might be brewing.

"Come on a nice holiday, have you?" the taxi driver was asking. Cassie turned, saw that he'd been addressing her directly as he handed her the little overnight suitcase she'd taken to the manor. Sam already had his big suitcase, the one which, he'd told her, he'd brought directly from New York.

"I, err . . ." Cassie glanced at the lighthouse, though it took no notice of her, its attention firmly on the ocean. "Sort of," she said eventually, deciding that would be easier than explaining. She felt the urgency pressing down on her, struggled not to bounce from foot to foot. She'd looked it up and she could get a five P.M. train back from Penzance to London, arriving after midnight but still back in time for work the next day. That meant they had to get on it though, and find the clue as soon as possible. "Do you know if we can get into the lighthouse?" she asked.

The driver's eyebrows pulled together. "You're not allowed to go in," he said bluntly, as if she should already know this. "It's a working lighthouse." He peered at her suspiciously, like there was something untoward going on here. "You're not staying in one of the cottages, then?"

Cassie felt Sam come alongside her, and jumped a little when he slung an arm around her shoulders. It made her feel small, pressed against him, though the weight of his arm settled her a little. "It was a surprise holiday," Sam said, and winked at the taxi driver, whose look of suspicion was immediately replaced by a grin.

He smiled at Cassie. "Ah, you're a lucky one then, aren't you?" And, after giving them his card in case they needed another ride, he waved them away. Cassie watched the car disappear down the winding cliff road with a mounting pressure in her chest. She pulled away from Sam.

"Why did you send him away?" she squeaked. "We're in the middle of nowhere and we need to get back!"

Sam's lips curved, like he wanted to smile, but he didn't give in to it, and ran a hand up and down her arm soothingly instead. "We'll be able to call another taxi, don't worry."

They fell silent, and standing there, close enough to touch, with him smiling down at her, felt suddenly intimate. More intimate than on the train journeys—which had taken forever, given they'd had to connect in London—where they'd been sur-rounded by other people and other conversations.

Cassie shifted, staring up at the lighthouse. "So what, do you think a clue is stuck on it somewhere?" That was what Tom had done when they were younger after all, stuck the clues on ob-jects or doors, before he'd gotten more ambitious. Very ambi-tious this time, apparently.

Sam looked at it too. "There was nothing else? On the clue?"

"Greg," Cassie said. "He said he had a friend called Greg."

Sam clapped, rubbed his hands together. "Right. Well, we best find Greg then." They both looked around, as if a Greg might immediately materialize, but there was only someone walking their dog, a little way in the distance. "OK," Sam said, "well, we'll have to ask." And with that he marched into the little complex, heading for one of the smaller buildings on the side of the lighthouse. Feeling incredibly conspicuous, like there might be someone peering down at her from the top of the lighthouse, Cassie followed him.

There was no answer at the first door, so Sam immediately proceeded to the second, which opened almost immediately. A man stood in the doorway, with scruffy gray hair and gray stub-ble that was on the verge of becoming a beard. He was also very short. Cassie only noticed that because he wasn't much taller than she was—and she was only five foot.

The man frowned. "You the curtain people? You're a day early."

"We're, ah . . ."

Sam glanced at Cassie, who shook her head, wondering what, exactly, "curtain people" were. People who made curtains, presumably? Or installed them? Though that wasn't the right word, was it? Hung curtains? Was there a job for that?

Sam changed tactic. "Are you Greg?"

"Yessss," the man said, drawing out the word. He raised his eyebrows—also gray—but didn't offer anything more.

Cassie stepped forward. "I'm Cassie. Tom Rivers' sister. He said to ask for you when I got here—I think you might have an envelope for me?"

Greg stared at her, then frowned. "He didn't warn me. He was supposed to warn me when you would be coming, so I could get prepared."

"He was going to warn you?" It made sense, she supposed—he'd have been following her progress, keeping tabs on where she was with it.

"That's right."

"He . . ." Cassie swallowed. "He couldn't."

His eyes turned shrewd. "Why not? Something happen?"

Sam glanced at Cassie and she knew he was wondering if he should step in. She nodded, unwilling to be the one to say it out loud.

"Tom died," Sam said quietly. The words cut into her, like always, but Sam's pain, the way it simmered in his voice, cut into her too. Would either of them get used to it? It must get easier, surely? But every time she thought it would, something happened to remind her that the pain of it was still there.

Greg paled, looked between them. "I . . . I didn't know. I'm . . ." He shook his head. "That's terrible." He stepped aside, ushered them into what turned out was a charming little cottage, all light and airy. It was messy though, with big pots of paint out, and when he led them into the living room, Cassie saw plastic on the floor around the edges. The wall on one side was half painted, light blue over the white that had been there previously.

"I'm doing it up," Greg explained unnecessarily.

Cassie walked over to the window, which was next to a white

bookcase, mostly empty except the bottom shelf, which was filled with books that weirdly all had blue covers. She looked out—you could see the ocean from here.

"I usually just manage the bookings but, well, I got roped in." Cassie turned back to see Greg looking at her quite intently. "Your brother . . ."

Why was he looking at her like that? What was he going to tell her? Cassie hugged her arms around herself as Sam came to stand next to her, not touching, just offering silent reassurance.

"He saved my life."

Cassie's arms dropped to her sides. "What?"

Greg gestured to the one sofa, light blue and apparently un-affected by the redecorating, and Cassie obeyed, going to sit down, Sam following her. The two of them looked up at Greg, who pulled a hand through his gray hair, shook his head rue-fully. "I met him at a bar in Penzance—that's where I live usu-ally, you see. We were both on our own, both down."

"Down?" Cassie asked, leaning toward Greg as she spoke. "What do you mean, down?"

Greg shrugged. "Well, I don't know the details, I could just tell he was upset, you know? Had the signs you get when you're drinking alone, something getting you down." Cassie bit her lip. It didn't sound like Tom. To her, he'd mostly seemed happy and content, seemed like he had things figured out, with a long-term girlfriend whom he loved, a job that excited him, always off on adventure holidays. She looked at Sam, but he was frowning, like it was news to him, too. Some things, it seemed, Tom had told neither of them.

"Anyway," Greg continued, "we were both a bit drunk and a bit sad—my wife had left me, you see, though it turned out it was only temporary. She's back with me now, we were separated for a total of two days." He smiled at Cassie faintly, and Cassie did her best to return it, though she just wanted him to carry on with the story. "So, me and Tom, we got chatting and had a few drinks. He mentioned your parents," he added, giving Cassie a little look.

Cassie's heart gave a painful thud. Their parents? Tom had been talking about their parents? Is that why he was down? But whenever he talked about them with her, it was always fondly, trying to get her to remember the good things about them— things he could remember, by virtue of being those few years older than her.

"We left together when the place shut. And well, outside on the road . . . Well, like I said, we'd been drinking, and to cut a long story short, I nearly stepped out in front of a car and Tom, he pulled me back." Cassie waited, but he said nothing more.

"That's it?" She had been expecting something grander, like Tom climbing a building to save him or something. Not something that could just be a drunken memory, one embellished by alcohol.

"I'm telling you, that car would've hit me if it hadn't been for your brother."

Why hadn't Tom told her? Maybe he'd not thought anything of it, pulling a stranger out of the way. It had clearly stuck with Greg, though. And it was a horrible, wrong thing to think but there was a moment—a tiny, fleeting moment—where Cassie felt bitter about the fact that Tom had saved Greg's life, but his own had not been saved. That Greg should have been lucky, when Tom was not.

"Anyway, look, I'm working on the cottage, but you're welcome to stay here." It took Cassie a moment to register the change of subject, so she didn't get the chance to decline the offer before Greg carried on. "I'll go to my place in town for the night. One of the bedrooms is out of action at the moment, though," he added with a frown, glancing between Cassie and Sam as if trying to figure out whether that would be a problem.

"I'll sleep on the sofa," Sam said quickly. Unable to look at Sam, because of the suggestion implied there, Cassie opened her mouth to say it wouldn't be necessary because they wouldn't be staying, but Greg talked over her again.

"All right, good, and there's food in the fridge, some anyway, and you help yourself to anything. Some nice wine there too, OK? Not the cheap stuff either—Tesco Finest."

"But we can't kick you out of your house!" Cassie said, louder than was perhaps necessary. "I mean, sorry, it's so incredibly kind of you, but really, all we need is the clue—the envelope, I mean—and then we'll be out of your way." She wanted to check her phone, see if she was still on track to make it back to London, but knew that would seem rude. "He did give you an envelope, right?"

"He did, but, well . . ." He got up, left the room.

Cassie looked at Sam. "Is that it?" she whispered.

"I think he'll—"

Greg reappeared and Sam stopped talking. "Here," he said, and thrust an envelope into her hands. There was no number in the corner of this one and Cassie found her stomach lurch. Had she gone wrong somewhere? "He told me to give this to you first."

Cassie felt both Greg's and Sam's eyes on her as she opened it.

Whoop! You made it this far!

There was a doodle of a lighthouse in the middle of the page, a speech bubble coming out of the top of the lighthouse, with the words *Welcome, Chipmunk* inside.

I wondered if you'd do it . . . Just kidding (sort of).
So, now you're here, I'm setting you one more task . . .
Oh, the power. Here it is: stay the night. Yes, that's right,
I can practically hear you scowling from here. But be a good
little sister—stay the night, and you'll get the next clue in
the morning. I know you won't want to. I know it'll freak you
out, staying somewhere unplanned, far away from home,
on your own—but if you do it then it will prove you can do
something spontaneous like this, and the world will not
come crashing down around you.

Good luck! (Try and have fun?)

Cassie gripped the note tighter. She could hear his voice, playful, teasing. It gave her those same conflicting feelings she always had, each time she opened the next clue. The pressure on her chest, her heart, as she thought of her brother, and the fact that she'd lost him. And that spark, the *flutter* almost, as she read words that connected her to him. Words that made her feel his presence lingering around her.

She read the note one more time, then looked up at Greg and blinked. "He wanted me to stay overnight?"

"Yes, that's what he told me."

"But I can't," she said flatly. "I've got work tomorrow." As she said it, she realized how stupid this all was, how reckless. She should never have just taken off with Sam—the seven-hour trip down here had been exhausting, and now she had to do it all back again, and Greg wasn't even going to give her the damned clue. She should have planned this more properly, and then she'd have been prepared. She took a breath, tried to stay calm. "And you're clearly not in a position to put us up in any case." She gestured around the room, but he shrugged.

"I've got a place in town, like I said. It's no bother. Besides, if it's what Tom wanted, I'll make it happen."

"But . . ." Cassie stared at him helplessly. "I've got *work*," she repeated. "I can't stay in the middle of nowhere without planning, without telling people, without—" She looked at Sam, sitting next to her. "Why are you grinning?" she demanded.

His grin just got bigger. "Because you're cute when you're flustered." She narrowed her eyes at him and he held up his hands. But he didn't push. He wasn't going to make her do it, she realized. The decision had to be hers. He'd let her turn around and leave, without the clue, if she wanted to. She looked to the window, to where the ocean was waiting. *If it's what Tom wanted.*

This was probably exactly the reaction he'd have expected from her, too—to freak out, refuse to do it. But he must've thought she *would* go through with it, because otherwise she'd never get to the gift at the end.

Sam took her hand, squeezed it. She looked down to where their fingers laced, so easily, together. "He's trying to show you something, I think," he said. "Why don't you let him?"

"But my job, Sam. My boss already hates me."

"So what's the problem, if he already does? You're not going to make it worse in that case. Just call in sick."

She frowned. "I've literally never faked being sick in my entire life." She usually agonized over it even when she *was* ill, torn between not wanting to pass the cold or whatever on and not wanting to look like she was faking it, terrified that people wouldn't believe her.

"I'll call in for you?"

She snorted. "What am I, nine?"

"No," he said softly. "You're definitely not nine." Their gazes met, held. Then she had to look away quickly, because it felt too intense, and Greg was still there, watching them with a bemused expression. Tom had thought she'd be alone, which would have been even more daunting. But the prospect of staying overnight somewhere with Sam made her stomach churn with a different kind of nerves.

Still, Greg was right. And there was no question about it— not really. She wasn't going to fall at this hurdle, not when she so desperately wanted to get the next clue. If it was what Tom had wanted, then she had to do it. So she squared her shoulders. "OK. I'll stay."

Chapter Thirty

After telling them he'd be back tomorrow with the clue and wishing them a good night, Greg left the cottage, leaving Sam and Cassie in the kitchen, alone. Sam smiled at her. "Well, I don't know about you, but I could do with a quick nap, before we do anything else." *Do anything else*—what was that supposed to mean? Nothing, she told herself firmly. *Stop reading into everything.*

Sam insisted she take the bed to nap, which was far comfier than it looked, with about four more pillows than were totally necessary. She fell asleep more easily than she'd thought she would, given the way her stomach would *not* stop churning, and when she woke it was after six P.M.

She gathered her washbag from her suitcase, found a towel in the drawer under the bed, and padded down the corridor to the bathroom. Where she nearly collided with Sam, who was coming out of the bathroom, towel wrapped around his waist, muscled chest fully on show. Jesus, would you *look* at him? She felt a blush rise to her face, even as her mouth went a little dry. She made herself look up, into his eyes, and she swore she saw him trying to stop a smile. And why wouldn't he be smiling? He must know how good he looked naked. Naked. He was naked, under that towel.

Stop it, Cassie!

She cleared her throat. "I'll, er, just have a shower, if that's

OK?" God, what was she doing? Why was she asking for *permission?*

In the bathroom, she told herself to get a bloody grip, even though she felt like a complete mess of emotions. She gave herself a stern look in the mirror. "You can do this," she said firmly. She could stay here, next to a lighthouse, on a cliff edge. She could stay here, with Sam, miles away from her home in London. It would be fine. There was no reason her stomach should be churning this way—she was probably just hungry.

She got dressed in the jeans and loose black top that she'd worn on the way to the manor, then agonized over whether to put makeup on. It was just the two of them, so it would be obvious she'd done it for him, but in the end she put some on anyway, keeping it subtle, because she was too self-conscious not to.

Sam was fully dressed by the time she got back to the kitchen, though she couldn't decide if she was relieved or disappointed by that. He was holding a wicker carrier bag, which he held up to her. "I've packed some food. Thought we could go out, have a picnic somewhere on the cliffs."

"A picnic?" For some reason, she found that quite endearing.

"Sure, why not? Might as well make the most of it, right?"

"Right," she agreed. God, why couldn't she sound as casual as him?

They left the lighthouse behind and walked along the cliffs. Cassie was grateful for the sound of crashing waves below them, because it negated the need to say much, meaning she could let go a little. She felt her shoulders start to relax as she breathed in the smell of the sea, the wind tugging its fingers through her already messy hair.

Sam picked a spot seemingly at random, and they both sat down. There was no picnic blanket, but the grass was warm and dry after a day in the sun. Cassie stretched her legs out in front of her, tilted her face toward the evening sun as Sam scrambled around in the plastic bag. He produced a bottle of white wine—Tesco Finest, as Greg had said—and two white mugs with a turquoise stripe at the bottom, just like the lighthouse itself. Cassie laughed a little as he poured wine into them, handing one to her. He smiled apologetically. "I couldn't find any wine-glasses." She smiled at him, and took a sip. The cool, crisp flavor seemed perfect for a summer's evening. She'd have to remember to send Greg something to replace it, once she got home—no matter what he'd said, she didn't feel entirely comfortable help-ing herself.

Sam unpacked the rest of the bag, handing her a peanut-butter sandwich on white bread, which made her laugh again, a whole carrot, which he'd topped and tailed but hadn't peeled because apparently he hadn't been able to find the peeler, and two rice cakes.

Sam grimaced a little as he took stock of their makeshift pic-nic. "Sorry. It was the best I could do with what was there."

"No, I love it. Peanut butter is my favorite, anyway. I don't buy it at home because otherwise I eat the whole jar in a matter of days and that can't be good for you."

Sam smiled that crooked smile. "I know, I remember. Me and Tom caught you eating it out of the jar at Claire's house more than once."

"Right," Cassie said, though in truth she'd forgotten that, and felt a little jolt at the fact he'd remembered.

The sun was starting to set now, turning a deep yellow, mak-ing the sky around it colorful, orange giving way to pink, purple, and blue, the light reflecting on the calm ocean out on the hori-zon. It was so unbelievably beautiful that it felt a little surreal that she was actually here, watching it, on a little corner of the earth.

Having finished his food, Sam shifted and leaned back so that his posture mimicked hers. Their hands were close, almost touching, and Cassie felt like she could feel the pulse of his fingertips stretching across the space to meet hers. The skin on her forearms prickled.

"Did you know Tom had come down here?" She spoke into the silence between them, silence that did not, for once, feel awkward. He hesitated, then shook his head. "Me neither," Cassie admitted. "Why do you think he came?"

Sam continued to look out at the sunset. "I don't know. We talked about coming to Cornwall to go surfing one year, but never did it. But maybe he came on his own—if he'd told me, I'd have wanted to come, I guess, and if he wanted to be alone . . ." There was a moment of quiet between them after he trailed off.

"It makes me sad," Cassie murmured, "that he was low and couldn't tell me. I didn't know he still felt sad about our parents." She frowned, and for a moment she thought of the story Linda had told her at Tom's funeral, about the whisky, the fact that Tom was so clearly trying to be like their dad—a dad who neither of them had really known—in some small way. "That sounds silly. I don't mean that—of course he was sad, it's not something that ever went away, for either of us, but I mean—"

"I know what you mean," he said softly. "But I think he wanted to be strong for you. You were so special to him, Cassie." He turned, looking at her now instead of the horizon. "You're . . ." But he broke off and turned his gaze away from her again. She let out a slow breath.

When it became clear that Sam wasn't going to continue, Cassie spoke again. "Do you think he's, you know, out there?"

Sam didn't speak right away. "I don't know," he said slowly. "I guess I don't really believe in all that, but I also don't *not* want to believe it." She nodded—she felt the same. And if Tom *was* out there, then he'd like this, she thought: to see her and Sam to-gether, sitting in companionable silence.

The sun was nearly gone now, sinking below the ocean, its reflection making it seem almost whole again. A cool breeze caressed her cheek and she shivered a little. She should've brought a jacket or something—she knew better than to be cocky and set out without one in England. Sam clearly noticed, because he reached out, put an arm around her and pulled her gently to his side, without saying anything. The warmth of him enveloped her, chasing away the slight chill in the air, and her skin prickled where his bare skin touched hers. After a moment, she dropped her head onto his shoulder. It felt easy, natural, to sit with him like this, a little like the friendly relationship they'd had when they were teenagers, before she'd decided to close her heart off from him. Only this time there was something more there, and her body felt tense, expectant.

"It's so breathtaking," Cassie whispered, as the last of the sun disappeared, leaving its warmth behind in the air before night came to steal the color away.

Sam kissed the top of her head. "Yeah."

She tilted her head up to look at him, smiled, and saw his face soften into a smile back at her. Her heartbeat quickened as she met his gaze, blue eyes even bluer out here, by the ocean. She felt rooted there, unable to break the eye contact. His expression changed, those eyes becoming more intense, more focused, and his eyebrows pulled together into a soft frown. Not angry or confused, Cassie would guess, but questioning. Then, slowly, he leaned toward her, closing the distance between them, and kissed her. Lightly at first, barely a whisper, but then she reached up, cupped the back of his neck.

And she was kissing him back, her other hand coming up to his shoulder, pulling him closer toward her, and, God, it was like falling, drowning, all thought going from her head so that the only real thing in the world was him. All these years later, and Sam was still the only one who could do this to her, could set her body alight like this.

She couldn't be sure how long it was before he broke away, and she was relieved to see that she was not the only one breathing heavily. He ran his hands down the sides of her arms, pulled back slightly, and she shivered again, whether from the touch or from the sudden departure of his warmth, she couldn't be sure.

"Come on," Sam said, a little huskily. "You're cold and it's getting dark—we'd better get back."

"Right," she said, trying to keep her voice steady. "I don't fancy getting lost out here."

He got up, held out a hand and pulled her to her feet, then dropped her hand again, almost like he didn't want to touch her. She folded her arms as they walked back along the cliff edge, so that she couldn't do something stupid like reach out to try to take his hand again.

Was it just her, or was the air in between them humming with electricity? It could just be her. But then, he'd kissed her, hadn't he? He'd definitely been the one to make the first move. She tried not to think of the last time this had happened, all those years ago. Tried not to think of how he'd so clearly regretted it then. Tried not to keep glancing at him now as they approached the lighthouse, wondering what he was thinking, whether he regretted it this time, too. Her skin was prickling with energy as he unlocked the door, held it open so she could go in ahead of him.

They headed to the kitchen, Sam putting the mugs in the sink while Cassie hovered, curling her fingertips around the wooden chair in front of her. It seemed too light in here, compared with the darkness settling in outside. She headed for the cupboards, needing to do something. "Tea?" she asked, perhaps a touch too brightly, as she moved some things around to see if she could find any. For God's sake, why was she asking him if he wanted tea?

She glanced over her shoulder, saw him shaking his head. "I can't drink caffeine late at night—I won't sleep."

"Really?" For some reason that felt like a funny thing for him to admit—a weird vulnerability that she wouldn't have expected.

"Yeah. For a while now."

"Oh. Right." She closed the cupboard door. She didn't really want tea either, now that she thought about it. They stood, looking at each other. There it was again, that damn sparking electricity, taking up the space between them even as they stood on opposite sides of the kitchen.

"I'll, err, go and get the bedding for the sofa, then." He shoved his hands into his pockets as he came past her, headed into the hallway and then upstairs. She heard his footsteps creaking above her, and found herself twisting her hands as she waited for him to return, getting herself a glass of water just for something to do.

Because what was she *supposed* to do? There was something there, between them. There always had been, if she was being honest with herself. But that didn't mean they had to act on it. She'd learned the hard way, hadn't she, that Sam was not to be trusted? She crossed to the window over the sink, stared out. It was a full moon tonight, the light of it shimmering across the darkness.

She jumped at the sound of Sam coming back into the room, and turned to face him. He held up a sheet. "All I could find," he said, with a little smile. "Maybe they're redoing the spare bedding too."

"Oh," Cassie said. Why couldn't she think of anything to say? Why couldn't she stop *looking* at him, for God's sake? Why couldn't she stop thinking of his chest, as he'd come out of the bathroom?

"It's OK. It's warm enough tonight and I'll use the cushions as a pillow." He hovered in the doorway of the kitchen. Waiting for something, she thought. He waved a hand in the direction of the living room. "Well, ah, I'll just go and set up, then. So, good night?"

Cassie burst out laughing. She couldn't help herself. The tension—bottled within her and dancing between them—bubbled over, so that she couldn't stop.

Sam frowned at her. "What?"

She pressed her lips together to stem the laughter—the whole *ridiculousness* of it. "Sam. It's, like, nine P.M. or something."

His lips twitched into that crooked smile. "Well past bedtime for me."

She laughed again, shook her head.

He took a step toward her, into the kitchen, still holding that sheet. "Do you, err, want another glass of wine or something?"

Their gazes locked, and she felt her heart thud. She listened to it, waited. Then she took a deep breath, stepped toward him so that they met in the middle of the room. She knew what she was doing. Knew that this could only go so far. And knowing that—well, it meant she was safe this time around, didn't it? "No," she said, her voice calm, certain. "I don't want another glass of wine." She closed the distance between them, tugged the sheet from his hands and tilted her head up to keep her eyes on his.

He reached out and brushed her hair back from her face, leaving pinpricks of warmth behind. She didn't need to say anything, didn't need to explain. For better or worse, they'd always been able to read each other. "Are you sure?" His eyes were so damn intense, and she felt like she might explode if she didn't do something about the little space that remained between them soon.

She nodded. "I'm sure."

And then he was kissing her again, and she dropped the sheet on the floor where they stood, her hands needing to be free so that they could touch him. She ran them up under his shirt, and felt that glorious toned muscle beneath. She felt his hands mirror hers, sliding up underneath her top, her skin turning to fire where he touched her. And Jesus, *this*. No one else had ever made her feel this.

He moved his mouth to her neck, she groaned softly at the light scrape of his teeth. He brought his lips back to hers, his hands traveling up her back, and wherever he touched, her skin throbbed. *More*. Her whole body was sparking, alive, and she needed *more* of it.

As if he'd sensed it, as if he'd heard her somehow, he deepened the kiss, pulled her even closer, and she felt the heat shoot to her core. He said her name softly, almost like an oath, then in one movement moved his hips to hers and literally plucked her off her feet. It made her laugh, a little breathlessly, even as she hitched her legs around his waist, even as she used the change in angle to press closer to him. For a moment they stopped, looking at each other, their faces close. The look in his eyes was enough to make her nerves a shivering mess.

Then he grinned, and leaned forward to take her bottom lip between his teeth. And when she groaned softly, he carried her to the bedroom.

Chapter Thirty-One

Cassie woke curled next to Sam, his tanned, muscled arm around her, his breathing heavy, chest rising and falling. She stayed still, biting her lip, not sure what to do. This was *Sam* lying next to her in bed. And they were both naked. Which had felt great last night, when she was caught up in the moment, but now . . .

How was she supposed to play this? Casual and breezy—is that what he'd expect? Was this just another one-night stand to him—had he been off sleeping with multiple women in New York, since Jessica? Jessica. It gave her a jolt to think of her. He was supposed to be getting *married* to her, less than four months ago, and now here she was, sleeping with him. And before Jessica, he'd been all too happy to take various women back to his place—she'd watched it happen, watched the girls fall at his feet. She tried to push that aside. It wasn't fair, to judge him for that now—she'd wanted to sleep with him, hadn't she? It had been her decision. And it had been . . . well, amazing. Intense, passionate, toe-curling, the lot. The type of sex you only ever dream about. Or that she did, anyway. Maybe Sam had that kind of sex all the time. *No*, she told herself. *Stop that.*

But she wasn't sure she *could* pull off casual and breezy, and she couldn't lie, say she had to leave for work so that she could get out of here and figure out what to do, because they were on the bloody edge of the world right now with nowhere *to* go.

She edged away from him, figuring she'd go to the bathroom, make herself pretty at least, and see if she could hunt down some coffee or something. But his arm tightened around her. "Where are you going?" he grumbled, his voice all sexy and husky from sleep. "Come back."

She laughed, and it dispelled some of the awkwardness. He pulled her to him, kissed her neck softly, and she felt the same tingles from last night travel down the side of her body, right to her toes. He kissed her again, squeezed her arm, then murmured, "I'll be back." He got up, and she tried not to watch as he threw some clothes on. It was almost a shame to see him dressed—he really was something, naked.

When he was out of the room, she pulled a pajama top on then popped to the bathroom, quickly brushing her teeth and checking herself in the mirror. When she clambered back into bed, she got her phone off the bedside table so she'd have something to distract herself with while she waited for him to come back.

She unlocked it, read a WhatsApp from Hazel. **Where are you?? Did you stay for an extra night? Did you stay alone??**

Feeling her lips tug into a smile, Cassie sent a message back. **You're not going to believe me, so I'll just have to tell you in person. I'll be back later today. I think.**

Nooooo. The suspense is killing me!

Cassie grinned, then sobered when she clocked the time, feeling her stomach flip. She needed to ring Robert—she was supposed to be at work in an hour.

Sam reappeared in the doorway, hair disheveled, holding a tray of coffee, toast, and scrambled eggs. Cassie looked at the tray, blinked, then looked at Sam and smiled. "I don't think anyone has brought me breakfast in bed before," she admitted. And he looked so cute, all rumpled, trying to be domestic. Something tightened in her chest and she felt a slight tingle of panic. She shouldn't—couldn't—go down that road, couldn't let herself start feeling that way about him, not again.

"Good, that means you have nothing to compare it to—if you did, I'm not sure I'd come out on top." He brought the tray over, set it down between them on the bed. He glanced at the phone in her hand. "Just do it," he advised. "You'll feel better once it's over and done with." Well, of course he knew what she was thinking.

Knowing she wouldn't enjoy breakfast while her stomach was a ball of anxiety, Cassie dialed Robert's direct line. "Robert?" she said when he answered. "It's Cassie. I'm really sorry, but I'm not going to be able to make it in today. I'm not feeling well."

"Not feeling well?" he asked incredulously, as if he'd never heard of such a thing.

"Yes," Cassie said, hated that her voice wasn't firm. "I've got . . ." Sam pointed at his stomach, made a face. "A stomach flu?" She realized she'd made it into a question and continued hurriedly, "I think. I feel really nauseous anyway, and I don't think it's a good idea to come in. Hopefully it's just a twenty-four-hour thing."

"But . . . But . . ." Robert spluttered. "You can't be ill, I've got no one to cover for you."

"Can you get a temp?" Cassie asked, though she knew from memory that there was nothing major going on at the hotel today, and Josh could handle it. "I just don't want to be throwing up all over the guests," she said, as firmly as she could manage. Sam gave her a thumbs up. "Actually," she continued, talking over Robert, feeling bolstered by Sam, "I've got to go. I'm feeling a bit . . . I'll update you tomorrow."

She hung up, then stared at her phone. "I can't believe I just did that."

"You were great! Very convincing."

Cassie narrowed her eyes. "Liar. But he can't disprove it, can he?"

"Exactly. That's the spirit."

She ate a forkful of eggs. "They're good!" she said, and meant it. She'd had enough experience with Hazel's attempts at scrambled eggs to know that they could come out extremely rubbery if you did it wrong.

When they'd finished breakfast, Sam took the plates and piled them on the bedside table. "I'll have a shower, get ready," he said.

"Get ready for what?"

He shrugged. "Something fun?" He kissed the top of her head almost absentmindedly before leaving for the bathroom. And that kiss, the casualness of it, the way it seemed so natural, made her stomach lurch again.

Her phone beeped as he left and she jumped, worrying that it would be Robert. She looked down at it, saw a message from Josh.

Heard you're ill, that sucks, followed by a sad face. Then, immediately after, another message: **Are you actually ill, or did mystery sponsor show up and turn out to be a massive hunk and now you're eloping together?**

It made Cassie grin. She glanced up at the open door to check that Sam wasn't on his way back, then replied.

You're closer with the second.

WHAT!!!! Are you pulling my leg here?

I'll tell you at work tomorrow!

But I need details!!!

There was a knock at the door, and Cassie scrambled out of bed, yelling to Sam that she'd get it. She opened the door to see Greg on the other side of it, wearing a gray shirt today. Maybe all the gray was deliberate? "You did it, then?" he asked, a little gruffly.

Cassie grinned—she couldn't help it. "So it would seem."

Greg handed her an envelope, and this time, Cassie saw the number in the corner. "As promised." Cassie took it, smiled her thanks. "Now, you enjoy your day here, OK? You might as well, now you've come all this way. And you're welcome to stay another night—the place is yours until tomorrow."

"Thank you," Cassie said, trying to get across all her gratitude. "You've been so generous."

Greg waved a hand. "It's the least I could do. And you're welcome back anytime, you hear me? I've written my number down so you can get hold of me." He pointed to the top of the envelope. Cassie felt a little jolt, seeing something on the envelope other than Tom's number, but it settled after a beat. This was a man Tom had had a connection with, for whatever reason, and it was no bad thing to have a piece of him there too.

She said goodbye to Greg, and took the envelope into the kitchen, staring at it. This was it. The last clue, the one that would take her to the end, would reveal whatever gift Tom had gotten her—the very last one he'd give her. There had always been the same number of clues in Tom's treasure hunts. So this one, it would be the one to take her to the final hiding place, and after that it would be done and her connection with Tom would be broken. No more clues in his handwriting, no more hearing his voice as she read the notes.

She heard Sam coming down the stairs and quickly shoved the clue half under the fruit bowl on the kitchen table. She smiled as he came into the kitchen, hoping that the flash of warmth in her cheeks wasn't obvious. "Greg says that we've got the place for another night, if we want it." She said it as casually as she could, like it was no big deal, making it clear that she didn't expect anything from him.

His eyes crinkled. "Excellent. Get dressed then, let's go exploring." He was already dressed, of course, wearing jeans and a blue T-shirt—casual, so much better than those fancy lawyer suits. Not that she had anything against suits per se, but Sam seemed more *him* when he was like this, without the bravado he'd picked up in London.

"OK." Because why the hell not? She'd come this far, after all. And while she was here, she'd let herself roll with it—just this once.

They walked along the coastline, no real destination in mind, enjoying the warm day. The sea was different shades of blue and turquoise, and Cassie watched as a few different birds dived into the water to catch their lunch. Next to her, Sam squeezed her hand, their strides somehow matching, despite the difference in their heights.

They found a little café nestled up on the road above the beach and sat outside there on a blue picnic bench, under bunting on the old stone building. A woman, who Cassie guessed was in her fifties, came out beaming, showing off very white teeth, which weirdly matched the white top she was wearing underneath a blue apron. "What can I get you, my loves?"

"Err . . ." Cassie began, and looked at Sam, who was sitting opposite her.

"Cream tea is one of our specialities, if you're looking for something nice and tasty? I can make it an iced tea on a day like this, do a couple of sandwiches to go with your scones?"

"Sounds brilliant," Sam said.

The woman brought out the iced teas first, the glasses already beaded with condensation, and Cassie took a sip, realizing she was thirstier than she'd thought. She hadn't thought to stop for a drink along the way, too caught up in this weird fairy tale of a day. When the woman brought out the scones and sandwiches, set it all down between them on white plates with flowers around the edges, they thanked her. Cassie ran her eyes over the spread as the woman walked away, her stomach tightening a little in hunger after the walk. Then she laughed out loud.

"What?" Sam was looking at her with that little crooked smile, trying to figure out the joke.

She shook her head. "I just can't believe I'm here, sat outside in Cornwall, with you, having afternoon tea, of all things."

His smile got bigger. "Me too. A week ago I was in New York, with no idea where I'd be next."

Cassie bit her lip. So far, they hadn't really talked about the last few months, had carefully avoided the subject of when they'd last seen each other. "How was it?" she asked after a beat. "New York?"

"It was . . ." He reached out, took a cheese and cucumber sandwich, but didn't eat it right away. "It was brilliant, in lots of ways. I ended up working at this youth-center-type place, teaching kids to climb." He shrugged a little, like he was embarrassed to admit it.

Cassie cocked her head. "I can imagine that."

"You can?"

She nodded. She could imagine *this* Sam, the one she liked,

doing something like that and being good at it. She remembered, with excruciating detail, how patient he'd been when he'd
tried to teach her how to ski. "I can," she said firmly. "I bet you
were good at it."

He looked down at his sandwich, a slight flush at the base of
his neck, all flustered and uncomfortable.

She hid her smile, decided not to press the subject. "I bet
your mum missed you," she said instead.

"Yeah. I bought her a spa day, to try to make up for it. I think
she's going with Linda, actually."

"Really? Linda didn't tell me." She needed to ring her, check
in, see how the pub was doing. Linda was working to convert
the upstairs to proper rooms, Cassie knew, taking one of her
suggestions on board. "And . . . Your dad?"

Sam looked out toward the ocean. "I haven't spoken to him."
His face tightened, like he wanted to end it there, close the discussion off. But then he seemed to make a decision and sighed,
looked back at her. "He was at . . . the hotel, back in March." It
was carefully phrased—the word "wedding" very clearly avoided,
though Cassie still had to fight to control the way it made her
stomach turn.

"Really?"

"Yeah. He wanted to . . . I don't know. Apologize. Be there.
Whatever. But I, well, I left."

"I remember," Cassie said, a little wryly. Her tone made Sam
grin, and some of the tension left her body. "Have you tried
talking to him since?"

He shook his head. "I'm not sure I know how to, after all this
time."

Cassie considered him. "I know it's not the same," she said
slowly, "but I'd give anything to speak to my parents again.
There's so much I wish I could ask them, so much I wish I knew

about them that I don't, that I never will." He reached for her hand, but she shook her head. "It's OK. I'm not . . . I'm OK," she repeated. "I just meant . . . Will you regret it, not at least trying, while you have the chance? Maybe you won't—I don't know your dad, and maybe he's truly not the type of person worth giving a second, or third, chance to. But if you know, deep down, that there's a part of you that *will* regret it then . . ." She smiled gently. "Well, then maybe you should try."

Sam said nothing for a moment, just looked at her, brow a little furrowed. Then he sighed. "I've been so worried, my whole life, about ending up like him. That I'll do what he did—have a kid and let them down or something. I travel, sure, but up until recently I did it for holidays, and stuck to one place, held down a job." His face twisted into a little grimace. "I've been trying so hard not to be him, but what if I am?" Jessica's name was there again in the offing, but it was like neither of them wanted to mention her directly.

"Well," she said, as calmly as she could, "maybe the fact that you're aware of it, aware of his mistakes, means that you won't make the same ones." They both looked out at the ocean for a moment, then Cassie picked up a sandwich of her own, turned it round and round in her hands. "Amy's pregnant," she said quietly. Sam's gaze snapped to her face. "It's Tom's." Sam nodded slowly, and Cassie stared at him. "You knew," she said.

"Yeah. Yeah, I knew." She remembered, then, how he'd told her to drop the subject of Amy, back in the bar, the last night she'd spent with Tom before he'd died.

She felt tears burning the back of her eyes, but blinked them away. "Then you know . . ." She took a breath. "You knew he was going to leave her. He *had* left her. He left her, because he didn't want . . ." But it felt too damning to say it out loud.

Sam looked at her for a long moment, eyebrows pulled together. "I think he would have changed his mind, in the end," he said eventually.

She looked down at her sandwich again. "You can't *know* that though, can you?"

"No, but . . . Look, he didn't tell me exactly what he was thinking. I knew that Amy was pregnant, and I knew Tom was freaking out. I think he idolized the *idea* of your dad, growing up, but he, I mean, you guys, you never actually had one, did you?"

Cassie frowned down at her plate. "That's not—"

"I'm not saying it excuses it or whatever," Sam said quickly. "I'm just . . . Well, I can kind of relate." He gave her a lopsided smile. "You guys had Linda, and Claire, and—"

"Claire wasn't exactly much of a role model," Cassie said with a sigh, then immediately felt guilty about it. Claire hadn't done anything explicitly wrong, had she? They'd been looked after, had a house, comfort. Had a place where they could stay together—because who knew what would have happened if Claire hadn't taken them in.

"Well, Linda then. But there wasn't, I don't know, a 'dad' figure, you know? And Tom, well, when he talked to me about it, he was saying he didn't know *how* to be a dad. And I guess I'm saying, I kind of know why."

Cassie said nothing, though her heart ached at the idea that Tom had felt he could tell Sam all this, and not her. Maybe that was because, as much as she'd always tried to look out for him too, he'd usually been the one looking after her. So it was a different relationship from the one Tom and Sam had had. And maybe, instead of feeling jealous, she should feel grateful that Tom had had someone like that in his life.

"I really think he would have gone back to Amy, Cassie," Sam said softly. "He loved her. And he wasn't enough of a fuck-up to leave her alone with a baby." He gave her that same crooked smile that she knew so well. "Not like me."

She sighed. "You're not a fuck-up, Sam." He raised his eyebrows, and she laughed. "Well, not *all* of the time, at least."

"I've ruined so many things, Cassie," he said quietly. "Even if I didn't mean to, I have."

She didn't say anything, wasn't sure what exactly *to* say. Because she knew, didn't she? She'd been there.

He took her hand, held it on the table. Her fingers laced with his automatically. "But I don't want to ruin this."

Cassie's stomach lurched, a mix of emotions she couldn't quite identify. She felt heat, more than just from the sun, flash down her spine, and she sat up straighter, more rigid. "Sam . . ." But she wasn't sure what to say. She wasn't sure she was ready for this conversation. "Let's just enjoy the rest of the day, OK?"

He squeezed her hand, nodded, and let her fingers go. And even in the warmth of the day, her fingers registered the loss, the chill that took over from where his hand had been.

Chapter Thirty-Two

The sky was turning gray above them as they sat on the grass outside the lighthouse, close enough to see the sea but far enough back that there was no chance of accidentally falling over the edge. Sam had tried to make them sit a bit closer, but she'd refused—the view of the rocks below was beautiful, but not something she wanted to see up close. The gray sky didn't mar the beauty of the place. Instead it took on a new character, going from peaceful to wild as the wind picked up and the air cooled, threatening rain. The sea below was moving from placid to angry—not a full-blown rage, not yet, but building toward it.

Cassie ate a third slice of the oven pizza that they'd found in Greg's freezer. She sighed. "I'm a little sad this all has to end, that I have to go back to reality." She was getting the first train back to London tomorrow. Because she was close enough to, she dropped her head on Sam's shoulder, and he put his arm companionably around her.

"Me too," he murmured, and she wondered if he felt it too, the sense that it all just worked here—that *they* worked here. It was like there was a spell around the cottage, the lighthouse, the coast, and while they were inside it, they were safe.

"What will you do now? Go back to being a lawyer? Go to London?" Up until now she'd tried to hold off asking him any of these questions, because she wasn't entirely sure what she wanted the answer to be. She didn't want him to disappear, but she also didn't want to make it painful, and they both still had so much to sort out. For her part, she knew she couldn't put herself in a vulnerable situation. Whether or not he'd changed, there was a part of her that still didn't totally trust him, as much as she wished, in that moment, that she did. So would it be better or worse if he was close by? Could they work toward being friends, after this? Or would they drift apart, with only this memory of a few romantic days in Cornwall, like something out of a film?

"I'm not sure," Sam said slowly. "I quit my job, remember?"

She nodded, although it wasn't entirely accurate. He'd jilted the boss's daughter at the altar, not quit his job, and there was a difference.

"Do you want to be a lawyer again, though? Did you enjoy it?" She shifted slightly so she could look up at his face, read his expression. She'd never actually asked him this before, she realized. He'd certainly acted like he'd enjoyed it, though—the money, the status, the social circle.

"Parts of it," Sam admitted. "But I don't know, now . . . Something about it doesn't feel right anymore. But I'm not sure what is right. I'm not like you—I don't have a passion, so without a job, a purpose, I'm worried I'll just . . . drift."

She couldn't really imagine Sam drifting. He'd always seemed so sure of himself, of his place in the world. Sure of what he wanted, and how to get there, even if she didn't like or agree with it. It was funny that he thought of her as the one with passion, drive, purpose. Did she have that? She supposed she did, to some extent. She loved being in events, loved the thrill of it. And once, she'd been so sure what she'd end up doing, before she'd gotten caught in the cycle of London life, work. But really, it hadn't been her work, ever, that kept her grounded. It had been Tom. So she got it, that drifting feeling, even if she didn't say it out loud.

"Another beer?" Sam asked, holding up his empty one.

"Sure."

She pulled her knees to her chest as he went back inside, wrapping her arms around them. She wished she could stay here, listening to the sea, indefinitely. Back at her flat in London, all she had to listen to was the sound of banging doors, distant arguing, sirens, and traffic.

Sam came back out with two beers—and the envelope. "I found this," he said, holding it up.

"Right." Cassie cleared her throat. "Greg dropped it round earlier." It had been stupid, to think he wouldn't notice it, or would forget about it. It was the whole reason they were there, after all.

He handed it to her with the beer, sat down next to her. "So, are you going to open it?"

She stared at it, at the number in the corner. Then she looked at Sam. "I'm too scared to," she whispered. When he frowned, she carried on. "If I open it, then that will be it, done. It's been like . . . Well, not like having him back, but it's been something of him to hold on to, you know? And when I finish it, when I get to the end, that'll be over." And what if she couldn't handle it? What if she broke?

"I get that," Sam said. "Really, I do. But, Cass, you can't let fear rule you forever. That's what Tom has been trying to show you, right? That you're braver than you think?"

She put the letter down next to her, on the other side of Sam, away from them both. "I can't, Sam."

"Can't or won't?" Although his voice was calm, there was a subtle bite to it.

She frowned. "Why are you pushing this?" It wasn't right—he should understand where she was coming from, surely. He kept saying how he got it, how he missed Tom too—well then, he shouldn't be trying to make her do it when she wasn't ready.

"Because you can't be scared of everything all the time, Cassie!" He threw a hand into the air as he said it, and she jerked away. It wasn't what she'd been expecting, and hurt lanced through her.

And before she could stop herself, she was snapping back. "Me? I'm not the only one who's scared, Sam."

"What's that supposed to mean?"

She made a scathing face, falling back into old patterns even as a part of her hated herself for it. "You don't want me to let fear rule me, but look at you—you're scared of ending up like your dad, but at the same time you're scared of making a proper commitment, just like him. You left Jessica at the altar because you were so scared to go through with it, didn't you?" She bit the words out, then, because that wasn't enough, got to her feet, paced a few steps away from him.

"It wasn't right, Cassie. Me and Jessica, it wasn't right." His voice was weirdly calm now, and she turned to him, folding her arms.

"Have you even spoken to her since?"

A pause. "Well, not really."

"Right." Why should that make her feel worse? Only that, if he'd talked to her, figured it all out, this would feel less like an illicit weekend and more like it could actually have meant something. "Well, then, don't talk to me about being brave, Sam, because it's just hypocritical."

Sam got to his feet too now, and she could see the rigidity in his body. The sky above was darker still, and Cassie felt the first few droplets of rain fall onto her face. He took a step toward her, his jaw tight, so that she had to tilt her chin up to look at him. "Fine," he bit out. "Maybe you're right. But at least I'm brave enough to do one thing—at least I'm brave enough to admit what's going on here, like you don't seem to want to."

Something shot straight to Cassie's gut and she stumbled backward a step, shaking her head.

"Yes, Cassie. At least I'm brave enough to tell you that I love—"

"No, don't," she said, her voice high, almost unrecognizable as her own. She backed away another step, wrapped her arms around herself. "That's not fair, that's not . . ." Her breathing was coming quicker now, even as she told herself to calm the bloody hell down. But it was too much. She didn't want to hear it. She didn't want to let herself go there, couldn't bear the fallout if it didn't work out, couldn't hear it or say it, because it would open her up, leave her vulnerable when she was still only just piecing herself back together. She'd vowed not to give Sam her heart again, hadn't she? And she was damn well going to stick to that.

"No," she repeated. "I . . ." This time, her headshake was frantic. "I can't do this. Not again." She couldn't give her heart to him, couldn't open herself up to *really* love him, because it would give him the power to break her. And she knew she couldn't break anymore, not after Tom.

"What do you mean, again?"

She made a noise that was part sob, part incredulous laugh. "We've been here before, Sam! I told you, five years ago, how I felt and you . . ." But she couldn't finish, so she turned on her heel instead.

He grabbed her arm, stopped her, even as she threw off his hand. "That was different," he said firmly.

"Oh really?" she spat back at him. "Why?"

He frowned. "Because back then, we were—"

She raised her eyebrows scathingly. "What? Kids? I knew how I felt *then*, Sam. And you knew it too. You knew it, and then you thought of the most hurtful way to tell me to get over it, to prove some kind of point." Tears sprang to her eyes too quickly, the hurt of that time coming back to her, even after all these years.

He was staring at her. Was it her, or had his face gone slightly paler? "I didn't want to hurt you," he said, his voice hoarse.

"Well, you did."

"No, I . . ." He took a breath, his shoulders heaving with the effort. "I mean, I knew I'd end up hurting you in the long run, if we went down that road. I knew I'd fuck it up. And I couldn't bear it—to lose you when that happened."

"To lose Tom," she said, and it came out as a half-sob.

He nodded, took a step toward her. This time, she didn't back away. "Yeah, to lose Tom. But you too, Cass. I felt so much for you, even then. I felt too much, and I didn't know what to do with that. I thought I was doing the right thing—thought it would be better for both of us, to end it before I made things worse."

"And what, you thought it was OK to just unilaterally decide that? You could have talked to me about it, Sam! And instead you . . ." She closed her eyes, shook her head. "That's not the point." She was getting distracted with memories of the past. She'd put that aside, moved on. She didn't want to circle back to it now.

She felt the touch of his hand on her cheek, opened her eyes to see him standing there, so close. "I loved you then, Cassie. I think I always have."

Her throat closed on that, and her heart—her damn betraying heart—felt like it was swelling, beating more deeply, the rhythm of it lighting up her whole body. But that was why she couldn't go there. Because if she did, and if it didn't work out—if he hurt her again—then how would her heart survive it?

"And what, because you're ready now, it's OK?" It was barely more than a whisper.

He opened his mouth to say something, then closed it, shook his head. "This is real, Cassie, this is—"

"No." Her voice was a snap, and it cut him off. She took a breath, stepped away from his touch. "No," she said again. "I gave you a chance then, Sam, and I . . ." She turned from him, picked up her clue off the ground, and sped back to the cottage without another word. Her eyes were burning, and she felt like she might break down into sobs. She tried to take slow, calming breaths as she ran inside, grabbed her suitcase. She'd already packed, of course, just to be organized.

Then she found the taxi driver's card, called the number. Sam probably thought she was just calming down, or getting a glass of water or something. And that was fine, that was better, because she didn't want to face him. She couldn't do this. She just couldn't.

It was only when she heard a car arriving that she went back outside. Sam was frowning, looking from the taxi to her. It was raining more heavily now, his hair starting to darken with it, droplets clinging to her skin as she crossed to the car and put her suitcase into the trunk.

"Cassie," Sam said, slowly. "What the fuck are you doing?"

She drew herself up, made herself look at him. "I can't do this, Sam." Her lips wanted to tremble, and she pressed them together to stop them. "It's too much. And we're both . . . We're not . . ." She opened the door of the car. "It's just too much, OK?"

She gave him no chance to reply, got into the taxi as quickly as she could, told the driver to go. Sam didn't try to stop her. Didn't run after her or call her name. When she turned to look back at him, one last time, he was just standing there in the rain, watching her go. And it was only then, alone in the car, that she allowed the tears to fall.

Three Months Later

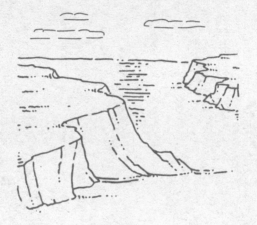

Chapter Thirty-Three

Cassie sat on the cobbled street outside the little restaurant, sipping a glass of the best red wine she'd ever tasted and contemplating just one more slice of the cheese platter that Claire had ordered. The evening sun was still warm, even in mid-September, and her shoulders were bare in the flowery dress she'd bought on impulse just before she, Hazel, and Linda had left for Bordeaux. All around her were beautiful buildings, sand-colored, the pink evening light making them glow. Across from the restaurant there was a tall building of flats, each with its own balcony. A woman stood there, her face tanned, wearing a bright red-and-green dress, and she was laughing on the phone, talking loudly, apparently unbothered by the tourists that hovered below.

"Go on," Claire said, nudging the cheese platter toward her. "I've seen you eyeing up the brie." Cassie cut into it—if you couldn't indulge in extra brie when on holiday, then when could you?

Claire looked more relaxed than Cassie thought she'd ever seen her. Since moving to Bordeaux she'd gotten a tan, and she'd stopped dyeing her hair, so that the natural brunette now showed through the bottled red. She didn't even seem bothered about the gray that was woven through—and she shouldn't, thought Cassie, because it suited her, looked kind of fashionable, like it was intentional. She'd put on a bit of weight—

probably from all the wine, cheese, and pastries, if Cassie's week here was anything to go by—and she looked good with it. Healthier.

Across from Cassie, Linda sighed, pushing her chair back from the table and folding her arms across her stomach. Her rings glinted in the evening sunlight. "You know, Claire, I think I might move here too." She picked up her wine, took a sip. "I could open a restaurant here instead."

Cassie exchanged a look with Hazel, who was sitting next to her. The thought of Linda running something out here didn't quite fit, and Cassie saw from Hazel's face that she agreed. Besides, despite what she said, Cassie knew Linda would never leave the pub. But the fact that she'd left it for a few days to go on holiday, the fact that she seemed to be getting on well with Katie, the manager, was definitely a positive thing.

"Well, you're welcome here anytime," Claire said. "It's been so lovely to see you. To see all of you. Like having a little slice of home here." Cassie shot her aunt a look. She hadn't thought Claire really cared about that. Claire gave her a little smile, like she knew exactly what she was thinking, and Cassie took another sip of wine. It really was good, though she had no idea what it was, apart from the fact that it was local to the region.

She felt more content than she had in a while, the edge taken off her in a way that made her realize how much stress she'd been carrying around recently. Robert was making *everything* at work seem stressful, making her wonder if there was something going on at management level that she and Josh didn't know about. And OK . . . maybe, she admitted to herself, some of that stress came from the fact that she couldn't stop replaying that night in Cornwall. Couldn't stop seeing Sam's face as she drove away from him in the rain. Hadn't been able to shake it, even though weeks had passed.

He hadn't called. *She* hadn't called either. There had been no more emails, obviously. And she'd completely let go of the idea of the house in Wales.

On top of that was the fact that she still hadn't gotten up the courage to open Tom's final clue, and the little envelope with the number five in the corner had been hanging over her since the summer.

"I'll do it too," Hazel announced, lifting her glass in a salute. Her green eyes sparkled above the rim. "Move here, I mean. They need advertising people here, right?"

"Sure," Claire said. "Those that speak French, I'd imagine."

Hazel waved her wineglass, the remaining liquid sloshing a little dangerously. "I'll learn."

The waiter came along at that moment to clear their plates away—an attractive man in his twenties, Cassie would guess, giving off tall, dark, and handsome vibes, with cheekbones that looked like they had been sculpted.

"*Merci,*" Cassie said as he took her plate.

He gestured to her near-empty wineglass. "*Un autre vin?*"

"*Non, merci. Un café au lait, peut-être?*" He gave her that warm smile, which she returned. She'd only just gotten brave enough these last two days to try out her high school French. In all honesty, she wasn't totally sure she knew what a café au lait was, but it was one of the only things she remembered from school in terms of beverages, and she knew it was coffee, at least. Maybe she could come back, learn some more French. The prospect was strangely appealing, and she found herself mentally checking her work diary to see when she'd be able to come and visit again.

The waiter had turned from Cassie to Hazel now, his brown eyes becoming slightly more intent—something Hazel seemed oblivious to. "*Et pour vous?*"

"*Vin!*" she announced. "*S'il vous plaît. Nous sommes en vacances!*" She said it all with a very English accent, which made both Cassie and the waiter grin. But Hazel looked at Cassie. "See? I'll be fluent in no time."

The waiter cleared the remaining plates, but hovered on Hazel's side of the table. "*Pour combien de temps?*" Hazel looked at him blankly and he switched to English, proof that he'd been humoring them with the French. Cassie liked that he had, though, that he'd given them the chance to try, without making them feel stupid about it. "For how long are you here?"

"Oh, until Friday."

"Do you have plans, until then?"

"Ummm . . ." Hazel looked around at all of them. "I don't know. Do we?" She focused on Cassie, who shrugged and looked across at Claire, passing on the question.

Linda jumped in. "Here, love," she said to the waiter, "why don't you give her your number?" She got out a pen, handed it to the waiter along with a napkin.

When he left, Cassie burst out laughing. "Getting hit on in France! It's like something out of a romance novel."

Hazel waved a hand at her.

"Well, you wanted to move here, didn't you? Maybe you can get a French husband while you're at it."

Hazel rolled her eyes overdramatically. "Don't be ridiculous. Though if you're all being boring tomorrow, maybe I'll take him up on it and go on a wild romantic day."

Cassie narrowed her eyes at her.

Hazel frowned. "What?"

"You're not even going to give him a chance, are you?"

"Cassie, he lives in *France*."

To be fair, that was a valid point, but Hazel never gave anyone a chance—she'd yet to go on more than one date with any of the various guys she'd gone out with this year, as per usual.

"Well," Claire said, "if anyone wants my recommendation, a French boyfriend is definitely the way to go."

"Hear, hear," Linda said, raising her glass and finishing off the contents. He wasn't here tonight, because Claire had insisted on a few girls-only nights, but they'd met Claire's new boyfriend the other day. Boyfriend—it sounded so odd, for her aunt. And Blaise didn't really seem like the word "boyfriend" fit, either. He was this sexy, older Frenchman, who whispered into Claire's ear and made her blush. It was kind of nice to see— Claire had been single since Cassie could remember. She supposed she'd not been with anyone when Cassie's parents had died, and then she'd suddenly became a parent to two young children, which couldn't have done wonders for her love life. If she'd ever had a boyfriend before now, she'd kept it quiet, and Cassie had never really thought to ask. She was realizing that it wasn't just Claire who hadn't made an effort. They both could've tried harder, over the years.

"Oh look," Linda said, gesturing across the cobbled street. "They're closing up that shop, the one with the pretty scarves. I wanted to make sure I went in there before we leave. Will we be able to come tomorrow?"

Claire hesitated. "Well, I thought we could take in the vineyards tomorrow, if you're all up for it?"

"Aha!" Hazel said. "So we *do* have plans!" Everyone ignored that.

"Well, I'll just run over now. I'm sure I can convince them to stay open."

"I'll come too," Hazel said, and the two of them got to their feet and crossed over, Linda waving at the pretty Frenchwoman who was closing the shop in a way that left no doubt about the fact that she was a tourist.

It was odd, given they'd spent the whole week together, but Cassie still felt a little awkward, sitting alone with Claire. She supposed they'd never quite figured out the rhythm of their relationship, beyond the caregiver-child basics.

The waiter came out with their drinks order, and as Claire thanked him, Cassie's phone buzzed from inside her handbag. She bent down to get it, and saw it was a WhatsApp from Amy. A photo of the baby—her nephew. Amy had given birth around a month ago. Cassie had gone to see her early on, when Amy was still a bit exhausted and out of it, but she hadn't been since—Amy's parents were staying with her, to help, and she hadn't wanted to intrude. She smiled as she looked at the photo, a little lump forming in her throat. Could she see Tom in him? She wasn't sure.

"What are you looking at?" Claire asked, and Cassie turned the phone so she could see.

"Tom's son," Cassie said quietly.

Claire stared at the photo, and her expression was unreadable. Then she smiled at the phone. "My grandnephew. Is that right? I always get confused."

Cassie put the phone away—she'd reply to Amy later—and Claire sighed. "Your mum would've loved it here."

Cassie paused in the action of picking up her coffee. A tiny coffee—was it supposed to be this small? She watched her aunt. Claire never voluntarily offered up information about her parents.

"Your dad too, of course," she continued, "but your mum . . . I can totally picture her, sitting out here, drinking, having everyone laughing, making friends with all the staff."

"Just like Tom," Cassie murmured, and Claire nodded, her eyes shining.

"Yes." She twisted the stem of her wineglass on the table. "Cassie, I've been wanting to say this for some time now, but I couldn't quite bring myself to. And I suppose, being here, moving, it's given me some space and I've been reflecting a bit on some things. So, I just wanted to say sorry."

Cassie frowned. "Sorry?"

Claire stopped twisting her wineglass and clasped her hands together in her lap. "I wasn't there for you, or Tom, the way I should have been when you were growing up."

"Don't be silly," Cassie said immediately. "We were perfectly well looked after."

"Yes, yes, I don't mean physically. I mean emotionally. I know that I never got close to either of you, in the way I should have. But it was just . . . so hard." She took a deep breath. "I was a year younger than you are now, when Abi died."

Cassie felt a jolt. So young. Or, at least, she still *felt* young. Young, and a bit of a mess, certainly not ready for kids yet.

"And then I had two children to look after, children who reminded me of my sister and I . . . well, I broke a bit, I guess. I couldn't talk about it, didn't feel like I could admit some of the dark thoughts I was having, so I closed off. I know that. I couldn't stop it, but I knew it was happening."

Cassie didn't know what to say. She watched Claire's face, lined now, and tried to remember the younger version of her. She didn't really remember Claire as a person when she first went to live with her. She'd only been five, and all she really remembered was crying, screaming, hiding from Claire when she was called because she wanted her *mum*, not her aunt. And Tom. Always in her memories, there was Tom, comforting her.

"Abi . . ." Claire carried on. "You won't remember this, it was a long time ago, but we were close."

No, Cassie thought, she didn't remember. She barely remembered anything before her parents died, and it was something that she hated. The fact that she didn't know them, couldn't visualize them as real people.

"We argued, a lot. But we were close. And when she died . . ." Claire pressed her palms into her lap. "Well. It meant that I wasn't there for you as I should've been, and then by the time I'd sorted my own emotions out, it was too late and I didn't know how to connect with you. Either of you." She looked across the street, to the shop Linda and Hazel had disappeared into. "Thank God for Linda. She picked up the slack."

Cassie tried to figure out what to say. "Look, it's not one-sided. We—I—didn't try to connect with you either. I didn't want to," she added quietly, hating to admit it. "You weren't Mum, and even though you never tried to replace her I still wanted her, not you." That was the way it had always been with her and Claire—their shared history of grief and trauma driving them apart, rather than pulling them together.

"I didn't try to replace her, but I didn't keep her memory alive for you either," Claire said, a hint of bitterness, of self-loathing, perhaps, creeping into her voice.

"I wish I could've known them," Cassie said on a sigh.

Claire's eyes were overly bright, shining with tears. "I wish you could have, too." She smiled, though it was tinged with sadness. "I was so excited about being an aunt. I helped pick the name Cassie, you know. Tom, well, that was your dad's choice from the beginning, so your mum got to pick yours. She wanted Christina, at first."

"Christina?" Cassie asked incredulously.

Claire laughed. "I know."

"So I have you to thank for my name?"

"I guess you do." She paused, then picked up her wine, took a sip. "Your dad, he was the kindest person I knew. My boyfriend broke up with me—this was before you were born—and Abi and me, we went out to get drunk and shake it off. But Abi, she passed out early on, so David stayed up with me instead. He was so tired. I still remember it. He was studying for his master's at the time, I think—they both were. But he stayed up with me, talking all night, until I fell asleep."

"Really?" She hadn't heard that story before. She knew her parents had met at university, that they'd gone on to do their master's in conservation together, because Linda had told her, but she had never really thought of Claire being on the scene too. Which was ridiculous, now she thought about it.

"Yeah. And your mum . . . Well, she was my best friend." Her expression flashed and Cassie saw the pain, still there after all this time. "I saw a lot of that in you and Tom. It was wrong of me, but it's part of what made it so difficult to be there the way I should've. Because the two of you, when you were together, reminded me of Abi and me as kids."

Cassie let her emotions wash through her, didn't try to block them. She was learning that grief was circular, never really going away, coming around and around again. But each time, she was getting more and more able to deal with it.

"Abi . . ." Claire continued, apparently on a roll, "she was so full of life, so daring. Always wanting to try new things."

"Like Tom," Cassie said automatically, because this part she knew—Tom had inherited her mum's bravery, her zest for life. She'd heard it so many times, from various people. Tom himself had taken that on board, too.

Claire frowned a little at Cassie. "Like Tom, yes, but . . . She was like you, too. Or you're like her, I should say. You know she was worried about marrying your dad?"

Cassie felt a little jolt. "What?"

Claire nodded. "She was so scared about falling in love. You saying that to Hazel, about her never giving men a chance? Well, that was Abi. She almost didn't go through with it."

"What, really?" She didn't know how she felt about that—both that her mum had been scared and that she'd maybe not wanted to marry her dad.

Claire smiled softly. "Yes. But she loved your dad, so much. She was just worried it might be *too* much."

Claire took a sip of her wine, and Cassie let that resonate. Scared of loving too much. Sam's face flashed in her mind, even as she tried to push it away.

"And she was scared of swimming, as a child."

A memory came, of her mum clapping as Cassie floated in a pool, armbands on. It was hazy, but it was there. So maybe it wasn't all gone—there were bits of her parents she still held with her.

"She got over it, of course, but she had to work at it. And Tom, he was like your mum, yes, but he had bits of your dad in there too. They were both always willing to give people a chance."

Like Sam, Cassie thought. Tom had been willing to give Sam a chance, where Cassie wasn't.

Claire reached out, took Cassie's hand across the table. "Your mum, she got over her fear about your dad. Obviously, otherwise you wouldn't be here. She was strong, so much stronger than me. I let the grief of losing someone I loved stop me from getting close to anyone else—including you and Tom." She shook her head. "Don't become me. Don't let what's happened to you stop you taking chances elsewhere."

Cassie stared at Claire—when had she become so insightful? Claire squeezed Cassie's hand and Cassie squeezed back.

She jumped at the sound of the chair scraping out next to her, and looked up to see Hazel there. She hadn't noticed her and Linda coming back. "What do you think of our new scarves?" Hazel asked, flipping a purple scarf with a blue-and-silver pattern on it over her shoulder dramatically. "I got one for you too." She held up a deep-red scarf, dropping it around Cassie's shoulders. "It goes with your hair."

Cassie smiled, running her fingers over the soft fabric, and Claire made admiring noises as Linda and Hazel presented their purchases.

Don't let it stop you from taking chances. Claire was right. She thought of Sam, trying to tell her that he loved her. How she'd run. How her mum had nearly done that, too, apparently. Then she thought of Tom, trying to tell her she was brave. And she took a breath.

One thing at a time.

The time had come to open Tom's last clue.

Chapter Thirty-Four

"*It's just not the* same, is it?" Hazel said, leaning back against one of the faded red chairs in the Costa Coffee they were currently sitting in. The sounds of coffee beans grinding, milk being frothed, and a particularly unhappy toddler filled the coffee shop. Cassie wrinkled her nose as she took a sip of her oat milk latte—something Josh had gotten her into.

"Not quite." They'd come for a breakfast coffee before work, trying to re-create Bordeaux vibes. But a cramped Costa in the middle of central London wasn't having quite the same Zen effect as outside under the sun in France. Cassie glanced at her handbag, to where she'd stashed Tom's last clue. She'd promised herself she'd open it this morning.

"So. Have you spoken to Sam?"

Cassie jerked her head up to look at Hazel. "What? That's a bit random."

"No, it's not," Hazel insisted. "I wanted to ask in France, but I didn't want to upset you on holiday."

"And now?"

"Now I think it's time," she said simply.

Cassie gave Hazel a narrowed-eye look but when Hazel just sat there, waiting patiently, she sighed. "No, I haven't spoken to him." Hazel knew most—but not all—of what had happened in Cornwall. She knew Cassie and Sam had slept together, but

Cassie had kept the details of the argument to herself, and she'd tried to keep how she felt about it all concealed, to some degree. But Hazel knew her, and she'd picked up on some things—just as she'd picked up on things when they were teenagers.

"Has he tried to get in touch?"

Cassie squirmed. "No." And he wouldn't, she thought, not after she'd up and left him in the middle of bloody nowhere. She wouldn't have gotten in touch, either, if their situations had been reversed.

Hazel leveled a look at Cassie, leaning forward in her chair. "Cassie. Don't you think you should give him another shot?"

Cassie scowled. How long had Hazel been planning to push this on her? "This is Sam we're talking about."

Hazel nodded, her black hair swishing with the movement. "Yes, Sam. Sam, who gave up his savings to save the pub for you, who came back from New York for you, went with you to Cornwall."

Cassie pressed her lips together and said nothing.

"Don't you think he deserves another chance?" Hazel said softly.

Another chance—what, to break her heart again?

She didn't say that out loud, though, thinking it might sound a touch melodramatic, so instead she scoffed. "You're one to talk—you close yourself off all the time, you never give *anyone* a chance. How is that any different?"

Hazel didn't look at all fazed by the accusation. "I like to think that when the right guy comes along, I'll be ready, but in the meantime I genuinely am happy being single. It suits me, and I don't buy into you needing a guy to make you happy."

"Then why—?"

Hazel held up a finger. "You don't need a guy to make you

happy," she repeated, "and I'm sure you'd find a way to be happy on your own, because you are brilliant and courageous and kind and fun, with or without a guy. You've pulled yourself through the worst year imaginable, and I know you're still healing, but if you can get through that, then there's no doubt you could make a life for yourself without someone there, and I'll happily come spend time going on walks in the country or whatever with you, just the two of us, until we're too old to walk and then we'll get those little scooter things."

"Well, good," Cassie said, feeling a bit stumped. This wasn't where she'd thought this conversation would go.

"But," Hazel said pointedly, "you already have a guy. A guy who wants to be with you, who is definitely not perfect but who clearly cares about you. A guy who, let's be honest, you've been in love with for most of your life."

"I have not—"

Hazel held up a finger again and Cassie bit her lip. Maybe, she admitted, there was some truth in that.

"If you don't want to be with him because you don't love him or don't think you could love him in that way then that is totally and completely fine. But I'm not sure that is the reason. And I wouldn't be your friend if I didn't say so." She finished her coffee and got to her feet. Then smiled, and gave Cassie a swift kiss on the cheek, something which was quite uncharacteristic for Hazel. "I have to go. A motorbike advert calls. Unless . . . do you want me to stay to open the clue with you?"

Cassie hesitated, then shook her head. This last time, as with the first time, it was something she had to do on her own. She watched Hazel go, her words playing on repeat in her head. How long had she been wanting to say that? Then she squared her shoulders, and reached into her bag for the envelope. One thing at a time. Today was about Tom, not Sam.

And so, she opened the last envelope. There was no accompanying note this time, just the clue.

You may be surprised
At where this will end,
And how you take it,
Well, that will depend.
Go to the place where you dread to be,
And find the redhead who can give you the key.

P.S. I believe in you.

She read it a few times, frowning.

I believe in you.

Her heart tugged with those words. Pain, yes, but also something lighter and brighter, something that was surfacing more and more these days when she thought of Tom. It didn't make it any easier to figure out the clue, though, and she bit her lip as she read it one last time. That was OK, she told herself. She just had to give herself time. Because she found that, like Tom, she believed that she would figure it out.

Cassie smiled automatically at the people waiting in the hotel reception, who were clearly impressed with the Art Deco vibe, before taking the lift down to her little basement office. Josh grinned at her as she let herself in. "Welcome back. How was . . . What? Why are you staring at me like that?"

Cassie only continued to stare at him.

At his ginger hair.

Redhead. The place you dread to be.

Josh lurched for his phone to look at himself in his camera.

"No," Cassie said. "No, it's not you, it's . . ." She hitched in a breath. "Tom."

Josh frowned. "What?"

"Tom, he—"

But she was interrupted by Robert coming in. He glanced at Cassie. "Nice holiday?"

"Yeah," Cassie said, her voice sounding a little strangled. Work. Tom had been sending her back to work. "Yeah, it was—"

"I'm sure it was great. But look, I need you to get your head back in the game, OK? We've got a birthday party for a one-year-old to pitch for later today, and I need ideas." He left it at that, sweeping out of the office in a way that Cassie was *sure* was deliberately overdramatic.

Cassie walked up to Josh's desk the moment the office door shut. "Did Tom give you something for me?" she demanded.

Josh's expression changed. "You finished the treasure hunt?" She nodded.

He reached out, took her hands in his. "You figured it out."

She gripped his hands back, felt tears pricking her eyes. "He got you involved?"

Josh looked like he was about to cry, too. "I wasn't sure you'd do it."

"You've had it all this time? The gift?"

He nodded. "But I couldn't give it to you. I knew you had to get to the end." The phone rang and Josh picked up. "Hang on," he said, in a very unprofessional voice. He put down the phone on the desk, fumbled in his desk drawer, and got out a letter, which he handed to Cassie. Then he picked up the phone again. "So sorry about that, new assistant, doesn't know what he's doing. Can I help?"

And while Josh was dealing with the inquiry, Cassie read, hearing Tom's voice in her mind.

My favorite sis,

Congrats—you've got to the end!

But—there's a caveat. There's one more thing you need to do in order to get your epic Christmas present.

I've roped Josh in—I like him, have I ever told you that?—and he's under explicit instruction not to give it to you until you do this last task, however long that takes. I know, I know! I'm mean and a terrible big brother, etc. etc. But I reckon you'll thank me for it.

So your last task is this: quit your job. Yes, you heard me! Quit your job. It's holding you back, and your boss doesn't deserve you.

Whether you do it or not, I love you. But I hope you do. Because I think you're destined for something else.

P.S. You'll know by now about Amy, I'm sure. The baby—can you believe that, an actual baby?—is probably nearly here by the time you get to this point, if I'm right with my bets on how long this will take you. I didn't handle it right at first—you'll know that too. I got scared, about being a dad, about whether I'd know how to do it. I'm still a bit scared, truth be told, about letting them both down. I wasn't looking for this, but I think I've figured out that sometimes the best gifts in life are the ones you don't expect. So I want to go back, be there for Amy—and for my child. I'm going to take this time in Argentina to get my head straight and make sure I go back to them in the right place because I can't let her down again the way I

did when I left. I don't want my child to grow up looking
at me the way Sam looks at his dad.

But the point is, I'm not going to let being scared stop
me—or I'm going to try not to. When I get back, I'm going to
tell Amy how much I love her, how excited I am to meet our
baby. And how sorry I am, for not saying that immediately. I
love her so much, and I made a mistake, running like that. So
what I'm saying—badly (I know, I know, I'm usually more
articulate than this)—is that I don't think you should let fear
stop you.

P.P.S. If it's a boy, what do you think of the name Elton?
(Just kidding. I do like the name Noah though.)

Cassie stared at the letter, her heart murmuring in her chest,
the paper gripped tightly between her fingers. She focused on
the last bit first. He'd made a mistake with Amy. Relief coursed
through her. He'd planned to come back, and hadn't had the
chance to tell her, to explain, before he'd died. He'd wanted the
baby, had wanted to be with her. He hadn't abandoned her. Sam
had been right.

Then, she took stock of the rest of it. He wanted her to quit
her job? That was completely insane. "He's telling me to resign,"
she said out loud, her voice a little hoarse.

He gave her a little smile. "Yeah."

"But . . . I can't. I can't just quit!"

"Why not?"

What kind of stupid question was that? she thought silently.
There was a whole multitude of reasons. Money. Career. Security.

Josh seemed to read all this on her face. "You'd get another
job like this, if that's what you wanted," he said reasonably. "But

you're trapped here. Tom knew it. I know it. You are brilliant at what you do, but you don't love it here."

Cassie stared at him. "So you're not going to give me the gift? Even after . . . everything?" After they kept it from her—him, Linda, Hazel. All of them part of it. And even though Tom couldn't have known that this would be the last treasure hunt she'd ever do, it felt somehow right that her friends had been involved. It felt right that they'd kept the clues to themselves, had allowed her another gift entirely, in figuring it all out herself, no matter the ups and downs.

"I have to think it's what Tom would have wanted," Josh said gently.

Cassie stood there, the letter still in her hand, her mind reeling. Robert bustled back in, frowned at her. "Why are you still standing up? Have you even logged on yet?"

She took in his ugly, pouting face, his receding hairline. And she realized. They were right. *Tom* was right. She didn't want to be here. She wanted to be doing her own thing. She was scared. But that didn't make her a coward—she could be scared and brave. So she straightened her spine, and spoke before she could think better of it.

"No."

Robert stared at her. "What?"

"No. I haven't logged on, because . . ." She looked at Josh, who nodded. "Because I quit." She realized then that she had no idea how to officially resign. Saying "I quit" was the type of thing that sounded good, in theory, but actually left you with no idea what to do next. Surely there was a way to officially resign? Notice to be worked? And, God, she was overthinking it—her brain was definitely doing its best to take away from her moment.

"I quit," she said again. "And I'll . . ." What? What did she say now? "Well, I won't be working here any longer."

Robert's face went from blank to seething, his jaw clenched, eyes flashing, and she knew he was ready to jump on this, that he was about to tell her to get out, in that case. She knew that would ruin it, would make her panic about it, so she grabbed her bag and practically ran out of the office door, up the stairs to the reception area.

She heard Josh following her, spun to face him. He was grinning. "Here," he said, thrusting an envelope into her hands. "You forgot this." He gave her a wink, then dashed back to the office, no doubt to face Robert's fury.

It was just like the others: a small, white envelope. No number on it, but a little man doing a victory dance was drawn on the front. There was a speech bubble coming from the little man's mouth.

You did it.

She blew out a breath as she stepped out of the hotel onto the pavement. She had. She'd done it. She'd gotten to the end.

She opened the envelope, and when she saw what her gift was, what Tom had been gearing up to all this time, she felt all the blood rush from her head.

The house. In Wales. Tiff's house.

Tom wanted her to buy it. And he'd given her the means to do it.

Chapter Thirty-Five

Cassie stood next to Amy in the little second bed-room of her flat, which she'd converted into a nursery. Amy's little boy was asleep, tiny pudgy hands clenched into fists, little chubby legs wriggling every now and then. Tom's nose, she decided. He had Tom's nose. Maybe he'd look more like him as he grew up, although right now that was all she could see. But that little part, well, it proved it, didn't it? There was a part of Tom still here, right in front of her.

She dashed away a tear as she watched him sleep and Amy put an arm around her. "Sorry," Cassie whispered, and Amy shook her head. They stayed like that for a moment longer, then crept out of the bedroom and into the living room.

Cassie made Amy sit while she made them two herbal teas, then carried them to the sofa and sat down next to her. Amy's parents were out at the moment, so it was just the two of them, but Amy had told her that her mum was staying another two months to help out. Even with the help, Amy looked knackered: dark circles under her eyes, her curly hair done up loosely in a bun on top of her head—no headband—her face pale. Still, when she smiled at Cassie, it looked genuine.

"I'm sorry I haven't come by more," Cassie said.

Amy blew on her tea. "Don't be silly. I wouldn't have been much fun before now, anyway. Although, I still don't feel normal. Mum keeps saying I'm going to have to get used to a new normal."

"I knew your parents were here," Cassie explained, still feeling the need to justify, "and I didn't want to, I don't know, get in the way or intrude or whatever."

"Don't be silly. You're his auntie, you could never intrude."

Cassie felt her eyes burn a little at that, took a sip of her tea to hide it. "So. Have you settled on Albert for sure now? That's the name you were going for last time we spoke, I think?"

Amy wrinkled her nose. "Oh yes. The Albert phase. I don't know what I was thinking there. It must have been the hormones or lack of sleep or something."

Cassie's lips twitched. "So no Albert?" She had to admit, she was a little relieved about that.

"No. I've been toying with Leo, but I'm not quite sure. It's ridiculous that I still can't decide, I know, and I have to soon, but it's just, nothing seems quite *right* somehow."

"In that case," Cassie said slowly, "there might be another name to consider." She slipped Tom's letter out of her handbag, saw Amy frowning at it. "It's the letter Tom left for me, when I did the final clue." She held it out gently. "I think you might want to read it." She waited while Amy read, watched her frown even out, watched her blink as she took in the words. Watched as she hitched in a sobbing breath when she got to the last part.

"He was going to come back."

Cassie nodded. "He was. He loved you, Amy."

Amy met Cassie's gaze. "Thank you for showing me." She held the letter back out to her and Cassie reached out to take it, but Amy's fingers tightened on the paper. "Sorry," she said. "I know it's yours, I just . . ." Cassie gently pried Amy's fingers away, then looked down at the letter. She made a crease with her nails, then tore off the P.S. section, handed it back to Amy.

Amy looked down, and then, with another sob, took it, gripped it in her fist. "Thank you," she whispered, then took a shaking breath. "So, Noah, hey?"

"Not that there's any pressure," Cassie said quickly. "I just . . . I thought you might like to know."

"I quite like it, I think."

Cassie smiled. "Me too."

Amy placed the note on her lap, like she couldn't bring herself to put it away just yet. "So. Wales?"

Cassie laughed, the sound a little incredulous. "So it seems."

Tom had spoken to Tiff in December last year, apparently. He'd talked through prices, said he'd be in touch again during the following year. And then, Tiff had told her when she'd rung, she'd heard nothing. Obviously. Tiff hadn't realized that Cassie was Tom's sister, hadn't connected the dots to the chap on the phone last year. But, yes, it was still for sale and yes, she'd love to talk through the details with Cassie directly.

Tom had used his half of their inheritance, put it in an account in her name, ready and waiting, should she want to use it. It was an *investment*, his note in the envelope had explained. He would be a shareholder in the business.

"You're really going to go through with it? Just up and buy this place? Leave London?"

"I really am." Linda had convinced her, had told her it didn't *have* to be permanent—nothing had to be permanent. But if she didn't try, how would she ever know? There was a lot of work to be done. Things wouldn't be ready for some time. But she had plans—and now, she had money to start her on her way, plus her own inheritance money. She was going to try. If she failed, that was OK. But she was going to try. She was going to be brave.

And with that in mind, there was one more thing she had to do.

She stood outside the front door, staring at the slightly peeling green paint, trying to psych herself up to knock. *Come on, Cassie.* If she could quit her job, abandon her London life for bloody Wales, and start a whole new business venture, then she could do this. Because Hazel had been right. It was stupid to pretend that Sam didn't have a place in her heart. She'd tried to shove him out. Tried, and failed.

She'd found out where he lived from his mum. He'd been in London for three months now, apparently. Since Cornwall. They'd been in the same city, all over the summer, and never seen each other. Which made sense, she supposed, given the size of London, but still, it didn't stop the nerves on her skin from prickling at the thought that he'd been here the whole time.

She brought her hand halfway to the door, paused. *Get a bloody grip, Cassie.* She knocked.

It took five agonizing seconds before the door opened. And when it did, Cassie's heart stumbled, then seemed to fall into her stomach.

Jessica. It was Jessica standing there, one hand resting on the doorframe. Her auburn hair seemed to shine as she pushed it back from her face, and Cassie felt, in that moment, ridiculously short and frumpy, next to Jessica's tall elegance.

"Cassie!" she exclaimed, perhaps a little too enthusiastically, then smiled uncertainly. "How are you?" she asked in that sexy Irish lilt.

"I'm . . ." But she couldn't think what to say. They were back together. They were *living* together.

"Jess?" It was Sam's voice, calling from inside the house. The sound of it reverberated through Cassie. "Who is it?"

"It's—"

"No," Cassie said quickly, cutting her off. It had been stupid, she realized, to come here. Stupid to think that Sam would just be waiting around for her.

Jessica frowned. "You don't want to see Sam?"

"No," Cassie said again, knowing that she must look utterly ridiculous, showing up at Sam's doorstep and then refusing to see him. "No, it's OK. Sorry, I . . . I have to go, actually." She backed away a step. Thank God. Thank God *Sam* hadn't answered the door, that she hadn't blurted out some stupid declaration of love, or asked him to come to Wales or something equally ridiculous.

"OK," Jessica said, looking perplexed. "Do you want me to give him a message?"

"No, that's OK," Cassie said, already turning to walk away, to get out of there. Did Jessica know? Cassie wondered. Had Sam told her what had happened in Cornwall?

"Cassie?" Jessica called from behind her, and Cassie turned back. Jessica smiled, and it was impossible, right then, to hate her, even though she wanted to, because there was such genuine warmth in that smile. "You look really well." She hesitated, like she wanted to say something more, but only smiled one more time, and closed the door.

Cassie refused to look back as she walked away, kept her head high, just in case anyone was watching. Of course. Of *course* Sam had gone back to Jessica—he'd been due to *marry* her in March, for God's sake. And she was beautiful, and clever, and kind. Would they get married? she wondered briefly. Sam had clearly lost it a bit after Tom died—just like she had—but now that he was healing, would that still be in the cards?

Stop it, she told herself. There was no point going down that road, even as her stomach churned, nausea swelling and burning the back of her throat. It was her fault, wasn't it? She'd accused him of being too scared to go back to Jessica, and now he'd done just that. She'd driven him back to his ex-fiancée, because she'd refused to admit that he was right, that she loved him too.

And now it was too late.

She took a breath, squashed down the feeling. She'd had the chance to say it back to him, to see whether they might finally be able to make something between them. She hadn't taken it, and now she would just have to live with that.

So she'd go to Wales, and she'd find a way to pour life into that beautiful house. She'd honor Tom with that. And she'd leave Sam Malone, and her feelings for him, firmly behind.

Chapter Thirty-Six

Sam hovered on the stairs on the way back from the bathroom, reading a message on his phone. A reply, to a message he'd sent a few days ago.

That would be great, I'd love to see you. How about next Thursday?

He stared at the message from his dad. But he'd gone there—it had been him who had gotten in touch, who had made the first move this time. He remembered what Cassie had told him, back in Cornwall. About wishing she'd had more time with her parents. It was part of the reason he'd reached out.

Great, he typed back. **See you then.**

Maybe he and his dad would never be best friends or have a perfect father-son relationship. But maybe they could have *some* kind of relationship. And maybe he could let go of the anger that he'd been carrying around for as long as he could remember. He could try, at least.

He shoved his phone back into his trouser pocket and walked into the kitchen of the little one-bed flat he was renting out in Peckham. Jessica was standing there by the kettle, waiting for it to boil. Whoever had been at the door had clearly gone. Wrong house, probably.

Jessica was scrolling through her phone, still wearing her smart dress and tights from the day, her auburn hair falling in waves around her shoulders, looking perfectly made-up after a day at the office. How did she do that? he wondered. He was sure he looked like a mess after a day at his desk, then fighting for space on the Jubilee Line home, before hitting the overground that did, at least, have more space. She glanced at him as he got two mugs down from the cupboard and put a teabag in each one automatically, before noticing the subtle raised-eyebrow look she was giving him.

"Right," he muttered, and bent down to get a teapot—dusty from lack of use—out of the bottom cupboard. She always liked tea to be done *properly*, Jess.

"So," she said, perhaps a touch too brightly. "How was your day?" She poured hot water into the teapot, then carried it to the small kitchen table, where they both sat, waiting for the tea to brew.

Sam grunted and shrugged noncommittally. He was back working as a solicitor. He'd caved in the end, mainly because he'd had no idea what else to do. He was no longer at Jessica's firm, but her dad had not, apparently, wanted to ruin his reputation completely, so he'd taken a job at another firm right in the middle of central London. He'd only been at it two months, and the grind was already getting to him.

"You?" he asked, feeling the weight of the brief silence. The awkwardness hung between them—and really, what had he expected? Actually, he'd expected a lot worse. He'd expected her to shout at him or something, given it was the first time they were meeting up since he'd left her. It was why he'd invited her to his house, rather than meeting up somewhere public—both so she could rage at him, if she wanted to, without worrying about what other people were thinking, and so that he didn't have to deal with other people knowing just what a dick he'd been. But she'd been polite, calm. She'd always been in control, Jess—probably why she was so good at her job—but she seemed settled now, too, in a way he wasn't sure he'd ever noticed before.

"Oh, you know, the same." She waved a hand in the air.

But she loved it, Sam knew. She'd always loved what she did, and he had no doubt that she'd take over from her dad one day as head of the firm.

"So," Jessica said, the word loaded.

"So."

She laughed a little. "Oh God. I didn't expect this to be so awkward."

Sam smiled wryly, but said nothing. Because he *had* expected it to be awkward—but then, he'd walked out on her, not the other way around. Sam's phone vibrated in his pocket, and he slipped it out, grateful for the distraction as Jessica poured the tea. His heart did an automatic little lurch, like it seemed to do nearly constantly when he got messages these days.

Stupid, to think it might be Cassie. Why would she randomly be texting him? She never had before. But it still felt as if a part of him was waiting for her to get in touch. Then again, maybe it was better that she didn't. Maybe it was better that the whole thing, whatever that was, stayed closed.

He opened up the message from Sheila, frowning because they'd had barely any contact since he'd left New York.

Hey honey. Someone sent me this, just passing it on in case of interest. X

Along with the message there was a link, which, when Sam clicked on it, turned out to be an advert for a job. A job, working as a climbing instructor. It was a short-term thing, for two months this autumn. Teaching, running workshops, that kind of thing. The pay was terrible. And it was in Wales, in the middle of fucking nowhere. He couldn't do it. It would be irresponsible of him, when he'd only just gotten his shit together again.

Jessica glanced down at his phone. "What's that?"

"It's . . ." He looked up at her as he put the phone to one side. "It's a climbing job—someone in New York sent it to me in case I was interested. But I'm not," he said quickly, feeling the need to explain, for some reason.

She met his gaze head on, in that very direct way of hers. "Why not?"

He ran a hand across the back of his neck. "I don't know. Because it's silly. A job for a twenty-year-old, not someone who should be halfway up the career ladder by now."

"But you *are* halfway up the career ladder. And you hate it."

He grimaced. "It'd be like my dad," he said quietly. "Taking a short-term job, jumping around all over the place. It's flighty."

"It doesn't have to be. Not if it's something you love, something that means something to you. Did you enjoy it?"

"Yeah. I guess I did." It had certainly been better than being stuck in an office, at any rate.

"Well then." She gave him a small smile and he knew it meant this was the end of the small talk.

"I'm so sorry, Jessica."

"So you've said," she said wryly. And he had, over message, but still . . .

"I mean it," he said. "I shouldn't have hurt you like that. If I could take it back, I would."

She nodded slowly. "Would you go through with it, if you could do it again? The wedding," she clarified, when he stared at her.

"I . . ." He swallowed. "I would do things differently." It wasn't the whole truth. He knew now, as he'd known then, that marrying Jessica was not the right thing to do. But it felt callous to say it out loud, and he didn't want to hurt her any more than he already had.

She nodded again, processing. Then she picked up her tea, took a sip. "I was so mad," she said. And for a moment, the calm expression dropped and her eyes flashed. "God, if you could've seen. I smashed up the wedding cake." She laughed a little, even though there was nothing remotely funny about it.

"I'm sorry," he said again, wishing that he could come up with something more adequate. But there was nothing, really. Nothing that could take away what he'd put her through.

She set down her tea. "I know you are." She ran a hand through her waves, then shook her hair out, the auburn shimmering. "And I know I kept pushing. After Tom, when you fell apart like that, I didn't know what else to do but pretend it was fine and push ahead with it." *Fell apart like that.* He supposed that was what had happened. She drew her shoulders up. "And so, I have things I'm sorry about too. I'm not saying it's my fault," she said. "At all. But it wasn't right, to have the wedding then, and I should've acknowledged that sooner, should've tried to be there for you in the way you needed, rather than just thinking about what I wanted."

God, she really was something. How many people would be able to deal with being left at the altar and stay so calm, so rational?

"For a while, afterward," she continued, staring at her tea, "I thought that we should get back together." His stomach lurched a little, though he said nothing, let her continue. *Closure,* she'd said, when she asked to meet. She wanted closure. So the least he could do was listen to what she had to say. "After I got over the mad part, I mean." Her eyebrows pulled together. "Well, mostly over it, in any case." She looked up from her tea. "But I've had some time to think and I . . ." She blew out a breath. "I don't think we were right together, not really. I don't think I was the one for you." It was what he'd said to Cassie—or a version of it, anyway, when she'd accused him of not sorting things out with Jessica.

Jessica cocked her head at him, all beautiful angles and sculpted cheekbones. "I think . . . I think I was trying to make you fit with what I wanted."

"And I wasn't? What you wanted?"

She laughed, and it sounded so genuine. "The problem is, I think you were trying to make yourself fit too. Even now . . ." She leveled a look at him. "I love my job. I love what I do, and I want to stay in London, stay with my dad's firm. What about you?"

"I don't . . ." He couldn't finish the sentence. Couldn't say that the vision she'd just conjured up in his mind made him feel all itchy and sticky, like he needed to get outside for some air. She nodded, and he knew he didn't have to finish. She got it.

"I was hoping I'd be enough, in the long run, to make you stay, but I've realized, with a bit of time—and maybe, OK, a bit of therapy . . ." she shot him a grin that he did his best to return, "that it wasn't fair, on either of us. You didn't love me, not in the way that I need."

"You deserve better," he said. "I was never good enough for you."

She reached out across the table, laid her hand over his. "It wasn't just you. I don't think *I* loved *you* in the way you deserve, either. Because if I had, I wouldn't have pushed ahead. I would have seen what you needed. I thought . . . I thought I under- stood about Tom, but really, I just wanted to make it better the way *I* thought it should be, the way I wanted it to be, and I . . ." She shook her head as she broke off. "You're a good person, whether you believe that or not, and you do deserve to be happy. And me . . . I wasn't going to make you happy." She paused, then said, "This life, it's not going to make you happy, either."

He let it settle. Wondered briefly what would have happened if Tom were still here. Would he have gone through with it? Would Tom have convinced him to walk down the aisle, to keep walking this path, as he'd once thought he would? Or would he have made him see, before the wedding day, that it wasn't right? Tom was never one to push, so maybe he wouldn't have said anything, unless it became clear that Sam wasn't happy. But he had a flash, then, of telling Tom that he and Jessica were engaged. Remembered Tom's face, considering.

If you're happy, I'm happy.

That's all he'd ended up saying, but Sam wondered now if there was something more. If Tom had known, back then, that it wasn't right.

He slid his hand out from under Jessica's, reached out to tuck her hair behind her ear in a friendly gesture. "I'm sorry. I wish it was different. I wish I could've been the one to give you what you need. I wish . . ." He broke off. *I wish I could love you* sounded just a tiny bit harsh, didn't it? Even if, on some level, he knew that he'd never loved Jessica deeply enough, never loved her in that way that made you hurt. Never loved her in the way he loved Cassie.

"You know what my dad says," she said wryly. "Wishes won't get you riches."

He let out a huffing laugh. "Right. Though it's not really *that* great a saying, I have to admit." He sighed. "I don't know how you can even consider forgiving me."

She raised her eyebrows. "Who said I've forgiven you completely?" She laughed when he grimaced. "I think fifty percent forgiveness is about all you can hope for."

"I'll take it," Sam said immediately, and Jessica grinned.

Then her expression grew more serious. "I've told you," she said. "I had my own visions of that day, and I didn't take into account that you'd just lost your best friend, that you were grieving, that you had your own demons. We were both being selfish, I suppose." She wrinkled her nose. "I don't recommend that you do it to anyone else, though—being left at the altar sucks." She gave him a little punch on the arm, and he laughed, though the sound was weary.

"Noted." He got to his feet, feeling odd now, sitting there. "Will you be OK?"

"Yeah. I think I will." She stood too and they both walked automatically to the front door. "Will you?"

"Yeah," he said. And one way or another, he would be. He'd figure something out.

"Think about what I said, OK?" He frowned. "About the climbing job. Because, well, following a dream, an ambition . . . Going after something you enjoy, it's not flighty, Sam. Running toward, well, that's different to running away, now, isn't it?"

"Since when did you get so wise?"

She rolled her eyes. "I have *always* been wise." She opened the front door, started to step outside, then looked back at him. "Sam?"

"Yeah?"

"It was Cassie, at the door earlier." His heart jolted. Literally jolted, sending his body into mini spasm, just at the sound of her name. Jessica's lips curved into a soft, understanding smile. Like she knew, somehow, even though he'd never said anything to her. "I just thought you should know."

Chapter Thirty-Seven

Sam sent his dad a quick message, explaining that he might be a bit late to meet him, figuring that, all things considered, his dad could wait thirty minutes, if need be. He shoved his phone away in his pocket, then rolled his shoulders a few times to relieve the tension. He looked up at the block of flats, toward the window he knew was Cassie and Hazel's living room.

He reached out, pressed the buzzer, and was let in. He tried not to think as he climbed the stairs. Thinking about what he should say would just fuck up his mind. It had taken him five days after Jessica had told him it had been Cassie at the front door to work up the courage to come here, and he wasn't backing out now.

It was Hazel who opened the door. She frowned. "You're not my takeaway."

"Err, no."

She looked at him for a moment more with those very direct green eyes, then stepped aside. "Well, come on in, Malone." She closed the door behind him, gave him a hug. There was something so simple, so easy about Hazel.

"So," she said. "Coming over for a girls' night in? I've got some face masks stored away for emergencies if you fancy it?"

"Ah . . ." He glanced around the flat, down to where he knew

Cassie's room was. He'd never been in there, but he'd seen her come out of it while he and Tom waited for her.

Hazel walked to the little kitchen/living space. He followed automatically. "Cassie's not here." She picked up a bottle of red wine off the counter, poured two glasses and handed one to him without asking. "It's from Bordeaux," she added.

He took the wine automatically. "When will she be back?" And would it be weird, to wait for her indefinitely? Why hadn't he thought about that beforehand?

"She's in Wales," Hazel said bluntly. "She left yesterday."

"She's in ..." It hit him then, straight in the gut. "The house." He remembered Tom talking a bit about it, at the end of last year. He hadn't gotten the ins and outs of it, but he remembered— that was what the treasure hunt was leading to. A house, in Wales, for Cassie to start her own business.

So that must mean..."She finished it? She finished the treasure hunt?"

Hazel smiled, nodded. "She did."

Was that what she'd come round to tell him? Had she wanted to make the point that she'd done it, after he'd accused her of being too scared to get to the end? It hadn't been fair of him, to snap that in her face. And he hadn't been thinking of that, not really. He'd just wanted her to own up to her feelings for him, because he knew that, unlike the twenty-year-old girl she'd once been, the one who'd held such certainty about him, this Cassie was too afraid to go there.

"And she's gone? Already?" Hazel nodded. So much for her not being brave, Jesus.

"So she quit her job and everything?" For a moment, he wanted Hazel to say no, that she'd just gone to Wales to scope out the landscape. Then he felt immediately guilty for it. He wanted this for Cassie. Regardless of the fact that it meant she wouldn't be here, near him, he still wanted it for her.

"Yep."

"Wow."

"I know. Our girl's got guts." *Our girl.* Did she mean anything by that? he wondered. Either way, it sent another punch to his stomach.

"Yeah," he murmured. "Yeah, she does." So, she'd left. She'd actually left. Maybe, then, she'd just come to his door to say goodbye.

"How long is she there for?"

"I don't know. For good, I think, if it works out." *For good.* She was gone, for good.

He took another sip of his wine, suddenly feeling like he needed it. "How is she?" he asked, and Hazel smiled.

"Good, I think. I'm going to visit her—and the house—next week." She hesitated. "You could come too, you know."

Could he? Just show up, with Hazel, like that? "I . . ." He cleared his throat. "Thanks. I'll think about it," he lied. It now felt ridiculous to have come here in the first place. *She'd* left *him* after all. She'd made it perfectly clear she didn't feel the same—or didn't want to feel the same. She'd walked away from him in Cornwall—and then she'd done the same when she came to his house. He was stupid, to cling on to hope. She was doing what was right for her, and he was proud of her for that. And maybe, now, he needed to do what was right for him, too.

"Thanks, Hazel." He put the remainder of his wine down on the countertop. "I, err, best be going."

"All right." She gave him a quick, hard hug then stepped back. "I'm still rooting for you, don't you worry."

"Huh?"

She smiled. "You know what I mean." His stomach did that little squirm thing. Maybe at the thought that she was implying that she knew everything—and, let's be honest, Cassie probably *had* told her everything. "You know, you can be a bit of an idiot sometimes, but I always liked you."

Sam snorted quietly at the half-compliment, then sighed.

"Not like her, then," he said, before he could stop himself.

But that only made her grin. "Now you know that's not true."

But he didn't, did he? That was the problem. He couldn't separate what he'd *felt* from her, and what she'd said.

He walked down the two flights of stairs, stepped back out into the autumn chill. Watched a bus pass him, jammed full of people. Then he got out his phone. Opened the message from Sheila, stared at it. And, with something he couldn't quite identify in his gut, he clicked on the link.

Three Months Later

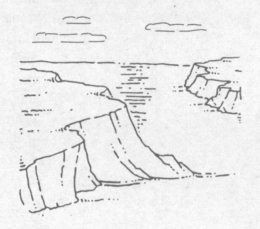

Chapter Thirty-Eight

Sam's breath misted out in front of him as he crossed the church graveyard, merging into the gray around him, brought on by the overcast sky threatening rain—or snow, if the hopefuls on the radio were to be believed. He passed the old crumbling gravestones, ones which had long since been forgotten, and headed across to the newer part of the graveyard, the dampness of the grass seeping through his shoes.

There was a nod to it being the week of Christmas at the church, with a Christmas tree outside, modestly decorated with white fairy lights, and there were wreaths on some of the gravestones from where loved ones had come to visit. He saw, from a few steps away, that there was no wreath on Tom's, though. Should he have brought one? No, he thought, Tom wouldn't have cared. He doubted he would have cared about the flowers, either, but he couldn't show up empty-handed.

He reached the gravestone, set down the bunch of flowers he'd bought from the local flower shop. He'd gone with the florist's recommendation, something bright, but not too in-your-face. There was a metal container with holes in the top, but there were already flowers there, someone else having recently come to visit. So he set his next to them, on top of the stone. His eyes traced Tom's name, gold on orange-and-black granite. Cassie would have chosen it, he realized—she was the next of kin. And it suited him. It was bright, stood out, like he'd done in life.

It had been a year now since Tom had died. Exactly a year. And it felt both like no time had passed, like there might be a chance it hadn't really happened at all, and like an impossible, infinite amount of time had gone by, time weighted by the absence of his best friend.

He hadn't been to the grave since the funeral. He'd made excuses to himself—he'd had wedding prep, been in New York, London, then had this climbing gig in Wales. But really, he just hadn't been able to face it.

"I'm sorry about that, mate," he said quietly, resting one hand on the cold granite. "It's been hard, getting by without you. And I miss you." He blew out a breath, watched the mist hover before disappearing. "God, I miss you. You would love Wales. I know, I know, it sounds boring, doesn't it? But it's actually cool and kind of beautiful. And it's fun, teaching the kids. Fun seeing some of them want to hate you when they come because they've been shipped off by their parents or are trying to play it cool, and fun winning them round. You would've been great at it."

He was going back to Wales now: he had decided to commit to moving there, seeing how it went. He'd come to visit his mum for a bit but he knew that, for now, Wales was where he wanted to be. And though he was slightly playing it by ear, the manager at the temporary gig had been impressed with him, asked him to stay on. He thought that he'd like to set something like that up himself one day. Set it up as a charity, maybe, work with disadvantaged kids and give them a chance to get out, do something physical. He still had lots to figure out on that front, but he reckoned he could do it.

He'd managed to find a little cottage in Snowdonia, close to both the beach and the mountains. He was loving the country-side more than he'd thought he would, having always been drawn to the city as a teenager. But he felt like he could breathe, really breathe, for the first time in a long time. A little like when he'd been in Cornwall, with Cassie.

"Cassie's OK too," he whispered to Tom, feeling like he had to reassure his friend. "But you probably know that. She's prob-ably been here, right?" Today? he wondered. Would she have come too, on the anniversary of his death? "But if she hasn't, don't be too hard on her. It broke her a bit, when you died, I think. She loved you so much. But she's tougher than she looks, and I think, I really think, she'll be OK. I . . ." His throat closed. It felt odd, to talk about her like this, almost like he was lying to Tom, somehow. What would he have thought, about Sam hav-ing feelings for her? Feelings that he hadn't ever been able to make go away. "I guess all I can say is I'm not going to hurt her. That's why I've let her be, OK? I'll figure it out, but she's going to be OK." He said it firmly, then clapped the top of the grave-stone, the way he would have clapped Tom on the back.

He turned, picking up two more bunches of flowers. Smaller, but still beautiful. He'd brought them for Tom and Cassie's par-ents, who were buried here, right next to their son. He remem-bered coming here one year. It had been Mother's Day, and Cassie had made a card for her mum at school. They'd put it in a plastic wallet to protect it from the rain, set it on the grave, and they'd stood, Tom and Sam each holding one of Cassie's hands. Too young, really, to know what to do, to say, but they'd all stayed there together in solidarity, looking at the picture that Cassie had drawn.

Sam had gone home to his mum afterward and hugged her, stayed with her while she was cooking, worried about leaving her alone, and she'd let him be, singing to herself as she made spaghetti bolognese, like she knew he didn't want to talk, just be there.

He'd always admired the two of them, for getting through it, for growing up without their parents and being OK. Then Cassie had lost Tom too. And still, she'd managed to get through the year, had quit her job, moved somewhere completely new. Jesus, how strong did you have to be to come through that still fighting? The thought of it made him miss her more than ever. Physically miss her, something inside him aching at the thought that she was out there, living her life away from him.

"I'll see you, mate," he whispered, his voice thick and a little pained. He brushed his hand over Tom's gravestone, a hard lump in his throat that wouldn't go away no matter how many times he swallowed. And that was OK. It was OK to feel like that, to want to cry. Because it was evidence that Tom had meant something, wasn't it? Evidence that he wouldn't be forgotten.

He took a deep shuddering breath, then turned away, back through the graveyard, past the Christmas tree outside the church and along the gravel pathway to the parking lot. He nodded to someone coming up the path the other way, someone else with flowers in their hand and a lost loved one to grieve.

He got to the parking lot, the sound of his shoes crunching on gravel strangely soothing, and held up the key to unlock his car. Then he jerked to a stop.

His dad was there, getting out of his car, slamming the door behind him. They'd met up once, in London, and it had been awkward and uncomfortable. But they'd talked, a bit—just small talk, nothing serious—and most noticeably, neither of them had yelled at the other. His dad had promised to be in touch more, but Sam hadn't really believed him. Too many years of being let down for things to be smoothed over by one drink. Yet here he was now.

"What are you doing here?" It came out a little harsher than he'd meant it to.

His dad cleared his throat. "Your mum, she thought I might find you here. She said you were on your way back to Wales, but stopping here first."

Sam shoved his hands into his pockets, not knowing what else to do with them. "Well, yeah," he said. Because it was true, he'd give him that.

"You spending Christmas in Wales?" Clearly batting for small talk, then.

"Yeah." It had felt right, to spend it there this year. He'd felt like he needed to be away, because last Christmas here had been so shrouded in grief. He wasn't running, and he remembered what Jessica had said: running toward was not the same as running away. And so it seemed right, to be spending this Christmas and New Year's somewhere where he was starting something new, making a new path in life, as his mum would say. She'd gotten it. And actually, she and Linda were going out to spend New Year's with Claire in Bordeaux. Linda seemed determined to make a little friendship group there, though why now, he had no idea. Maybe it was Tom. Maybe it all came back to Tom. His mum hadn't mentioned Cassie's name, so he supposed she wasn't going, though what she was doing for Christmas and New Year's, if anything, he had no idea.

His dad was still looking at him, shifting from foot to foot. "I just came to see if you fancied getting a coffee or something, before you leave."

Sam hesitated, then shrugged. It was going to take both of them working at it, after all, for anything to change. "Yeah. All right."

He continued to his car, assuming that his dad would get in his own, follow him. "Sam, wait." He turned back. His dad hadn't moved. "I should've stuck around more before now," he blurted out.

Sam raised his eyebrows. "Yeah," he agreed. "I suppose you should've."

His dad gave him a slightly sheepish look. "Your mum, she told me to be honest."

"Did she now?"

His dad looked down at the ground. "I never really found what I was looking for. Or if I did, I didn't fight hard enough to keep it." He looked up. "I loved your mum. I did. But then we had you and I . . ." He shook his head. "I was scared I'd fuck it up. A kid, big responsibility, that."

Sam flinched. A big responsibility, yes. One he should've stuck with. But then, he thought of Tom. Of how Tom had panicked when he'd found out Amy was pregnant. How he wasn't sure he could go through with it, be a father, not yet. Sam thought he would have come around. He was almost sure of it. But even so, Tom, the best person he knew, had panicked and bolted at the thought of it. It was easier not to judge when it was your best mate, not your dad. But still.

"It was better," his dad continued, "to not do it at all than do it badly. And then, well, I got scared to come back, because you were growing into this person I didn't know. And I was worried about letting you down if I stayed."

Sam nodded slowly, not sure what to say to it all. It wasn't like they had a precedent for these kind of chats.

His dad took a deep breath. "I'm sorry, all right? It doesn't mean I wasn't wondering, all this time, how you were doing. When I heard you got that fancy lawyer job in London, I couldn't believe it. It just made it harder—no way you'd want to know someone like me, not when you'd turned out so much better, actually made something of yourself."

Sam ran a hand across the back of his neck. "Well, I'm no longer a fancy lawyer, if it makes you feel any better."

"Never liked lawyers," his dad said quickly, and Sam laughed, something in him loosening.

"Any reason we're having this conversation in the cold? Or shall we go and get that coffee?"

His dad followed behind him in his own car to the nearest coffee shop. As he drove, Sam couldn't help replaying the conversation. One part in particular stuck out. *I didn't fight hard enough to keep it.* And Sam knew, that was him. That was what he was doing, with Cassie. And yes, maybe she didn't feel the same. Maybe she really didn't love him. But if he didn't even try, if he didn't fight for her, then how would he ever know?

Chapter Thirty-Nine

"*Ready?*" *Hazel looked at* Cassie and Josh, all of them sitting around a white-clothed table. "On three." She counted, and they all pulled their crackers at the same time. Cassie, sitting in the middle of the two of them, was left with the straggly silver-and-gold ends of both of theirs. Hazel handed Cassie her extra one, and they all took out the contents.

They were in a Thai restaurant in central London, one of the chains—a smaller chain with really good Thai food, but still a chain. It wasn't exactly ideal for a Christmassy lunch, but Cassie and Josh were both broke, and had needed to come somewhere cheap: Cassie, because she was spending time getting the house event-ready, and consequently living off savings and earning no money, and Josh because he'd left the hotel too, claiming that it was unbearable without Cassie there, and was concentrating on his master's instead. Hazel had offered to pay for them both and take them out for a "proper" Christmas lunch, but they'd refused on principle. So there they were, ordering rice, noodles, and Thai green curry on the twenty-third of December. The restaurant had made an effort—crackers on the tables, tinsel in the window, and a little Christmas tree at the register. It was a slightly odd yet somehow great combination.

Following Josh's and Hazel's lead, Cassie put her red paper Christmas hat on, then cleared her throat as she extracted the little slip of paper from the cracker. "What did Adam say the day before Christmas?"

Hazel rolled her eyes. "It's Christmas, Eve."

Cassie put it down. "Yeah. Well, I don't think it's *that* obvious," she said, feeling oddly defensive of her joke despite the fact she hadn't come up with it.

"Hey, I wouldn't have got that either," Josh said, "so don't worry. OK, do mine. What's the most popular Christmas wine?" He didn't pause for either of them to guess. "But I don't like Brussels sprouts! Get it? Whiiinne," he added for effect in a whiny voice.

Hazel wrinkled her noise. "My favorite wine is Malbec."

Cassie prodded her in the ribs. "Your turn."

She flapped a hand at Cassie. "No, I don't want to tell jokes, I want to hear about Wales. Is it devastatingly moody? Is the house looking gorgeous now? Are you incredibly content and feeling very smug? Come on, make us jealous." She settled back in her chair, clasped her hands together in front of her, like she was settling in for a good story.

"But not *too* jealous," Josh added, moving his paper crown so that it sat a little crooked on his red hair. "Like, have a heart for those of us stuck in London running in and out of temp jobs too."

"Or those of us in advertising meetings where you spend forty minutes discussing which blue color scheme to go for."

"Right, so, like, maybe it can be eighty percent brilliant and twenty percent not?"

Hazel looked at Josh a little musingly. "Maybe seventy-thirty?"

"Yes," Josh agreed, then looked at Cassie. "Go."

Cassie laughed. "It's . . ." She lifted both hands in the air, let them fall back to her lap. "I don't know. It's hard work, but it *is* brilliant. I think it'll be ready to open in March—and you both have to come. I'm going to try and do a kind of launch party, invite the press, that sort of thing."

"We will one thousand percent be there," Josh said firmly, and Hazel nodded.

Tom would still be an investor, Cassie thought, even though he wouldn't be around to see her try to make a go of it. She planned to do one retreat a year—a wellness retreat, with an emphasis on living harmoniously with nature, something he would have been proud of—in his name.

"Well, I guess this means you're not coming back to the flat then," Hazel said with a sigh. "Does this mean you're officially giving your room up?"

Cassie bit her lip. "I think it does." They'd agreed not to make it official until Cassie had spent a couple of months in Wales, in case she hated the whole thing—a kind of security blanket. She looked at Hazel, felt her eyes well. The thought of not living with her best friend gave her a pang. She'd just done it for three months, yes, but this would be more permanent. She'd lived with Hazel since leaving university; they'd grown up together.

Hazel was looking like she might cry too, but she straightened her spine, gave Cassie a mock-warning finger waggle. "Don't back out now. Do you really want to move back in, go back to working for Robert?"

Cassie grimaced. "No."

"Well then," Hazel said, with a firm nod. She'd cut her black hair recently, into a chic bob, and it swished with the movement. "We'll still see each other. All the time."

"I'll hold you to that," Cassie said with a smile.

"Does this mean you have a spare room?" Josh piped up. "Because the guys I'm living with are all parting ways and, well . . ."

Hazel looked at him, and her eyes widened. "Really?" He nodded, and she flashed a grin. "Oh God, you're so in. That's way better than having to find someone random."

Hazel's phone beeped and she picked it up. Smiled a little before she wrote back. "Who is it?" Cassie asked.

Hazel hesitated. "Chris."

"Chris?" Cassie's eyebrows shot up. "As in, the Chris you've already been on two dates with?"

"Yes, Cassie," Hazel said in an overly placatory way. "That Chris. And you can stop smiling like that now."

Two waiters came out with the food and the bottle of prosecco at the same time. Cassie looked from her newly poured glass of fizz to the vegetable Thai green curry in front of her. "Not *quite* the right vibe, is it?"

Josh waved that away. "We'll make it the right vibe." He held up his glass. "To Cassie and her new adventure." The three of them clinked glasses.

"And Happy Christmas," Hazel added.

Cassie clinked again with the other too, but she felt a twinge in her gut. She hadn't figured out yet what she was doing for Christmas. Christmas without Tom. She'd been trying to ignore it, her new project a welcome distraction. Claire had invited her to France, and she was thinking she might do that—see if she could get a last-minute flight tomorrow. It would be a good combination of being with someone who knew Tom, but also not being where they'd grown up together. Hazel had also offered to spend Christmas with her somewhere completely different, just the two of them, if that was what she wanted, but Cassie knew that Hazel would go out of her way to make it lovely and fun, and then she'd feel the pressure to live up to that. With Claire, she was only just beginning to learn, she could just be. Either way, though, she was going to have to figure out a way through it.

She still had the prosecco in her hand, suspended in midair. Hazel met her gaze, gave her a small smile of understanding. "To Tom," she murmured, and held her glass up a third time.

Cassie pressed her lips together when they wanted to tremble. "To Tom," she whispered. She took a sip, put the glass down, and felt Josh take her hand on one side, Hazel the other, so that they were all linked. She took a breath, breathing in the chili and coconut, then let it out slowly.

One of the waiters came over, black hair slicked back, looking far too young to be working in a restaurant. "Umm . . . Miss?" He looked from Cassie to Hazel, eyebrows pulled together, clearly not sure who to address.

Hazel immediately sat up very straight, and gestured confidently to Cassie, who frowned. But her attention was diverted by the waiter when he spoke again.

"Something has been delivered here, for you. It came on a bike," he added, in a voice that suggested that was most perplexing. "For your table number."

He handed over an envelope. An envelope, exactly like the ones Tom used to put his clues in. Her heart jumped. One more clue? But that didn't make sense; she'd gotten to the end. And Tom couldn't possibly have known they'd be here now. "Umm . . . Thank you," she said to the waiter, who nodded and, after hovering for a moment, perhaps hoping she'd open it in front of him, slunk off.

Cassie turned the envelope over in her hands, looked at Hazel. "How do you know it's for me?"

"I just do. Open it." Her voice held that demanding tone that

Cassie knew all too well, so she gently tore the white seal, and took out a sheet of paper from within. Her fingertips tingling, she read the short note.

Cassie,

I've thought long and hard about how to do this, and in the end, tradition seemed right. So here's the thing. If you want to, I've got one more Christmas treasure hunt for you to do. But unlike Tom's, this one has only one clue, and there's no secret of what's at the other end: me. The choice is yours. If you solve it, if you come, then I'll be waiting. And if not . . . Well, I guess I know your answer.
    Sam

Sam. His name reverberated around her mind as she read it one more time, and the tingle in her fingertips spread along her arms, straight to her chest.

"He's . . ." She hitched in a breath and looked up at Josh and Hazel. "It's Sam. He wants me to . . . follow a clue." She stared at them both, dumbfounded. "How . . . How is this even possible? How did he know I'm here?" Probably not the most important thing to focus on right now, but her head felt fuzzy and her heart was ratcheting up speed, making it difficult to think.

Hazel and Josh exchanged a look—a look that very clearly suggested they were in on something that she was not.

"Well," Hazel said slowly, "I may have given him a little hint."

"You told him?" God, why was her voice so squeaky?

"Yes. The treasure hunt was all his idea, though," she said quickly. "I just gave him a little helping hand."

Cassie let that settle for a moment, then looked at Josh. "And you knew too?"

"We may have . . . discussed it. So?" He leaned forward. "What's the clue?"

Cassie frowned. "There isn't . . ." But she saw, then, another small piece of paper in the envelope, and slipped it out.

If you want to see me, all you have to do is ask.
P.S. Rhyming was Tom's thing.

Cassie's stomach lurched. That was so *like* him. She could hear his voice, a hint of playfulness in it, see that crooked smile. But it wasn't helpful in the slightest.

"What?" she snapped. "That's . . ." She thrust the clue into Hazel's hand, and Josh read it over her shoulder. "What the *hell* does that mean? All I have to do is ask? What am I supposed to do, ring him?" She directed the question at Hazel. If she'd been in on this whole thing, then she'd know the answer.

She wrinkled her nose. "I'm not sure if I should . . ."

"Hazel," Cassie said warningly.

Hazel leveled a look at her. "Ask, Cassie."

"But I . . ." She stopped, took in the expression on Hazel's face, and her heart did another overexuberant beat. "You? You know where he is? He really roped you in, didn't he?" She pulled a hand through her hair, trying to calm her own damn body down so she could think, process.

"He rang me," Hazel said calmly. "I think he was worried that you'd . . . Well, that you'd react a bit how you're reacting now, if he got in touch directly."

"What's that supposed to mean? I'm not—"

"He's scared, Cassie. I think he's scared of facing you, if you walk away from him again."

Her fingertips thrummed and she laced them together in her lap to keep them still. She closed her eyes, allowed the noise of the restaurant to fade away. Thought of Sam's face, of the intensity in his voice, trying to tell her he loved her. Of the realization she'd come to in September, when she'd tried to see him, the sickening feeling she'd had as she'd walked away from him, leaving him with Jessica. Jessica.

She opened her eyes, looked at Hazel. "But he was with . . ."

"No," Hazel said, knowing immediately what Cassie was referring to. "He wasn't. He's not."

Cassie let that roll through her, the fact that she'd jumped so instantly to the wrong conclusion. Hazel was still looking at her, waiting. "Where is he?" Cassie whispered, and Hazel's grin was instantaneous.

"I knew you'd pick right! I never doubted you."

Josh raised a hand. "I did."

Hazel gave him a small slap on the arm. "Stop it." She grabbed her handbag off the floor, rummaged through it, then produced a key, which she handed over to Cassie.

Cassie frowned as she took it. "Is this supposed to be the answer? Because this could be for anywhere!" A hint of panic was creeping into her voice now. Panic, she knew, that was coming from the thought that she might not get it, she might not make it to him, and he'd leave, and that would be it, really it, this time.

"Don't worry," Hazel said soothingly. "He's not trying to make this difficult." She turned the key over for Cassie, showed a small sticker on it, where a postcode was written down. "If you can get yourself there, you can let yourself in with the key."

"Let myself . . . Oh." A house. He must be in a house somewhere, waiting for her. She bit her lip. The nerves in her body were prickling, urging her to move, but she stayed sitting for one more moment. Hazel and Josh were both watching her, waiting. And Sam's voice came to her, one more time.

At least I'm brave enough to admit what's going on here.

She realized, then, that there was no choice at all. She'd never had any choice in what to feel for him.

"OK," she said with a whooshing breath, getting to her feet at the same time. "I'm doing it, I'm going."

"Yay!" Hazel said. "Good luck."

"What, no dessert?" Josh asked, with a playful smile, earning another "Stop it!" from Hazel. Leaving them behind, the key clutched in her hand, Cassie ran from the restaurant and toward the person she knew, in that moment, that she could not live without. And even if that scared her, even if she thought she couldn't stand it to lose someone else she loved so much, she knew, right then, that it didn't matter. He'd already carved out a place in her soul, so now all that was left to do was to try to hold on to that, for as long as she could.

Chapter Forty

The taxi drove her down the dirt track that the postcode had led her to, bouncing a little on the uneven ground, the long grass in the middle of the road—and "road" was a generous term—scraping the underside of the car, though the driver didn't seem all that concerned about it. The headlights, combined with the sliver of moonlight filtering through the clouds, illuminated their way in the dark. Cassie leaned forward to see out of the front windshield, her heart jolting with each bump of the car. Ahead of them was an old stone cottage that looked on the verge of crumbling down, a small stone wall around it, separating it from the vast hills in the background, hills that seemed to stretch on eternally. Chalky rocks nestled in the grass seemed to shine in the moonlight, and frost, already settling in for the night, sparkled as they drove.

The taxi pulled to a stop, and without the noise of the engine, Cassie could hear the wind swooping over the countryside. Other than that, everything was so quiet, like they were miles away from anyone else. Whether or not that was true, she couldn't say, having completely lost her bearings in the five-hour journey it had taken to get here. "You sure this is the one, are you?" the driver said, in his brilliant lilting Welsh accent.

Wales. After spending three months here, it turned out that

Sam had asked her to make the trip back to Wales from London. Farther into the rural countryside than she was now based, but Wales, nonetheless.

Cassie stared at the cottage. There was one light on in the downstairs window, but otherwise it looked empty. She wet her dry lips. "I think so," she said, a little uncertainly.

"You want me to wait, do you?"

"Yes, please," she said in a small voice. Because what if she was wrong, and Sam wasn't here at all? What if she'd misread the postcode, despite having checked it a thousand times? What if *he'd* gotten it wrong? She took a deep breath, her heart speeding up, adrenaline coursing back through her. She felt both tired after the journey and impossibly wide awake and was now regretting the coffee she'd had on the train, sure that it was making her jittery. And God, why hadn't she thought to change before she got on the bloody train? Why hadn't she thought to bring makeup, so she could turn up in a more presentable state?

She checked her phone, though the battery was nearly dead. Almost 10 P.M. What if he wasn't awake? What time did he usually go to bed? She had no idea. *She* sometimes went to bed at 10 P.M., didn't she, so it wasn't out of the realms of possibility?

"You going, love, then are you? Only I've got supper waiting for me at home."

"Right. Yes. Sorry." She got out, immediately sucking in a breath against the cold. Jesus, it was bloody freezing, the air crisp and harsh in her mouth, practically burning the back of her throat. It was enough to get her moving fast toward the white gate that led through the stone wall to the path up to the front door.

She was too cold to hesitate, and maybe that was better, not to think about this. Still, her fingers shook slightly as she put the key into the lock, turned. It clicked open. Oh God, it actually opened. It had worked: she was here; she was doing this.

Somehow, she managed to turn back to the taxi driver, give him a little thumbs up. She heard the engine start up again as she stepped inside, shutting the door behind her. There was music playing somewhere, but it was dark in the hallway. Light was coming from down the corridor and she blinked as her eyes adjusted. She bit her lip, hovering. Why hadn't Sam come to see who it was? Hadn't he heard the door? Was this some kind of test? A trick?

Stop it, Cassie, she told herself firmly. She was here now. She'd traveled five bloody hours at the drop of a hat—there was a reason for that.

Slowly, feeling the need to tiptoe for some reason, she followed the light into a sitting room, the music, lively violins, getting louder as she walked. Maybe that explained why he hadn't heard the door. She stopped in the doorway. There was a fire crackling away in the fireplace, the flames eating away at the wood, the smell of smoke in the air. The relief of being warm shuddered through her. Or maybe that was the relief of seeing him, of knowing it was real. Because there he was. Just the back of his head, but still. Sitting there, on a red sofa, facing the fire, with a glass of what looked like whisky in his hand.

Whoever owned the cottage had put up some Christmas decorations—unless Sam had set them up himself, which she doubted. There were white fairy lights above the fireplace, tinsel over the top of the windows, candles burning in the corner. Those, at least, must have been him.

"Sam." She said his name quietly, could barely get it from her lips. He turned, lightning fast, and she held her breath. He stood in one fluid movement, staring at her, and she stayed completely still, unable to move.

"You came." His voice was a little hoarse.

"Yeah." She let out the breath. "Yeah, I came."

And then his face split into a grin and he crossed to her in two big strides. He reached out, running his hands down her arms, which were still encased in her coat. Even through her coat, her skin sparked to life with his touch. He quite literally picked her up off her feet, spinning her in a small circle and kissing her and it felt so right, so unbelievably *right* to be there, in his arms. She laughed, putting her arms around his neck, pulling him closer, and he kissed her again, and God, *this*, the taste of him, how could she ever have thought she'd be able to put it aside?

He broke away suddenly and she frowned up at him. "Wait," he said and darted away, his movements a little frantic. He grabbed something off the little coffee table, then came back to stand in front of her. His expression was a little careful as he looked at her, as he held something out for her to see.

A necklace. *Her* necklace, the one he'd given to her all those years ago. The chain dangled from his fingers, the stone swaying slightly.

She stared at it, dumbfounded. "You kept it."

Sam ran a hand across the back of his neck, the way he did when he was nervous, or anxious about something. "Yeah. I guess I was always hoping there would come a time when I could give it back to you."

She reached out, traced the little silver chain with her fingers, remembering the moment he'd given it to her, outside Linda's pub. Remembering how she'd thrust it back at him on that skiing holiday.

He was watching her, she realized. Watching her to gauge her reaction. So, without saying anything, she slipped off her coat, gave it to him. Then she turned around, holding up her hair so that he could get to her neck. So that he could fasten the necklace around it. She felt his fingers tremble against her skin as he clasped it in place.

She turned back around, tilted her chin up to look at him, and felt her lips settle into a soft smile. Saw his chest relax as he let out a breath—as, putting the coat to one side, he drew her to him, put his arms around her. She rested her head on his chest, listening to his heartbeat.

"I'm sorry," she said quietly. "I'm sorry I didn't say it back last time."

He eased away from her slightly, gave her that crooked smile that she loved. "Say what back, exactly?"

She laughed a little. "Need me to say it out loud, do you?"

He shrugged, but she could feel it—the slight brittleness there. The worry he was trying to hide. "It would be nice."

She reached up, framed his face with her hands. "That I love you. I love you, Sam Malone."

She felt a breath loosen within him as he drew her close once more and she felt, really felt for the first time, how much it must have cost him, waiting for her, wondering. "Well, that's good. Because I love you, Cassie. It's always been you." She let it slide through her, the fact of it, let herself breathe him in as they stood there, together.

"You're here," he said again, running a hand down her back like he needed to keep touching her. "You're actually here."

"Yeah." Her voice was a bit shaky. She tilted her head, looked up into his face, met his gaze, firelight dancing in the blue. "Maybe I'm braver than you thought."

"No." He shook his head, kissed the top of her hair. "You're braver than you thought."

This time, it was she who kissed him, drew him to her as close as they could possibly manage. And this time, they did not stop.

Twelve Months Later

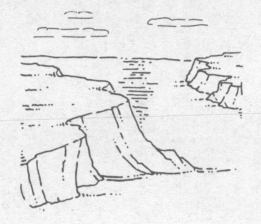

Chapter Forty-One

Cassie stood at the bottom of the Patagonian mountains, staring up at the epic, snow-covered peaks, which gave way to rough, grassy terrain nearer the bottom. Next to her, Sam held her hand, but neither of them said anything. They just stood, taking it in.

It was Christmas Eve, though the fact of that was almost impossible to believe with the warmth of the day, the sun beating down on them, and with no sign of celebrations around them. It wasn't as unbearably hot as she'd expected it to be in the height of the Argentinian summer, though, and there was a strong wind tugging at her hair and whisking away the sweat from the walk.

"Do you think this is an OK spot?" Sam asked, his voice quiet. Cassie looked around. They were at the bottom of the mountains, gray rocks and small bushes surrounding them. A lake formed the backdrop, bright turquoise and glistening in the sunlight, and you could see mountains all around, the clouds circling their tops, land and sky taking measure of one another.

"I think so, yes."

They set their small backpacks down, and Cassie took out her flask of water as Sam got out the handcrafted wooden star. A star, not a cross, because Tom had been the light in both of their lives.

Cassie hadn't found out exactly where Tom had died, where he had fallen. She could have asked Toby—Sam was still in touch with him—but she'd found she didn't want to know. This trip wasn't about revisiting his last steps, but about celebrating his life, and honoring him in a place he'd always wanted to go. He had his grave, but this . . . this would be for her and Sam.

She watched as Sam dug a little hole, stuck the wooden spike in, with the star on top. It was unobtrusive, small enough that hopefully no one would mind, but it was something that would be lasting, that would show he was loved. And she liked the fact that the star was imperfect, the edges a little crooked. Because they were all imperfect, weren't they? And that was OK. It was OK that they all—Tom included—made mistakes. It didn't make Tom any less perfect to *her*, or any less loved.

She didn't say anything out loud, but she found herself talking to him, in her head. Telling him that she'd done it—she'd gone through with it, completed the sale, and now that house in Wales was hers. She'd launched it both as a B&B and an events venue in summer, and she had her first wedding booked for the spring. Her first wellness retreat—the one in Tom's name— would be this summer.

She glanced at Sam, who was standing next to her, staring at the star. He'd be talking to him too, she knew, and she wondered what he was saying. He'd gotten into climbing because of Tom, and now he was setting up his own center, working with disadvantaged kids, trying to give them an experience they wouldn't get otherwise. He was so good at it, and he loved it. So, Tom had guided both of their lives, really. And he'd given them each other, in some ways. Cassie didn't know if they would have ended up together anyway, if they would have found their way to one another eventually no matter what, but she didn't dwell on it. The point was that they were together now.

She bent down to her backpack again, setting her water aside. She'd thought so hard about what to bring with her, what to bring for Tom. She'd been to his grave, of course, taken flowers, talked to him there. But here, in the place where he'd died, the place where he had been doing what he loved, she'd wanted to bring the right thing. In the end, she'd settled on photos. The first one was of Tom, Sam, and her as teenagers. In it, Tom was laughing, Sam was grinning, and she was making a face, clearly trying not to smile. It was something simple, but a memory of a time when he was happy, when the three of them had been together: two of his favorite people in the world, he'd said.

She set the photo down at the bottom of the star. And next to it, she stuck a photo of Amy and Noah. Amy was smiling down at Noah, propped on her hip, looking toward the camera with her eyes, trying to get him to smile. Tom's family. Next year, they were all going to have Christmas together. Amy had promised to come and stay with Cassie and Sam in Wales.

Without saying anything out loud, Cassie and Sam found a rock nearby, and sat down together, taking a moment to just be. He put his arm around her. She was crying, soft tears running down her cheeks, the salt of them pooling in the corner of her mouth. She let herself cry, though, and he stroked her hair gently, saying nothing. He linked his fingers with hers, kissed the top of her head. He didn't ask if she was OK, and she knew it was because he got it—because the answer to that was so much more complicated than a yes or no.

When she felt the wind caress her cheeks, dry the tears there, she let out a breath. Sam stood, pulling her to her feet. And it was only then that she felt able to put down the last photo, the one that made her feel the closest to him of all. A photo of the house in Wales—*her* house—taken just before she and Sam had left for Argentina. In it, the house was covered in an early snow, and the whole place was decorated for Christmas, for the Christmas event that she'd agreed to host for the village. Fairy lights on the outside, two little Christmas trees on each side of the green front door.

Sam had smiled when she'd shown it to him on her phone, before she printed the photo. He'd told her that it looked like the house was *glowing,* and though she'd laughed, she secretly agreed with him. You could see the dim lights from inside the house, and it was like it was happy to be in use again. Like it was grateful that she'd taken it on and made it shine once again.

She set the photo down for Tom. So he could see that she'd gone through with it. That she'd gotten to the end of the treasure hunt. And that she loved her last gift, more than she could put into words.

"Bye, Tom," she said softly. She felt Sam's grip tighten a fraction on her hand. "I love you."

Then they began walking, back the way they came. Back to the little lodge where they were staying, and the old woman who had promised them a feast. Back to welcome in Christmas Day, and to celebrate the fact that they were both still here, still together.

"Thank you," she breathed, barely loud enough to be heard. But the wind carried her words away, whisking them into the air. And she felt sure, for a brief moment, that Tom could hear her.

Acknowledgments

Writing any book is such a mammoth effort, and it really could not happen without an entire team of people. Thanks first and foremost go to my brilliant editor, Sherise Hobbs, who brought so much passion, creativity, and patience to this book—I know she feels as proud as I do, to see the book written, and without her support this book would not be what it is now.

Thanks to the incredibly smart Bea Grabowska for her attention to detail as well as her insightful and creative suggestions and general support throughout the whole process. Thank you, Katie Green, for a meticulous copyedit (and making me realize that time lines are clearly not my strong point!). Thanks to my agent, Sarah Hornsley, for her help, energy, and enthusiasm.

In rights, Rebecca Folland and Flora McMichael deserve huge thanks for championing this book internationally, which is as much of an excitement this time around as it was with my debut. Thanks to Emily Patience for helping *Always, in December* to reach readers last year—and preemptive thanks on that count for *One Last Gift* too!

On the U.S. side, thanks to Hilary Teeman and Caroline Weishuhn for their enthusiasm for Cassie and Sam and, as last time, for some brilliant last editorial suggestions to really make the book shine. Thanks to Morgan Hoit for her endless positivity and passion and helping to bring the book to U.S. readers, and to Melissa Folds for some wonderful reviews for *Always, in December* last year and for getting as excited as I do when reading them!

It is an odd thing, writing acknowledgements before the book has been published, because there will undoubtedly be so many more people to thank by the end of the year! So I'd just like to take a moment to thank the incredible and generous authors who took the time to read and quote for *Always, in December* last year: Jo Lovett, Emma Cooper, Holly Miller, Josie Silver, Claire Frost, and Cathy Bramley, as well as all the amazing bloggers and bookstagrammers who helped to make *Always, in December* a success by sharing thoughts, reviews, and beautiful photos. I can't name you all here because it would take too much space—and I'd be terrified I'd leave someone out—but it really does mean the world to see you taking the time to do this.

And thanks, as always, to any reader who has taken the time to read this book. Without readers, authors would not be able to write, and it is such a passion and a privilege to be able to do so. So, thank you, if you have read this far.

One Last Gift

EMILY STONE

A Book Club Guide

Questions and Topics for Discussion

1. In the prologue, we learn that Tom has made a scavenger hunt every Christmas since Cassie can remember—a tradition that she looks forward to every year. Are there any holiday traditions with your family or friends that you hold especially dear, or that give you the same feeling of anticipation and joy that Tom's scavenger hunts give Cassie?

2. It becomes clear quite early on that neither Cassie and Tom nor Sam have "conventional" family structures. Do you think that has anything to do with why they might have all gravitated toward one another? Do you have anyone in your life whom you would consider "found family"? If so, did anything in particular bring you together?

3. Cassie and Sam's feelings for each other are initially revealed on their ski holiday, but any chance at a relationship quickly comes to an end. What did you think of how Sam and Cassie reacted in that particular situation? What do you think it says about their personalities that they reacted in the way that they did?

4. Losing Tom is a terrible shock for Cassie, and she blames Sam for her brother's death. Do you think that reaction is fair? Why or why not?

5. Sam, too, is grieving his best friend's death. Do you think that is why he makes the seemingly impulsive and life-changing decisions that he does? Why or why not?

6. When Linda gives Cassie the letter from Tom, why do you think Cassie can't bring herself to open it at first?

7. Why do you think that saving the pub is so important to Cassie?

8. Tom left most of Cassie's clues in the care of her closest friends. If you were one of her friends, would you allow her to work the clues out for herself, or would you let her know that you had one? What do you think the benefits (or the drawbacks) are of each way of handling this unexpected responsibility that each friend bears?

9. Sam's travels seem to have given him a new perspective on life; have you ever experienced a similar change in perspective after taking some time away from your "real" life? Did you make any lasting changes to your life as a result?

10. As Cassie reaches the final clues in Tom's scavenger hunt, he pushes her to do things she never would have thought herself capable of. Can you relate to that? Has there ever been anyone in your life who has encouraged you to venture outside your comfort zone?

11. What did you think of Tom's final gift to Cassie? What does it reveal about his understanding of her?

12. Sam and Cassie knew each other for nearly their entire lives, but it still took several decades for them to end up together. Why do you think it took the time it did? Do you or any of the people in your life have a similar story?

EMILY STONE is the author of *Always, in December* and *One Last Gift*. She lives and works in Chepstow and writes in an old Victorian manor house with an impressive literary heritage.

Twitter: @EmStoneWrites
Instagram: @EmStoneWrites

RANDOM HOUSE BOOK CLUB

Because Stories Are Better Shared

Discover

Exciting new books that spark conversation every week.

Connect

With authors on tour—or in your living room. (Request an Author Chat for your book club!)

Discuss

Stories that move you with fellow book lovers on Facebook, on Goodreads, or at in-person meet-ups.

Enhance

Your reading experience with discussion prompts, digital book club kits, and more, available on our website.

Join our online book club community!

 g randomhousebookclub.com

Random House Book Club ™

Because Stories Are Better Shared

RANDOM HOUSE